THE STORY OF A LAKE

THE STORY OF A LAKE

by

NEGLEY FARSON

THE BOOK CLUB
111 CHARING CROSS ROAD
LONDON, W.C.2

This edition 1939

PRINTED IN GREAT BRITAIN BY PURNELL AND SONS, LTD. T.U.)
PAULTON (SOMERSET) AND LONDON

To

TORSTEN LANDBY

CONTENTS

MAIL DAY

LYND opened his eyes and stared at the clock. It took him some time to make sure it had stopped. His eyes did not focus so well these days after a drinking bout, and there was often a distressing time lag between what they saw and the realisation of what that meant. He lay a little longer in his blankets, debating when it would be worth while to begin another empty day; then he held up his hands and thoughtfully began to rub the fingers of one hand slowly down over the outstretched fingers of the other; it was an uncanny gesture—as if he were putting on a pair of invisible gloves.

This was the first thing he did every morning. Back in London the doctors had told him that this spreading numbness in his fingers was a form of arthritis; the alcohol was beginning to poison his nerve centres at the roots. It did not sound alarming. There was no immediate retribution. Arthritis was what Lady Mallard had; the reason she wore a white woollen shawl around her shoulder when she and the General took one of their deadly dull winter walks along the Plage at Mentone. It would never get Tony Lynd. But out here, where his fingers often felt flabby as flannel when he grasped an oar, and the axe had a tendency to turn in his hands and cut off a foot, this semi-dreadness could make trouble.

The clock did not count. That had been the most disturbing confession he had had to make to himself in B.C.; to admit that time did not matter. That, self-sufficient as he had thought himself to be, in little less than two years he had reached a point where it made no difference to him what day of the week it was—except an occasional Wednesday or Saturday, mail days, when he would row seven miles down to the store for any letters or supplies—and that even the months had no meaning. It was true that there were certain months of the year when the laws of the Province said that he might not fish or shoot for certain food. But, then, he had not always rigidly obeyed those laws. And they had entirely lost their importance since he had taken to living out of tins.

Anyone who had known Lynd well would have been shocked at the sight of two Hardy trout rods sagging from pegs along the log-cabin's wall; at the spectacle of a good Greener gun standing, still put together, on a spring day in the corner; at the pile of London and New York newspapers, their wrappers still uncut, flung in a careless heap beside the stone fireplace.

It was spring, and as he lay there a warm billow of air brought in the scent of the hot sun on the blossoms of old Mead's deserted apple orchard. Lynd frowned. When he had first come here he had decided to put that orchard in shape; that had been one of his early enthusiasms. Old Mead had been a genuine "remittance man"—an authentic outcast. When Lynd had bought the place the settlers on Scaup Lake had taken a particular pleasure in recalling one or two mouldy jokes of the pathetic old exile; how the recluse was fond of saying, "My loving family is paying me two dollars a day—for the rest of my life—so long as they never have to see my sweet face again," or "My father rose from mill hand to manor. But he couldn't rise to becoming the father of an English gentleman—no, by God!" This last, when the old outcast was in a belligerent mood, in one of his drunks, which, as the rows of inverted whiskey bottles lining his paths testified, must have been his usual state. On $2 a day, in pre-War British Columbia, a man could do himself very well—even drink himself to death.

Mead had been found dead in his blankets the third winter of the World War, when, no smoke having been seen coming from his cabin for over three weeks, a search party coming over Bald Mountain had found him frozen stiff. That had been twenty years ago. And since that day no one had lived here until Lynd bought the place. A genteel white marble

tombstone, cut and sent up from Port Mary as per a letter of
instructions from Bradford, stood at the foot of the apple
orchard. It read:

RICHARD HENRY MEAD

MAY 14, 1859

MARCH 31, 1917

"Which," grinned the man who had taken Lynd up to see
the deserted place, "is about all you can say for him."

Lynd, when he came to know the personality of old Mead
which still lingered around the place—things shown by the
fragrant, useless apple orchard and the rose which still
climbed over the logs from beside the cabin door—was furious
with the old outcast for currying favour with the other Scaup
Lakers by saying such demeaning things about himself. It was
obvious that in telling him them, the locals expected some
sort of such revelation from him. Why not keep quiet about
it? And he sensed that the curiosity, uncertain envy and
malice implied in his lower Scaup Laker's remark about old
Mead would soon come to be applied to himself.

The cabin stood at the end of a lonely North Arm that,
about five miles up from the store, struck off from the twenty
miles of open main lake. The arm was about a mile long. No
one else lived there. Mead, warned by the early settlers of
how the lake rose with melting snows, had set his cabin on a
high delta of land about fifty yards back from a long curving
crescent of rocky grey beach. It lay in a pocket of sun made
by the long arm of Bald Mountain and the high wall of fir
forest that stood behind it. Its apple orchard of some twenty
trees throve in the warm lee. That was all.

From the mouth of the North Arm Lynd's cabin was just a
lightish block of logs at the base of the dark forest. Mead had
had grand ideas, and its main room was as open and airy as
a studio. A bedroom and the kitchen projected backward
towards the forest from either end. Lynd had kept himself
busy, and free from thinking about other things the first

winter, by putting in practically an entire new floor. He had
stained this dark brown with some walnut stain he had
bought at the store. He had also stained the window frames,
from which blue-and-white checked curtains now billowed
in softly in the warm spring air. The back wall of the cabin
was lined with rows of unpainted shelves filled with books.
A lazy Morris chair stood beside a long centre table, on
which now stood a midge-bespattered reading lamp. And
while he had seen no reason to improve on Mead's old
wooden bunk in the bedroom, and he had not run to sheets
which would require too much washing, he had hinged a
large semicircular flap to the side of his bunk, so that he
could lie there and read at nights. A lamp stood on that now,
with dead midges all around it, which he saw, as it had a
glass bowl, had burnt itself out. That meant another half-
inch of wick to clip and clean. One of those tasks that simply
could not be neglected—like keeping a plentiful supply of firewood on hand. By the lamp lay a Tauchnitz copy of *Lord
Jim* he was re-reading to console himself these days. And
beside that stood a bottle of Black and White, in which there
was still a good inch. He grinned at it sourly, and then drank
it neat.

When he stood up he noticed that he had on nothing but
an old checked lumberman's shirt. Always a sign that he had
begun drinking heavily before he went to bed. Sometimes it
was only by looking in the glass that he could tell how long
he had been "out." It was one of those concave shaving
mirrors which magnified, relently, every hair and line.
Rubbing the black stubble on his jaw, he estimated that he
must have been "out" this time for at least two or three
days. It was interesting that his beard should come out
black, when his hair was still a sandy red. It was also interesting, and something to think about, that though he was still
a year on the right side of forty, that black beard was beginning to be flecked with sprouts of grey. They did not show
anywhere else. As there was no barber, of course, on Scaup

Lake, he had had to cut his hair himself. The result was a bang across his sullen brows such as the ancient Roman senators used to fancy: he had to cut it that way to keep the hair out of his eyes in the wind. Only when it rained did he ever wear a hat. And very often not then; he loved the rain on his face. His face, weather-beaten until it was darker than his hair, gave a startling brilliance to his blue eyes. This added to a natural fixed intensity, which often caused people to stir and move uncomfortably, as if he were deliberately staring at them in the store. Those eyes were very bloodshot now.

A cat, which had been dozing in the sun against the hot cabin-logs, came in tail-erect, with ratchety purrs, and to attract attention rubbed itself against his slender legs. He was a neatly built man, slim-hipped, with good shoulders, and, in spite of himself, the amount of daily tasks he had to perform in this country merely to keep alive had kept him fit. Although the pain in his stomach now felt as if the cat itself was inside it, he leaned down and gave it a pat on the head. "All right," he muttered, "you'll have your breakfast in a minute.

Still in his shirt-tails, he walked through the big main airy room, glanced with satisfaction at the billowing curtains and entered the small room at the far end.

The far end of this room held an ordinary kitchen range. To its right was a long washing sink, with sloping sides and a zinc basin. Above it were long rows of wooden racks to hold the drying dishes. The sink was cluttered now, as Lynd had fallen into the weak habit of using every plate, cup and saucer in the house until not one clean one was left; then he would set to in a prodigious and often painful burst of energy to wash the whole lot.

The other wall was lined, like a store, with rows of tins. Sockeye salmon, Campbell's soups, Boston baked beans, peas, asparagus, peaches, apricots, pears, Carnation milk and a row of powdered Klim. There were big tin canisters labelled coffee, tea, sugar, salt, pepper, matches. There was a little set of spices. And a little luxury row of Japanese crab, anchovy paste, and Norwegian goat cheese. But this last was almost too redolent with memories to allow him to touch it. A ham, still in its wrapper, and two sides of bacon dangled in their cheese-cloth from the cedar shingles. There was enough there to stand a siege—or one of his black moods.

He broke open a tin of Sockeye salmon and put all of it on a plate for the cat. Then he shook out some Klim powder into a bowl, poured a couple of ladlesful of water into it from a bucket in the corner, and, sitting down with the bowl clasped between his bare legs, stirred a spoon around it to make some artificial milk. He did this automatically, never looking at the things he reached for or picked up. As he rubbed, he sat with his head on one side, a cigarette dangling from his lips, his amazing blue eyes fixed vacantly on some place in the jagged rim of green forest he saw outside the window. When the milk was ready he poured it into a deep soup plate and walked to the cabin's front door. He called: "Here, puss. . . . Here, puss. . . . Puss, puss, puss. . . ."

Four kittens which had been playing in the scented grass between the cabin and the blue lake appeared from the tall grass and tumbled towards him. He put the plate down and went inside. . . .

As he was trying to start the primus to make some tea a low hum from up the lake became a roar and finally drew him to the door. Staring up along the long strip of shimmering blue, he saw a white launch slide past the mouth of the lonely North Arm. It was the *War Eagle*, the big logging camp's boat, her cabin black with loggers. That told him two things; it must be somewhere around noon—and this was a mail day. It was either a Wednesday or a Saturday. Everyone who could on Scaup Lake would be going down to the store. Well . . . let them go.

2

Shorty Murdoch had just shot his pig. He had raised the animal to maturity, and now, he knew, every additional bit of food he collected for it would be just so much sheer waste of effort. It would not put on another pound. Worse than that; with the coming of hot weather the animal might even lose weight. So he shot it.

It was a murderous act. The pig and he had become quite friendly during the lonely winter months. They understood each other. In some ways they looked alike; they both had the same pale pinkish flesh that goes with red hair; they both had white-lashed, pink-rimmed eyes; they both walked around with the same air of questing greediness. They were both silent, except for an occasional grunt.

Murdoch was a little man and did not trust himself to knock the pig out with one blow of a sledge. He had backed the animal, pathetically trustful, into a corner of his plantation and shot it with a ·22 between its inquisitive pointed ears. He was standing there, after he had slit its throat, thinking of how, in Chicago, they would have used all that gouting blood, when a casual-looking man, bearing a shotgun over the crook of his arm, stepped out of the low, second-growth pines. Even in his old rubber boots and torn tweeds, anyone could have told at a glance that Copey Debenham was an English gentleman. His very manner oozed that complacent information.

But Shorty Murdoch did not smile at the sight of him. He did not believe in hereditary paramounts—not out in British Columbia. He had been born in a Glasgow slum. Mr. Debenham couldn't come any of that on him out here. It was all very well that when, and *if*, the man's three healthy elder brothers died he would automatically become Lord Debenham. Meanwhile he was just the laziest man on Scaup Lake; and the Debenhams were notorious on Scaup Lake for not paying their bills. They even had the gall to joke about it; they'd tell you to your face, if you cared to listen to such sinful boasting, that the chief reason why they were out here on Scaup Lake was because their English creditors could not get at them.

"Ha!" said Copey, sitting down comfortably on a stump, "so you've shot the blighter?"

"I have."

Copey smiled.

Now, if there was one thing that he should have known better not to do, it was that. Shorty had reason to be sensitive about his yearly pig. The reason was this: in this part of the world where it was very hard to make any money at all, and Shorty often had to sacrifice his dignity and independency by going up and working for a week or so as a bucker in a logging camp, his pig-idea had been a stroke of genius. Every year he had a young one sent up from Port Mary. He fed it with scraps he collected from the colony of house-boaters around the store. He always took a bucket with him when he went down for the mail. It had, also, what it could get from rooting around his wretched plantation. And in the process of time that pig became fat. Then he killed it, cut it up into sections, and went about the lake in his Siwash dugout selling the pieces to the other settlers. The Treads, the old man was the original settler, always took both the hams, which they knew how to cure, and held them over for the winter seasons. And the Treads, also irked with the necessity of how to make money, always paid him on the nail. So did old Dr. Feather and his wife who, usually, could be persuaded to buy all the chops. The rest of the pig was problematical. The fore-legs he very often gave free to Mrs. Swinton, the French wife of the English game-warden, the only person he could converse with on the lake. They had some rare talks about birds and beasts, and the salads you could find, and life, and the other Scaup Lakers in the Swinton house-boat of nights. But with this fresh meat Shorty reaped the most immediate profit from his brilliant idea. For, after he had sold it to the settlers, he paddled around the lake for the next few days, dropping in on them just at meal-times, and ate most of it back. *That* was why Mr. Debenham smiled.

"I was thinking," said that good-natured Englishman, quite unconscious of the hostile thoughts in the Scot's head, "I was thinking we might use all of that pig?"

"Ah . . ." Shorty stared at him and fell back, as if to protect his beast. "Ye were, were you—well, there's others to be conseedered. Don't forget that."

Copey filled his pipe.

"I suppose you know," he said, making a bad job of trying to conceal his emotions, "that Aline's coming back? That she gets here this afternoon. . . ."

"Does she?" said the Scot.

In spite of himself, Shorty Murdoch was unable to hide his surprise. The departure of Aline Debenham, Copey's eighteen-year-old daughter, for England last autumn had been a major event on Scaup Lake. As everyone knew, it was much more than just a mere trip home to see her relations—it was meant to be a real departure from the lake. A complete break with it. Cecie Debenham had made it plain that the reason why they had scraped up every penny to fit Aline out for this adventure, and buy her tickets home, was that, while she was over there, in the life she had been born to, Aline should find a man. She would marry and escape the lake life. There had been great things talked about in the programme for her; hunting down in Somerset, perhaps a trip to Switzerland for the winter sports; the London Season with all its occasions, dances, dinner parties, the Derby, Ascot, being presented at Court. Her aristocratic English cousins had promised to do their bit. And now she was back! But all the Scot said was:

"Wha' are ye doin' with that shotgun at this time of the year?"

Copey grinned. "Trying to shoot one of my own geese," he lied. "They broke loose when the lake flooded. Haven't seen one of the silly blighters since. Have you?"

"No," said the Scot disgustedly. "But ye'd better tell Bessie to wipe her mouth before Swinton comes along."

Bessie was, after Aline, Copey Debenham's greatest love. She was an old black spaniel, fed to the point of bursting from whose greying muzzle two dangling grey pine-grouse feathers now gave the show away. She was innocent of all this and turned her soft brown eyes up lovingly to Copey as he leaned down, laughing, to rub her chin. "Good old dog," he said, with a rich, familiar warmth in his voice. "You little traitor, you!"

Bessie wagged her stump of a tail, and Debenham got up. "Well," he said, "if you do want to sell us the lot of that pig—and we'll pay you cash for it—this time, anyway—take it over to Cecie." He snapped together his gun.

"I've only got three grouse," he said, "and I need a couple more. Aline's bringing a friend with her—a girl who's never known the delights of British Columbia. Ta-ta. . . ."

3

Captain Heinrich von Hauptmann arose and patted his hairy stomach. He stood naked, in all his glory, under God's sun. "Elsa," he said, "you will now bring me my moccasins." A mousy creature who had been trying to split a stick of kindling wood, with a knot in it, left the axe where it was stuck and went into the house. It was a startling house, for that part of the world. It was like a post-card of Bavaria: gables, carved chamois heads facing each other on the roof ridge, even to the stones weighting down the low, flat shingles. A châlet. Instead of logs, it was made of boards, painted red; and in a part of the world where all doors swung open to the wooden latch, this one bore a Yale lock. To protect, perhaps, its treasures inside: the staring heads of buschbok, antelope and African buffalo; the glass-covered case of Mannlichers and triplex sporting guns; the knick-knacks of coloured crockery that every German holds dear.

The Count leaned over as far as his stomach would permit and laced a pair of yellow, calf-high moccasins over his bulging bottle legs. Then he pulled something over his head. At first you might have thought that the Count, as they had dubbed him here, was going back to bed again. This long, dangling garment of greenish khaki. But then a broad leather belt strapped around the Falstaffian middle transformed this mystery and showed that Captain Heinrich von Hauptmann was now wearing a one-piece shirt and kilt. It had a large open V over the chest; but this bronzed expanse was covered by a majestic greying beard. The Count then put the other piece of wearing apparel, a French *beret*, on his neckless, shaven head. "We will now," he announced, "out the boat."

When the German thought that his wife was having too unsuccessful a struggle in trying to shove a bluff red row-boat into the water he halted his puffs on a long *Jaeger* pipe to lend a hand. Then, handing her the precious china-bowl, he stepped into the skiff, faced forward, and began his monthly eight-mile push down to the store.

As he rowed, or pushed rather, he sat with his head a little cocked to one side, as if his brown eyes were fixed on some remote object in the flawless sky. Scaup Lakers had noticed this peculiarity and had said that he did that perhaps because Captain von Hauptmann had a stiff neck. He always held himself very rigid. But that was nonsense.

What he was really doing was freeing his mind from his body. He had found, after long practice, that he could accomplish this feat. When he was doing something irksome and monotonous, or merely sitting still, if he concentrated—if he just thought, and thought, and thought—his mind would lift. Quite consciously. He could feel it floating, hovering, until finally it drifted away from him. It was a blissful sensation. Like riding off in a balloon. In reveries like this he could utterly forget what he was doing; and many a time he had pushed the whole eight miles down to the store, only to wake up there with a hurt surprise from the pursuit of the deer across sun-reddened snows in his beloved Bavaria; the great slab of the Zugspitz, cold and grey, when there was a boom as the avalanches broke and the snow poured like waterfalls over its sides. . . . Yes, life could be very beautiful, and he had seen a lot of it.

They were very useful, these day-dreams. They helped him to endure life. Elsa understood that. She had quickly learned that there were certain times when he ought not to be tampered with, when she should not get in between him and his thoughts. She was a good wife. A good *Hausfrau*. Food was there when he wanted it—she was sewing now, he understood, for some of the other settlers so that they could have enough money to buy some of the essential groceries they must have from the store. For his part, for the complete life, he would have preferred a more healthy woman. One of those buxom Baltic girls. A peasant. Someone with great big breasts and deep-thewed hips and two great ropes of yellow hair plaited down her bare back. Ah!...That would be magnificent. They would make love in the woods, in the dappled shadows of the scented pines; or she would stand full length on a rock, her strong body glistening in the sun against the blue lake.

He had thought of that this morning as he had walked down for his morning dip. The lake lay there as usual, enigmatic, smiling blandly in his face. Not a ripple ruffled its dawn composure. All the leaves of the alder bushes still drooped with the dew and sleep of night. He had shouted as he jumped into it, shattering the reflection of his own body. Anything to break this basking silence. . . .

And to think that there were any amount of lovely, neurotic, frustrated women walking around Munich at this

moment who would simply have leapt at the chance! Yet—
they would never find him. Life was so perverse.

4

Old Dr. Feather and his wife had been on the lake thirty
years. He had been the first man to come up there, after
Tread, ten years before, had walked up the deer-trail to
find that only Siwash were living there. The Siwash were
gone now; a kind Government had put them on a reservation. But he and Tread were still there. Like two old stags.
Although that was certainly not the simile that would leap
into your mind when you looked at old Tread; for he was
the meekest, most anæmic man who had ever swung an axe.
Everybody had wondered at the tenacity of the old man;
what, in the first place, had ever possessed this obvious bank
clerk to leave Canterbury in old England; and why, for forty
bitter years when he had had to arise with the sun and fight
the jungle until it went down every night, had he hung on
here? In answer to one of von Hauptmann's earlier questions
—before the German had succeeded in making an enemy of
every man on the lake—old Tread had opined laconically:
"I guess it's because I've always been my own boss."

Every mail day old Tread dropped his wife at the Feathers'
place while he and the Doctor went on down for the mail.
It was the only chance she ever got to talk to another woman.
Mrs. Swinton, the game-warden's wife, was always there.
And so was Miss Gay, the Feathers' lady-help. She was in a
terrible state of nerves to-day, and had already broken a
plate, because she had heard that Mr. Murdoch was coming
over with a bit of his pig. Miss Gay, whose red knitted
jumper looked as if it had been pulled on over a flat board,
had wisps of forlornly drooping black hair, frightened grey
eyes, and a full and hideous set of porcelain teeth. She had
often tried to impress upon Mr. Murdoch that beauty was
only skin deep.

The rest of the women were talking about Aline Debenham.

"The dear little *dhoti*," said Mrs. Feather, who had dandled her as a baby. "I do hope she has had a good time."

"Well," yelled Mrs. Swinton, curling her lip, "she would not be coming back if she had, would she? No?"

She had to scream; because, even with her black tinned ear trumpet, old Mrs. Feather could only make out what you said by one or two words that came through here and there; and now she smiled and said: "I'm sure she has."

She was a splendid woman. She knew Thibet—but she had never once been inside a theatre. She had gone out to India fifty years ago to marry her soldier man, and never been home since. She could be pardoned, therefore, when she took her scissors and cut out all the lingerie advertisements in the magazines that circulated on the lake. She was deaf to protests that on the other side of the offending bits of offending female figures were usually the ends of stories people wanted to read. They were positively indecent, she said. And—what *had* become of corsets?

"In a way," said Mrs. Tread slowly, "I'm really sorry she is coming back. It will upset the boys, and she will never marry one of them, anyway. I've tried and tried and tried to tell them that. But they won't listen."

The grin on the Frenchwoman's face became absolutely lascivious as she said: "Poor Billy. I can't see what either Matt or Billy can see in that girl. Empty-headed little thing. *Just* like her mother!"

As this was in the ordinary conversational tone, old Mrs. Feather got none of it. She was content to sit there and see that her guests got enough to eat. They began these talks at lunch and usually ended them after tea-time—as no one could ever tell when the mail would actually get up. But if she had known that the two Tread boys were being discussed as imperilled by laughing little Aline Debenham—

why, she would have made people ashamed of themselves who thought a thing like that. The little *dhoti*. . . .

Mrs. Swinton, whose rat-like eye had been fixed on the largest piece of Miss Gay's marble cake, with a whole walnut on it, reached over and took it quietly before anybody else could get it. She giggled:

"I always like to eat my cake *with* my lunch."

* * *

Von Hauptmann had tried to make Elsa join in these luncheons. She would have been welcome. Despite the awkwardness that Mrs. Swinton would have probably made. The Feathers' house was open to everybody on this lake. And her staying away only emphasised what a pariah, even on the lake, the old German had made of himself. But after one sad occasion, when he had dropped her there, and brought her home as nervous and unhappy as she could be, he did not force her again.

Things had drawn them together. Her panic when the German mark broke, and they found they were penniless, had frightened even him at first. He resented it. It terrified him to see the care with which Elsa cherished each possession, every plate, every knife, every bit of furniture in their house, how she clung to them—as if she was afraid she was going to lose them now. She was so happy in her home, a house of her very own. He could understand that. She had, after all, only been one of his mother's upper housemaids before the old lady sent her out here to marry him. Elsa had gone through the German Revolution, a thing he had not known because he had been in B.C. since before the War; and she talked about it out here as if she had escaped from a perpetual nightmare. He had always travelled light himself. He gave few gifts to fortune. But she made him apprehensive. For his guns, for a few of the mementoes of his wandering life, for his carpenter's shop with its fine set of tools that he had, in the affluent days, ordered regardless from Germany.

For a long time he had been afraid to go into that room; the tools were a challenge to him. With them he might earn his living now, ask the other settlers to let him do some odd jobs. But he could never humble himself to ask them.

He knew what they thought about him; some of it, at least. How Mrs. Swinton had gone around telling everybody he was out here because he had done something "queer" out in German East Africa. Well, generalities could be very useful sometimes—as long as she kept to that.

They would never know of the boy who had died under his drunken flogging.

The yellow glare of the unpainted board shack of Smedley's Post Office and General Store drew him back to the present. In a few minutes he would have to face the lower Scaup Lakers. The thick lips behind his mask of beard and moustache set in a sullen pout. He slapped back the French *beret* irascibly on his bullet-shaped shining skull. The lake, narrowing to become a river that tumbled thirty miles down to the sea, caught his skiff and sucked it into the river pool. With heavy, arrogant thrusts he drove it in between the other boats lying at Smedley's wharf.

5

The "people around the store," as they spoke of each other, considered themselves the only legitimate inhabitants of Scaup Lake. This was because they all had a job of some sort, a reason to explain their presence there. This differentiated them completely from the upper Scaup Lakers, who, the people around the store contended, were all either trying to run away from retribution or themselves. There were only six settlers on the whole twenty miles of upper lake.

Instead of the aloof secret lives in lonely cabins of those mysterious characters on the upper lake, the lower lakers lived in one of the strangest, most *gemütlich* colonies in the world. This was nothing less than a series of shacks, all lying along the river bank, end to end, all built on the top of cedar rafts. Eight of them in all. Tread had started this type of house-boat when he had first come to the lake. Finding the jungle too thick, his first years to cut a clearing in, he had simply felled some cedar trees into the water and built his shack upon them. This amphibian life had taken root so that to-day a row of gangplanks stretched to the river bank from these house-boats below Smedley's; and children had been born and had grown-up to full-sized men on them. Beside the planks leading to the bank, a plank-walk extended from house-boat to house-boat. Just like a street. These shacks were painted and some of them even had flower boxes at the windows. People with children had fenced in little yards on their rafts. The obliging and sometimes dangerous river washed away everything that was thrown, or fell, overboard. Two hundred yards below the last house-boat smoked a white rapids. From then down there was not another habitation until Scaup River raced under the railway bridge twenty miles below. This was at Quamicot, jumping-off place for Scaup Lake, where Ken Cullen took his one-ton motor lorry down every Wednesday and Saturday to bring up the post and supplies.

*　　*　　*

Smedley's POST OFFICE & GENERAL STORE, as its green-lettered sign read, was the vanguard of progress on Scaup Lake. It represented enterprise. Smedley was a young Montreal Canadian, smelling, as all grocers must, of fresh crate-wood, cheese, lamp-oil, and ham. So did his ravishing sister, Zonia, who, a few months back had married Brinsley Greville, the hatchery man. Greville was an undoubted English gentleman, although a very faded one; and was too utterly distinguished and weary to have a social complex of any sort. But it was Zonia who first had the courage to point out and complain about the social abyss that existed between the upper Scaup Lakers and the people around the store.

"Oh, let them be," muttered the bored Greville, speaking of the upper Scaup Lakers one night. "They came out here to be alone. That's why I came."

"Oh, it's all right for you, Mr. Smarty," retorted Zonia; "you're a man. But what about *me*? Who do you think I've got to associate? Nobody. Nobody but that peroxided Mrs. Ken Cullen, who, I'll bet you all you want, was a Vancouver tart."

"You don't have to bet," smiled Greville. "I know she was."

"Well then? . . . "

It was a good thing, thought Greville, that Zonia could not guess the thoughts that were running through his mind. He had often meditated upon the peculiar attractions of Mrs. Cullen. Her gifts were, when you came down to it, based on the fact that she really had been a tart—she knew how to please men. Such being the case, in a place where there was no practical value in the maidenly virtues, Ken Cullen had shown damn' good sense in marrying her. She was a recent addition, but it was already plain that she was making the uncouth former little garage mechanic from Vancouver one of the happiest and most contented men on the lake.

"And I'll bet she was a damn' good one, too," Greville heard himself say.

"Now don't you be common," said Zonia.

Greville loved being called common by Zonia. Its irony cheered him up. "I've come to the conclusion," he said slowly, "that nothing but vice—flagrant and frequent—can make it up to a man for living in this charming hole."

"Then why don't you go home?"

On the return from their honeymoon, to Seattle, Zonia had found some faded photographs and an old copy of *Country Life* at the bottom of her new husband's trunk.

Stowed there, no doubt, where they wouldn't arouse trouble-some memories. After much plaguing, he had admitted that the photo of the boy on the fat Shetland pony was himself, that the one with a moustache was himself at the University; and he did not have to answer questions about *Country Life*, for the leading article, big as life itself, was a long account of Stoke Folliot, the Greville home, with photographs of the house and park and even a mention of himself, who, according to the article, was "ranching in Canada."

"Did you *ever* have a ranch?" persisted Zonia. Greville smiled: "Well . . . hardly. You know what the English are—incurable romantics. Every younger son who goes out to the Colonies, to the wide open spaces, is supposed to be ranching, or shooting big game, doing something dramatic."

"Did—you—ever—have—a—ranch?"

"No. I was a clerk in a Toronto department store. My lady-like demeanour got me a job in the ribbon department. I worked there five years. Then I thought I'd stood just about all of that hideous existence that a man can take, so I came out here—and married you. Now you know every-thing. Put those photos back."

It was the longest speech she had ever heard Greville make. Even longer than when he talked about fish.

A fish, before her marriage, had been an impersonal thing. She did not like to talk about fish in bed. She often suspected that Greville's midnight musings about why God made the Pacific salmon die, after they had spawned only once—bedroom scenes seemed to bring these thoughts naturally to his mind—were only red salmon drawn across the love-trail to cover up his own lack of staying power. She was a lusty girl. And Greville, in self-defence, complained that it rather put him off when she brought the aroma of the Smedleys to bed with her.

Zonia's thoughts on the morning of her marriage were not so much upon the delights of owning the aristocratic hatchery-man as they were that, once she had become Mrs. Brinsley Greville, Cecie Debenham would simply have to invite her to some of the week-end house parties that she gave during the summer months. Gay people from Victoria or the mainland whom she saw, usually waiting around Smedley's store until the Debenham launch could be made to start and come down lake to get them. And although her brother had long ago refused to let the Debenhams have any more credit at the store, and they were, as a consequence, having their essential supplies and delicacies sent up from some trusting firms in Victoria, she did live in this hope. Otherwise Scaup Lake was going to be an impossible place.

All her efforts to make Brinsley pay a visit to his people, so that she could enjoy the sights of London and Stoke Folliot, were met with the weary evasion: "Oh, I've got two sisters. They'll never marry now. One of these days we'll ask them to come out here and see us."

6

As Brinsley Greville had suspected, Virgie Cullen was a lively bit. She was sitting this morning in a pink silk dressing-gown, with pink, ostrich-feathered mules, close to the Cullen house-boat stove while her husband read a letter that Bill Tread had just brought down.

"DEAR KEN,—My daughter is coming home to-day. Mr. Lyon is bringing them up in his car, as it is a new one and he says he can't drive over twenty-five miles an hour (25!), I don't know what time they will get up. Aline had her trunks sent up to Quamicot, booked to you —could you fetch them in your motor-truck? And if you get back to the lake before they get here, could you bring them up to the house in your boat? Our boat won't run, as usual. (You will have to fix it when you come.) And would it be too much trouble to you to go to the Chinaman and get our laundry? . . . And when you are down in Quamicot will you go to Wright's and see if you can buy a bottle of Maraschino cherries? . . ."

"Huh!" laughed Virgie Cullen. "That dame doesn't want much, does she? So she calls you Ken, does she?"

He grinned and shook his head: "Ah, go on! Don't be silly. You know how it is. I do jobs for *everybody* on this lake. Why, I'm one of the family. They all know me."

"Yeah? And what about this guy Lyon? He's always coming up. Do you think that Debenham is wise?"

"Wise to what?"

"Or do you think he does know—and just doesn't give a damn. I'll say that life up here can take the ambition out of a man!"

"You've got a fine mind," said Ken. "Isn't there anything else you can think of?"

"Sometimes," said Virgie. "Give us a kiss. And don't forget that bottle of Green River when you're down."

The Cullens enjoyed life. Midnight shoutings and rockings of their house-boat were often followed by Ken appearing in the morning with some fresh scratches on his face. He was proud of them; no man on the lake had a lively woman like Virgie. Once when Mrs. Debenham asked him where he got his cut lip, he explained:

"Oh, we fight all right, all right. . . . Mrs. Cullen can fight like hell. But it's better that way. Quick come, quick over; that's our motto. Better than going around moping all day—don't you think so?"

"Your life sounds fascinating," said Cecie.

* * *

The Chinaman had three bulky bundles of laundry with which he was loath to part.

"Money!" squeaked Ah Foo. "Money, money, money! Missie Debenham say pay next time. Maybe no pay. Washee stop along me."

Ken seized the bundles. "Ain't you ashamed of yourself, Ah Foo? All right, keep your shirt on. I'll see that they give you something on account."

"Is it the Chink, or the combination of him and wet clothes that makes that smell—or do you think Ah Foo hits the pipe?" Ken asked of Billy Tread, whom he found waiting for him outside.

That pink-cheeked youth had no time for Celestials; hastily swallowing down his Adam's apple, he began: "Listen, Ken—let *me* take them up. Why should you bother? Gosh! Haven't I taken Aline up and down the lake hundreds of times? . . . ."

"Okay by me, kid." It was fun to tease Billy. Not so with Matt Tread; you never knew what that lanky grouch would do. "But, you see," said Ken, "Mrs. Debenham *asked* me to take 'em up. So, if I get back here before them I guess that's the way it is. I'm not going to eat your girl, Bill. Want to ride down with me, and lend me a hand with those trunks?"

"No," said Billy. "Maybe they'll get here before you get back." He followed in Ken's footsteps like a dog.

*   *   *

When they got back to the store they saw that something had happened. People were running. Four loggers were carrying a man up on a door from the *War Eagle*, which had just come in. "Our high-rigger," said one. "He's just cut hisself down." The door was padded with blankets and on these lay a twisted man with a cold white face. "He's not dead. Not yet," said a logger; "but he's hurt pretty bad. Come down a couple of hundred feet." The crowd stood around and looked down.

"Can't he hear?" said someone.

"Hear hell! Could you hear if you fell couple a hundred feet out a tree? Why this here Finn would a been dead if our time-keeper hadn't patched him up."

"Time-keeper! Huh?"

"Wot I said."

The time-keeper, a bald, pale-faced little man, who looked like a clown in rubber boots and a lumberman's shirt that was several sizes too large for him, came out of the store with Smedley, who pointed to Ken. "This man's in a bad way," said the time-keeper quietly. "I've put a tourniquet on his left leg—the bones are right through his flesh there and they'll probably have to take it off as soon as you get him to hospital. Do you think you can get someone to ride down with you and loosen that tourniquet about every twenty minutes?"

Ken looked around. "You, Billy," he said; "come on here. You studied first aid, didn't you, during the War? Hop in here."

With solemn efficiency, the four loggers lifted the door from the ground and carefully slid it into the motor lorry. Virgie Cullen, who had rushed up in one of her husband's overcoats, stood on the edge of the crowd, craning her neck. When she saw the time-keeper talking to Ken she ducked out of sight. She stood there by the nose of the car and watched the little man trot hurriedly back down the bank and into the *War Eagle*. When the motor lorry had gone off, she asked a bystander:

"Was that bald-headed little man the time-keeper? The man who patched that Finn up?"

"He sure was, missus!"

"Well . . . I never!" said Virgie Cullen.

7

"Why do you have your toilet paper printed in Greek? It seems almost too erudite."

Cecie Debenham looked apprehensively at this ironic
Bl

young creature whom Aline had brought back. Miss Felicity Correl had red hair, green eyes that always stared over your shoulder as she listened to you—she had not said one word at dinner—and the most beautiful nose and jaw that Cecie thought she had ever seen. But cold as a classic marble.

"M-my dear," said Cecie, with her almost imperceptible little stutter, "*was* it? We have to cut up every bit of newspaper we can find, you know. . . . I suppose it was a bit that came wrapped up around Aline's halva. We get that from Seattle."

Miss Felicity Correl gave her low choking laugh. "I'm glad to find something in your house," she said, "that isn't old England." Cecie wasn't sure whether this was meant to be insulting or not, until the girl added: "I'm *so* sorry." Then she knew it was.

The girl sat there with both beautiful legs stuck out before her while she examined the room. Cecie, up until this moment, had been very proud of that room. It was all there; the same old chintz chair-covers; the same repoussé silver photo-frames, with self-conscious relatives staring out at you from army uniforms or Court dress; the silver whatnots on the writing table; the same piles of *Tatler*, *Sketch*, *Bystander*, *Field* and *Country Life*—England. It might have been a drawing-room in any country house. This had been Cecie Debenham's answer to Scaup Lake; and now she saw that this girl saw something funny about it. . . .

Miss Correl suddenly frowned thoughtfully. "It is *so* nice of you to have me," she said, leaning forwards: "What is that you're making?"

"A pull-over for the Growler," said Cecie. "It's only to stop him from wearing the one he had on to-night at dinner, the one with the holes in the arms. He will never buy *anything*."

The Growler, Copey's unwilling partner, had dispelled the all-England atmosphere of the house by appearing before dinner, and not changing, in a pair of white rubber boots, canvas slacks and a shockingly tattered primrose pull-over. He had come in to fetch Copey, who had seized the mail, captured the London *Times*, and had immediately become lost in his favourite authors—Messrs. Knight, Frank and Rutley—on the back page.

"Have you seen Alice?" demanded the Growler, hardly waiting to be introduced. He limply touched Miss Correl's hand.

"She's gone," he said to Copey. "If you want her, you'd better go out and get her. I'm helping Nanny get the dinner."

*   *   *

"'Alice' is our cow," explained Cecie Debenham after Copey had groaned and followed the Growler out. "Milking her is supposed to be Copey's job. M-my dear, I don't see how she does it—with never a bull. . . ."

Miss Correl gave a long rasping laugh. "Doesn't seem much love lost. Does there?" she said, nodding her aristocratic head towards the door which had just closed behind the two men.

"LOVE! M-my dear—wait till you been *in* this house about one week. He's *impossible*. Wait till you see him in action, scraping all the bits off the plates after dinner like a . . . like a *white*-wings! It makes all of us quite sick."

Mr. Bertie Lyon, who was in the room at the time, gave a guffaw and said to Felicity: "You know the story, don't you —how Copey sold him a pup?"

Felicity had heard it. "I heard it the first night I met Aline," she said now, rudely. And as she thought of how Copey Debenham had bought this ranch from an advertisement in an English sporting magazine, and found that it was three feet under water during the rainy season every year— and of how, by inserting a duplicate of the self-same advertisement, offering a half-share, he had caught Mr. Hiscock, a retired Darjeeling tea-planter—as she thought of human tragedy Miss Correl laughed hoarsely. "It's frightfully funny," she said. "No wonder he is called the Growler."

"He's a little beast!" said Cecie.

*　　*　　*

Now, when she was obviously trying to make herself pleasant, Cecie found this young woman very interesting, in spite of her first reactions. She seemed genuinely interested in life on the lake and asked intelligent questions. Cecie began to think there was something other than a sneer, something sad in that hoarse, painful laugh . . . as if Miss Correl had found the world so awful that the only thing left to do was to laugh at it. She could see that she was honestly amused by the story of old Mrs. Feather—how she cut out all the lingerie advertisements. Aline's letters for the last few months had been full of nothing else than Felicity Correl: apparently she knew everybody, went everywhere—and didn't give a damn. That was the cubbish way that Aline would have put it. Cecie had wondered at the time what "didn't give a damn" meant. Now she felt that she was getting somewhere within grasp of it: the perpetual sneer on the face of this lovely young woman was not directed against her, this room, Copey, life in B.C., or any one specific thing— it was just against life. She looked a thoroughly disappointed woman. Hard as nails.

Aline had insisted on going across in Billy's boat to see the Treads. Lyon had gone out to help Copey and the Growler, who were trying to see what had gone wrong with the little petrol motor that ran the electric lights. They sat there by lamp-light before the crackling little fire, and then Cecie took a deep breath and asked:

"Why did Aline come home?"

"Bored," said Miss Correl.

"*With England!* Besides—Aline couldn't be bored. She's not introspective enough."

"London's frightful," said Miss Correl.

"S-so's B.C.," said Cecie, resuming her knitting. "Everything's frightful, isn't it . . . if you let it be?"

She worked hard. She was furious. She wanted to say: "Look here, my dear—I've seen just as much of this world as you have. Good and bad. And if you've taken that idiotic child of mine and made her think it was smart to think that life is dull . . . I could strangle you."

"If you don't mind," said Felicity, who seemed to sense that something was in the air, "I think I'll go to bed. I have headache."

"I—I'll get you some aspirin."

"That's *so* kind of you!" said Felicity. "I have some."

A few minutes after Cecie had shown her to her room, and how to bolt back the shutters so that they would not bang about all night, Copey came back and sank into a chair. He had a whiskey and soda in each hand, and handed Cecie hers. "Well? . . ." he said.

Cecie looked at him. "Copey, do you know what I think? I think that fool Aline has been made to come back here . . . just because that *terrible* creature wanted a trip abroad! . . ."

8

The lake which had faced that dawn with the unbroken smile that taunted Captain von Hauptmann had gradually become angry. Miss Felicity Correl heard it roaring in the black night. She had blown out her lamp, and probably for the first time in her life she faced a scene in which there was not one light in all the darkness. Just black night. As she leaned there in her dressing-gown her eyes became oriented and she could make out the white line of the surf where it broke on Copey's beach. She heard the Tread boat come back, and Billy's love-sick voice shouting another "Good night" to Aline. She heard Aline pass her door on tip-toe. She saw the reflection of her light on the ground and then, after an intolerably long time, that went out. Felicity sat there, her face in her hands. The wind shrilled around the corners of the house; and then she felt it shake the house and begin to thunder like muffled drums in the brick chimney.

"Oh . . ." she moaned. She leaned out so that the gusts of wind whipped her hair as she tried to stare through the dark. "So this is where you are? . . ." she said.

*   *   *

As she leaned there she noticed that she was looking at some trees along the rim of a mountain a long way off from her. They seemed to be lighted now by some glow that came from behind them. Like a false dawn. Then the glow became brighter and the line of trees became blacker, a ragged silhouette. The clouds above them began to glow a dull red. She stared at it uneasily. Then she hurried back into the room and lit the bedside candle.

Copey gave a startled rumble in answer to her repeated tapping. "What is it?" he asked. "What's the matter?"

"I don't know," she said through the door. "I think you had better come and look."

She hurried back. Copey came in from his room on the other side of the corridor. "It looks like a fire," she said, pointing to the glow. "Is it?"

"Fire . . ." Copey stuck out his head. Then he drew it back with an expression of extreme annoyance on his face. "I should just say it is a fire! It's a brute. That's either Lynd's . . . or the old German's place. Now I suppose we've got to turn out and try and do something. Damn it!"

THE YEARS BETWEEN

LYND found her again at Bombay.

There had been a farewell party at the Yacht Club, and he had decided to sit up for what remained of the night to see his last Indian dawn. It came up red and steaming, with the drenched palms over on Elephanta Island barely able to raise their drooping heads above a lull in the hot July monsoon. Smoking, his eyes had been fixed on a native lateen rig that during the last hour had won its way in from the Arabian Ocean and was now trying to beat up against the yellow, sluicing harbour tides. It was only in the silent hours like these that he dared to return to the secret places of his own heart. To that shrinking, sensitive, perhaps cowardly person who was just as real as the outwardly hard-boiled American newspaper correspondent a few of the British had been trying to get drunk a few hours back to cover up their shyness in giving him a royal good-bye. They too had revealed glimpses of their true selves behind the official mask; and, as the bottles were emptied, one after another of them had mentioned the fact that he was not altogether a bad chap, that they forgave him for some of the hard things his crass ignorance of the situation had made him say about them, and that, taken all in all, it was jolly nice to have an outsider, an American at that, recognise some of the difficulties that they were up against.

He smiled as he remembered this and sat down to begin his last dispatch. There were so many things he would like to say about the British and what he had seen here, but the formality of a newspaper cable heartlessly precluded them.

He would like to tell people that, in Lahore, he had met a bank manager who said he was proud to be the chairman of a club which had black-balled Rudyard Kipling—"because he had a touch of colour in him!" That he had gone

B1

over and patted Zam-Zammah himself, a side-step as he was
reporting the Mohammedan riots. That a large part of *Kim*
was Kipling's early life; that the old Afghan horse-dealer was
true—so was Lurgan Sahib. That mysterious antique-dealer
in Simla, to whom Kim was sent to "learn the secret things"
did have Black Magic (some ability to hypnotise); he was a
British Agent. . . . And then Lurgan Sahib lost his magic
. . . took to drink (probably in terror of the Indians' revenge
—when they found his magic was gone). "And it was my
bank," said the manager, proudly, "who served a writ on
Lurgan—and put him in jug!"

Tony had found many of such *sahibs* in India—especially
among the younger ones. But there were others. . . .

Now, that old British General at Peshawar, for example.
There had been something magnificent about that old
warrior! Here was a distinguished British commander who
actually resented the intrusion of the aeroplane into what he
obviously regarded as his personal and very friendly fight
with the Afridis. It wasn't sporting, said the General. It
wasn't fair. Not the way to treat an Afridi, who, after all,
expected you to fight like a gentleman. And, to bar this
modern contrivance which he thought gave him unequal
odds over an honourable foe, the General, in his official
reports, was actually trying to prove it was useless.

"Look at that fellow!" growled the General as Tony
leaned beside him across the sand-bags of Matta Fort and
they watched a circling aeroplane, whose observer or pilot
was vainly searching for some Afridis on which a bomb to
drop. "He's never going to hit anything! They call me a
bow-and-arrow soldier . . . but I've been trying to tell them
tanks and aeroplanes are no damn' use in this Mohmand
country. Got to go up it on your hands and knees . . . same
way as I did when I was a boy. The Afridi understands that
kind of fighting. Damn' nice chaps, these Afridis."

Lynd laughed now as he recalled that charming incident.
He could not write it. It was too utterly human for the

Indian cables which, at nearly a shilling a word, allowed barely enough space to cover the bitter political problems. Nevertheless, here in India he had witnessed something that had immensely gratified and strengthened that secret Tony Lynd, the other man he was afraid to have people know. This old General was a fanatic defender of chivalry in warfare, a virtue that had vanished from the European conflicts where people shot their prisoners and gassed babies as they slept. He was a return to the heroes of childhood. He vastly admired that old General and hoped it was not true what he heard: that he was going to be broken for his backwardness.

The world nowadays was full of such dirty tricks.

As he typed, the sweat dripped off his forearms and blotted his carbon copies. He winced again as he recalled that eye-scorching aerodrome at Karachi—and the British complacency that had offended his dignity even as he stepped out of the Baghdad aeroplane. He stared once more at that amazing sight of the yellow Mohammedan forts, with their castellated towers of sunbaked mud, rocking in the heat haze of the Great Sind Desert. He watched again the peacocks and the grey monkeys playing around the Jain temples as they went down through the jungled hills of Rajputana. He was thrilled once more by the mêlée of colour and castes he saw all along his first railways stations, the shrinking black Untouchables and the proud Hindu women with diamond studs in their noses. He saw the glistening black-mud flats of the Gujerat with the shockingly urban sight of the factory chimneys of Bombay rising up across them. Was it to see these that he had travelled to the East? He recalled his fright as he faced the mob at Sholapur, mouths dripping blood red from betel-nut—as if they had already been slashed; and that awesome sight of the Akali Sikhs, striding barefoot through the dusty streets of Mogra—with the polished quoits, an almost forgotten deadly weapon, on their blue-turbaned heads. Kipling's India; he recalled his rick-shaw rides along Simla's ridge, that South Kensington the implacable British have created in the Himalayas, and how hopefully he searched for a modern Mrs. Hauksbee. . . . Well—he had found a Colonel's daughter who would prob- ably grow up into something like that. *Sahibs ?* Yes—she had actually used that very word when informing him what he should consider people of her own kind; and he recalled his rage at her unforgivable, unpardonably complacent ignor- ance of Indian hopes and hates . . . and how he had felt at the time that another afternoon's talk with a self-satisfied young lady such as that would have turned him into a rabid Gandhi-*wallah* . . . or a murderer.

When he came to the little Mahatma himself, Lynd smiled as he recalled how two thrusting young subalterns in the Taj Mahal Hotel had informed him that on the night Gandhi was arrested, a woman had been found in bed with him. "Well, all the more power to him!" laughed Tony. They could not understand his continued mirth at their narrative until he informed them that he had been there himself on that dramatic night—he had achieved a world scoop on the Gandhi arrest—and that what they were trying to tell him was the most footling form of official propaganda. He could still see their amazed faces.

The little Mahatma himself had been an immense comfort and assurance to that secret Tony Lynd, the man he never wanted the world to see. The courageous simplicity of the little 104-lb. figure who had stripped himself so clean of material things that the world could not touch him any more. The man who with the mere power of an idea was defying the mighty British Empire. Here was a model for any man, his own secret self, to live up to. He had been so absorbed with Gandhi's personality that he forgot the journalistic questions he had come all the way to India to ask. And when he did remember them they all seemed so vulgar and trivial, so utterly beneath the problems that Gandhi was proposing that he was glad not to have voiced them.

*   *   *

For the last ten years he had been darting about Europe as a foreign newspaper correspondent. And he had had ten eventful years of Russia and the Near East before that. The result was a kaleidoscope of impressions that had blurred his memory of almost every single event. They were like a fast-run movie strip. It was the chief irony of his most interesting profession that he had been forced to see so many lives without ever being able to live an uninterrupted life of his own. He had been so satiated with sensations that he often felt merely numb when he should have been deeply shocked. One of the things that constantly surprised him was the instinctive kindliness and decency he found everywhere in mankind and the way it was corrupted into the most shocking cruelty by political creeds. The cause of class or country was a sufficient excuse for otherwise well-intentioned people to commit the most atrocious barbarities. After twenty years of watching the human tragedy, it was only natural that an impartial observer, a professional neutral such as his job made him be, should have become callous—he could not have lasted otherwise—and that he should carefully have protected his own intimate personality; that secret side of a man that he seldom shows except when moved deeply either by anger or love.

It was thus that he had learned to travel the world; outwardly the congenial, he hoped competent, and not too cynical newspaper correspondent—and inwardly that sensitive, shrinking, perhaps cowardly creature that he knew so well, still searching for the impossible in love, still clinging to many of his childhood ecstasies and still uncalloused. . . .

The six pages of cable that he typed so painstakingly this morning were the work of his strictly professional being; a concise résumé of the Indian situation during the six months that he had known it. In a few hours people would be reading it in the streets of New York; three hours later in San Francisco. In a week they would have forgotten it.

He smiled as he thought of that, and turned to a bearded Mohammedan servant who had quietly entered his room and had been laying out a fresh suit of white drill on the bed. In a beard that was blood-red with dripping betel-nut, Abdul's gash of a mouth, opened now in his ghastly smile, showed that it possessed only two teeth; and Tony smiled gravely, as he always did at this morning apparition. Lynd was thinking that that blood-red mouth, perhaps, would be one of the Indian memories that would last the longest. Like Kim and his holy man, he and Abdul had travelled the length of India together. And they may not have been feigned, those tears in the faithful Abdul's eyes, as he took that last cable he would ever carry to the Post Office for Lynd *sahib*.

Another show had ended at which Tony had been merely a spectator. Another strip of memories had been added. A zinc travelling ice-chest, which he could not think what on earth he would ever do with; two solar topees, one of which, at least, he would throw over the rail at Port Said—to fulfil the traditional gesture of white man's defiance to the East, that you have done with it; a complete outfit of aertex shirts, white cotton drill suits, Chinese pongee—even unto white mole-skin dinner jackets, which he also wondered what he could do with unless Fate sent him to South America, or he was forced to spend a summer in the United States. He hoped he would never forget that lovely sight of the green rushes of the Kabul delta shining in the sun . . . he hoped he would one day meet that old bow-and-arrow General again who had given him and poor Budgin hell for standing by Kabul's streams, debating whether there were any trout in them, when the Afridis began to snipe . . . and he would like to remember the yellow peaked turbans of the Dogras, peering down over the blockhouses, as he fulfilled one of his life's ambitions and went up Khyber Pass. . . . This last scene had certainly not been one of travel's disappointments. Now he reflected that all bills were paid, all his bags packed, all farewells had been said. He was done.

While Abdul was away at the Post Office he lay for a long time, luxuriously, in the cool, stone bath. Then he clop-clopped back in his slippers along the row of servants, squatting on their hunkers before their sleeping *sahibs*' doors, and carefully began to dress. He dressed without haste, sitting on his bed under the comparative cool swirls of air from the revolving wooden fan. One thing at least awaited him on the Arabian Sea—he would escape from the hot, horizontal rains of the July monsoon.

Only one farewell remained, and it was perhaps characteristic of him that his final good-bye should be with the pariah white man of all India—Freddy Wayson.

Freddy's was the most brilliant mind he had found out here. But it was too clever. Freddy had a wit that was beyond his own control. When London newspaper editors discovered that it was also beyond their jurisdictions—and that it might even be turned against them—they fired Freddy. When he had run the gamut of Fleet Street, Freddy Wayson came East. There was a brief period of scintillating respectability when he edited the *Pioneer*; then there was an even briefer pause while the *Civil and Military Gazette* was awakening. Then that extremely respectable journal also parted with him. And Freddy was on the loose. A bad thing for a disgruntled Englishman in India. Especially with a brain. He began to attack the *sahibs*. He was simply snapped up by a Hindu Bombay newspaper, whose previous editor had drunk himself to death; and, after a few of its new excoriating editorials, the *India Daily Post* swept the country like a prairie fire—and Freddy Wayson became the loneliest Englishman East of Suez.

No *pukka sahib* would speak to him—although India officialdom rushed to buy each day's *Daily Post*, for fear of what Freddy might have had to say about them. He was not allowed to cross the threshold of any *pukka* club—although traitor Freddy was always the liveliest topic of conversation on their cool verandas. He was even shunned

fearfully by the white correspondents who lived in the Taj
Mahal Hotel—because they had been warned against the
danger of being seen with renegade Freddy by the *pukka
sahibs*. In Freddy, Lynd had found an exhilarating antidote
against the sometimes boring circumspection of official
India; and the engaging Freddy Wayson had found a man
who could appreciate his sense of fun.

"But it's no use, my lad," Freddy had confessed the previous night on the Taj Mahal terrace as they drank their
evening round of cocktails. "I'm out with my own kind—
but don't think I'm in with our little brown brothers. Far
from it. The wily Oriental gentlemen . . . these Wogs . . .
they take you at the evaluation they see your own kind set
upon you. When they see you are not allowed to enter any
of the *pukka* clubs. When they see you being ignored when
the Editor of the *Times* is entertaining a visiting party of
M.P.s and their toothy misses at a dinner table right beside
you. When they recollect that they've never, never seen you
on the lawn of Flagstaff House, to whose odious teas they
have been condescendingly invited—you're out with them.
They become patronising to you, old chap . . . damned,
infuriatingly patronising. . . . And that's a thing I don't
like."

Freddy wore the blue-and-red striped tie of the Cold-
stream Guards, in which he had been a lean and husky
officer during the War. But he was fat now, ridiculously
bulging, showing fat pink knees below the absurd khaki
shorts he almost slept in. No *pukka sahib*, after sundown,
would have dared dress like Freddie, the renegade. "I'm
worth my weight in gold to these Wogs," said Freddy
disgustedly, "but don't think I'm in love with them . . . or
like to clasp their fish-like hands. I'm just fed up to the teeth
with Mother England's human exports. It makes my tail
twitter to see Ealing lording it over the glorious East. . . ."

Freddy came in, to grace the occasion, actually wearing a
pair of pongee bags, and immediately questing about Lynd's

empty room for the whiskey bottle: "Where is it, old boy?" Without asking what, Tony pointed to where a half-bottle of Johnnie Walker lay in the bag waiting for his pyjamas. Abdul also came back. He was afraid of Freddy, although he liked Wayson *sahib*, who always teased him, and particularly was he afraid of the way Wayson *sahib* and his master could drink. As he saw Tony accept the glass that Freddy held out to him, Abdul raised his hands: "Ah, *sahib*, *sahib*. . . . We have not had our breakfast yet!"

The bottle was emptied; the bags were piled into a motor car with the faithful Abdul; and Freddy and Lynd strolled across steaming Bombay to the pier. The natives, already taking hashish to escape the hot monsoon, stared at them with lack-lustre eyes. . . .

* * *

The big P. & O. boat had come down from China and was already a Noah's Ark of white types from the Orient. Most of them were only going home on temporary leave. "But there," said Freddy, as they climbed up the gangway, "is a h'officer and a gentleman who is looking on India— and *glory*, me lad—for the very last time!" He pointed above them to where a red-tabbed General, with a face like a red mullet, was waving an affectionate farewell to another Indian servant, like Abdul, staring upward from the congested pier. The pier was full of these tearful farewells. After Lynd had said "Good-bye" to Mrs. Abdul and all the nine little Abduls, Abdul and his wife hung a wreath of sickly-smelling jessamine around Lynd's neck, an expensive wreath for the Abduls, covered with silvered glass balls. "I feel like a prize bull," muttered Tony to Freddy as they climbed up towards the faces that were grinning down at them from the big *Kasr-i-Hind's* rail. "You stink like a crematorium!" unsympathetically replied Freddy. On the obscurity of the deck, after a final wrenching farewell to the Abdul family, Tony flung off his wreath and read the last-minute note that the old Mohammedan had tearfully placed in his hand. It read:

"SAHIB, If you do not come back to India yourself, please send me another *sahib*. For I have no one but God and Your Honour to protect me. . . ."

"Pretty good!" said Freddy. "for an old rascal that's been cheating you up and down the length of India!"

Tony smiled. "I know, I know," he said. "He always took what he considered was his just commission out of all money I gave him to pay for anything. But I feel sure he never took more than that. And I know damn' well that he never allowed anyone else to cheat me. I was his own monopoly."

"You're getting sentimental," jeered the fat Freddy.

*   *   *

The smoking-room of the big *Kasr-i-Hind* was a mêlée of pith helmets, "Cheerioah, old chap," "See you in Piccadilly," and a few red-rimmed eyes. Some of the older faces from China were as sere and serene as the Orientals themselves. The thoughtful melancholy of those who had not struck it rich, or who were genuinely torn by their parting with the East was trodden underfoot by the hasty gaiety of the crowd that had come down to drink the Bombay passengers off. There were two tables in the corner, Tony noticed as they were searching for a place to sit down, that were full of Malay planters—lobster faces with fish-white foreheads—already well under weigh at this hour of the morning on the long carouse home. An Indian Civilian or so looked disparagingly around, self-consciously trying to lend dignity to the scene, remembering no doubt the one they had just quit where their very entrance into a crowded room would have brought everyone in it leaping to his feet. Their supreme conceit irritated Freddy, who remarked:

"This whole crowd gives me a pain in the tail. They're bloody suburbia, all of them. Look at them! Kind of people who'd live in Cheltenham! Now they're *sahibs*! Oh, God! Get a steward."

Twisting his fat body in the revolving chair, Freddy pointed out various celebrities in the scene. "There's my boss—the Chimpanzee. He's talking with Chundra Dass, another slick advocate. I'll bet you the Chimpanzee is trying to get Chundra Dass to bring him back another secretary . . . that's what he calls his procession of white girls. . . . Old Chundra Dass is thinking of what he is going to do to himself in Paris. Old Chundra Dass was knighted for his estimable services to Empire on the Skeen Commission. Glorious bit of satire, old boy. Didn't think our people could be up to it. . . . What old Chundra Dass really did was use some private official information he was privy to on the Skeen Commission to help himself make a killing on the Stock Exchange. Only he made one mistake . . . market reactions, when he let the cat out of the bag. What happened was, the market boomed instead of crashed—and old Chundra, who had sold himself short, lost his shirt on it. . . . He'll never forgive the British for that, old boy. . . . Ha-ha. . . ."

Lynd was not listening. After twenty years he still thrilled to the romantic confusion accompanying a ship's departure. He was listening to the engines slowly rumbling beneath them, the hiss of the water pouring from her exhaust ports, the rattle and clank of donkey engines as the last cargo slings were slung inboard; already he saw her proud bows lifting in the swells of the Arabian Ocean, the sun play on her decks and blazing on her superstructure. For eighteen days now he had nothing to do but just lie in a deck-chair and read. . . .

"Now what I want to know," said Freddy, demanding Lynd's attention, "is where you're going to get a bit of nookey on this boat. You've got eighteen days for it, you know. And there's nothing like a boat for it, is there, old cock?"

Tony gasped. How could people talk so casually about women? A fat slob like Freddy. Didn't it make them secretly uncomfortable? Or was it just he who always felt so dismayed when such discussions were begun? He did not know why it was, but all his life he had cringed before talk like this. Was he afraid? And of what? Had something happened to him somewhere along the line that made him afraid to talk frankly and freely about women? He never could feel quite sure. At times he felt almost ashamed of this maidenly modesty within him, "this shrinking violet," as he often contemptuously thought of his own innermost self. At other moments he felt sure that he had gained a lot, simply by not losing this original romantic ideal about woman's sanctity. The enthusiastic belief in sheer goodness that had so often crucified his idealistic soul in boyhood's calf-loves. In his heart he felt certain that he was right to have these old-fashioned ideas about women; and he was furious with the fat Freddy for being so cheap about love. He said uneasily:

"Oh, they all get off, Freddy. The pretty ones always get off the ship. They always do."

"You're right there, old boy!" He saw the fat back of Freddy's red neck; Freddy, apparently already engaged in the amorous pictures he was enjoying of himself clasping the various pretty girls in the smoking-room. "By God— *there's one!*" said Freddy.

Tony looked. And saw Luba.

* * *

It was dismaying after all these years to find that the very sight of her could strike him such a blow as this. He was shaking so that he gripped the table not to show it. She was sitting with two Lancer officers and had apparently just come in. One of the officers, a sallow man with a long greyhound head, was telling the steward what drinks they wanted. While his lean head was turned, the other man, a colonel by his pips and crown, reached swiftly across the table and tried to hold Luba's hand. Lynd saw her hastily draw it away from him. It was just like Luba, always timid about showing even the slightest emotion in public, and not even capable of showing anything more than a frivolous portrayal of her feelings in private. And it was so queer, to see little Luba sitting there in a solar topee. . . . It would happen like this, after all these years, just as if it had been arranged this was the way they should meet.

"Seen a ghost?" asked Freddy.

"A little bit."

"Who is she? She's damned pretty."

"Oh, a girl I knew in Russia . . . ages ago."

"Hmmm! . . . Must have picked her out of the cradle then."

Lynd seized a passing steward and told him to bring them a bottle of Johnnie Walker. "As long as I'm staying on the boat . . ." he explained to Freddy. When it came he poured himself out such a stiff drink that even Freddy Wayson protested. "You've got eighteen days, you know," remonstrated Freddy. "You'll never see Marseilles, if you begin at that rate. Well, here's how—the next time we meet in Piccadilly."

Lynd nodded. Eighteen days, he was thinking. . . . Well, Luba, this time you're not going to get away from me. I made the mistake once of being afraid of your innocent love. But I've had fourteen long years of regrets, and time enough to think better about it. This time you won't find me so childishly puritanical. Fourteen long years, my darling; and now we've got eighteen long days to make up for them. His sudden chill that she might only be coming down to see the officers off was lifted when he heard the gong sounding round the deck for "All ashore," and, as he was still absent-mindedly letting Freddy Wayson shake his hand, he watched Luba kiss both the officers what he thought was a much too long and friendly farewell.

The man with the head like a greyhound laughed loudly afterwards.

*   *   *

"One of them is my husband, the other is the man I'm coming back to marry," said Luba after dinner.

"But you can't do that! Not out in India—not in that regiment! One of those men will have to resign."

"Oh, can't I?" said Luba, and it seemed that there was an undertone of hatred toward all men in her voice.

With Luba safe on the ship, where she could not flutter away from him, his old hesitation and indecision with her had immediately returned to him. He both did and did not want to speak to her again. He was afraid what it would lead to. Therefore he had kept her in sight all that day without ever once going up to her. It was only before dinner, when she came into the smoking-room and sat down by herself, and he saw the Malay planters stop their chatter and look hungrily in her direction, that he decided to wait no longer. He knew that his knees were shaking as he went across to her, and he was grateful to see her flush and then grow pale as she clutched her slender neck and gazed up at him.

"Well?" he said, sitting down in a chair before her.

"Tony! You—you gave me such a fright!"

"My sweet."

He looked around for a steward. They watched the others get up and go into the dining saloon. "You haven't changed . . . not much," he said. "Oh—Fofoiser!" she laughed, and endearingly called him by the pet name she had for both her yapping Pomeranian and him. "How nice of you!"

"You've bobbed your hair," he said slowly. "But your eyes are just as dark as ever. You—you look a bit thinner, not quite so much like a plump little Tartar girl. You are really very pretty, my sweet. And just as silly?"

"Yes, Fofoiser?"

Tony nodded. "My God, my darling . . . if you knew how I've thought about you. . . ."

Luba looked around the empty smoking-room. "I think we had better go," she said. He got up and walked with her out on the deserted deck. Automatically they both walked to the rail together and leaned there, staring down at the racing water along the ship's side. Finally, he said: "Luba, come to my cabin."

"Yes, Fofoiser."

* * *

". . . And so," he said, "that's part of it, what it has meant to dream of you all these years. You see what it has been like. But I do want you to know one thing, my dear; it will make a difference. This . . . well, I suppose you might as well know this is the first time I've been unfaithful to Christina. Never . . . not in ten years, have I touched another woman, I have always hoped it would be you . . ."

"And it has, Fofoiser."

"Yes . . . it was you."

* * *

The event that he had been torturing himself with for fourteen years had taken place. He knew now that the picture would never trouble him again. He felt a traitor as he thought this; but even in the middle of his love-making, in the ecstasy of this unbelievable reunion, Luba had stopped to exclaim: "What a big cabin you have, Fofoiser!" She was stupid. He knew enough now to realise that, and that the regrets he had been burning his brain with these last fourteen years were for a girl who would have driven him insane had he married her. But he knew it too late.

With Luba's arresting combination of yellow hair and dark fringed eyes, she could look spectacularly "Russian and tragic," when she wanted to. But that only made things all the more exasperating when you realised that there was nothing at all behind those Tartar brows.

"Oh, damn the cabin. And don't, Luba . . . don't always go on calling me by the pet name for your dog. Can't you think of something sensible sometimes?"

That dog! He had often felt it was indicative of Luba's stupidity that she should own such a miserable snip of weeping, shivering, unpleasant hair and flesh—and love it! It was called Minka.

"Fofoiser! How can you be so mean! Don't you know that we had to leave Minka behind to face the Revolution in Moscow? She's probably dead now."

"Oh, Luba. . . ."

He got up and put on his black-silk dressing-gown, the one with the white polka dots that Chris had bought him. She had bought half a dozen of these in the ten years she had been married to him. Poor Chris—he probably was a swine to talk to Luba about her. Chris whom he had made suffer for so many things she never knew about, when his brain had been fevered with vain regrets for Luba. Luba . . . the little flibberty-gibbet! . . . who, instead of realising what an unbelievable thing had happened, that they had actually lain in each other's arms after all these years . . . couldn't talk about anything except her damned sniffling dog.

How Christina would have laughed, if she could have seen this trick being played by Life on two other people. But she certainly wouldn't see anything but horror in this scene. He shook his head at the thought; he had planned it for so long and so determinedly that it had never occurred to him that he wouldn't seize Luba, even by force, the first minute he saw her again. The utter amorality of his intention never occurred to him. He had been frustrated too long. Especially when it was he, in his puritanical young manhood, who had sent innocent young Luba from his room the night she tried to get into bed with him. That regret had been too much to live with her fourteen years—without the determination to wipe it out at the first moment.

"Honest, my sweet," he laughed, as he looked at Luba now, lying there so unashamed, "if you could only know the deaths I've wanted you to die all those years. . . ."

"I saw you once, Fofoiser."

"Good God! Where?"

"Weber's. Paris. I was sitting just by the door where you came in. You—you looked around for a table."

"Well, why didn't you *speak*?"

"I couldn't. I put my face behind the menu. I think the man I was with thought I was mad—because I started crying. You had a woman with you." With her genius for mimicry she described Christina to the line; Christina's rather arrogant way of staring around her as she entered a restaurant—with her slender chin stuck out; her pet name for him—"Peter!"—and the peremptory way she used it. No one but a person who had seen and heard Christina in action could ever invent that.

"That's Chris," he said.

"Yes, I know. Your wife! I saw the photographs in the *Daily Telegraph* of your marriage. She is General Sir Hercules Mallard's daughter. Is that right?"

"Very much—at least he is. Exactly the type of man who would drive you Russians crazy. He's so correct."

"I'm not a Russian."

Here was another point on which he had long ached to have it out with evasive Luba; her unbelievable family! So he said:

"Yes, you are, my sweet. I know your father, Roderick, is supposed to be an Englishman. But he was born in Russia and if there is anything more Russian than a Russian it is

an Englishman, like your delightful father, who has been
born out there, never had to do a stroke of work in his life,
and out-Russians the Russians in their idea of life. There is
no use mincing words about it; I don't like Roderick. I
think he and your mother have ruined your life. Mine, too,
as far as that goes. . . . They were just damn' selfish."

"Your life, Fofoiser? Aren't you in love with your wife?"

"I love her—if you can get the difference? I'd have
probably been very much *in* love with her, if it hadn't been
for you. Poor Chris—I've made her suffer like hell for things
she has never done or known anything about! Times when
my nerves were on edge because I was wretched about you.
I've been a hell of a husband, I can tell you."

"And is she in love with you?"

"Absolutely. That's the worst part of it."

The boat thrummed beneath them. He could hear the
soft swish of the sea-water along her sides. He leaned forward
and lifted Luba's warm, fragrant body in his arms. Their
lips met.

*   *   *

Luba did not lack a sense of the dramatic. That was the
Russian in her. The next days as they lay in deck-chairs and
watched the dolphins chasing each other across the glassy
sea, he was given the story of her years. At times the tale was
almost too excruciating to be bearable. He wondered if such
things could really happen. Luba, when she began a story,
left nothing to the imagination. There had been a little
Jew-boy, for instance, off Golden Square, in a sweat-shop
where Luba had been forced to sew for a time. She always
had to keep the table between them. He had taken it as his
right—his father owned the establishment—to exercise the
droit de seigneur with every girl in the shop. Most of them had
been too terrified of their jobs to resist him, or too stupid.
When Luba had exhausted her evasiveness, and been forced
physically into a corner, where he was starting to unbutton

her dress, she had slapped him. After that she had hunted about London for another job. "I would have had one in the chorus of the Sphere—but the man engaging us said to me, 'You understand, of course, don't you, Miss Power, that you will go away with me occasionally for a Sunday? I have a cottage at Bosham where we can drive down Saturday nights.' Virtue means nothing to me, Fofoiser," added Luba plaintively. "I went down. But then he said I couldn't dance!"

Lynd shuddered. "I wish you would spare me these details."

Then there were women who demanded to be fitted, and have last-minute alterations made, in the big London hotels. "And some of them were so *dirty*, Fofoiser!" Luba climbing aboard buses, carrying heavy bags all around London. Luba at Nice, where she had gone to stay with an old Russian aunt—and a young Russian had climbed up the rain-spout and into her window one night.

"He was so handsome! And I thought he was so sporting to climb up that spout. So I let him do it."

"My God, was—was that the first one?"

"Yes, Fofoiser; he was a Prince. Prince——"

"Well—for—God's—sake!" He jumped up and stormed around the cabin. "Don't tell me his *name*! Haven't you any sense? Good God, Luba! I don't understand you at all!"

"Why, Fofoiser?"

*   *   *

"We're just flotsam and jetsam, aren't we, Fofoiser?" asked Luba one sultry morning as the *Kasr-i-Hind* cut through the listless green sea on her stolid run to Aden. She played deck-tennis with the unkillable Malay planters in the mornings and was now sitting in the shortest of all shorts, with decorative beads of sweat on her impudent little nose, where he had had their chairs placed on the shady starboard side. He had been lying there, trying to read a book, but really letting his mind wander over the colourful story of their unlucky love—since they had met and lost each other in the shambles of Romanoff Russia. "Have you ever thought," she said happily, accepting the long cool Tom Collins that the steward bore on his tray, "how we've been tossed about? It's just like a book, isn't it, Fofoiser?" Her bird-like laughter cut through the soggy air; and he saw one of the British *memsahibs* look up from her book and give Luba an angry stare. The word that she was a "Russian" had gone about the ship—in fact he had heard her, the second day, telling one of the breathless Malay boys how she had had to flee Russia and leave Minka behind her to face the Revolution.

Luba was obviously not a success with the English girls. She was too natural, for one thing—too likely to do or say something that they would not understand. She delighted Tony with her mimicry of their disapproving stares.

"They spend all their lives *acting*!" she exclaimed, unveiling an unexpectedly bitter dislike for them. "Always *seeming* to be something. What is it, Fofoiser? It would kill them just to be themselves!"

He understood what she meant. It was expressed in the self-conscious stalk of the Indian Civil Service officials on their daily promenade around the deck. As if they were on parade. "They always *see* themselves as something, don't they, Fofoiser? Even when they are talking to you, you feel that they are only listening to themselves. . . . Even their accent is artificial!"

He was already re-discovering that, despite Luba's incredible silliness about the hard facts of life, she still had this genius for refreshing caricature. He remembered how she had mimicked him when, as an eager, puritanical American youth, he had first turned up in Tsarist Petrograd. She had mocked his purity; Luba, who, at that time, was as virginal as a nun! But it had been just because she was so completely unaware of a certain side of life (which she now seemed to know only too well) that her chief source of amusement in those days was teasing her embarrassed father about his infidelities. Jokes which used to drive Lynd quite frantic, in love with her as he was. And now she was also innocent of the fact that nearly every comment she made about the British on the boat pointed out only too clearly the contrast between herself and his present life with Christina. There he had the two extremes: Russian Luba and his English wife. Two extremes also in his own life.

The contrast, he had to admit, only made Christina show up all the better. It left Luba where she was. And made him seem so much the worse. It was an ironic see-saw of values. Christina, for instance, would never in a thousand years see anything but wrong in the fact that he had slept with Luba. Christina took his faithfulness to her as a matter of course. Not as morals, which was just the awkward part of it—but just that he *was* faithful, and was expected to continue so. He, on the other hand, had not the slightest pang of conscience when he took Luba in his arms. She was too decent. There was no sin there—not in that nice little body and mind. No matter what she did, Luba could not be sinful. And no amount of angry reasoning could make her so. She might have been, he reflected, if she had been more intelligent; because then she would be scheming. Luba was too childish and inconsequential not to be innocent.

"I was just thinking," he said, "how stupidly we have been letting other people, and events, shove us about. A lot of it was my own fault. I suffered from being too pure—I was not practical enough about life. I hate to think what a naïve young fool I must have seemed back in Petrograd, but then you see—I was like that. I thought a woman's body was the most sacred thing in the world—especially when you loved her! And you see what happened—I just went crazy when I found out what the Continentals thought about women—or to be more to the point, when I learned what the Continental women thought about themselves. I was trying to catch up for the wasted years—too long a Puritan, you know?"

Luba chirped with laughter. "Well, you certainly had a reputation when you first met me. Didn't you, Fofoiser?"

He frowned: "Did I not! But then look what I did when I fell in love with you. The puritanical ass I became at once! You see, basically, I hadn't changed at all. That's the reason, when I found her, that I married Chris; she's so straight. With Chris, of course, I went straight too; the same way I wanted to do with you! That's what worries me now."

"What, Fofoiser?"

"Well, now that you and I have found each other again —and gone the whole way, I don't suppose we are going to back out of it, are we? And that can't help but make a difference in my relations with Chris. Even if she doesn't find it out."

"Yes, Fofoiser. I suppose you will have to tell her."

"I shall never tell her. What is the use of making poor Chris feel rotten?"

Luba said: "But what about me, Tony? Am I to be just your mistress?"

"What do you mean? Do you mean you want me to chuck Chris?"

"Oh, no . . . no . . ." She frowned. "But——"

"Well, I wouldn't do it, Luba. I know that."

"Yes," sighed Luba. "So do I."

* * *

They had tacitly kept off going into the details of her own marriage. He knew Luba well enough to know that, sooner or later, it would come out, all with a rush. And Luba waited for the Red Sea to do it.

There had been a lull in the monsoon the day they left Bombay. The hot, slashing rain had let up for a few steaming hours, and the false relief gave a new breath of life to them, although the sun was steaming overhead, and the oily sea merely reflected its smouldering heat. It was an effort to move. After Aden, the Deck Committee decided to hold a gymkhana.

It was thoroughly British, both such a decision and the zeal. Several of the enthusiasts maimed themselves, or other people, that dreadful afternoon. Lynd was one of them. A Malay boy, playing deck football, barged into Tony and twisted his ankle. That night he sighed gratefully and had the steward lash Luba's deck-chair to his. He need not dance.

The port side was gaudy with a drapery of limp signal pennants and Union Jacks. The officers were glittering in mess jackets of spotless white, with decorations up. The Malay planters wore white dinner jackets with black cummerbunds, as did Lynd. With air-scoops projecting from every port-hole and red-mouthed funnels gaping to draw air down to the engine-room, where, Lynd felt sure, it must be cooler than it was on deck, the ship's orchestra struck up the waltz from *Bitter Sweet*.

Luba was particularly lovely in an apple-green dress that, he thought, was a bit too *décolletée*. She seemed to like such display, which was rather surprising after the *gauché* little cub he had known in Petrograd, trembling when she touched his hand, still wearing the plaited pigtail of heavy golden hair down her back, even after she was engaged to him. She wound it around her head when they went to the family box at the Ballet. Such nervous, unhappy days. . . . It gave him a feeling of possession now to have the Malay men bring her back to him. By taking possession of her little silver mesh-bag and vanity-case he knew that she would have to return to her chair after every dance; for no face, however lovely, could remain without treatment for more than one dance on that stifling night.

It was after the first dance that he thought he noticed it; when she came back from the second he was sure; when he saw the third expectant partner approaching, another of the Malay contingent, he thought he had better speak:

"Your dress is running," he said.

She froze like a hare. "*Are you sure?*"

"Yes," he said quietly. "Lean back, and I'll dismiss this fellow." He looked up. "I'm afraid Miss Power is feeling she'll have to give this one up," he said, asking the other man to have a cigarette, facing the glare he knew he would get as the other man walked stiffly off. "Now," he said to Luba, "you cut along and change."

"I can't! Fofoiser—please let's go to your cabin!"

*   *   *

The door had no sooner clicked behind them than poor Luba flung off a shoulder strap and stared at her back. There it was—a green, and as he found out, an almost indelible tatoo.

"But haven't you worn this dress before?" he said, after vain scrubbing with soap and a bath sponge had produced only a smear.

"Of course!" she choked.

"Well, I haven't seen you in it."

"You have, Fofoiser—it was white."

*   *   *

She and the bath stewardess had dyed it the day before in the bath. It had cost Luba five shillings, as the stewardess had to keep that bathroom out of commission all day. She didn't want the Englishwoman in her own cabin to know her expedient. Suddenly her lovely eyes were filling with tears. . . .

"Fofoiser!" she said desperately—"you don't know

what it has been like. What I've been through in *India*!
There isn't an evening dress down in my cabin that my
cousin Kiki hasn't worn first . . . and you know how fat
Kiki is! . . ."

"But your husband? That regiment? . . ."

"That," cried Luba, "was just the most awful part of it."

* * *

The tale that followed was more harrowing than even
her London experiences as a modiste. An unreal winter in
Paris with the White Russians, none of whom seemed able to
fit into the Western world. She watched several of her girl
friends cynically become the mistresses of rich Frenchmen.
Kiki married a fat little *bourgeois*, a scent manufacturer, and
had a villa at Nice. One girl Luba had grown up with in
Moscow simply took the shortest way out. Luba had fled
to Paris after her London humiliation, quite prepared to do
anything rather than continue that purgatory in the sordid
dressmakers' shops. In Paris she discovered that the tragedy
of the White Russians had become a drug on the market.
Their sufferings had been too much for the pleasure-loving
Frenchmen to bear. A White Russian mistress was now
demodée. Jobs were even scarcer and more humiliating, if
possible, than those in London. She was in the last stages of
despair. Then, at Nice, after the Russian taxi-driver, *né*
Prince, had relieved her of her virginity, she had what she
believed was a fantastic stroke of good fortune.

It was a handsome English officer, just going back after a
long home-leave to India. He fell instantly in love with her,
said he would not go back without her, and . . .

"You know what the English are like, Fofoiser—how they
look down their noses and apologise because God has given
them everything? Well . . . he talked like that. And I
believed him. I think it was the easy way he talked about
his servants that did for me; merely clapping his hands.

CL

to have half a dozen 'boys' leaping to obey his command. Well, I was tired, I wanted to rest. . . . So I married him.

"But he was such a liar, Fofoiser!

"Do you know," said Luba, clutching his jacket lapels in her eagerness. . . . "In Poona, when we had to give cocktail parties—and we simply had to give them sometimes—I used to get the gin bottles first and dilute them with water . . . when the servants could not see me! . . . Very few people got drunk at our cocktail parties, Fofoiser. . . ."

At the club, she said, after they had finished tennis, instead of doing what the other people did—sit around on the lawn and have a few drinks before driving home—they left right off. "People used to think that we were still honeymooning. . . . The idiots!"

He understood, now, some of her bitter dislike of the Englishwomen on board.

"My husband had nothing to live on but his pay! The whole mess knew it. But he was such a fine polo player that they paid for his ponies for him. And that's all he cared about. . . . I begged him; I said: 'If you'll chuck the Army and get a decent job, I'll do anything. I'll work too. But I just can't stand this damn' sham. . . .' But he wouldn't."

She looked over her shoulder and stared ruefully at her stained back. "There is not one evening dress in my trunks that has not been worn by someone else first! Well . . . he's got his polo ponies. But he hasn't got me."

"What I don't understand," said the bewildered Tony, "is this other fellow—the other man? How does he come in? I saw you kiss him good-bye."

"Oh, Bumby? Fofoiser—he's my husband's colonel. He has given me the money to go home and get my divorce. Then he is going to marry me."

Lynd held his forehead. Perhaps it was the Red Sea, the intolerable heat affecting him; but this was all madness.

"What does your sweet husband say to all this?" he asked.

"Edward? Oh, he's relieved. He said so."

"Luba!"

"He did, Fofoiser. The night the Colonel couldn't keep it in any longer and said he simply had to tell me he knew everything, and how mean Edward was, and how much he loved me—Bumby, I mean—well, I went straight to Edward and told him. I said I had just had a long talk with Bumby. . . . Of course, Bumby was frightfully upset about it all; my speaking, you know. . . ."

"I should think he would be," grated Tony. After a time Luba became really too tragic to take seriously.

"But he put a good face on it and told Edward that he had meant every word he said. And Edward came back to me and said that everything had been arranged."

"Easy as all that, was it?"

"Well . . ." Luba flung up her head. "No, it wasn't. Edward was horrible! Right at the very last minute. He came down to Bombay to see me off, and at the Taj Mahal, that last night, he began to cry and say I had ruined his life, and—well, he asked if he couldn't sleep with me one last time. What could I do? Then he handed me his wedding ring, and said: 'You know what you can do with it!' Wasn't that simply beastly, Fofoiser?"

"Oh, for Christ's sake, stop calling me Fofoiser!"

*　　*　　*

He was sorry the next morning for the things he had said. He had been violent. It was unbearable to have to sit there and listen to Luba go on talking about herself like that. If she did not value her body, he did. God help him. She was just like all the White Russians; impossible figures in the nightmare of their life after the Revolution. But all this isn't true, they kept saying to themselves; this isn't really

happening! Laugh. The reason why so many Russians could
survive the almost unbelievable tragedies of their lives was,
he thought, because they did not *believe* them. They all lived
in a state of suspension—waiting for reality to dawn. They
lived, meanwhile, fantastic lives, never coming-to to see
this one. A Surrealist scene of poisonous colour and dis-
torted shapes against which the lovely figure of Luba
seemed unaware of its danger. He wanted to shake her—
wake her up to this present life.

That was what worried him. This White Russianism of
Luba's. There was no use trying to persuade himself that if
he again became involved with Luba he could either take
her out of that existence or keep free from it himself. Something would be bound to happen. Luba carried the contagion
of calamity. It was written in the book, her destiny;
and he did not want to drag Christina into it.

When she had gone to her cabin he stood there for some
time with an arm on either side of the port staring out at the
low brilliant stars. The sea had been as smooth as a bucket of
oil ever since they left Bombay, and steaming. He slipped
into a suit of cool white drill and went up on deck. The men
in the *Kasr-i-Hind* were going about the business of the ship.
Lascars had long since folded up the deck-chairs against the
dun cabin walls and were now sluicing the deck. Their head-
man wore a blue knitted toboggan cap, with a dangling
tassel, and had a decorative scarlet sash around his feminine
waist. Lynd climbed to the boat-deck and went forward. He
saw the face of the helmsman, gaunt-shadowed from the
binnacle light below it, staring ahead. Out on one bridge-
wing the white shape of a ship's officer leaned, chin in hand.
Three sharp double-clangs from the mast over his head told
him it was three o'clock.

Against the low moon he saw the black butterfly of an
Arab dhow. He thought of life in the mud-walled Mohammedan cities, and of the relations of men and women. They
lived. Women, cool water, a green oasis; this was what the

Koran said was Paradise. He thought of the frustrated life
the white man lives in India; the way the young officers
lashed themselves into a fury over polo or tennis as a form of
flagellation to ease their souls and bodies from the sexual
strait-jacket their careers would impose upon the best years
of their lives. The Tommies could sleep with a native girl
or some blowsy white prostitute—the Government recognised that—but the officers could not. Not until they
reached the comparative obscurity of Bombay or Calcutta,
not until they reached "Home." . . . This was the one thing
that was on the minds of most of the young men in the ship
at the present moment. It was what the Malay boys were
thinking about when they kept on making dates with each
other, all within the radius of half a mile or so around
Piccadilly Circus. To have a woman again. He thought of
his friend who had recently shot himself behind those mat
doors, soaked with water, of Maiden's Hotel in Delhi . . .
how the Mohammedan servant had come running into his
room that morning; "Oh, *sahib, sahib, sahib*! . . ." There
was no newspaper equivocation about that servant's statement: Budgin *Sahib* had blown his brains out. And both the
bare-footed Mohammedan and Lynd knew why: a girl in
Simla. Lynd had been sitting with Budgin in that Indian
South Kensington when the girl walked in, in smart jodh-
purs, where they were having ices—and he had seen Budgin
go sallow. . . . Budgin, afterwards, had admitted Lynd to his
despair: "I suppose it's worse somehow out here. . . . You
know—all this heat, and life without women? When you
find one you know you love, you feel as if there just *couldn't*
be anyone else."

Well, Lynd had felt that way too. About Luba. And then
he had married Christina. What followed had been the most
extraordinary adventure of his life. One side of their married
life, the side that most people assert is the all-in-all of it, had
been as absent as if there were no such thing. Within a month
of his marriage night he was appalled by the tragedy he had

et himself in for, had let both of them in for. For, even then, he had no idea whatever of deserting Christina. It was just how could he reconcile things. A man like himself! And then Christina had taught him other things. He had found a beauty with her in life that had no connection whatever with the marriage-bed. In spite of it, in fact; in spite of the daily little annoyances and the unescapable tautness from living day to day with someone with whom you rarely sleep. A monk, he often thought, had far the easiest time. Christina and he clashed; and they did not have the safety valve of physical relief. They did not kiss and make up. They either talked or laughed themselves out of it. His way was to laugh, laugh at himself. They could talk, because, mentally, he and Chris had become hand in glove. He had never known anyone capable of inspiring such devotion and faithfulness. Therefore, he had been straight. Part of this faithfulness was because he had suffered himself from undependable people, and he had resolved that he would live life so that Christina, at least, would always have someone certain to count on. Part was to prove the value of this to himself. In short, he had lived a life—ten years of it—of constant tribute to Christina. And he had never dared tell her about it. If she had known how often he had got up and walked to the window and simply bitten at his fingers at nights, then she would have suffered unbearably because she would have known that she had not satisfied him, and even the companionship they did have would have been spoiled. Now, when he felt that they could talk such things over, if the occasion came—such as if she discovered his relations with Luba— he could never explain things to Christina even then. He could not rob past days of what she had blissfully accepted as complete romance. So he was forced to continue silent. He would never be able to defend himself if Christina did find things out—not even to save her pain.

When the physical urge became too strong at times he had deliberately deadened it with drink. This had been misunder-

stood by even the best of his friends. He had to grin accept-
ance when one said: "What you need, old boy, is a strict
nursery governess. Chris." He knew how furious Christina
would be if ever she heard herself being alluded to as something so unprepossessing as that. He also knew how far off
from the mark that was. Chris, for all her South Kensington
background, was no nursery governess. And he did not need
one. He just still wanted Luba. It was, after all, no particular
effort for him to remain straight with Chris—with no Luba
around. Other women did not upset him too much. In his
profession as a newspaper correspondent he had had lots of
opportunities, in plenty of foreign capitals, to be unfaithful.
And with very pretty women, too. He had even gone to the
point of making all arrangements to be unfaithful—like the
girl at the Pera Palace in Constantinople, wife of a naval
officer, who had obligingly explained that her husband was
off on patrol duty in the Black Sea and that Lynd should
give up his room in the Tokatlian and take one beside hers.
"We will have only a balcony between us," she had said
invitingly, with her lovely velvet eyes. "You won't even
have to go out into the hall to come in." Instead, after pack-
ing and giving up his room, he had suddenly told the taxi to
drive to the ferry for Haidar Pasha and had gone up to bury
himself in Angora's muddy streets. As facts were, he had
been just as faithful to the ghost of Luba as he had been to
the living Chris. And now he had Luba.

He paced the empty deck. There was no harm in this. In
London things could be so arranged that he would see Luba
occasionally. They could have fun together. Perhaps,
together, they might get some of the happiness they had
missed. He might make up a bit for some of the things that
had happened to her, and she could drag him out of this
soggy, desperate mood where he seemed to be losing an
interest in life. He would be even happier with Christina,
less nervous and on strain. He would treat her more kindly,
now that his senses would be at ease. There was, of course,

that incredible Indian background of Luba's, and Colonel Bumby, or whatever his name was. But if the man chose to get mixed up with this White Russianism he could take his chance. Luba would in all likelihood carry the contagion of calamity to him. Colonel Bumby was an amazing figure, but he might have an even more amazing fate in store for him.

* * *

At Marseilles Luba went on to Nice to fetch her father and mother, who were staying with the Russian aunt. The finances of the Powers were quite beyond Tony; he understood that Roderick had just lost a job of some sort and was just about to get another job of some, sort, which would require their early return to London. They had, apparently, a flat in Hammersmith. Lynd gave Luba the address of his club, and had just time enough to be shocked by her profligacy in buying a first-class ticket to Nice and leap into his own Paris train, thoroughly upset by the nasty thoughts that ticket invoked about Bumby's munificence. He had never asked the Colonel's name. He did not, on their four fleeting days across the blue Mediterranean, want that serene peace shattered by any more of Luba's dénouements. And now, as he thought over that Indian scene, Colonel Bumby, whoever he was, became a more and more unintelligible figure. By the time Lynd reached Paris he decided he would stop off and spend the night there, to re-orient himself before he went on to join the Mallards.

At a sidewalk chair, watching the suicidal French traffic racing along the Boulevard des Capucines, he felt home again. Paris had been the hub for his last ten years' world wanderings. He knew that if he only sat long enough before the Café de la Paix someone would come along whom he knew. In this case it was Patrick Byron of the *Evening Chronicle*. Byron, a strikingly pale young man with a Shakespearian forehead, had an English girl with him, blonde, very county, and not his wife. "Miss Merrivale," he said, introducing them casually. "We're sharing a room together at the Hotel Gotham; Paris is so crowded. Alone?"

"Very much."

Miss Merrivale sat down and eyed Lynd with youthful insolence. Then she said candidly: "I've got to pee." When she had gone up the red stairs Patrick said:

"I've sent that bitch of a wife of mine to Scandinavia. She wouldn't go any farther. Where's Chris?"

"Dieppe. I'm going down there to-morrow."

Lynd smiled at Patrick. All London laughed over Patrick's love-frustrations and the patient, understanding tolerance of the faithful Booboo. Patrick was always either shipping her off to some far end of the world, or breaking his neck and the hearts of travel agents trying to take short-cuts around the globe to meet her somewhere on the way back. What Booboo thought on steamship trips about this new girl—it was always a new one with the unassuaged Patrick—who was occasioning her seeing another part of the earth, Booboo never said. As Patrick bought the tickets, Booboo seemed content to use them. Then she would return; the Byrons would have another new address, a flat or a house in a mews, give a sensational cocktail party or so, and Booboo would be travelling again. Pale, romantic Patrick Byron, with his luminous brown eyes and waves of chestnut hair, and wit, was the most successful young philanderer in London. Yet, Tony thought, he was one of the most lonely and unhappy men he knew. In Patrick, somewhere, there was a lesson to be learned.

In that sexual free-for-all of London in the 'twenties Patrick had taken what he wanted. The contraceptive, which seems a much greater invention than either radio or the motor car, had freed the English girl, usually not passionate enough to risk going the whole distance, from her fears. The generation of young men, most of whose eligible elder brothers had been killed off by the Great War, reaped

Cı

the harvest that was thus presented to them by the absence
of sturdier men who might have made good husbands, had
they lived. As most of this younger generation had grown
up under mortal terror of being conscripted, it was their
line to mock the more manly virtues. To be called a
"hearty" by the sparrow intellectuals who came down
from Oxford or Cambridge was enough to damn any
anxious male. To possess a maidenhead was considered
bourgeois by a Bright Young Thing nurtured on Soho night-
clubs, Moscow and Karl Marx. Young, uncertain and lovely
girls were afraid not to be promiscuous, not to talk smut,
not to use every word in the harlots' lexicon just to show
they were not prigs. The age of consent seemed to have been
reduced to puberty. And men like Lynd felt the hopeless
envy of having been born ten years too soon. These golden
lads and girls would one day come to dust, but—well, Lynd
had always found it a hard job to convince himself that they
were not right in living regardlessly before it came to that.

When he left Patrick and the relieved Miss Merrivale to
go on some place, he walked across to the respectable Hotel
Chatham where he had put up, and felt positively grateful
to Luba for the ease with which he went to bed. This was
certainly the first night he could remember in Paris when
he had not been, or wanted to be, out on carouse. Usually
drowning his frustrations in drink. It was with delight that
he slid down between the cool sheets and picked up his book.
He could be normal now.

*   *   *

He knew now that he had been torturing himself these
last ten years over a person who had never existed. No
woman of human flesh could fulfil the Luba he had invented
in his hot imagination. He had been more than a Mohammedan dreaming of the Courts of Paradise. Yet there had
been much in Luba, and her early setting, to drive him to

such reproachful reveries. His plastic years, the fantastic Russian scene; or was it because he always felt that neither of them had ever had half a chance with the other—their lives had been bungled for them by someone else? Was it only his fury with her incredible family? It had probably been more rage with them, and life in general, than love for Luba that had made him drive himself mad with certain pictures all these years. Everybody had been such a fool.

He had been very young and sentimental—and dangerously decent—that night in Moscow when Roderick Power had kissed him on both cheeks and placed Luba's hand in his. He shuddered now as he remembered how he had gone up to his room and got down on his knees and prayed, for the first time he could remember, that God would make things come out all right, this time. He had been leading a very dissolute life in the Hotel Astoria in Petrograd, full of the Allied staff officers and the *cocottes* of all the Russias, with the telephone ringing all night in his room, and usually a different woman to bed with him. A little prayer, perhaps, was not too out of place at that time. Roderick had been at his most Russian on the night he and Luba became engaged, and disgustingly lascivious, thought Tony, after one remark he made. Even on that night the romantic Tony had resolved he would have to warn Luba about her father's values. Which would have made Roderick laugh. Roderick was theoretically a Scotsman, and travelled on a British passport; but he was the third generation of his rich family to be born in Russia and he had come a long way from the braw and bitter stock of the original Glasgow adventurer who came out to Russia and found favour at Alexander's Court. Roderick was a dilettante. He discussed the Ballet, not football. And he had a mistress in every fashionable Moscow street. He could afford them.

Luba's mother was from a big naval family with estates at Vlasnitca outside Moscow. Tony had met the Powers on the

train going down to the Black Sea. As the War had prevented
them from spending their usual winter on the Italian Riviera,
they were going to the Crimea. In the two days in the *wagon-
lit* with them, and basking with Luba after they swam
luxuriously in the turquoise waters off Yalta, he fell in love
in its purest and most adolescent form. When his telephone
bell rang after midnight when he returned to Petrograd, he
answered a rude "*Niet!* No!" to the friendly young girls
who would like to come into his room, several of whom had
been there before. Thinking that, in Russia, he had found
this one true love of his life and never dreaming of any possible disaster, he had gratefully returned to his original ideas
about women. When a letter from Vlasnitca, written in
Luba's immature rounded hand, asked him there, he took
the next train.

*   *   *

Vlasnitca was an estate of interminable dusty roads occasionally running through the little log huts of villages fringed
with acacia trees. Of fields of golden wheat waving under the
great bowl of the blue Russian sky. Of the lovely sight of
green swampland, beyond which white stands of birch stood
out silvery bright against the dark pine woods. The old
wooden house of the Chardoffs faced a rush-bordered lake
full of fat lazy fish. Luba, anxious to show off her new
stallion, met him at the railway station on the estate in a
two-wheeled trap and raced him like Mazeppa to the house,
scattering the laughing peasant girls like chickens from the
road. . . .

On the way Luba reined up long enough to tell Lynd,
"Daddy is having an affair with Annutchka . . . one of the
maids. So if Mummy seems queer, you will understand,
won't you? Don't let on I told you. Daddy knows that I
know—but he doesn't know that Mummy knows too, or
isn't quite sure." Luba laughed joyously, tantalisingly innocent, and Lynd scowled; it was not his idea of the way to

bring up a young and rather too beautiful daughter. He shook hands stiffly when Roderick, a slender, poetic figure, extended his limp fingers. It was the first time Tony had seen Luba since that ecstatic night when Roderick had placed her hand in his.

That night when they were left alone in the old country house drawing-room, romantic with the history shown by the miniatures and paintings of Chardoffs in ancient naval uniforms, Luba flung herself down in impatient surrender on the couch before him and whispered urgently: "All that you wish, my lover. . . ."

He was so taken by surprise that he did not know what to do. He was almost rough with her, the way he made her sit up. Suddenly an awful feeling of sadism took command in him. The complete surrender of Luba invited him to take revenge upon her for all the female tricks that had been played on him, for early and forgotten loves. He did not even kiss her, but sat there and held her trembling hands, and watched her as she writhed. . . .

The next day, as they were walking towards the delicate woods of silver birch, Luba said: "You know the peasant girls here all swim naked in the streams. Daddy often gets his spy-glass and sneaks up on that knoll to watch them. He thinks they don't know he is watching!" Suddenly, she pulled him down beside her on the grass and pressed her pretty mouth against his. "Kiss me!" she panted. "Kiss me. . . ."

He stood up. "You've been reading too many romantic novels," he said.

That night, in a shaft of moonlight in his room, he saw her standing there. She had on nothing but a gauze-like nightgown. As she leaned down to kiss him her heavy plait of hair fell around his neck, with its girl's bow still tied on it. He gasped.

"For God's sake! go back . . ." he said. "Hurry. Get out!" He almost pushed her out of the door.

And then that incredible mood left him. The next night he tried her door. It was locked. He had meant that this one perfect love should be just right. Now he was furious to know what he had refused to take. The next night, when the Powers left them alone, he seized her hungrily in his arms. But she leapt up. She gave a hysterical little laugh and went upstairs to where her people were sitting in Roderick's study. He went in, and on some excuse induced her to come back; then he said:

"You locked your door last night?"

She nodded, looking down.

"Why?"

"I—I don't know. I think I was afraid. Please, please, please, please," she begged, when he seized her roughly again. "Let me go."

"Don't you love me?"

"Yes, yes, I do. But——"

He put down his hands and sighed. In both ways he had been wrong. Now he had made her think there was something bestial in love. "But why," he asked her wonderingly, "when you can joke the way you do about your father and the servant maids? . . . Why? . . ." He was heartbroken to think of what he had done.

Her insolent little Pomeranian strolled into the room. Luba's whole expression changed as she picked it up. "Fofoiser!" she cried. Then she held it across and tried to get Tony to kiss its infuriating little nose. "Isn't Minka *lovely?*" she said.

He clenched his hands.

*   *   *

Walking the next evening with his desperate thoughts through the apple orchard he came on Luba's father and the maid. They were sitting in the semi-darkness of the gardener's shed. Roderick removed his hand from the girl's blouse and asked him to sit down.

"Enticing, full-budded creatures, aren't they?" he said to Lynd. "These peasant girls! No, don't leave us. She is frightened, anyway, and now I'll have to wait. I love Russia in the spring. I like to take off my shoes and walk in the grass like a peasant—and eat cucumbers. Have you read Artzibasheff?"

Lynd nodded moodily. The girl, except that she was bigger, was almost a replica of Luba. The same fair mass of hair, the same dark-fringed eyes, the sharp chin and pert nose. It was almost as if Roderick were fondling his own daughter. He wondered if Roderick had tried that? He would be capable of it. "I don't know whether you know it or not," he said sullenly, "but both Luba and her mother are looking at this hut from Luba's window."

"Oh, my God, my God, my God—don't say that!" said Roderick. "There *will* be a row! Oh, my God, no—*no*!" He seized the peasant girl by the wrist as she tried to jump up and bolt.

"What can I do?" asked Roderick of Lynd.

"But Roderick Ivanovitch!" protested the peasant girl in chipping Russian, "I must get back to the kitchen. Olga Formarova will miss me."

With surprising strength for one so slender, Roderick seized her plump arm at the elbow and flapped her back on the trestle they had been sitting upon. "Smoke," he said to Tony. "We will smoke until it gets dark."

Lynd grinned: "But it doesn't get dark in this part of Russia in the spring . . . only a half-glow at midnight."

"Well then, well then, well then. . . . *I* have the idea! Why of course—Tony, my dear fellow, you go back and talk to them. Distract their attention."

"What?" asked Roderick nervously, when he saw Lynd's smile.

"That sounds better," said Lynd.

*   *   *

"How *could* you!" said Luba, when he came back to the old house.

"How could I—what?"

"Side with Daddy against Mummy like that!"

"You're crazy. What on earth are you talking about?"

"You know perfectly well what I mean. Daddy has Annutchka down there. You were with them. I saw you smoking in the tool-shed. We both saw you!" said Luba, stamping her little foot.

"Oh . . . my God! . . ." Lynd shrugged his shoulders.

* * *

That night Mrs. Power did not come down to dinner. Luba bantered her father back into something less like a state of terror. "Daddy, you must be more careful! . . . Mustn't he, Tony? Oh, naughty Daddy! . . ."

Lynd tried to eat, but the delicate little sterlet, which he loved, seemed not worth the trouble. Luba flushed, and then looked away when he met her eyes. Then she said she had to run up and see Mummy. She took her sweet with her.

"Life's ghastly, isn't it?" sighed Roderick.

"Very."

"This beastly War. . . . It has me held a prisoner here. Do you think it will stop?"

"Yes, I think it will stop."

"Damn' nuisance. I'm not allowed to travel."

"Yes, it can be inconvenient. People——" Lynd was going to remark that the people in the trenches might be finding the War irksome, but suddenly all desire, even to be rude to Roderick, left him. He stared at the maid.

Annutchka was serving them. Roderick did not look at her as she removed the plates. He handed Tony an ancient Russian decanter etched with the eagle of the Romanoffs. "Culture!" he said despairingly. "This is a country of barbarians—rabble. This is real brandy; I sent a man up to

Petrograd to get this. Pinkus Solomonovitch is bringing me four bottles of whiskey from Tula. He found them there. Well, here's to *Kultur*—I hope the Germans win."

* * *

The next morning was particularly beautiful. When Lynd looked out the window the poppies were blazing scarlet in the yellow fields of wheat. He was still at the age where his clothes felt good on him as he dressed and the beginning of each day brought an exultant expectation with it. He resolved, when he saw Luba, that he would carefully persuade her back to something like a normal state of mind. She came towards him through the long open rooms with the warm scents of the fields in them, very desirable in her light dress. He could not resist going up and putting his arm around her. She wriggled away.

"We mustn't!" she said.

"Why not, my sweet? It's marvellous to-day, isn't it?"

"Mummy says I'm not to kiss you," she said.

"Your mother? . . ."

"Yes, Fofoiser."

"But look here——!"

"Minka *takoi!*" She had already leaned down and clutched the scampering Pomeranian. "Ooooooo!" She held it up before her and kissed its little nose. "Minka, Minka, Minka! . . ."

That afternoon the coachman, Pavel, drove him along the dusty roads to Vlasnitca railway station. The lake fell out of sight below a hill of glowing wheat. The last of the white columns of Vlasnitca gleamed in the sun. They had to wait while a long line of dusty peasant carts pulled into the ditch to let them pass. Pavel was cursing them. But Tony was reading something that made him almost order the old fellow to turn back. It was a little pig-skin wallet that Luba, at the very last second, had pressed into his hand. "Don't read it!"

she whispered, "until you are on the train. I've written something inside the flap. I want you to keep it all your life! Promise?"

He nodded. But he had broken both promises. Under the pig-skin flap he read: "*I will love you all my life, Fofoiser.*" And three weeks later the purse went through a port-hole as his Swedish steamer passed Sandy Hook.

Letters, strangely dispassionate—for Luba seemed provokingly unable to express herself—followed him to the United States; but they were already full of the dramatic news about Roderick's decision to leave Russia and of the family's plans for spending the next winter at Nice. Luba wrote as Roderick talked—absolutely unaware of everything that was happening to them, and all the rest of the world because of this War—and in a rage against such shallowness he did not even let her know that, before he left Petrograd, he had volunteered for the British.

He went up to Canada to begin his training in the Royal Flying Corps.

Ah, what damn' fools they had all been!

The Hotel Chatham is quiet, on a side street off the Boulevard des Capucines. The toots of the French taxi-horns seemed in another world, as far off as his own hot-headed passion of those Russian days. He was glad to have had them, anyway, with all their pain. He smiled as he dog-eared the book and switched off the light. With the pillow curled into a comfortable ball under his head he gave a long contented sigh and went to sleep. . . .

* * *
* * *

At Dieppe he saw the fair head of Christina above the black caps of the battling French railway porters. He smiled as he saw her neat form pushing its way through their blue blouses. No wretched Frenchman could impede Chris. She put up a downy cheek to be kissed. It wasn't coldness; it was just that her lips were made up. And Chris just didn't like to be disarranged. In all the ten years they had lived together he had never once rough-housed Chris. Actually, her slender fingers were cutting into his arm and she was whispering, "Peter, Peter, *Peter!* . . ." Almost choked with the delight of seeing him. He made the expected remark about her trim, tailored, flannel suit, noticed how nice her high primrose jumper looked under her cool chin—she did look so decent!—and then said impulsively:

"Listen, Chris. Let's tell the porters where to take my stuff. You and I go somewhere and have a drink—first?"

"No," said Chris. "They're waiting lunch for you."

There was, she said with a confident smile, a whole special lobster for himself. "Oh, Goddam the lobster!" he said under his breath. Chris certainly knew how to throw cold water on him. If only she could ever, ever understand the importance of these little things. What they meant to comradeship!

*   *   *

The Mallards, this branch of them at least, were a highly respectable and proper family, and he had often felt his own disregard of life's formalities to be inexcusable in their presence. As it happened, of course, their propriety had made him an active social anarchist against even the most innocuous conventions. He railed against the interest they took, the obeisance they paid to possessions, meals, plans, schedules and all the material things. He could not bear, for instance, to witness the pain with which Lady Mallard surveyed a foreign menu—for fear that she *might* order something she might not like. It was positively obscene, he felt. He could not bear the General's anxiety over their baggage when they travelled, nor his needless reticence about the War—for he had been a Fifth Army Colonel, and had seen some gory sights.

When Tony had first come up to London to meet Christina's parents he had been highly impressed with that life. On his first night in the cool sheets of that well-appointed house, with the fresh little maid bringing tea into him in the morning, he felt like a barbarian in such a place after the board bunk-houses of Eastchurch where he was waiting to be demobbed. He knew that the General had not thought it quite right that Christina should come in and bandage his knee before he got up in the morning. But then the only possible way to do that was before he got his trousers on; and that was the way he met her, when he was a crash-case and Chris was a V.A.D. in the Royal Naval Hospital at Chatham. And, if Chris married him, as she said she was going to do, she would be bandaging that bit of raw bone for many a long day to come.

When he did get into civvies he stayed with the Mallards while the R.A.F. tried to repatriate him. Just to be perverse, he had, before he met Chris, taken advantage of the clause that the Service would put you back after the War at the same spot from which you had volunteered—and he had demanded Petrograd. He did not need to fear Russia now, now that Luba was no longer there. (He had heard through a mutual Anglo-Russian friend that the Powers were in Paris, living at the Crillon, where they were spending their last pennies in a frantic effort to marry Luba to anyone with money enough to keep them all.) And the result was that it was months before some worried officer in Bolo House gave up the transportation problem and wrote the little slip that offered Captain Lynd a free steamer ticket to the United States, or nothing, as an alternative. Months which he spent, as it happened, for the first part in Chatham Hospital, and then, after obtaining permission to leave Eastchurch Aerodrome, at the Mallards' South Kensington house.

In those days he had loved that complacent, secure existence. Of mornings he would tuck his silk handkerchief up his
sleeve, take his stick and saunter down the right side of
Brompton Road towards Harrods. Then he would cross at
Knightsbridge and stroll along the Park. He would then,
unless he happened to stroll up Bond Street, carry on down
Piccadilly to the Circus. Here, he knew, unless he turned
down sharp right to the clubs of Pall Mall, he had reached the
boundary line. The frontier of South Kensington and also
of a perfectly definite form of English life. The rest was just
England. Very fine, too; but South Kensington, where Christina lived, was a Valhalla on earth for a certain type of secure,
complacent, and very adventurous Englishman—and his
values; Army, Navy, foreign, colonial, Civil Service officers
and officials, some of the retired warriors so ancient, living
in those cavernous mansions off Cromwell Road, that they
seemed to have begun their careers in almost the bow-and-
arrow days. Builders of Empire. Men who had never
thought of life other than in terms of adventurous, colourful
careers in one of the Services—with a safe pension at the end.
Entire successions of families living lives of leisure on the
fixed incomes earned for them by some former adventurous,
and very often unscrupulous Englishman, who now thought
of mere respectability itself as life's chief reward. A whole
class of people who had never had to think of life in terms of
making a living—the way he and gallant Chris would soon
have to do.

He had been unaware of most of this complacency when
he first stayed with the Mallards. He was too fresh from the
War and the chaos of his own career not to appreciate such
dignified and assured security. Later, when he and Chris
were struggling to keep their heads above water in the mad-
house of New York, he had often thought long and enviously
of that sheltered life—and loved Chris all the more for
the way she faced the present one. But, in after years,
when he was safe, he was often stifled by such society.

In Dieppe the schedule was adamant. The Mallards made even the French give them tea an hour before their bath and breakfast. Then there was a pause while they came out on the front, and the General eyed the sea. He would have liked to have had his spaniel. But as there was no dog to take him for a walk, and no garden in which he could dig, and feel he was doing something, he took a deck-chair on the beach and read the London *Times*. Chris, her mother and Lynd went for a stroll along the Plage. Lady Mallard was a good-looking woman, with silvery hair and a clear face that a life of innocence and the open air would keep perpetually young. She was excellent company; and Lynd had nothing to complain of on these walks. He was lucky, he knew full well, to have such an engaging, sophisticated, friendly mother-in-law. Like the General, she was a person to be admired. They made a fine pair, walking about the foyer of a theatre. Lynd was proud of them. They weren't even dull. They were just too damned interested in the material pleasures, Tony felt, and had been all their lives, ever to have lived. He could not conceive of the General and Lady Mallard ever getting into bed together. The scene would be indecent.

There might have been some truth in this resentful, frequent thought of his. It might account for Chris. Chris wasn't bothered overmuch about piggish decency in life; she was, from what he heard from other women, notorious for the stories she could tell. But, fundamentally, Chris could not be abandoned. She always felt, at crucial moments, that she must hold something back. Some reserve. Some strange propriety in her make-up made him always feel that his advances were uncouth. She submitted. . . . But, after a while, he began to feel it was almost indecent to watch Christina undress. Yet she was a lovely creature. Even on that cruel pebbled beach of Dieppe he found it necessary to stop limping and admire her firm slender figure as she went into the sea. And she swam like a duck.

Analysing his own self, he had often wondered if his own life, in his profligate early Russian days—before he met Luba—had not ruined him entirely for a decent married life. Perhaps he expected too much from a woman—too reckless a passion?

There was nothing you could put your finger on in the Mallard ménage that gave him the sense of stifling anger that he felt after three days at Dieppe. He just knew that if he did not get away he would blow up. That night he said:

"Look here, Chris—I'm going across to London tomorrow. Do you mind?"

"Oh, Peter! . . ." Her voice broke.

It was always painful to make these escapes. It was awkward even to get out of their house in Cheyne Walk and get down to the club. Chris did not fuss. She always let him go. But he always knew that she could not understand. And he could not tell her. "Just put it down," he often laughed uneasily, "that I am like a cat—I like to prowl at nights."

"Very well," she used to say with rueful bravery to joke. "You will find me where you left me."

And he knew he always would.

*   *   *

*   *   *

They had arranged that instead of taking his vacation in France, as he had planned, they should go up and fish the Shetlands. Christina would come over later. He would live at his club. He loved to walk the streets of London again, for all its love of pomp and pageantry as friendly and familiar as a great village. It was satisfying to be back at his desk, and feel that he could ride at anchor for a time. In these last ten years a couple of months on end had been the most he could hope from this haven he called home. And one of the first things he did now was walk along to his tailor and resume

the fittings of two suits he had ordered the week before he
suddenly flew from Croydon one dawn for Karachi.

"But these are winter suits!" said the tailor.

"Well, winter will soon be along," said Tony, "and spring
won't be far behind—I hope. What was the last one like?"

He had found foreign journalism an exhilarating and not
particularly difficult profession. Nothing like the exact
knowledge was required, as for his early engineering training
or his hectic years of export work after that. As most of the
world's politicians and statesmen were busily engaged
calling each other either fools or knaves, and the most
distinguished economists clashed on every dogma, it was
largely a matter of taking your choice. Politics was not an
exact science. No one could prove you were wrong. More
often than not you suspected you were not right yourself;
and while he was amused by the highbrow attitude of the
intellectuals among his colleagues, profoundly discharging
their typewriters at foreign governments, he considered
that anyone with an ability to write concise English could do
their stuff. They, of course, did not agree with this flippant
estimate of their greatness. His worst argument in the whole
six months of this India assignment was the silencing of a
Left-wing London journalist who lunched at the little Italian
restaurant which a cosmopolitan group of the foreign
correspondents had made their rendezvous in Soho.

"You saw too much of Government House," said the
young university graduate, darkly, criticising Lynd's favour-
able reporting of the British in his India dispatches. "Too
many *sahibs*! Ha-ha. . . ." He laughed, and looked around
for the approval of the table.

"No," smiled Tony, "too many Hindus. When you've
seen as many squabbling lawyers as I have, my lad, all
fighting for the coastal shipping and the fat plums that will
fall when the British are driven out . . . and Parsee mills
working fifty-seven hours a week with indentured child
labour . . . you won't guff so much about patriotism as you

will about the pocket-book. That's what most of your heroes are fighting for. Anyway . . . I'm tired of defending the suppressed majorities."

A Pole and a Frenchman laughed silently. Both of them were more valuable to their governments than any two ambassadors. The Pole, knowing that Lynd was coming that day, had ordered a whole special *langouste* for him. It was his silent gesture of friendship. "And Gandhi?" he asked.

"Wonderful . . . " said Tony. He went on, picturing to the Pole, who was a philosopher in his way, the extraordinary lesson in life of sitting for hours talking with the little holy man. He related Gandhi's own story of the power of Civil Disobedience. Although they always talked shop at these luncheons, it was tales like these which were considered the most noteworthy . . . their personal experiences with mortal figures, the weak traits of dictators, and the highly libellous stories that they roamed the world to write and expand at that luncheon table. A sedate little Galician stockbroker sat there, never said anything, went down into the City afterwards, and very often made a killing on some advance information he had learned. They found the Galician helpful because of his early laments heralding any financial crisis. He had a nose for disaster. But it was funny, Lynd often told himself, that not one of his kind ever used the useful information they possessed to speculate themselves. They were all comparatively poor men.

The joy of journalism, if such taut, impartial work can be said to harbour that, came when you became partisan and deliberately tried to steer the situations you were reporting. The intellectuals among London's journalists were practically all of them Left-wingers, fanatically devoted to this critical attitude attacking Europe's post-War governments. They had plenty of provocations for their quixotic typewriters. There was one American whose sporadic returns to Paris or London were nearly always to announce proudly that he had been either escorted or thrown across the frontier of another country he had been "covering." With every fresh political scandal he uncovered, the world became just one country the smaller for him. The German correspondents nearly always considered themselves as unofficial ambassadors of their country, and added their propagandish views to conversation at the luncheon table. There were official luncheons at which the foreign journalists entertained British Cabinet Ministers or visiting statesmen, applauded their lofty platitudes, and forgathered afterwards to joke about clay feet. The whole scene, with its intimacy with the people who were running the world, and the dismay that such a close-up knowledge aroused, was Tony's daily life. But the greatest lesson he had learned from ten years was not to take either himself or his work too seriously. Dispatches die in one day.

Lynd had been unusually lucky in having a proprietor who was wealthy enough to be politically independent and idealist enough, after he had picked them, to give his men a free hand. As far as work was concerned, Tony had had ten happy and very adventurous years. He was shocked by the cable he found lying on his desk. It seemed innocuous at first, merely reading:

"HANCOCK SAILING MAJESTIC BE PREPARED."

"Marjory," he called out into the other room. "Who the deuce is Mr. Hancock?"

"Coo! Mr. Lynd—don't you know who Senator Hancock is? He owns the paper."

"Owns—the—paper!"

"Why, yes," said Marjory. "It all happened while you were in India. . . ."

The sale had, as it happened, been closed while he was in the Arabian Sea on the way back. Huntingdon Ridley, the old owner, had been told he had cancer and only a few years to live. In a panic, he had sold off everything he possessed and gone to Tahiti. "Coo, Mr. Lynd! The papers have been full of it!" said Marjory.

"I've been eighteen days on the boat, you know," muttered Lynd, wondering why he had not read it on the ship's wireless. "And I have not looked at a paper since Marseilles. Tell me more."

"Well, Mr. Lynd—two Senators have bought it. Mr. Merrill was proper wild when he got the cable. He's going to leave. He says you've all been sold down river . . . if you know what that means. He says you're working for the Republican Party now. He says Senator Hancock is a—well, you know what I mean?"

"I suppose he is. All Senators are," said Lynd. "Who is the other one?"

"Oh, a man from Georgia: Mr. Anson P. Ricket. He's not a Senator now."

"Never heard of him."

"Mr. Merrill said he was so tight that he didn't dare sneeze—if you know what that means, Mr. Lynd? But he doesn't amount to much; Senator Hancock owns seventy-five per cent. of the stock. Mr. Ricket is just the Editor."

"Only the Editor, eh?" Lynd smiled. "Who was the kind soul, do you think, who warned me about Senator Hancock? This cable?"

"I don't know, Mr. Lynd. Several of the men have already been fired. Some are leaving, like Mr. Merrill. Maybe, that's one of them?"

"HANCOCK SAILING MAJESTIC BE PREPARED."

Lynd stared at the five words. They might mean a dramatic change in his life. Then he turned to the first of the eight British papers he ran through every morning. "Well, Marjory," he laughed, "I've always said that the best thing about being a foreign newspaper correspondent,

or in the export game, was that usually you were three
thousand miles away from your boss. Well . . . that dream's
busted."

"Coo! Mr. Lynd—you *are* a one!"

*   *   *

Sitting on the club fender that night, Lynd took stock. He
had had a pretty fair amount of ups and downs in life. He
wasn't particularly worried about this one. He knew that,
in the slump, all the American newspapers were reducing
their staffs. There were hundreds of good journalists walking
the streets of New York. Some of them would be selling
apples soon. There would be small chance of stepping back
into that game. Russia, the War, selling insurance in the
United States; he was an engineer, but he was thirty-four
and had forgotten all the engineering he had ever learned.
He smiled as he thought of the words in *What Price Glory*:
"Think fast, Mister Captain—think fast!" Then he realised
that he was really looking forward to an upset—it would be
exciting. Instead of sitting on the sidelines of life, he would
have to get into the game. As he looked backwards along
these last few safe years, they did look as if he had been
lying in a backwater, although, geographically, he had
travelled and flown over vast sections of the world. And
to exciting events. But he had always been a spectator. At
the most, when he had happened to get into a tight jam or so,
they had been temporary; and it had only required a certain
side of courage, and nimble wits, to get himself out. They
had not even approached the excitement when he first
watched America, the land he had known for twenty years,
drop below the dark green swells of the Atlantic—and he
was bound for a new Old World. And no theatre or
pageant he had ever witnessed had provided the thrilling
spectacle of his few bags and steamer trunk shoved under
his bunk in his cabin of the old *St. Louis*, when, staring at

them, he realised that they represented all the material possessions he had in the world. World reporting had not been, strange as it seemed, a personal adventure. No assignment to cover some important and exciting world event for his newspaper could equal what it would be like when, and it might not be very long now, he received a cable telling him that he was out of a job and there weren't going to be any more assignments. Not from that paper.

* * *

He was not afraid of life, the adventure of living. He had fallen, and landed on his feet, too many times. Nor was he fatuous about this. A materialist, he had often assured himself, pays for his possessions by the constant fear that he will lose them. By travelling light, and giving few hostages to Fortune, Lynd knew there was very little that bad luck could take away from him. He had thought of that when he was squatting before Gandhi, out in India. The little man had practically nothing that anyone could take away from him. The British couldn't touch him. They could rob him of his liberty; but a man like Gandhi would gain a great emotional adventure by being put in jail. Tony had always found this so during his different sojourns in hospital; he had had as much fun there as anywhere else. In many ways he, too, was harm-proof against life. Yet, having gained this immunity, he had not yet been able to gain the one central motive, or *motif*, that should be the theme of his life.

He was conscious of this and spent most of his waking moments in a search for this missing motive. His professional studies of the countries his work called him to naturally provoked such personal questions. You can't spend a year writing the life of Soviet Russia without meditating whether you would like to be part of it yourself. When he saw the fierce enthusiasms of the Russian youth, compared to the flaccid young men one met in London or New York, he

envied their work. It was impossible to wander through the
Rhineland in 1924, and not say to yourself that, if you were
a young German, you would be wearing a brown shirt.
Here was cause, a purpose to living! Fascism, National
Socialism, Communism—all presented such causes. He had
no cause, nothing bigger than himself—in serving which he
could lose his own puny identity. He lived for himself, and
now Christina and himself, alone. They did not even have
a child to which he could dedicate himself.

When he looked about in the so-called democracies, he
saw little that could inspire him as a cause.   Neither England
nor America had the slightest vestige of it. In his own
country, rotten with corruption in the high places, there was
little indeed to inspire anyone to enlist in the service of the
State—except graft. In England, an island dedicated to the
protection of invested capital, there was no national appeal
that awakened any enthusiasm in the youth. Even the jobs
beyond the seas, the Cause of Empire, had begun to wane.
The Empire-holders (or losers) at Westminster did not
inspire. Labour, under the easy-oozy sentimentality of
Ramsay MacDonald, had lost its direction; it was no longer
a Cause, merely a complaint. In fact, from the constant
contact that his profession brought him into with people in
high places, Lynd had long ago realised that there were
very few of them capable of being admired, and that the
service of the State, in such opportunist hands, was more
often than not an ignoble cause. Politics, in the minds of
most intelligent journalists, soon became a synonym for
falsehood.

Being unable to change this state of affairs, Lynd had
found his greatest reward from journalism in the various
excursions he could make now and then, more or less as by-
products of his work, into the intimate lives of the people
in this world. He got more knowledge of the plight of the
British fishing industry by a few nights he spent in the cabin
of a stinking herring drifter in the North Sea than he could

by reading all the pamphlets written about it. But chiefly he got more enjoyment for himself. Here, watching the sullen fishermen as they shot their nets at sunset, with the last bit of sun lighting up a headland on the far shore, he felt that he was feeling the texture of life, as if he were handling it. These men had not had the corners rubbed off them. There was a solid reality in such scenes. They gave the pulse of the world to his own senses; the mental and physical satisfaction of being present in another phase of life. This contrasted, for instance, with sitting in the stalls and watching a play in London. And even there, if he could have gone back-stage, he would again be having one of these views of life—of people in action. France, to him therefore, did not mean castles on the lovely Loire or the cynical politics of the Quai d'Orsay so much as it meant standing in some French market town on fair day and experiencing his constant delight and admiration of the solid lives of the French peasantry. Paris he often thought of as the little shops where the husband and wife worked together, sharing their small establishment's triumphs and disasters—and therefore understanding each other. That was life. A great deal more important than what M. Tardieu said to M. Leon Blum. Germany, with its genius for forest life, meant the cold blue shadows of snow swirling around the grey spikes of mountain peaks and the satisfying sight of Bavarian farmers laughing over their steins in some deer-antlered village tavern. In the year he spent under the Soviets he had kept as far away from Moscow as he could, drifting down the lonely Oka and then on down the Volga to Astrakhan on the Caspian, recapturing on those lazy days when the skyline never changed some of the complete sense of repose that Russia would always mean to him. Red Moscow was a shock.

Astrakhan, Samarkand, Tashkent, Bokhara; these names had lured him. Scarlet poppies of the Crimea in the fields of waving wheat; sunset from the Alexander Hut as the snows reddened along the Italian frontier; the backs of brugda sharks sticking out of a dawn sea between Norway and the Faroes; the great rivers of Norway, pouring, hundreds of miles through their pine forests, white with waterfalls to the sea; mud flats and the lonely cry of a curlew over a Kentish salt-marsh. . . . These were the things that he kept as his rewards of living. These intangible possessions were why he could find no answer when his friends said: "But what do you get out of such a chaotic life—what has it all brought you to?"

There was no answer.

These were some of the things he had seen with Christina; the things that had no connection with the marriage-bed. They were their mutual belongings. They could not be taken away. Disaster might only drive them back to search for them again. He, to-day, had little more material possessions than those he had shoved with such a feeling of adventure under his bunk in the cabin of the old *St. Louis*. A car, a few more suits perhaps, reams of books. . . . That was all; he had always regarded the little house in Cheyne Walk, with everything in it, as Christina's. It *was* Christina, that house!

That was one hostage he had given to Fortune; he would have to protect that—although Christina, with her incorrigible urge for the world beyond, would probably make infinitely less fuss than he imagined when it came to the point of giving it up. She had never been a drag but just exactly the opposite when things came to a crisis. It was he who would be sorry for her, not she for herself. That was the most comforting thought—now.

Christina and he had never been happier than when in adversity. Then they looked after each other.

*   *   *

Senator Hancock missed the *Majestic*, and Lynd could well understand why when he saw him. He telephoned the office one day suddenly from a big Strand hotel. It was four o'clock in the afternoon; and when Lynd went over he saw that Mr. Abner P. Hancock was in bed. He was a bulldoggy little man, with a face both the colour and texture of a ripe strawberry.

"See these pyjamas," he said almost the instant they had released shaking hands. "Cost one hundred and forty dollars! Real Japanese silk!"

Mr. Abner Hancock was drinking Courvoisier '65—with Poland Water.

"Mr. Lynd," he said, "I like your looks. You look like a real man. I want you to do something for me."

"Anything I can," said Lynd.

"I want you to get the *Berengaria*."

"Where is she?"

"She's just sailed from New York. Get her on the telephone. Ask for Miss Salome Svenson."

Lynd said he would try, and got on to Trans-Atlantic Telephones. There was a delay; then a voice asked him his number and said they would call back. When the phone rang someone said that they could not contact with the *Berengaria* she was between two zones—she had left New York; but there was a gap of a hundred miles or so before she came around the curve of the earth and they could contact her from the English side. Sorry.

"*To hell with the curve of the earth!*" exploded Abner Hancock. "*I* want Miss Salome Svenson!"

"Well, I'll try again," said Lynd.

"That's right," said Mr. Hancock: "Gettem on the phone an' let *me* speak to 'em!"

Lynd tried, but this time he asked to be put through to the person at the head General Post Office in charge of the Trans-Atlantic Telephone Service. Finally a bored voice spoke in the receiver: "Oh, yes? . . ."

"Gimme that." Hancock grabbed the mouthpiece. "Whoosat speaking? Head General Post Office—yeah?

DL

Well, listen—I wanna telephone to the *Berengaria*. Yeah?
Wassat—can't get through to her before some time around
midnight? Say . . . you listen to *me*. . . . Yeah—well, I don't
give a damn who you are. Wassat—*you don't care who I am
either*. Do you know who you're speaking to? This is Abner
P. Hancock. . . . American Senator, yeah. Yeah. An' you'll
damn' well find *out* who that is by to-morrow morning.
Yeah? Hullo, hullo, hullo . . ."

Abner Hancock stared wonderingly at the dead piece of
guttapercha in his hand. "Why, the sunnavabitch cut
off! . . ."

Abner Hancock crawled back into bed. "Gimme a
drink," he said: "I got to figure this here thing out. Help
yourself."

Lynd tried the Courvoisier '65 with Poland Water and
found that he liked it. He sat there, eyeing Mr. Hancock,
his new master. He did not feel joyous about the future.

"I'm sixty years old," said Mr. Hancock, as if in a
dream—"an' I've got a million dollars for every year. . . .
No English sunnuvabitch can beat me . . ."

When Mr. Hancock had jumped up to seize the telephone
Lynd saw that he was built like a pear stood on two tooth-
picks and judged that he was about five feet four inches
high.

He looked at the puffing face before him. Its eyes were
closed. Mr. Hancock was bald, but had black eyebrows that
a bird could nest in. Drink, dissipation, rich living, pride
had swollen his face so that it seemed his skin could hardly
hold it. He had a beautiful bar-room tan. The purple veins
seemed like snakes struggling to wriggle away from it all.
Taut nerves had ploughed his forehead until the deep seams
looked as if a carpenter's steel marker had been drawn
across it. There was a deep dent where some distracted
nerve muscles had pulled one side of his brow deep against
the top of his pug nose. The nose had little paint-brush tufts
of black hair projecting from the nostrils. He had a stubborn,

bitter little chin. And over all, as it rested now, this face of Abner Hancock, U.S. Senator, wore an expression of almost imbecile credulity.

"Wonder how it is," mused Lynd to himself, "that dumb-bells like that can make so much money, and smart guys like me have such a tough job to get along?"

"I've got it!" said Mr. Hancock, suddenly sitting up-right. "I told you no British sunnuvabitch was going to lick me. . . . Abner P. Hancock can beat 'em all—yes, with one of his hands tied behind his back. Now you listen, Tony."

Anthony Lynd started at this quick adoption of his most intimate name.

"You lissen ter me—see? Now this is not a request, it's not an order—it's a command. Right! Now—get Halifax on the phone—get Halifax to connect us with New York—tell New York to connect with the *Berengaria* . . . Go on—get started. Push!"

Lynd got the G.P.O. again and asked about the chances of making those connections. Pause. Yes, said a voice, that could be done. Lynd nodded at Mr. Hancock.

"And tell 'em it's for Miss Salome Svenson—see? Miss *Sal*-ome Svenson—careful how you pronounce that; it's Eyetalian."

Lynd did as ordered and then came back and smiled at Mr. Abner Hancock. Part of the question he had just asked himself had been answered.

*   *   *

"You stick around," said Mr. Hancock. "Might need you to help me handle these British bastards—not that I don't think they're good guys, you know. Only . . . they try to high-hat you. Say—wait till you see this girl. . . . I broke her in. Loves me for myself alone. Mr. Lynd—let—me—tell —you—Miss *Sal*-ome Svenson's finest girl whole world. Gimme drink."

Lynd sat by the window staring down at the traffic on the Thames. Christina was coming back to-morrow, and, my! what a surprise he had in store for her. Mr. Hancock fell asleep. Lynd looked at his baggage. Mr. Hancock had evidently not felt like unpacking just yet; the room was a leather-shop's display window of pigskin bags. Around six o'clock the phone rang. It *was* the *Berengaria*. . . . He shook Mr. Hancock, placed the receiver in his hand and tiptoed swiftly to the door. As he closed it he heard:

"Say, Baby—how's Papa's darling? Say, *Baby*—if you knew what a helluva time old Daddy's had getting on to . . ."

*   *   *

Downstairs, Lynd walked into the bar. "Hello, Mr. Lynd," said Charley. "Heard you'd been in India. Hot?"

"As hell," said Lynd. "Charley—what's the strongest . . ." Then he stopped. "Nope," he said, "I've changed my mind, Charley, I'm going on the wagon, right here, right now—right in front of your face."

"What's the idea, Mr. Lynd?—not that I don't wish some of the others around here would start doing it. It makes me proper sick, you know, to watch some of these *good* men going down the drain."

"Charley, I'm not going to touch a drop until a man who's living in this hotel right above us leaves town. So help me, Bob."

"Got to look after him?"

Lynd grinned. "No," he said, "I've got to look after myself."

*   *   *

When Lynd went upstairs again he found Mr. Hancock in a wildly jubilant mood. He wanted to eat. "Do you like lobster salad?" asked Lynd, knowing that he wanted some himself.

"Suits me."

Lynd rang up and got a table at Scott's.

"See those?" said Mr. Hancock, pulling up his $140 pyjama trousers to display a pair of bottle-shaped, badly varicosed legs—with green snakes and dragons tattooed all around them. A sort of climbing design. "Got those out in China—when I was a sailor before the mast in the *U.S.* Navy. Yessir, I come from humble beginnings. D'you know I've never been to school? Not one single day. I've been through the University of Life . . . d'ever hear of that one, Tony?"

Lynd said he had. He thought it was a damned good one. Only—graduation was difficult.

"Ha—you said it!" Hancock laughed, like a seal being thrown fish, in his bath. "That's a good one, Tony—I'll use that one. And it ain't got no post-graduate course, has it? Say—you can do a lot with that joke. Bring me in a drink, wilyer? Not too much Poland Water."

Lynd poured him a stiff one and brought it in. "Sit down," said Mr. Hancock. "Know"—a big swig—"know I told you I was sixty years old and got a million for every year—well, don't tell Sweetie that—that's Miss Svenson—she thinks I'm a regular kid, only fifty-five or so; and"—another gulp to drain the glass—"y'know, Tony, she ought to. I lay that baby twice every day. How's that?"

"Remarkable," said Lynd.

*   *   *

At Scott's, Mr. Hancock ordered two dozen of the finest "natives" for each of them. "Put some old lead in the pencil, eh?" He grinned at Lynd. "What's your idea of life? I mean what's your goal—what are you working for?"

"I don't know," said Lynd. "That's a question I've often asked myself. Never been able to answer it."

"What—you mean to say you're just drifting through life like a dismasted ship—'thout any port in view? I mean, what's your objective—your *ultimate* objective?"

Lynd thought. "Well, at the moment, I can tell you; I'd like to have a nice schooner, a five year's contract with the paper to sail her wherever I wanted to—and do, say, two articles a week. I'd call that a good life."

"All right," said Hancock, "I give her to you."

"Don't be funny."

"Mr. Lynd—when Senator Abner P. Hancock says a thing—it's better than a written contract. You can have that contract, and you can have that ship, yes—an' look here, Tony—we'll call her the *Ultimate Objective*. How's that for a name?"

"Swell." Lynd felt uncomfortable. In his excitement Hancock was raising his voice. People at even the far tables were turning and watching them. "And look here, Tony. I'll make just one stipulation—for one month out of every year me and Miss Svenson will come along—see? Mediterranean . . . South Sea islands . . . don't give a damn where. *You'll* be the captain. Ha-ha! I was always before the mast. Looka these . . ." Before Lynd could stop him, Mr. Hancock pulled up his trouser legs to display the snakes on his legs. "Blue-water sailor——"

At this juncture the polite head waiter thought he would take a hand. He came up to their table and bowed to Mr. Hancock.

"Excuse me, sir," he said. "Someone was telephoning for the Grand Duke Dmitri—are you the Grand Duke Dmitri?"

Hancock looked up. "Grand Duke Dmitri? *Me*—the Grand Duke Dmitri? Grand Duke Dmitri—*hell!*—I am Senator Abner P. Hancock, of the U.S. Senate. That's who I am."

It was lovely.

*   *   *

Lynd debated whether he ought to risk taking Mr. Abner P. Hancock along to his club. They were a fairly cosmopolitan lot. Then the Senator solved the question by saying he would like to go to bed. Lynd got him into a taxi and back to the hotel on the Strand. There, Mr. Hancock suddenly got a renewed grasp on life.

"Mr. Lynd," he said stiffly, sitting on his bed. "Get that telephone. Now this is not a request, mind you; it's not an order—it's a command. I want you to telephone every one of our correspondents and tell 'em to come here to London. Wanta hold a meeting."

"But, my God, Mr. Hancock—some of them are out in Japan!"

"'Sno difference. Fetch 'em here. This is Abner P. Hancock speaking. Yunnerstan'?"

Lynd thought a moment; his future hung in the balance. Then he turned to Senator Hancock and said, "Nuts!"

"*W-h-a-a-t ?*"

"Apple sauce!"

"What d'y'mean?"

"Here," said Lynd, "have another drink. I'll come here at ten to-morrow morning. If you still want that meeting— I'll telephone all of them. Well, good night."

"Say, Tony—didn't I beat that Goddam British Post Office? And didn' I tell that Goddam head waiter where to get off? Didn' Senator Abner P. Hancock do that?"

"You certainly did," said Lynd, not without admiration.

"Well then—goo'night."

Over in the Café Royal Lynd found Patrick Byron sitting by himself. His ordinarily pale face was now paler than ever, and his mouth was twisted. "My wife's leaving me," he said.

"Ummm—but I thought you always were saying you were going to leave her?"

"I know. I've said a lot of damn' silly things. But I'd rather not talk about it."

"All right," said Lynd. "Let me tell you a funny story. Let me tell you the story of the only man in my life whom I've ever seen flatten out a head waiter. . . ."

* * *

Lynd walked across to the hotel opposite the office, ran the ticker tape through his fingers to see if there was any Agency news, saw that there was none, and walked along to his club for lunch.

"Oh, Mr. Lynd," said the hall porter as he came in, "there's a young lady just been trying to get hold of you."

"Did she leave any name?"

"Nossir."

"What did her voice sound like?"

The porter gave an embarrassed grin: "Well, all I can say, sir—it sounded very sweet."

Lynd knew it was Luba.

*   *   *

The Powers' apartment was appalling. It was one of those depressing thoroughfares where the houses go on for block after block without any change in their frontage except the number on the door; where, any time after five on week-days, when the tram stops, the same men always jump off it; a street with genteel little gardens, about ten feet square, standing meekly before each red-brick house; a street of hopes and high talk—but from which few dwellers ever graduate. The young escape on Sundays on bicycles into the country, and pedal back with rooster-tails of flowers behind their saddles; the elderly men scratch about in their patch of garden, and then put on a tweed coat and walk along to the pub to have a gin-and-It before luncheon time; women, if they are gossipy, can talk to each other over the back fences. But there was no escape for the Powers.

Roderick had aged frightfully. He had become puffy, and, when Lynd found him, he was reading the football scores. When Lynd walked him along to the pub later and simply filled him with whiskey—Power admitted he could not afford to get drunk, unless someone else paid for it—Roderick, warmed by the sudden appearance of a man who so poignantly brought back the memory of old days, wiped his watery eyes and said: "It's been so long since I've had a woman, my dear boy, that I can't even remember what it was like."

Mrs. Power had retreated further into the corner than ever. For some reason, this slender, once-lovely woman had become crumpled and witch-like. Her stare had a touch of madness now. She sat in a dark room, looking out on a shaft, which was full of Pomeranians which they were continually breeding. Some man had given Luba two, a dog and a bitch; and the sire was now acting in the capacity of husband, brother, sister, grandfather, everything except as son to this smelly household. Their hairs flecked the carpet, were strewn on every chair, so that when Tony stood up he had the beginnings of a fur coat clinging to him. Mrs. Power had withered so that he now thought she looked like a marmoset. And as she sat in the corner, regarding him with beady eyes, Tony saw that she hated him more than ever.

On the mantelpiece were two Popoff vases.

"The last things we haven't sold, Fofoiser," said Luba. Her sense of the dramatic made her point out that; but she was not in the least depressed by it. Elated, in fact.

This was Saturday evening. And a fresh-cheeked young man came in, in razor-pressed flannel bags, and an un-wrinkled coat of Harris tweed. At his appearance Mrs. Power came to life. "Come here, Ronald," she said, dragging him by her voice to a chair beside her in the corner. Then, with great animation, she began to discuss the horse races at Kempton Park. She and Ronald had each had a shilling on the 2.30, which came in at 10 to 1. But they had lost on three others. From their conversation it was obvious that the young man came in there every night to talk to the Powers. Mrs. Power was jealous of Ronald; Lynd saw that; she was afraid that someone would lure him away from her—this man who meant companionship.

D1

"Not like the old days, is it?" said Roderick thickly. "Remember Vlasnitca?"

Lynd saw his cue, and played up to it nobly: "Well, hardly, Roderick—that was a marvellous estate! I wonder what's happened to your house . . . and all your peasants? I wanted to go out there, you know, when I was in Moscow in 1928, but . . . somehow, I just couldn't face it."

He saw Roderick's eyeballs turn under their heavy lids and fix themselves on Ronald's face. Mrs. Power was also looking at him, and now turned to Lynd with eyes of expectation.

Lynd said to Ronald: "You should have seen that place! The most lovely country house . . . deep pine woods and birch forests. . . . You won't find things like that in *other* parts of the world, will you, Roderick?"

Ronald's eyes were now also staring. "Really?"

"No," said Lynd—"not ever. That life has gone for ever." He turned: "But you had it, Roderick—you did have it."

He had done what they wanted of him. Ronald knew now that when the depressed Powers told him about their former grand life in Tsarist Russia, they were not lying. Mrs. Power sank back with a grudgingly grateful sigh.

"Oh, Minka *takoi* . . . Minka, darling . . ." Luba was holding up one of the point-nosed little Poms before him. "Isn't she *lovely?*"

* * *

Lynd got a room off Russell Square. It was sordid. They had to climb up three flanks of dirty stairs. And the man in the next room never seemed to be out of it either day or night. They could hear him rumbling about in there; and once or twice he knocked on the wall, when they forgot and laughed too loud. But Luba's spirit filled it with careless happiness. For some reason, that he did not understand at the time, Luba never wanted to be seen with him in any of the better-class London restaurants. So they tried Soho. Then they found a little Italian place on the way out to Bloomsbury where they quickly became part of the family.

As Roderick had a weak chest, the Power family, before the War, often spent their winters in Italy. And tomboy Luba, with that flair the Russians have for language, could talk the *patois* of Naples' docks. It delighted the Italian proprietor and his gaunt, black-eyed wife. The Italian woman hated England.

Luba knew every secret of the Zappi family, told the ripening daughter where she could buy cheap dresses that had been used as models, made alterations in them herself. When Tony and Luba had *zabaione*, Zappi left the rest of his customers and went down to make them himself.

And sometimes, as their room had a gas-ring, they brought back tins of imported German *weiners* and cooked them and ate them with French mustard and a couple of bottles of good German hock that Lynd bought from the Club.

These were the nights when the mysterious man in the other room rapped on the wall. He seemed a frustrated person.

And Tony came to notice that even though he had had all the whiskey that was good for him at the Club before he drove out to Linderwood Grove to pick Luba up, and then a straw-cupped flask of red Chianti at Zappi's over their dinner—he never got drunk with Luba. It was strange because, aside from that night when the Malay-boys forced her to drink gin *pahits* on the P. & O. boat, Luba hardly took anything. Tony drank nearly all of it.

In these happy moods, this whiskey which so often made him lose his senses merely made him feel more alive. He began to take a new interest in his work.

* * *

Senator Hancock, unable to sit still while the *Berengaria* was bringing Sweetie over, had gone over to Paris and went down to meet her. He took her off at Cherbourg. Lynd got a wire from him to say that they had gone to Italy, where the Senator was going to buy some Old Masters for his Washington house. He had told Lynd about these: "The White House won't be a patch on it!" he declared. As Tony had returned almost straight to work after the blistering heat of India, he still had a month's vacation coming to him. He suggested that they throw everything in the car and drive up to the Shetlands.

Chris, very sensibly, said they would take the less-romantic train.

*   *   *

He felt proud of her as she stood in familiar tweeds on Euston platform. This was her best life. They crossed from Aberdeen to Lerwick, and woke up in the morning to the gulls wheeling and crying like squeaking blocks and the harbour full of herring boats. It was good to be back among these raw scenes again. They went up the island to where the grey, granite house of a Scot stood at the head of a lonely *voe*. He was a black Scot, the same age as Lynd, who had been in the Seaforths during the War, and in two bloody bayonet charges. At night, when the wind roared up the *voe* and blew the peat smoke back down the rumbling chimney, the Scot, after a few whiskeys, would leap up and illustrate the way, reversing the butt, he had bashed out the brains of a German sergeant as he was hanging on the wire— so many of his own pals had been killed. But usually, as they ate the little pink trout cooked in oatmeal for breakfast, the Scot was dour and contemplative, his mind engrossed with his struggle of leading the crofters in their hard daily work to earn their living. He was the local laird—his father apparently had been afraid to strike any child in the district, for fear it might be his—and the equally dour Shetlanders had every right to look upon their communal struggle for existence as a family affair. The young laird, Tony's friend, accepted this.

In his more genial moods he would dwell upon the old Shetland custom of "bundling," where, in the crofts where the beds are let into the wall, the old couple sat by the peat fire in the same room of the croft while the young suitor was allowed to get into bed with the girl. "The only precaution they took," grinned the young laird, "was that her parents tied her legs together at the knees. But you know what they say—love will find a way!"

Lynd had never found fishing a restful sport. Neither fly-fishing for trout or salmon nor bait-casting for the American small-mouth bass; nor had he found anything restful about wading out shoulder-deep to cast a four-ounce sinker out beyond the great foaming combers of the New Jersey coast. He had known times when he had deliberately wanted to break his cast—to lose a fish—because the struggle had put such a strain on his nerves. But he had grown up with rods of one sort or another in his hands, and loved the life in different parts of the world that they made for him. He always took them with him. By marrying Christina he had obtained a good ghillie. She knew how to keep a boat just the right distance off a lee shore; she sat on the bank while he waded some of the gentle English streams. She appreciated a big fish. Up here, where the wind swept across the bleak moors and the great waves of the Atlantic thundered against the eastern cliffs, she lay in the heather and read books while he fished the peaty burns.

He loved the Shetland lochs. Lonely and forlorn. He loved the secret silence of their grey lichened rocks. Alone in this bleak moorland, he loved the companionship of Christina as he sat there, tying on flies, or admiring perhaps a fine sea trout he had just landed. And their lunches when the lochs lay blue and they sprawled smoking in the sun. It was a good life.

"One of these days," he told Christina, "we will buy a pub. We'll call it 'The Rainbow Trout.' Where shall we have it?"

"Casablanca."

"No. I've seen the place; it's an African Brighton. Don't let names get you. Where? . . ."

"You'd drink up all the stock!"

"Ha! I know it. And I'd always be fishing—wouldn't I? No—I would not make a good pub-keeper. But you'd be grand. Gosh! what meals you would give them!"

"None of that railway fish with tooth-paste sauce and cold mut. It would be perfectly simple to give them good salads."

"Of course. What the hell—don't the English know of any other vegetables besides potatoes and brussels sprouts—cooked in the bath-tub?"

"Peas."

"Peas! Your English peas, my—God! Those fluffy things. You want them firm, with the creases showing, cooked in butter. . . ."

"I wouldn't have a pub. You'd never be in it. You would always be racing up to London."

"Don't you believe it; the one thing I like is the country—and you know it. Why don't we have a cottage?"

They often talked this way—and both of them were afraid that they would never have that cottage. "You're such a dab at gardening!" he said; and he had a picture of the beloved, faithful Christina, gloves on her hands, staring down at some work in a flower-bed—happy as any lark in the sky. Why the devil didn't they have this at once—at once! Because this was dangerous.

He had purposely told Luba not to write to him while he was in the Shetlands. He had made the excuse that he was roaming the islands, and that up on the island of Yell or Unst, where he would probably go, mail only got there by motor boat. Never knew when it would come. There was nothing to say, anyway, he said when she persisted. He knew that the truth was he did not want one thing from the outside to enter into this holiday with Chris.

"You're selfish, Peter," said Chris.

"Me!"

"Yes, you are. You're splendid about money and material things. You're unique. But you're selfish about yourself— you never give me any of yourself. The little things, like tiny presents, they do mean so much to a woman. It would make no difference if they didn't cost a shilling."

"Oh, damn it all . . ."

"Absolutely. In Vienna, when you gave me the money to buy my belt instead of going around to select it with me. . . . And you never remember my birthday—or even our *wedding* day—when was it?"

Lynd tried to think. "June 10th!" he said proudly.

"Yes, it was, Those were wonderful days."

"Weren't they. And we've got just as many more ahead of us. Now listen, Chris . . ."

As he argued with her, and looked at that nice creature, those noble eyes of hers, he wondered what on earth it was that made this lack of the physical satisfaction poison all the rest of their life. For Chris was quite right; he did not feel that particular *interested* love for her that would prompt him to do the little things. Often, he felt merely sorry for her. He would protect her on the big things. But that was not love. . . .

One evening as they trudged home across the wine-red moors a boy came towards them. There are no trees in the Shetlands, and you can see a sheep for miles. The boy was running. He was waving a telegram. It read:

"PLEASE RUSH BERLIN."

They spent that winter in Germany.

*   *   *

Berlin was in a state of jitters that winter over a threatened Nazi *putsch*. The world was being thrown into a like state of apprehension by a sensational Press which had never had such a godsend for headlines as Herr Hitler. Lynd went the usual rounds of establishing his contacts for information. The Wilhelmstrasse, the American Embassy, the bar of the Adlon Hotel. The last was the most useful. Several of the most prominent foreign correspondents gathered there every day before lunch to have a goblet or so of cold beer, chew salted almonds, and try to pick each other's brains. Two Jewish correspondents, with apprehensive ears to the ground, were particularly brilliant in their analyses of the inevitability of Hitler—with them, the fear being father to the thought.

To see the little Charlie Chaplinesque figure who was giving Europe such nightmares, Tony went down to the first Leipsic trial, where three young Reichswehr officers were on trial, possibly for their lives, on the charge of having succumbed to Nazi propaganda. Hitler was giving testimony in their defence. "I never tried to corrupt the Reichswehr!" thundered Hitler. "I want the Reichswehr to be faithful so that I can use it when I get into office!"

Tony sat within a few feet of the inconspicuous little figure in the shiny double-breasted blue suit when the future ruler of Germany was jabbing his finger at the seven scarlet-robed judges of the Supreme Court. The judges automatically jerked backwards as Hitler stabbed his finger at them. Hitler's voice rose and roared until its reverberance was like that of an express train roaring at you through a tunnel. Through the mullioned windows of the Supreme Court Tony heard the shouting in the streets. The taut faces of the three young Reichswehr officers in the dock were grey as putty.

"And when I get into power," roared Hitler; "then, I tell you—*heads will roll in the sand*!"

When Tony returned to Berlin he expected a wire of congratulation from his paper. He had been the only American correspondent present when Hitler made that speech that rocked the world. But he did not get it. To one of the Jew correspondents at the Adlon he said:

"You win. In my dispatch I put that 'heads will roll in the sand' stuff where Hitler made it—*after* he had spoken for some twenty minutes declaring he was not going to *putsch*, he didn't need to. You, very sensibly, led off with it."

"Of course!" grinned the Jew. "That's good journalism. What do you think?"

"That I was cuckoo. Have a beer? Your cable reads better than mine anyway . . . mine was dull. Have you ever met Dr. Frank? No? Well, I sat up most of the night before the trial with him. . . . Very interesting. . . . He explained how he was one of the original seven Nazis, only a few years ago: 'In these next elections,' he said, 'we ought to poll around four or five millions. We are inevitable!'"

The Jew nodded solemnly. "Sure—you're right there. That's the real story. But hell. . . . You know what the papers want. I tried to get my crowd to print a story that Hitler is being backed by Fritz Thyssen and the big Rhine industrialists . . . and you know what they cabled: that I was seeing things!"

Lynd thought he was seeing things when he attended his first session of the German Reichstag—and found it a mad-house. When he saw the brown-shirted Nazis rush from their chairs on one side of that supposedly solemn assemblage, and a vociferous crowd of Socialists charge from the other . . . when he saw these two bodies of delegates making faces and shaking their fists at each other directly below the President's chair—while the President clanged a cow-bell up and down over their heads to quieten them—Lynd said to a brother correspondent: "Why, it's like waking up in a loony bin!"

"When you've been in this country as long as I have," muttered the other, "you'll think the loony bin is the only sane place."

* * *

Christina, in the afternoons, went to the various cocktail parties given by the correspondents themselves or the diplomatic corps, and she sat by his side at the official luncheons given by the Foreign Office. She spoke excellent German, and as they stayed on they went out more and more into German life and entertained in their own apartment off the Tiergarten. They saw Reinhardt's *Midsummer Night's Dream*, *The White Horse Inn*, and *Casanova*, in its vast theatre with the revolving stage.

Lynd saw another side of Berlin night life. Visiting correspondents from other European capitals or America did not want to waste their evenings on the conventional shows: "Let's see some life!" was their chronic request. For Berlin was very decadent in those depression days. In some shows the female performers brought no costumes whatever. Or perhaps a red rose to cover some of the little necessities of life. One hardened globe-trotter turned up and irritatingly dared Lynd to show him something new. Lynd took him to a dim little place with shaded lights and people talking quietly at the tables, where a man played dreamily on the piano. If he knew you, or thought you would buy him a bottle of champagne, he would improvise a song about you and sing it as you drank your wine.

"Tame!" said the disgusted American.

"Well, he is off form," said Tony, who had been thinking he had talked too much about this man's playing before they came here. He called the head waiter and asked: "What's the matter with him?"

"He jumped in the Spree and tried to drown himself," said the waiter.

"Yes, I knew he was in trouble—his wife left him?"

"No—she came back."

"Bah!" snorted the questing New Yorker. "Old stuff."

They strolled along under the neon lights and Lynd turned into "Eldorado." "I'm afraid there's not much doing," he said, as they checked their hats. "You can dance if you want to—there's a beauty!"

The globe-trotter looked. It was a lovely girl, her blonde hair shingled in an Eton crop; when Tony nodded she smirked and came over to their table. "Dance?" said the world-traveller. The girl smiled.

"Gosh!" said the globe-trotter when he sat down. "She's a forward minx. Know what she did to me? Yeah— took me out into the cloakroom, girls' toilet I guess, and——"

"You didn't think that was a girl, did you?" asked Tony.

The man stopped. His eyes stared. He was obviously trying to remember what he had just done—or had done to him. "My—*God!*" he said. "*Honest?*"

"Exactly," said Tony.

* * *

* * *

At Christmas Lynd got an unlucky second-man on one of the American agencies to sub for him and he and Christina went down to Garmisch for the winter sports. Lynd's bad leg prevented him from ski-ing, for which he was thankful. And Christina had never learned the sport. But she had only to see a mountain before the next thing was the demand that they should both climb it. She nearly killed him, trying to see how far they could get, in that snow, up the sides of the chill Zugspitz. They were snobbish enough to be furious when they found the Americans and British had also discovered a little inn they had intended to stop at just under this beloved and much-advertised German mountain; and so, after a few days of freezing walks and suffocating cocktails in the inns of Garmisch, they came back.

* * *

Before leaving Berlin Lynd had spent a small fortune on telephoning Luba at nights. They had managed to have a last night together before he left London, not going to their shabby room off Russell Square, but driving down to Maidenhead, where Luba, at any rate, ate a surprisingly big dinner and they went to sleep with the pleasant sound of the water running over the weir. Luba was gloomy, and it was with great fondness that he looked at her head lying on his arm and tried to get her to talk about things. Luba did not want to talk. She merely wanted to feel his arms around her as she fell asleep. She had asked him if she could keep the Russell Square room; it was frightfully difficult living nose-to-nose with her parents, she said. He could well understand that; and knew that even that sordid room might be sanctuary. He criticised himself as he lay awake and looked at her babyish face that night; he was getting all the fun out of this—and he was not suffering anything. By rights, if he was going to go on with Luba, he should get a divorce from Chris and marry her. But, he told himself coldly, he was human. It was a rotten thing to do, perhaps—to sleep with Luba when he would not go the whole length of marrying her. But he knew he would not. He would rather be a swine than ruin Christian's life. That was all there was to it. And Luba did not seem to want that. Colonel Bumby, he could not get Luba to speak of. Nor of this dangling divorce from her peculiar husband. So he did not know what was the position.

He could not afford it, but he sent Luba before Christmas enough money to take the Powers all away over the holidays, and begged her to take her mother out of the atmosphere of that blind-windowed room. It was enough to drive anyone crazy, and even Mrs. Power might take a more reasonable view of life if given fresh air. Luba wrote him a brief note. The Powers, quite characteristically, had gone to the most expensive hotel in Torquay—and spent it all in two days. But perhaps they were right to have two days where, such as they had once lived, money meant nothing, even if it had to be Torquay.

Luba was a bad letter-writer, more ineffective even than when face to face. She was irritatingly coy as if she were afraid to put down "love" in the written word. Her little messages were full of trivialities, not even good gossip, or even questions. It was just as if a child had been given a punishment to write a hundred words. But he loved them for the gay little spirit they showed—and her courage. Then they suddenly stopped coming. When three weeks had gone he tried to telephone her. The Powers had no telephone, not feeling they were able to afford such a thing, and he had been accustomed to asking for Luba via the woman next door. When he tried to press this woman as to why he could never get Mrs. Fayne (it was the only occasion on which he had to use Luba's married name) or had she been given his message, the vulgar voice at the other end at last said: "I do not interfere in other people's business. . . ."

Her words and tone, for it was obvious that she gloated in being able to say something to upset him, alarmed Tony so much that he decided to fly to London. He wired Luba to meet him, and got on next day's Cologne plane. As the green of England came below him, he looked down with a feeling of dread. There had been something wrong in all this, this leaving Luba alone to face life. He pictured her in London's eight millions; brave, pert-nosed, trying not to get down-hearted. He would have given years if he could have seen her as he peered down at Croydon enclosure while they were circling to land. She was not there. He missed the Airways bus back to London while he was telephoning, to see if there was any message at his club. Then he hired a taxi and drove straight to Hammersmith.

*　　*　　*

Roderick gave a start when he answered the bell, and seemed on the point of preventing him from coming in. Then he said, "Hello, old chap," and motioned Lynd down the corridor. Mrs. Power was crouched, more like an angry marmoset than ever, in her corner chair.

"Where's Luba?" he asked.

"I don't know," said Mrs. Power.

"Don't *know*? What do you mean?"

"Luba is not living here any more."

Lynd sighed with relief. "Well, will you tell me where I can get her?"

Luba's father and mother looked at each other and then finally Roderick gave him an address. It was in the next street. "Oh, that's all right; I'll just go around and find her. Or maybe we could telephone from here?"

The Powers looked at each other; then Roderick, with a sigh, wrote out a telephone number. Tony walked out into the street to the corner call-box and dialled the number. There was no reply.

"I don't think you will get her. Luba said that she was going out to-night."

Mrs. Power said that the instant he came back. And Lynd saw that she was glad to say it spitefully. He asked Roderick would he like to come out for a drink. Roderick looked out from under his swollen lids at Mrs. Power. And then bravely said he would.

"What *is* all this?" asked Lynd nervously when they sat before the pub fire.

Roderick's answer was more frightening than ever. "Don't ask me," he said, wearily. "Women, *I* don't know what to make of them. Luba always does what she wants."

It seemed unfair to try and pry things out about Luba behind her back; so Tony poured a couple more double whiskeys into the bloated Roderick, and dropped him as he taxied back to his club. At his club he put in another call. No answer. Then, braving the sophisticated porter's concern (that servant was too used to this kind of thing) he told him to call that number at regular half-hour intervals. "I can get a room here in the Club if I want it, can't I?" asked Lynd.

"Yessir—there's two vacant and I'll let you know if any other gentleman asks for them, sir."

He went up, sat on the fender by the fire. He no longer felt dispassionate and merely friendly toward Luba. He felt furious, frightened, and desired her madly. He finally had to take one of the club rooms.

*   *   *

In the morning the telephone rang beside his bed. "Here's your call, sir." It was the night-porter's voice and Lynd knew it must be very early without even looking at his watch.

"Hello, hello, hello. . . ." He heard Luba's bell-like tones, obviously anxious to find out who was calling her.

"Hello there," he said.

There was a silence before she answered, and then she said: "Hello."

"Look here," said Lynd, trying to make his voice sound light and cheerful. "Didn't you get my wire?"

"I—I, of course, yes—but I couldn't meet you. I . . . I was out of Town." It was a bad lie, and it shook him to realise it.

"Well, why didn't you leave a note for me at the Club? When *can* I see you?"

"Well, why . . . couldn't we have dinner at Zappi's to-night? Say eight? I shall be busy up to then."

"Not before then, then?"

"I'm afraid not, Fofoiser."

"Oh . . . all right."

*   *   *

When Lynd got to Zappi's at seven-thirty, he found Luba already there. She was laughing with the grouped Italian family; and the first thing she did was seize the young Zappi girl and turn her round and round before Lynd. "Look! Fofoiser, I made that myself—isn't it *smart*!" Lynd growled something about Carissima's dress and asked Zappi for a table. Luba was as hard to pin down that night as butterflies. Her mind would not rest on any subject. Finally Lynd said, "Let's go back to your flat."

"But I've got a *girl* living with me!"

"Doesn't make any difference. I'm not going to eat you."

There was a girl there. "Charmed to meet you, I'm sure," she said, mincing forward to touch Lynd's hand. She was false. She was something that was not true. There was the air of something horrible in this place.

"Do you mind?" Lynd said, looking pointedly at the door. "I want to speak to Miss Power for a few minutes—alone."

The girl looked at Luba, flung up her head and made as if to stay: "Well, me and Miss Power——" she began.

"Please!" Lynd, just touching her arm, nodded towards the door.

"How dare you!" said Luba, who had backed strangely into a corner. "How dare you treat one of my best friends like that!"

"*That!* . . ." said Lynd. "Why she's as common as dirt. That girl's the vulgarist little bitch I've ever seen. Your *friend?*" He frowned. "Luba—what is it?" he asked.

"I won't be treated like a tart!"

His eyes opened. Now he knew the meaning of this sinister atmosphere in the flat. The pretence of the girl.

"You are one," he said.

Luba hit him.

*   *   *

For a moment he was dizzy with surprise and rage. He stood there, holding his face; and then Luba, who had retreated back into the corner of the room, began to take off her skirt. "I've got to go out," she said fiercely. She looked trapped, flustered to the point of frenzy.

"I'm sorry," he said. "If you had been a tart, Luba, it wouldn't make any difference. I love you. But you're too damned stupid to be a tart. What the hell is all this? If you're tired of me, say so. I guess I can stand it. But I don't think that's it?"

It seemed hardly possible that anyone could escape some answer to that, but all Luba panted was: "Violet is my friend!"

"Vi-olet! Oh, Luba . . . for Christ's sake. That bloody little twerp!"

"Well, I must say!" said Luba, "you can use better language."

He put up his hand. "Stop it. I'm going. I'm not going to ask you any questions. Your life is your own—but just let me tell you one thing, Luba, for all your guts—you are the damnedest little fool I have ever known. If you've become so desperate that you have to take up with a girl like that, then it's a ghastly shame. If that's what you've come to! But what *is* all this mystery? . . . This flat? And why in hell's name are you wearing black silk underwear?"

Luba snatched up a black evening gown she had laid out on the bed and held it defensively before her breast. "Get out!" she said frantically. "Leave me alone!"

"All right. If you say so."

He picked up his hat and walked out of the flat. As he walked to the main street a long grey Lagonda turned up the cul-de-sac that now held Luba's ground-floor flat, and stopped before her door. It was not the kind of car you would expect in that kind of street. Lynd watched as a grey-haired man in a dinner jacket got out and playfully tapped on

Luba's window with his stick before skipping into the apartment house.

It looked like Colonel Bumby, or whatever his name was.

*   *   *

The Berlin man returned to his post, and Lynd and Christina returned to London and opened their house in Cheyne Walk. One of the first things he did was buy Chris a dachshund puppy. They had watched a German with three of them on a leash—all four of them staring into a window along Unter den Linden one day. They decided they must have one. The puppy—as Tony had happened to remember this birthday—was a secret present. Chris awoke to find it on her bed.

Over their coffee that morning they had a tantalising argument as to what they should name it. They wrote names on slips. "Zeppelin" was the winner. The funny little thing did not look that way now; but it would.

She was a bitch in more sense of the word than one. Forgetful one day, Chris locked Zeppelin up in the closet with her best dresses. Zeppelin jumped up, dug her sharp teeth into the finest tissue and silks, and hung there until it ripped. When, hunting her distractedly all over the house, she was revealed by her happy barks at their footsteps, tragedy was also disclosed. From as far up as Zeppelin could jump Christina's dresses looked like shredded wheat. Zeppelin had evidently tired of that some time back, and came out with an evening slipper in her mouth.

Lynd made up for all the birthdays he had forgotten in years that day when, after a lunch at the Ivy, he went with Chris to a new dressmaker she wanted to try in Conduit Street. It did not make the hour he spent there with Christina any better to know that this was one of the shops where Luba had worked.

*   *   *

He made no attempt whatever to get into touch with Luba. The days drifted along. He found London very dull. Most correspondents worked feverishly because they were afraid someone else would scoop them on a story; they were often bored with themselves. The mere round of his work brought a certain amount of occasions and functions. He got free tickets for first nights, to which he always took Chris. Christina could say immediately why she did or did not like a play; he could not say why—he just did or did not like them, that was all. Usually he did not. Chris was a theatre fan and often went to a pit with some friend. On such evenings he went to his club, was frightened out of it by the spectacle of the same womanless men trying to find something to talk about over their wine in the dining-room. And he went to every party he was invited to. These were many.

This was a bad sign for him. He had long ago wearied of parties and the necessity of making conversation. He no longer hoped for anything exciting from them. He always cursed himself afterwards for having gone. And, after you have been to a few official functions, you know that they are the most meaningless displays of bare bosoms and decorations and indifferent food. He often longed for *zabaione* at little Zappi's with Luba. Those meals had been heaven.

Chris and he did a certain amount of entertaining at Cheyne Walk, either killing-off parties or dinners at which six would be the most people and they could invite whom they liked. Chris was a witty conversationalist; they had friends among many of the younger set in the foreign diplomatic corps, one very amusing Bolshie; and there was a more or less continual appearance of some man he had known in the Near or Far East, or from the States. As far as such things went, he could not have asked for a better life. Chris and he always sat after everyone had gone, and he enjoyed her gossip as he drank a final good night whiskey.

She was trying to make him cut down these days. His insides were giving trouble, and one doctor that he went to even advised him to go to a psychiatrist. "Actually, it's a case of nervous indigestion," he said. "But you seem more mentally run down than anything else. Have you something that's worrying you?"

Lynd smiled. "Nothing, I'm afraid, that you'd call serious."

"Well, you never know," said the doctor.

"I'm just bored. That's all. Bloody bored."

"Quite enough," said the other. "Have you ever tried living in your mind? Excuse me if I say this, but you seem a lusty chap—you know, the kind of man who likes the good things of life; women, wine—and all that. . . . You feel you can't get along without them? But being bored is not a thing I should expect from a man with your work—a foreign newspaper correspondent!"

"A great surgeon!" said Lynd.

The doctor laughed. "But you see I am not bored—I enjoy every day of my life. My work is enough to let me lose myself in it."

"Wish to God I could say that! Let me try to explain something," said Tony, conscious that he was talking more for his own information than the doctor's. "In my profession we are supposed to see a lot of the world, a lot of exciting things. We do. We see so damn' many that we get bored with sensations. We lose our capacity to remain interested. The more stupid among us go blasé at once—a year or so in Europe, and they think they know everything. You were asking me a minute ago did I ever try to live in my mind— did I think, in other words? . . . Why, of course I do. I have to. My job keeps me reading, or studying something, making myself familiar with it, every day. . . ."

Tony laughed; it seemed an impossible task, to dissect the reason for this lack of interest in his work. "Perhaps it's a certain sense of the futility of it all," he said. "You see,

we all think at first that what we write is going to be read,
and that it will mean something. Well . . . after a time
you see the joke of all that. This town's full of diplomatic
correspondents, and journalistic intellectuals, sentimental
liberals, most of them, who think that European governments
tremble at their words. You see, the point is, we all think of
a newspaper as some great entity, as if it were omniscient—
well, when you know some of the woolly minds which
write the editorials in London, warning Germany to be
good—or the Soviets—and you know some of the hard-
boiled practical men who are running those countries . . .
the only thing is to laugh. The 'Power of the Press.' . . ."

"Do you deny it?" asked the doctor.

"Not a bit. That's the hell of it. I just know its shams
vis-à-vis the Boob Public. That's why I've learned now not
to take my job seriously. I'm interested in people—not
politicians. The Press only wants politics—what these
canting humbugs have to say. Politicians, apparently, have
special brains. They make the head-lines. But the more I
see of the people who are running things, the more I get the
horrid feeling that this little world of ours is going plump
to hell.

"This is very long-winded," said Tony, "but in talking
to you like this don't think I'm running down my own
colleagues. Far from it. It's these other people I'm talking
about; I wish you could know the dismay we feel at the
things we have to listen to from certain of these big people,
the horror with which we have to report some of their blab
lying—their unforgivable stupidity; the fake secrets they
think they are making you believe in, just because they
whisper them to you 'under the rose' . . . You would
understand then why, when some of us sit down to our
typewriters, the first words that come into our minds after
beginning 'PRIME MINISTER X SAID TO-DAY' . . . are 'God
help the world!'"

Tony laughed and stood up. "And so," he said, "I think

we all spend too much time thinking and talking about
politics. Perhaps we have to—but let the politicians do it.
They made this mess. What I'm thinking of, the more I see
of this world, the more I want a little life of my own. Something very small—a personal life—where a new set of habits
might do me a lot of good!"

The doctor smiled. "You are absolutely right," he said
hopefully. "You must change your habits."

"Ummm. . . ." Tony reflected. "I'm not sure I want to.
I'm not sure, if a man finds his life too dull, if he isn't
entitled to a lot of bad habits to make up for it. Why not?
If they give him happiness. I know what you're going to say;
that they will ruin his health. But health isn't everything,
you know. Some of the most unpleasant people I know are
vegetarians . . . simply odiously healthy people. No, I
think I'll go on the way I am."

While he had been reading obsolete *Punchs* in the specialist's waiting-room, Tony had reflected that his visit was
useless. No doctor had an answer for what was ailing him.
There was no medicine in the whole pharmacopœia that
could pass as a remedy for the missing Luba. The solution
must be found in the course of events. Life had always been
that way for him. A crisis nearly always meant that he
started to play life again with a new pack of cards. The
future, therefore, always promised to be interesting.

*   *   *

Lester Blackwood was an author who had become obsolete.
In his younger days he had written some excellent *belles
lettres*—days when people still quoted Walter Pater and
writers did not need to have anything to say, as long as they
said it beautifully. This was when he was in his mystical
period. He had been, at that time, very religious, and there

had been a tremendous vogue for his musings. But then people began to suspect that it was not their fault for being bewildered by Lester's profound regurgitations about the road to fulfilment through spiritual suffering. Lester was merely out-Lestering himself. He might as well have been talking to a dog. Then his public turned on him. When he frantically wrote an obscene novel, to keep pace with the "Twenties," and become popular again—people thought he had betrayed them! Lester Blackwood rapidly became a back number.

He lived in a cavernous flat out in Bloomsbury. Strange people were found there. Writers who might have been great —but had just missed it. A few painters with grotesque and unprofitable ideas for canvas. Hopeful young girls who were beginning to learn how to write. In other words, mediocrities.

Most of his old friends kept away from Lester Blackwood's parties.

* * *

But when Lester called him up and said that he *must* come, Lynd needed no urging. Not in this desperate mood. But even as he drove out in his little open Lea-Francis to Bloomsbury he felt depressingly listless. Perhaps, he told himself, it was the oncoming spring.

The party was even worse than he had expected. When he came in, a gathering of people, not one of whom he remembered ever seeing before, were sitting in a large circle around the board floor on white chamber-pots.

"Got the idea of the jerries from the Prater in Vienna," said Lester. "Haaaaaa! Think it's a good idea, don't you? Haaaa!"

Lynd shuddered and was glad to see that every pot was occupied. Lester pulled at his grey goatee, gave another one of his wheeze-laughs, and offered Lynd a glass of *slivowitz*, the Slav's plum brandy. When Lynd went into the next room to put away his coat, he found Patrick Byron lying on the bed, completely out, with his arm tight around the waist of a light-coloured negro girl. She grinned at Lynd, and, mocking her own darkie-accent, said:

"Dis yere baby o' mine has suah got some grip foah a woman—even when he's un-conscious. But, man! what dat boy can do when he's performin'. . . . Baby!"

"Want any help," smiled Lynd. "I can unhitch him for you."

"No, man, you run along. I doan like those things out there that they're sittin' on. I had one of 'em *break* under me once!"

As Lynd returned, a young woman stepped in. She was slender, and had a peculiar deer-like gait as Lester brought her across the room to Lynd. Her hair was reddish, dull in lustre, done in a French bang like—like that central figure in the painting of the Café Royal. Her lips were striking scarlet, and slightly twisted. She had freckles. At first, Lynd thought her distinctly ugly and unappetising.

"You two already know each other," leered Lester, ushering her across the room with his hand on her behind, a thing the young lady did not seem to mind.

The girl blew a couple of bubbles through her sneering lips, and asked: "Why?"

She spoke with an aristocratic drawl. It was not affected. "You two fell down the stairs together at Vyvyan Flower's party."

Tony remembered dimly a bottle party four years back in Knightsbridge when, because of repeated thumps on the wall from an outraged neighbour, it was decided to take all the drinks down into the basement to see the dawn. He remembered himself and a red-headed young girl beginning this spiral descent, imagining they could balance a table full of bottles, and their final toboggan—like a Cresta run! He even recollected some of the young person's remarks.

"And I was starting off the next morning for Spain!" said Lynd.

The girl gave a hoarse laugh a painful sucking in of breath: "Yes, I remember now—you insisted upon telling me all about that. You were going to get a *mule* and ride down the Pyrenees. . . ."

She seemed to be saying that as sarcastically as she could, and he resented it. "I *did* ride down the Pyrenees," he said.

"How frightfully funny."

Lester left them, and as there was nowhere else for them to sit they had to park themselves on a divan in the corner. "A bed built for love," said Lester as he pointed them to it. "Don't mind us."

It was a notorious contention of Lester Blackwood's that the only thing needed to seduce any woman was a place to do it. In pure friendship he would often offer the keys of his flat to his men friends who were without this convenience. Although it did get about that he climbed up the fire-escape to watch the performance.

"What do you think of this party?" asked Lynd.

"Perfectly *ghastly*."

"Then why did you come to it?"

A curiosity was stirring in him. This girl, who never looked you in the eyes but stared over your shoulder as she was talking with you, had a powerful fascination. It was snake-like, but—it was alluring. She spoke with the minimum of movement, no gestures, no movements of her body, and not the faintest alteration of the level tenor of her voice. Only her face was mobile; and to Lynd's question her brows met in a frown.

"I don't know," she said.

"Well, that's as good a reason as any other," he said. He got up and dutifully brought her back a glass of fiery *slivowitz*. "Isn't there anything decent to drink?" she asked. Lynd questioned Lester, who said there might be some

EL

whiskey left. There had been two bottles, but Pat Byron and the nigger-girl had come early, Patrick already half-soused; and they had drunk one of them right off. Lynd, going into the other room, was directed by the coon to the other bottle. It was on the floor by the bed. "I'm 'fraid he's done for *this* evenin'," she said, looking at the silent, sleeping figure on the bed beside her. "Can't you take him off my hands?"

"Later," said Lynd.

While he was sitting on the Turkish divan he saw the negro girl come out. She had on her coat and hat. She stood on her toes to whisper something in Lester's ear, kissed him, and left. Lynd went back and shook Patrick. He was completely out.

"I'm afraid he'll have to sleep with you to-night," Lynd said to Lester, who had come into the room.

Lester became unaccountably agitated: "No, no," he said; "I've got other plans! Tony, you will do me a favour, won't you? You will get him out of here?"

"Later," said Lynd.

He went back and joined the girl on the couch. "When you've had enough of this ghastly party," she drawled, "let's go out somewhere and find a quiet place where we can have a drink."

Lynd, remembering he had passed a pub at the corner and, telling Lester he would be back, a promise that Lester made him repeat, they left. In the pub the girl leaned with her elbows on the table, taking quiet puffs at a cigarette— and said nothing. Finally, at closing time, he said he must go back.

"Oh, well, if you *must*," she said disgustedly.

He explained things.

"Oh, that silly little misery," she said of Patrick. "I could wring his —— neck."

She had used the Army adjective as casually as any British Tommy would use it. Then, clasping her bag under her arm, she walked slightly ahead of Lynd to her car.

"It would be *so* nice," she said suddenly, "if we could meet somewhere and have a drink to-morrow. Here's my card." She gave him a business card which, he saw, bore the name of an Australian newspaper. "I'm the London correspondent for *that*," she drawled. "*Good* night."

* * *

Back at Lester's, Lynd asked him: "I say, who *is* that girl?"

"Felicity Correl? Humph—that's a poser. Father's an Australian who was knighted for his services to the Empire during the Boer War. Sold them some rifles that wouldn't go off, I understand. She was born in England. Flick was one of the Bright Young Things of the naughty 'twenties in London. But I think she's settled down now. Any rate, I've never got anywhere with her."

Patrick was a problem. Lester, looking anxiously at the clock, broke up his own party before one o'clock. "Now," he said, "you get that young man out!"

"Where does he live?" asked Lynd.

"I dunno." Lester shook Patrick. Then he shook him savagely. "Byron!" he yelled in his ear: "Where do you live?"

Patrick mumbled an address, fought off Lester, and rolled over to sleep. "Oh, that's all right," said Lynd. "I know the place—that's where he lived before."

As slithery to get a secure grip on as a slimy fish, Patrick was slid downstairs and across the pavement into Lynd's car. But, after Lester had gone back, Lynd saw the lights go out every time he put his foot down on the self-starter; the battery had run down, and the car wouldn't start. While he was trying to spin it he saw a figure come up the street, halt a minute opposite the car to stare at the huddled

Byron, and then dash quickly into Lester Blackwood's apartment house. As she had to wait until Lester answered the bell, Lynd saw that it was the negro girl.

*   *   *

In an ancient taxi they pulled up before Patrick Byron's address. The taxi-driver volunteered to help Lynd take Patrick up to the second floor. "I know where it is," said Lynd. He fished out Byron's keys and tried every one of them in the lock. Finally he found one that fitted and opened the door. He reached around for the plug and switched on the electric light. "Don't know where his bedroom is," he said.

There was a shout from a room somewhere, and then a little red-faced man, with grey hair, in blue-and-white striped pyjamas, stood covering them with a revolver.

"By *God*, sir!—what do you mean by this? Don't move, don't move—or I'll blow a hole through you! Who *are* you? What the devil are you doing in my house at *this* time o' night? Answer me that, sir—answer me that! *No*, Myra," he called back over his shoulder: "Don't call for the police. *I'll* handle these gentlemen. Now, sir? . . ." He pointed the revolver at Lynd.

Obviously, a military gentleman. An angry one.

"Speak up! Out with it? Why did you tamper with the lock on my door?"

The taxi-driver, who could understand none of this, had gone a gruesome white. He had let go of Patrick, who had piled neatly on the carpet. Lynd knew that if he laughed he would probably get a bullet in him forthwith. So he tried to explain things; his friend was ill, had given him, in a delirium, this address, where he had once lived, and obviously had still kept on his key-ring the key of the flat.

"Deliriums, be damned! Your friend, sir, whatever your name is, is disgustingly drunk. Get him out. Get him *out*, I tell you, and let me sleep."

*   *   *

"Well, sir," said the taxi-driver, when they had Patrick back in the cab. "That was a rare do, that was. Haven't seen the likes o' that in *my* experience—not in twenty-five years' drivin' this same here bloody little bleeding cab. I wouldn't try it again, sir."

Lynd was searching Patrick's pockets to see if he could find any letters addressed to Byron which might show his home, but they were all addressed either to his paper or to his club. He could, of course, take Pat to his club, but that would be a scurvy trick to play on a friend in a condition like this. "No, driver," he said, "I know one place where there can't be a mistake—my home."

*   *   *

It wasn't until the taxi clunked to a stop before the door of Lynd's own house that he realised that there was not a single bedroom free. Christina had one of her cousins staying, so their single guest-room was occupied. The only room he could think of—as Patrick was now showing signs of violence, and he might break something if left below in the drawing-room—was Christina's work-room at the top of the house. Aside from the sewing machine, there *was* a sofa there.

Stealthily, Lynd supporting the heavy weight of the shoulders, the taxi-man carrying the legs, they got Patrick up the stairs. "I'd be careful of him, sir," whispered the taxi-driver hoarsely. "'E might jump out."

"Oh, I know an old trick," grinned Lynd. "Help me to get off this heavy overcoat."

It was a heavy, navy-blue affair with a thick belt. Lynd reversed it, shoved Pat's arms through it the wrong way around and buttoned it up his back. Then he twisted the belt around, drew it tight, and buckled it at the back. Thus hobbled, Patrick could not do anything. They placed him face-down on the couch and slowly tip-toed downstairs, where, from a decanter on the sideboard, Lynd poured himself and the taxi-man a good stiff drink.

"Thank'y, sir. This has been a rare night."

Lynd went up to his single bed opposite Christina and went quietly to sleep.

*   *   *

"Mr. Lynd! Mr. Lynd!"

He and Christina were awakened in the morning by one of their two Norwegian maids. They always had their coffee in bed of a morning. But Elsa was not bringing coffee now. Her blue eyes were staring out of her head.

"Mr. Lynd," she said hysterically, "dere iss a *man* in de house!"

Lynd, who had completely forgotten the previous night, sat up bewildered and rubbed his eyes. He was usually a quick waker, but he had a bit of a bad head. "A . . . man? . . ." he muttered.

"Where?" demanded the practical Christina.

The Norwegian girl stuck a finger upward. "And his head's yust like dis . . ." Elsa tried to turn her own head around backwards. At that they heard the most awful rumpus from the upper stairs:

"Get the hell out of my way, blast you! Who do you think I am? Where am I?"

The voice of Gudrun came: "Yust you stand dere!" Gudrun was a peasant from the Nordland of Norway. They build them big up there. "Yust you stan' dere until Ay get Mr. Lynd . . ."

"Lynd? *Lynd!*" Christina and Anthony heard the sound of hysterical male laughter, and then Patrick's voice: "Tony —for Christ's sake come up here and save me from these savages. There's a girl got me stymied up here with a *broom!*"

Lynd led him down, just as he was, with his coat the wrong way around and buttoned up the back, and his arms flopping forward helplessly like a diver's do. Only his eyes showed above the back of his coat collar. It was a great breakfast.

*   *   *

"Tell me," said Lynd, as they taxied down to his office (he had telephoned a garage to fetch his car), "do you happen to know a girl called Felicity Correl?"

"Do I *not*! What's she to you?"

"Nothing—yet."

"Then you lay off her. I know at least three men that girl has made drink themselves into dip and dope homes. There's something uncanny about her. That girl is Death."

"Thanks for the advice."

*   *   *

When he got to his office and telephoned, her voice said: "O, *hel*-lo. . . ." It sounded so unpleasant and affected that he reached across with the instrument and put it down. Then he said: "I've got only a short cable to send this morning. I'm going across to the Foreign Office now. I could meet you at the Queen, if you want to; that's the pub by Scotland Yard. About half-past twelve? I say, if you haven't got anything else to do why don't we have lunch? Make it the Ivy, at one. What? Let's do both? Why that's great! See you at the Queen."

He was conscious as he put down the receiver that a definite change had taken place in his life. He never doubted that for an instant.

*   *   *

He was not as astonished, therefore, as he should have been at the Ivy, among the gay, theatrical company, when suddenly it had been decided that they should spend the next week-end in the country together.

"My car's bust," he said, describing how last night, trying to kindle it with a weak battery, he had broken the Bendix on his self-starter.

"We'll use mine," she said.

When he told her of Patrick's latch-keys and the striped gentleman, with the revolver, in pyjamas, she gave that hacking, sinister laugh, leaning forward with her hands against her forehead. "Sardonic," he decided, was a milk-and-water word for that laughter. She did sound like Death!

*   *   *

*   *   *

When Patrick Byron asked him afterwards what he thought of Flick Correl, he replied that he had found her most invigorating. Pat laughed.

"Flick's father is lovely," said Pat. "You know, if you go to Scotland Yard, they will tell you that the best pick-pockets in England are the Spaniards from Soho, the best sharepushers are Americans, the best confidence men are the Australians, and the best blackmailers, a vocation that requires the maximum of guts and heartiness, are English aristocrats. . . . Well, Flick's father is what I would consider an all-round gentleman.

"The College of Heralds," gurgled pale Patrick, enchanted by his own similes, "could sing lovely songs of sheep station fratricide and of bars *sinistre* on the Western Gold Reef . . . in Geoffrey Correl's pedigree. All of which merely became romantic when Geoff Correl bought Bentham and ran his own pack of hounds up in Yorkshire. We English have our principles, you know.

"I'll tell you the kind of man he is—he's a human rhino. The mill-owning *parvenu* who had built Bentham before him had a lake built on the grounds . . . with a flock of stone herons artistically fishing among its rushes. . . ." Patrick leaned back and laughed softly. "I was too young to be in on it, but my father tells me that when Geoff Correl wanted to give a pre-view of his lovely red-haired little girl to immediate post-War society, he gave a pretentious house-party at Bentham to which he invited, or blackmailed, half of England's future admirals . . . and you know what naval blokes are. When they were having breakfast Sunday morning, one of them drew the attention of the whole table to the lake—and there, me lad, every artistic little heron had a kipper on its beak. . . .

"Hah!" laughed Pat. "You can see what Flick's had to put up with! The old man's answer, however, was classic. Bentham was famous for its wines and long dinners, but for the rest of that house-party all the British Navy got for lunch or dinner was beer and kippers . . . breakfasts were the promise of what things might have been; for they were the same as Sunday's fatal breakfast . . . with cold grouse, and everything that is good to eat. . . . That story did him a lot of good in London, however, especially in the City, where he now has the reputation of being a man who can hardly wait to be hit—before he hits back.

"At the present moment he lives at his club—dyes his hair jet black—except for little grey tufts over the ears which he thinks make him look like Forbes Robertson—and if you look on the hall porter's desk as you go out in the morning you will always see a genteel little package from the florist for Sir Geoffrey Correl, containing an orchid, or a gardenia for his buttonhole. . . . If you're ever forced into the ditch some time by a vast cream-coloured Rolls-Royce, coming down the North Road as if it owns it, that's Sir Geoffrey's chauffeur. . . . He encourages them to drive that way."

"Hum. . . ." Tony let out his breath. "And his daughter?"

"Flick? . . . Ah. . . . Some smart-alec put it across *her* in the early 'twenties, in London, and the old boy was so furious that his treasure had been deflowered that he

E I

took her off on a trip around the world . . . to get her out of the picture. What happened out there no one knows . . . not for sure. People who came back from Pekin said she had made the hell of a scene out there by slapping the face of the young German Attaché—smack in the middle of a picnic party—and everyone had taken it for granted they were practically married! From what I know of Flick Correl myself I should say that poor Hun was *the* one love of her life! Why she hit him, Flick never said: I don't suppose even her old man knows. The Pekin people say the German just raised hell about it—he was a *Baron*. And Flick had slugged him!

"At any rate"—Pat looked at Tony seriously, as if even he was oppressed by the thoughts it invoked—"when the lovely Flick started to be seen at London bottle-parties again she was no longer the inarticulate, hoydenish, puzzling little Correl girl. . . . You know, the French say we're cold because we English hate to shake hands when we meet . . . well . . . Flick does a lot more than merely kiss you on both cheeks. . . ."

Tony felt mute and oppressed. The thought of the wilful way these young girls of the 'twenties distributed their loveliness—more lightly than their brothers would even shake hands; as Pat implied—nearly destroyed him. It was another blow that life was inexorably striking at his flickering youth. He must hammer the life out of these childish castles he was always building. They had always been sold from within . . . long before he got to them.

*   *   *

He had thought she might be joking at first, as he stood, feeling rather foolish, in front of the Goring Hotel. He had left his bag with the hall porter. But no, prompt on the stroke of one her blue Riley swung around the corner. She lived in Westminster Square. And he found himself speaking quite naturally as he asked the porter to fetch his bag. She wore a green-and-black checked coat with a scarlet knitted hat. They took the Kingston By-pass.

England was already taking on that golden haze that is her glory in the spring, of grass and field and budding beech-woods. Distances were powder blue. She drove expertly, too impatiently, he thought, as if it irked her to be thwarted by anybody else. They said practically nothing on the drive.

This was a relief after Luba's prattle, and even Christina's conversation, who knew and appreciated every changing view of the English countryside. He loved England deeply. Soon the apple orchards would be in white blossom, and the soft air would smell of growing hops, and the red-roofed oast-houses would bask in the lazy sun. God could not have designed a setting more blissful for love.

"What about a drink?" he said.

"Marvellous. We'll stop at the next nice-looking pub."

*　　*　　*

"In America," he said, to try and appear interesting, "our distances are sharp and clear. Hard. We don't have this pastel haziness. I don't know much about Art—but when I first saw the paintings of Constable I thought they couldn't be true."

She rewarded him by frowning thoughtfully, and saying: "Yes, you're right there—I remember thinking that when I was in the States."

"When was that?"

"Oh, years ago," she said.

She had a beautifully slender neck, with a lean jaw; although, he decided, her best feature was the line from her forehead to along her straight nose. He had plenty of chance to look at this profile, for one thing he noticed was that her greenish eyes never met his, but always looked over his shoulder as he talked to her—as if she saw someone there in the Land of Mist behind him.

There was something sad, reminiscent, regretful in this trait. She was a bitter woman, he decided.

*   *   *

He remembered little about that night, except that they were caught in a violent rain-storm as they were crossing a heath; and she suggested that they put up at that little pub for the night. It was a pub that was not used to having visitors, "grand people from London," even temporary honeymooners; and it was some time before a room could be got ready for them. It gratified him that she did not seem to mind in the least the lowly status of the pub—Christina was inclined to be fussy, even quarrelsome about such things—and this girl wolfed more than her fair share of the platter of bacon and eggs that had been put before them. The apologies of the fat landlady, he saw with pleasure, were not needed with Miss Felicity Correl.

The room they were given had just had its carpet taken up; and perhaps the one thing he would never forget about that night was that when he got up in the dark, he put his bare foot down on about six tacks at the same time.

"My God!" he cried.

Felicity reached about for the matches and lighted the candle on the chair beside them. She looked at him extracting the tacks and gave a laugh. One of those painful-to-hear intakings of breath.

"The safest place for you," she said, "is to pop back into bed."

Now that he was fully awake, he looked at the bottle of whiskey they had taken up to their room with them, and saw there was a good half of it left. Doubtfully dusting the floor with his foot for tacks he ventured across to the washstand

and brought back the pitcherful of water and the solitary glass. He sat there, on the edge of the bed, and talked. He began to talk a little wildly at last, and then they became engaged in a very original argument. Neither of them could remember what it was the next morning. But it had been interesting. It had been fun, lying in bed and talking like that.

The strangest impression that he carried away from that night was its peace. An assured ease such as he had never known with any woman. With others, you always had to be on guard against feminine misunderstanding that might shatter things. But not with this girl. But that two comparative strangers could, under such carnal conditions, talk as innocently and impartially as they had was a miracle that he would not like the task of making credible to anybody.

* * *

Felicity Correl, he soon admitted to himself, was unbelievably the one woman he had been looking for—the perfect combination of brains and beauty. If it had not been for her shocking past of the 'twenties. But, then, every girl of Flick's period and set seemed to have one. That was precisely what was the trouble with the world; there was a stupid contempt for her own virtue even in Felicity. Flick was so damnably unrepentant about it!

"Oh, for God's sake do stop preaching!" she said.

"I'm not preaching. I'm just trying to tell you something. Damn it all, can't you see that when an ordinary human being comes in here and sees that horrible nimbus of pansies and unbelievables all you bright young things have hanging about you—that he sheers off. He can't stand it, I tell you. It makes him sick. He's actually afraid to fall in love with one of you because the minute he does he will be introduced to half a dozen of those odious pups who all feel that they have the right to feel free and easy about you. . . . My God, with your brains! Haven't you got enough intelligence to see that?"

"I'm not going to be talked to as if I were in a reform home. So there."

"Go on, then! Be a . . . well, be a . . ."

He soon realised the danger of these talks with Flick. They never got him anywhere. And it soon came that the instant Flick felt that she was being lectured to she invented merciless affairs of her past that simply excoriated him. His imagination sizzled under the very memory of them. And then he discovered that when Flick found this out, she began to play it as a game. There was no limit to which she couldn't imagine things—for his destruction. He was appalled by it.

He had not known her a week before she told him the name of her first lover. This was while they were sitting in his car in Piccadilly, waiting for the green light to go on. The information had not shocked him at the time; he knew the man; he had the reputation of being a danger to young women; later, things came to a point where he would get up and leave the room when he saw this man enter it.

That was when he knew that he was becoming inevitably more and more fond of her. When he began to realise that this was probably permanent. Felicity felt this as well, and said one day, as they were waiting for another traffic light: "It's so nice to have something that will last!" He was aware when she said that that many other men must have left her. They would leave her because they had faced the same trial that he was headed for; they had fallen in love with her—and then found they could not face any longer her straightforward talk about her relations with other men. They were jealous of their forerunners. And so they had quit. And in this way, he knew, Flick had paid for her arrogant looseness, and was lonely.

There was an exciting and entirely satisfying interregnum

between that first country week-end, so strange in its frank-ness—or perhaps its casualness, because what she had said about herself then, and her relations with other men, had not affected him—and these heated days when at the very mention of one of Flick's affairs he would fly into a rage and try to leave the room. When Flick began to demonstrate how uninhibited she was he wanted to run away from her.

"No one else," she said, "has ever talked to me the way you do."

"Why should they," he said bitterly, "when you always seem to have been so obliging? Unless they happened to be in love with you. And *then* they'd say something!"

She fell silent at that. "Love" was a word that Felicity never used.

* * *

This second phase, when he knew that Flick was deliber-ately trying to destroy his sense of values, opened a stage of warfare that raged between them for months. They fought it out in pubs in their pre-luncheon meetings; they were still attacking each other as they sat in one or the other's motor-car, drinking tea outside the midnight coffee stalls dotted about London. No victories were ever granted, no defeats were ever admitted. The *casus belli* was Tony's continued criticism of Flick for ever having submitted to the life of the 'twenties, and Flick's furious retaliation against what she declared was his intolerably blind conceit.

In moments of expansion, this ease that he had discovered with her, Tony had told Flick some of the adventures of his own life. And he could never find one in hers that she, now, could not find one in his own to match him with. In this unique naturalness he had found with Flick, Tony had dis-cussed his affairs with a frankness that he had never felt free to use with anybody. It had been quite a new and pleasur-able experience, like two surgeons dispassionately discussing a patient's history. But it had been folly . . . for Flick preserved every item for ammunition, and used them over and over again.

The distracting part of these arguments was that Flick would not agree that she had done wrong, and therefore allow him to win past that to where he could place her back upon the pedestal. She would not go there. Instead, she flung his own deeds back to be weighed against hers. Not only that, she declared that he was a hypocrite to criticise her.

The result was a morose purpose unfolded within him to pay her back with her own coin. If she was going to glory in her waywardness, he could be dissolute too. In this hard way, with the bits in their teeth, they raced against each other. He could drink desperately, whole-heartedly now. It amused him to make Flick drink. It was rare now when they had their moments of peace together; it was neck and neck to whatever calamity lay ahead of them. They both felt that they were increasing the pace to a dangerous degree. They both became fascinated by the reckless danger of their lives. Neither of them would cry "Stop."

He was going to make Flick knuckle-under. And if she didn't, she would have to pay the price of his own collapse. Once or twice, when she had become alarmed at what he was doing to himself and tried to restrain him, he had merely laughed. "All right," he said. "You know. You know why I'm doing this."

"Know what?" said Flick.

"You know . . . trying to prove that every damn' thing you did was right!"

He was aware that his conduct had the element of madness in it. "Well, what in the hell would you do," cried Flick one night, "if I did admit I was wrong?"

"Not that I'm going to!" she added quickly.

*   *   *

The worst injury that Flick was making him inflict on Christina was not his unfaithfulness. The physical contact played the minor part in this mad carouse with Flick. Christina herself did not stress this. What Christina resented now was the shell of Tony that came home.

"Go ahead," she said to him petulantly one night, when he came in after dinner was half over. "I don't care *what* you do. Have a mistress. Have half a dozen mistresses. . . ."

Tony felt that Chris was tried beyond endurance.

"But I don't want half a dozen mistresses!" he cried. "Can't you see?"

"No. I can't."

Christina's cool lips were printed in a straight red line. Tony hated to see that. Christina could look lovely in storm, real storm, but he hated to see the droop of sadness in it. There was, he soon found, very little drooping to-night. "I've put up with a lot from you," said Chris. "But I can't stand Flick. That girl is insatiable. You're a perfect fool not to see it. I don't care what she does to you—it's what she's making you do to me that I'm complaining about. What on earth you see in her I can't understand."

"Well . . . er . . . we get along well together."

"Get along well! . . . Peter! Can't you see you've been in nothing but trouble ever since you've known the girl? Don't you know that all your friends are talking about it— the mad way you are drinking yourself straight to hell? You will, you know. You can't keep it up at this pace all the time. Something will happen to you some day. You do know that, don't you, Peter? And you don't want to make me *not* be in love with you, do you?"

He fell silent at that. He knew that he couldn't explain to Christina these oases of peace that he and Flick had strangely found. They were too incredible. He couldn't explain, although he did intend to make a stiff try, that all this drinking was largely because of his own pig-headed self. He would drink on, and on, and on. . . . Why? . . . Simply because

Flick had gone wrong in the 'twenties—and wouldn't admit it. Damn her. But that this should affect him so could also not be explained, even to himself; he was like a wild maverick, unbranded, badly needing a bit and halter. . . .

"I guess I've just got a lot of the original devil in me. You don't think I'm mean, do you? I try to protect you in other things."

"I don't think you're mean, Peter—I think you're just a damn' fool. And you won't see it. What you're doing, Tony, is dancing along the edge of disaster. . . . and you won't see it. I miss you a lot these days, and wish I could get through to you. Why don't you chuck it all and you and I have a trip around the world?"

He shook his head. The answer to his disintegration lay in London.

"No," he said; "there's no use running off. I've got to work things out here. Let's hope they come out right."

He looked at her. She had the perfect quality of repose. The book she had put down when she began this argument, she now picked up from the arm of her chair before the fireplace. He thought what a savage irony lay in most of life's realisations. How, for ten years, he had made unknowing Chris suffer because of an imaginary Luba that he was torturing himself with. Ten of the most incorrectly aimed years of his life. He could have built a good and sound life with Christina during that time, if Luba's ghost had not made less than half a man of him. But he had not made this life. And now the petty quarrels that had meant merely a passing annoyance and discomfort in those days, were becoming accumulative. They were taking on a momentum. Without seeming the least able to prevent them, these daily quarrels, all of his own making, were like an ebb tide daily carrying him away from Christina.

"You know what's the matter with you?" she said. "You're afraid of that girl."

"Oh, nonsense."

"You are. She's put a spell on you."

*   *   *

One night, when Christina was spending the week-end with some friends in the country, a habit he was encouraging more and more, he had arranged to meet Flick at Hubler's in Fitzroy Square. Most of their engagements were in pubs. He usually managed to buy a few drinks for her every day before lunch, and he was now deliberately avoiding luncheons he should have gone to in connection with his work, so that they could eat together as well; they always met before he went home to dinner and sat drinking and chatting in some pub until the very last minute. Often, he suspected, she was deliberately trying to make him late. Did it gratify her sense of possession—or was this all part of her programme to wreck his home? With Felicity he always felt like a man who is taking his boat through dangerous rocks. Her own punctuality, he had long since realised, was one of her greatest attractions to men. Men appreciate when they don't have to sit and wait and wonder what someone, whom they are waiting to go out with, is doing with someone else. They always suspect the worst. And to-night, he had to wait and wonder a long time.

He tried to hold back from drinking as he watched the minute hand of the clock slowly drag, so brazenly indifferent, around the cruel dial. Drink, with Flick, often sent him into a rage these days. He eyed with malevolence a harmless "Ho-bohemian" in the bar, a fair young man in sandals, green corduroy bloomers and a Tyrolean jacket. He recognised the puffy-faced woman on a stool as a former Bright Young Thing of the 'twenties, having her continual round of gins—she was out of it now. He recalled her story; how she had taken the second-rate Art critic she happened to wake up with one morning to the Registrar's office and married him.

This bar, at opening time in the morning, was a museum of once-lovely girls who had been the Girl Who Would Do Anything of their few exciting years. It required an enormous amount of brains, he thought, for a girl to have those reckless years, and then escape. Felicity had done this. She had, in fact, made him think there could be no God; Flick had sinned so contemptuously—and met no retribution. She bragged about that.

He would take it out on her to-night. He was not going to be stood up like this, kicking his heels in this pub for half an hour while she had a few more drinks with somebody else. He was just about to leave when Hubler came to the bar and said he was wanted on the phone. It was Flick, very tight, saying she would be along right away. They had been going down to Marlow and he tried to tell her that if she did not hurry, the hotel would be shut. The way she quickly cut him off and sputtered: "Oh, we can talk about that when I get there," made him think she was speaking in the presence of somebody else. He had half a mind to get on to the exchange and try to find out where the call had come from. But then he thought that he would rather not know. He had got that way now. . . .

Half an hour later, when he was again on the point of going, he was aware of a row going on outside the door. He paid no attention to it at first, until he heard fat Hubler protesting: "But I *know* de lady! She iss an old customer of ours. She iss a very respectable lady!" Then he had some idea of what he was about to see.

It was Flick. With her was a South African painter. Lynd knew him by sight. And that was all he wanted to know of him, because Flick had had an *affaire* with him. Now here they both were, the South African in a very noisy argument with the taxi-driver. Lynd watched the scene.

"Lousy barstard! . . ." the taxi-driver announced to the grinning crowd. "'E's been an' committed a nuisance in my *cab*! . . . 'E's been sick! 'E can tyke his choice. . . . 'E's goin to give me a quid to put things right after 'im . . . or I calls the perlice. . . ."

The scene blurred for Lynd. He saw Felicity's twisted lips and the open, starting eyes of the South African as the artist tried to wrench the fingers of the taxi-driver from his coat-lapel; and old Hubler all beard and fat cheeks below two upraised arms; and all around them a ring of lamp-lit faces laughing. . . .

"'It 'im, guvnor!" was the advice given by the crowd to the helpless South African. "Don't let 'im talk to yer like that."

"The likes o' *'im*—'e couldn't 'it nobody," a woman jeered. "Why don't the *loidy* stand up for her man?"

Felicity was earning the British crowd's disapproval by trying to walk out of this scene. She had got as far as Hubler's door when she saw Lynd standing there, facing her. She tried to put on her challenging sneer. He stepped aside to let her in. And then he walked rapidly around the street and got into his car.

*   *   *

As he let himself into the empty house in Cheyne Walk, he heard the phone ringing. It was Flick.

"Darling," she said, "do let me come around."

"Why?"

"Tony . . ."

"Yes?"

"Do."

"Oh, all right. I was just going to bed."

"Wait for me!"

He went down to the cellar under the stairs and brought up a bottle of whiskey and some glasses. While he was waiting for Flick he stared around his study. One wall was lined with books; there was a photo of one of his early sailing boats and another of himself in the R.F.C., and over his desk was the cast of a perfect 2½-pound trout he had caught only fifty minutes' drive out of London. He had once done a lot of work here. It pained him when he thought of how very little he ever sat in this room now, how little he was ever in the house.

He had brought the whiskey into his study because the drawing-room was essentially the property of Christina. Even when she was not there her personality pervaded it. And he did not wish to present it thus, defenceless, to the merciless Flick.

"You drive me crazy!" he said to Flick. "What in God's name are you made of?"

"Be sensible, darling."

"That's what I'm trying to be."

"No, you're not . . . you're just being silly. I know I was naughty to be late."

"Late! *Naughty!*"

"Yes . . . because that's all I did to-night that you can take any exception to. And you know what I mean. And look here," she said, making her eyes dilate and look fierce. "Why did you run off and leave me like that? That wasn't nice. Was it?"

He held up his hand. "Don't!" he said. "I know that argument; it's one of your old ones—that the best defence is a quick attack. Here's the other one: 'A person can get away with anything—as long as you have enough guts.' Fine. And here's the last: 'You're jealous of my past life.' That's three of them from your box of tricks, isn't it?"

He stopped and looked at her. "Well, I *am* jealous of your past. I am jealous of all the other men you've slept with. But——"

He paused, for he felt it was very important this thing that he had to tell her. And he knew he could not make it sound sufficiently impressive. "I am jealous," he said, "and I know that that gives you nothing but satisfaction. Secret now—but later you will try and throw it in my face. But I'll tell you why I don't think that you will throw it. Just think for a minute; you and I have become pretty much part of the other—and just weigh in the scales the satisfaction you'll get out of knowing I'm jealous—against the fact that I am leaving you. And that that is just *why* I'm leaving you —not because of your relations with other men . . . *but because I'm jealous of them*!

"We're both rotters," said Lynd, sitting down heavily.

*   *   *

The streets were glistening when he went to the door to let Flick in; and as they sat there now they heard the cheerful sound of the seep of rain on the trees in the garden and coursing noisily down the spout. They sat in deep chairs before the wood fire that he had put a new log on when she telephoned. It was now crackling merrily. "This is not merely an 'affair,'" he growled morosely—"this thing between you and me. Or is it? Do you want it to be?"

Flick sat there, her greenish eyes seeing something in the flames. She frowned: "Yes, you're right there. It is not an affair. I don't want it to be. But you *can't* live in the past," she said painfully. "I never live in the past. That's why these other casual affairs have never meant anything to me." Then, as if she felt she had surrendered some ground to him, her lip curled: "The first couple of times, with someone new—yes."

"Ugh!" he shuddered. "There you go again!" he said. "It's no question of morals with me. It's just my own blasted imagination."

"But that sort of thing doesn't do you any harm—not when you're *young*."

"Oh, doesn't it? Look what I have been saying just now; that I'm jealous. As it happens, I know half a dozen men

in Town who you say yourself brag have slept with you.
What the hell do you think I think when we meet and shake
hands? We ought to have an old school tie!"

At that, she choked and gave that hacking laugh.
"Darling, one of the reasons why I love you—you can
make me laugh!"

"Oh, go to hell!"

They were friendly again almost at once. He was
furious with her and felt that he would like to kill her; yet
he knew there was more solid companionship with her
now, even with this ghastly conversation, than he had
known with any other woman.

*   *   *

With a strange magic (perhaps the opiate quality that
Patrick had spoken of as Death?), her presence soothed him.
All would have been well this evening had he not gone into
the drawing-room to fetch something, as she was leaving.
Flick followed him and was standing by the door.

"I have never seen a room," he heard her say, "which
had so much *negative* good taste."

"Haven't you?" He spoke without looking up. "That's
too bad."

"Y—es. . . ." Flick uttered her most sarcastic drawl. "All
. . . this!"

He found himself trembling.

It was an old room, with a lovely Adams fireplace and
pale duck-egg blue walls against which the old mahogany
furniture stood out dark and shining, particularly a Chip-
pendale book-case which was the pride of Christina's heart.
On the floor was a faded, delightful old Indian carpet which
her father had given her. There were one or two good paintings on the walls, and a few which had been done by their
friends. Christina had a genius for flowers and the room had
been arranged to take them, although now, of course, there

were none here. Before him, on her desk, was a neat pile of her account books and a little photograph of Zeppelin, the dachshund.

"How would you arrange it?" asked Tony evenly.

"I would have just one picture . . . one good one . . . something that would dominate the whole room . . . that would inspire you to look at it."

"I see . . . a Matisse?"

"Yes . . . something like that."

He turned on her. "You unbelievable little sweep! You *parvenu*. The thing you can't understand . . . that's simply beyond your understanding . . . is that this room is *lived* in! This room isn't fixed this way to impress someone else . . . this room is for *us*. Damn it all . . . you, with all your cheap talk about paintings . . . Christina has more judgment in her little finger than you have in your whole mind . . . clever as you are. You make me sick; you talk like an Art student! . . . *One good picture* . . . oh, my God . . . it's the kind of thing an author would hunt about for weeks to show that a character was cheap!" He was wild that anyone should dare to criticise Christina's house. "Now you're showing some of the lousy sense of values you've picked up during life. Don't make me laugh."

"You've liberated me!" she said dramatically.

"Oh, shut up."

It was the first time since he had known her that he really felt her master. He saw she was crying, but it did not stir a chord in him. He was utterly cold. It was such a surprising sensation that he telephoned as quickly as he could for a taxi. He wanted to get Felicity out of his sight while this mood still held on. There was no knowing . . . he knew he wasn't safe . . . what she might do to make him weak again. She had flung herself, with every indication of remaining, on the sofa. He remained standing, finishing his drink, until he heard the taxi-man at the door.

"There's your cab," he said.

"Thanks. I'm glad you did that. I feel much happier now."

"So do I."

He helped her into the cab, told the man where to go, and went back into the house.

"By George!" he said. He stood in the door of the drawing-room before he flicked out the light. "*One . . . perfect . . . picture . . .*"

It was the first time for nearly a year that he went to bed with an easy heart.

*   *   *

But it was a false peace. Felicity Correl and he were both too well known to get away with any clandestine meetings in their London life. It might be all very well for them to see the actual unsinfulness of their relations—the way both of them rejoiced in just the mental companionship they had found with each other. But the world was not built to accept relations like that. A juicy bit of scandal like this was not going to be neglected by his eager friends. People began to "talk." And Christina, quite naturally, hit back.

"Well, I should think I would say what I damn' well like!" she told Tony. "What do you think I am? That I am going to sit down under a thing like this? Not much. Are you trying to protect her to *me*? My God . . . you're *unbelievable!*"

What he had tried uncomfortably to point out was the sordidness of such a quarrel. There was nothing nice about this. In Chris, Flick had taken on an enemy well worthy of her steel. They had, in their journalistic set, several mutual acquaintances. Well, Chris was seeing that they would not remain mutual any longer. She was already giving them their choice. Their small world was storming.

He really didn't give a damn that night, what Flick had said about the Chelsea house. He had brought that on himself. It was a nice house. He liked it. He had often said so to

Flick. And he had said it just once too often, it appeared. Even an angel could not be asked to admire her adversary's handiwork. What had sent him into such a maniac rage, perhaps, was that up until that very moment he had been foolishly imagining he could have this relationship with Flick without provoking an open warfare.

And he was now aghast to see how, by violating the conventions, he had made everybody's life public property.

*　　*　　*

He tried to lose himself in his work, and with his almost pre-natal dislike of politicians in general he found plenty of disconcerting information to cable, the way the soothsayers were trying to plaster over with mere words the appalling cracks that were appearing everywhere in the European façade. The slick legal phrases of Britain's Foreign Minister at the League were, he knew, not the answer to give to the seriously-intentioned Germany that he had just been reporting. And he worked off a lot of his personal suppressions by trying to make American readers aware of the Geneva fiasco. But this gave little more than a passing fillip to his days.

He wanted to get away from the London scene. When he saw a lull looming ahead in his work, he discussed the temporary escape with Felicity over a luncheon at the Escargot in Greek Street.

"For a while," he said moodily, "I'd like to forget there is such a thing as a lousy politician in this world. I'd like to get out of Europe—mentally, at any rate. Where could we go?"

She was nervous, and rolled little bread-crumbs with her slender fingers. He was jumpy also. He had not noticed it himself, how his nerves were going. But Flick pointed it out. "Haven't you still got a couple of weeks' vacation coming to you? You know the way you told me you were rushed off from the Shetlands to Berlin? Couldn't you snatch ten days now? And we could go off somewhere? The place, of course, is Spain! Spain would be marvellous—for both of us."

Easter was early that year. As it happened, he had already arranged that Christina should take the car and join the Mallards down in Cornwall. They had a cottage there. He wired the paper and got a reluctant consent that he should take ten days off. Chris had already left; and he and Flick drove down to Newhaven and between them drank a whole bottle of whiskey in a zestful argument they had about Life that night. But, now that they were safe and securely together again Flick got into another of her sarcastic, mocking moods. They did not sleep together that night.

* * *

It did not make matters better, on the motor-ferry over to Dieppe, when Flick announced that she had already made this trip to Spain, twice, with other men. For it was an announcement, quite out of the blue, when he was sitting there peacefully on a camp-stool, staring at the sea, trying to recover from the amount of whiskey they had put away the previous evening. His nerves were snapping.

"Why on earth do you have to say such things?"

"Because you're so damned pi!"

"Pi! Pious? Me? Now what's the matter with you?"

"Oh, all that talk you went in for last evening . . . how much better in bed Luba was than I am . . . that sort of thing."

"I never said such a thing! You know it! What I said was——"

"That everything was different when you l-o-ved someone!"

"Oh, shut up."

In that mood they reached Dieppe. Dieppe, with its memories of summer and Christina, and days . . . God knows why he had thought them so dull. "If you're going to be like this all the way to Spain," he rasped as they waited for the French Customs officials, "we're going to have a swell time!"

"There's your diplomatic friend. Why don't you ask him to come along with us?"

"I *will*!"

Hambro, in the American Embassy at Paris, was waving good-bye to them from the railway platform. A dyspeptic young man, every inch the gentleman. Tony rushed across to him. "Where are you going?" he demanded.

"Why—Paris, of course."

"Well, come along with us. We'll give you a lift as far as Rouen. *Portier!*"

He saw Flick's eyes expand with anger as he and Hambro, the porter, and the bags came back. It gave him tremendous enjoyment. "Lots of room," he said, jerking his and Flick's bags about to make room for Hambro. "Don't mind the back seat, do you? No . . . take that myself. . . . Miss Correl will drive . . . what, Felicity?"

"This *is* kind!" murmured Hambro, obviously startled by the look given him. "I—you wouldn't have lunch with me on the boat. N-now I'll give you a dinner in Rouen."

"*Rouen?*" said Felicity.

"Rouen. Of course Rouen," said Tony. "Now hop in . . . Customs over . . . papers passed . . . whoopsy-daisy . . . this is *marvellous*."

He lay back and laughed.

"I *say*!" said Hambro to Felicity. "You *can* drive!"

The young man was terrified. So were all Frenchmen along the road of that hurtling Riley. For a moment, hanging on to the bouncing back seat, Tony was afraid he might have overdone things. Flick, in her rage, was quite capable of steering them into the nearest motor-lorry. He knew that Hambro would have something to say about this in Paris!

Felicity, with the smile of a cherub, pulled softly to a stop before the Hôtel Des Quatre Nations in Rouen. "You must come on with us *much* further," she said to Hambro.

"Awfully good of you . . . but I simply wouldn't think of it. . . . I suppose you and Tony want to push on fast . . . eh? . . . Perhaps . . . I've victimised you enough already? . . ."

For a moment Tony had a qualm; Hambro wasn't so simple as he looked. But Flick was there ahead of him.

"Not on your life!" said she. "That dinner, Mr. Hambro?"

"Oh, of course . . . how silly of me."

It was an excellent dinner. Flick, rejecting suggestions, practically ordered it. She almost got the most expensive wine, until Tony, firmly aided by Hambro, picked one half-way down the list. The bill was unbelievable. And while Hambro was changing some English pounds to pay for it, Flick said she would like to have a brandy.

"Now," said Flick, when they had seen Hambro into the station, "will you be good?"

"I will," said Tony.

*   *   *

It was heaven to travel with someone who didn't give a Continental damn for time, dates, what time they ate, where or when they slept, what cafés they stopped to drink at or how long they lingered in them. Lynd revelled in the unaccustomed freedom of such casualness. Not like the Mallards. It is true, the Mallards did move about with an astonishing comfort, even in the most barbaric places . . . they knew what they wanted, and, if they did not get it, everyone else was made to feel sorry for it. In that they were no different from the usual Englishman abroad, who travels, always in the hope of reforming the Continent. But Lynd loathed all the fuss and bother. The Mallards said it was weakness on his part; but he would much rather not have eaten at all than send the ham-and-eggs back to be cooked separately, instead of the homogeneous mass the Germans always made of them. He hated arguments about food. Food wasn't worth it.

"Thank God," he said fervently to Flick, "you don't care for such things."

"My sweet," she said, in one of those rare but extremely precious moments when she spoke directly to him. "One of my few virtues is that I do not get on a man's nerves."

"You've had so much experience," he said bitterly.

"Yes, my sweet—so have you."

* * *

That, of course, was the whole root of the thing. The tie that bound them together when they quarrelled with each other—battles which would have sunk less veteran ships— was that they both had had experience. Painful thought— so many of Flick's virtues were the consequence of her wantonness. And in here—in these infrequent moments when Flick dropped her guard—Tony thought he some- times saw another Flick. An entirely different woman.

Spain, with Flick, was chaotic . . . a blur of disasters.

* * *

They drove quickly out of San Sebastian and up into the mountains where Pampeluna, with its buff walls and faded red roofs, stands upon its plateau. In a corner of the main square he found the Montoya brothers still running their famous little hotel. The Spaniards met them as the car came to a halt alongside the arcades. And when they saw who had come back, the Montoya brothers immediately took Lynd and Flick into their private office—its walls hung with photographs of famous bullfighters—where they hammered

Tony on the back with hysterical Spanish hospitality, and clapped their hands for a maid to bring two bottles of their best white sherry.

He saw at once that Flick, long used to being the centre of attraction, was jealous about the warmth of this welcome that he had received. It was from the Hotel Montoya that he had set off on a long mule ride down the Pyrenees four years before. Only a few days after the night in London when he and Flick had had that Cresta run down the basement steps at Vyvyan Flower's party. Since he had met Flick they had often discussed what a pity it was he had not brought her along then. For five wasted months he had wandered freely, wherever he wanted, all over Spain. From the winter snows of the Pyrenees to the white walls of Cadiz during Carnival time. He sighed now at the wasted opportunity.

Flick, with her lip beginning to curl, was, he could see, deliberately setting out to have an angry carouse. She began to bait the two Spaniards about the dullness, the painful propriety of all Spanish night life.

"You're so damn' hypocritical," she drawled. She was egging the Spaniards into suggesting some excitement. She would do anything. It would also be something that would shock the Spaniards. It was in her disregard for all the harassing conventions of life that perhaps Flick's chief charm came in. Disastrously, in this case. It began when the bewildered bullfighter brothers asked would Flick like to see "the Montmartre of Pampeluna." Flick, with that curl of her lips, announced she did not believe there was such a thing.

"You know what it means?" said Tony. He had suffered so long from Flick's baiting him for his alleged priggishness that he resolved now to give her the full blast of her arrogant freedom.

"Prig!"

"All right. Go as far as you like as far as I am concerned."

The white sherry was affecting both of them equally. Tony knew that although the badgered Spaniards had suggested it as a joke it would be catastrophic to let Felicity be "shown the town." The Montoya brothers would never have the same respect for him again. However, it would be worth losing even that to see Flick thoroughly shocked at last. And Pampeluna, he felt, could do it.

"You asked for it," said Tony.

It is not much fun to watch people being lascivious. The bullfighter brothers were unquenchable. Lynd hated Flick for watching it. In an ultimate house, which they had reached after a mysterious drive where the head-lamps shone on rows of tree trunks, they found a young Spanish aristocrat playing the guitar while the girls danced a brothel-version of the *flamenca* until they were entirely naked.

"I spik English," said the young guitar-player, sidling suggestively up to Flick as he twanged the strings. Then, seeing Tony's look upon him, he hurriedly apologised, "You may think it *infra dig.*, *señor*, to see me, a gentleman, playing the guitar in a Spanish cat-house . . . but, I assure you, I am in the tradition . . . all the great Spanish artists did that."

Tony's reply, whatever it might have been, was smothered in the plump breasts of a Spanish girl. For some time, during the dance of the *flamenca*, she had been eyeing him, pointing at his head, and making remarks about his hair to the other girls. That belligerent head of sandy hair, and the scylla-blue eyes, had fascinated her. Now she took a running jump across the room, landed in Tony's lap, and threw a scissors around him with her smooth, muscular legs. Pulling Tony towards her, she jammed her lips against his.

He had never felt so silly in his life. When he broke the scissors hold and pushed her off, she seized his arm, jerked him towards her and then, skipping around him, threw a double-Nelson on his head. By this time the brothel was in

FL

convulsions of laughter. The guitar-players were shouting
bets, mimicking the red-*béreted* bookies in the pelota games.
Tony was furious.

The girl, apparently, was the strong-man of Pampeluna;
and this wrestling game seemed her pet stunt. Even in his
anguish Tony had to laugh at the thought of how easily
she must have tossed the little Basques about. Finally, he
got a grip on her. She was young, very firm, frantic as a
wild-cat as he bore her inexorably to the floor. She bit her
lips not to cry when he put pressure on the hammer-lock.
Then he released it, kicked her legs from under her, and
jumped on her chest. In that position, holding her flat, he
raised one arm.

"*Bueno?*" he asked the uproarious room.

"*Si, si, señor . . . bueno, bueno! . . .*"

It was a great success.

But in the meantime the guitar-player had been making
advances towards Felicity. He had her backed in a corner and
was now walking around in small circles before her, chanting . . . "Oh . . . la-la-le-yayoooo . . ." Flick, frightened,
but unwilling to show it, looked past him at Tony. For a
moment Tony had a mind to let the young Spaniard scare
her some more; it would serve her right. She had asked for
this orgy. But when the female strong-man started to
embrace him again he decided they had both had enough.

"*Noblesse oblige!*" said Tony, when he paid the enormous
account that Madame presented for the sweet champagne.
He paused long enough to admire the 1901, Queen Victoria
penny which she wore, silvered, on her porch of a bosom;
then, leaving the bullfighter brothers somewhere upstairs,
he took Flick's arm and hustled her into the greying
street.

"It occurs to me," said Lynd, as they were walking
slowly across the square, watching the roof-tops of Pampeluna emerge against the greenish morning sky, "that you
and I, my sweet, have had just about as idiotic an evening

as anyone could. Still . . . it's harmless. That's the charm of these Spaniards."

He stopped. "Have you ever been in a place like that?"

She shook her head. "Never, my sweet. Never. That's the first time I've ever been in a place like that with anyone. I think it was awful."

"That's fine," he said, humbled. Then: "But why with *me*?"

"I just wanted to see if you would take me there."

"Why? What on earth would *that* prove?"

"Oh, you amuse me. I wanted to see your conscience at work. You're so funny."

"Well, it didn't work, did it?"

"No," she said. "But you still think it was wrong to take me there."

In silence they finished the last half of that long square, banged on the hotel door until a wretched Spaniard roused himself somewhere in the interior, and they went up to their room. A newly opened bottle of the famous white sherry stood on their dressing-table and Tony poured out two glasses.

"It's all right, Flick. You can say what you want; but you know that we are both of us egging each other on to have the usual drunken fight. I don't say we will ever admit it— but you and I have got something between us that both of us have been looking for all our lives. You know what I mean, too. A desire to live a decent normal life together. And not just this."

"Perhaps."

"You've seen too damn' much."

"So have you."

He handed Flick her glass, and put his arm around her waist as he did so. "Ah, my sweet . . ."

She put her head against his chest. "Yes," she said— "more than I've ever wanted anything—I want to lead a normal life with you."

She lay there with one arm around him as they slept. It was uncomfortable, but he did not shake it off. It was the hot middle-day when they dressed and came down to drink more white sherry under the red-and-white parasols of the Bullfighters' Club.

*   *   *

But it was not the sherry or the bullfighters that held Flick and Tony for three days around Pampeluna's yellow square. It was Jesus Christi Basiano.

"Jesus is an artist," Lynd told Felicity. "But his snows are green, his trees always painted red—and God knows what you will think of his skies. Nevertheless, he's a damned nice Spaniard."

He was very much flattered when, on the first afternoon after their arrival at Pampeluna, as they were having coffee outside the Café Suiza, among clicking dominoes and waiters with pots of goat's milk, a Baby Peugeot pulled up and Jesus leapt out.

"Jesus rode with me into the Pyrenees four years ago . . . didn't you, Jesus?" said Tony, introducing them.

Jesus, who could only understand the words Jesus and Pyrenees, nodded effusively: *"Si, si, señor!"*

"Only our language prevents Jesus from telling you how he loves me," said Lynd. "Usually I say, *'Si, si'* . . . and Jesus says, 'No, no' . . . don't you, Jesus?"

"No comprendo, señor."

Although Jesus could understand nothing, he would not be left out of the conversation; Tony had to try, at least, to explain everything. Any conversation between Tony and Flick therefore became impossible.

Jesus, an egg-faced little Spaniard, with two black dots that went for eyes, was staring anxiously from one to the other of them, for fear that he was being made fun of in some way. Lynd reached out his hand and Jesus seized it.

"My wife," said Tony.

"*Señor!* . . ." Jesus leapt to his feet. He stood back. He threw out his arms. With both hands he seized Felicity's and pressed it to his lips. "Ha-ha, *señor!*" He pounded Lynd on the back. "*Bueno, bueno!*"

"Now don't laugh, for Christ's sake," said Tony quickly as he saw Flick's lips begin to curl. "This man is a friend of mine."

With a picturesque melange of sign language, a few words of Spanish, and much serious gesticulation around the square, Jesus made it known that he had just heard Señor Lynd was in town, and that he had come at once. How long had Señor Lynd come to stay? And where was Señor Lynd going?

In his effort to protect Jesus from Flick's hovering sneer, Tony hastily answered, "Ujue *pueblo.*"

"Ah . . . ha! . . . *Señor, señor!* . . ."

To his horror, Lynd realised that by this unguarded remark he had invited Jesus to go with them.

Ujue, as Jesus himself had shown him four years before, was one of the last remaining bits of old Spain. It was a tiny village, a robbers' roost, perched on the tip of a lonely spur of mountains in deepest Navarre. Lynd had been saving it as the one place where, he hoped, the very romance of the scene would impress even a hard-boiled soul like Felicity with the wonder of their being together in Spain. He had counted a lot upon Ujue *pueblo.*

And now Jesus had entered the scene. And, knowing Jesus, he did not see how it would be possible to drop him.

So, for three days, he had plied Jesus with sherry in an attempt to knock him out. The result had been several bumpy rides in the Riley out into the countryside around Pampeluna where, knocking at a shabby door among the goats and children of some wretched village, Jesus would magically usher them into the palatial study of a Don. In this way, one afternoon, Tony and Flick spent a few unreal hours in the home of a great Spanish dramatic critic, preparing in the countryside his great work on the plays of Lope de Vega. On the next afternoon in a village where they had the barricades up in the main street for an early bullfight, they were taken into the presence of the Royal Blood itself; a listless Duke who was writing a history of the Carlist wars, all in longhand, of which there was to be only one copy—each volume of which he bound in red morocco himself. The Duke produced his wife with the ceremony of introducing them into a sacred harem. They were charming people; the Duke spoke the most exquisite English . . . but they would feed Felicity sweet sherry and plum jam. Lynd feared for Jesus. And Jesus, of course, now considered himself a member of the Lynd household.

"Jesus knows everybody," said Lynd despairingly.

"Wish he didn't know us," said Felicity.

Tony had never imparted to Flick the intention of Jesus to go with them to Ujue. The dashes out into the country, therefore, had an irritating purposelessness in her mind. On this morning she had decided to put a stop to it all.

"When," she asked, "are we going to leave this lousy town?"

"To-day," said Tony. "At once. Now. *Pronto*. Let's get our things down at once."

The night of the wrestling match with the strong girl in the brothel they had not seen Jesus because the two bull-fighter brothers had far too much respect for Jesus' gentility to ask him to come along. Since about eleven the previous night, when Lynd had driven Jesus to his little painted home over the meat-market, Jesus had not been on the scene. Perhaps the white sherry had done its work. Now, with some luck, there was a good chance to escape from him.

Flick, who knew nothing of his secret apprehensions about Jesus, was in a mood so savage, after the amount of white sherry which she insisted Tony made her drink, that she would not leave the table to pack her bags. It was accordingly the hour of siesta, that dependable hour when all good Spaniards should have been taking their noon-day doze, that Lynd brought the motor car around and began to stow their bags. Flick, her beautiful eyes very bloodshot, was finally persuaded to get into it.

It was then, as he was in the very act of turning out of that yellow square, that a figure leapt on the running-board. Jesus had arrived.

With an agility that both astonished and infuriated Tony Lynd, Jesus leapt into the air and came down on the moving car's back seat.

"*Si, si, señor!*" cried Jesus, exulted by his feat—and waved for them to go ahead. "Ujue!" he said.

Flick leaned forward and turned off the switch.

"Is this ghastly creature coming with us?"

"He is," said Tony.

"He is *not!*"

"Well, let's see you try to get rid of him." Tony, facing the inevitable, looked at Felicity with a grin to see what she would do.

He was not prepared for what she did.

"Heah! Heah!" Felicity addressed Jesus with those scaring tones with which one tries to drive off a midnight cat. "Get out!" She waved a hand at him.

Jesus, who apparently thought this was some kind of English game, sat there and smiled. His seriousness, hard to bear even at the best of times, was now, to Felicity, just a red rag. Tony laughed. He felt sorry for Jesus; but it was marvellous to see any mere man standing up to Felicity like that. He looked at Felicity.

"You think this is *funny?*" she said, and there was again that dangerous rising intonation in her voice. "Well . . . what do you think of *that?*"

She threw her bag and hit Jesus in the face.

In his consternation Lynd was unable to do anything before it was too late. While he was still clutching Flick's hand, Jesus leapt from the car. There was nothing sprightly, no gaiety in the bound with which he regained the street; he was horribly mortified. He was holding his hand to his face. Staring, unbelievingly, at Flick. The instant he saw Tony scrambling out of the car he took to his heels. Seeking sanctuary, Jesus headed for the nearest church. It was impossible to pursue him there, even for his own good. Lynd, horrified by the thought of what would be the feelings of the proud little Basque, if he were allowed to escape without having been forced to listen to the most humble apology, braved the church. In its dark, tranquil interior he saw a few women, in black, kneeling on little chairs they had reversed before the altar. A priest glowered at this sight-seeing foreigner—always in a rush, these gaping strangers—and vanished in a crypt. Somewhere, in the vast maze of yellow stone, Lynd heard chanting voices. But no Jesus. . . .

When he came out into the hot sunlight, his squinting eyes focused themselves on Flick's red mouth. A decisive moment, he realised, was at hand. Something that would have a vital effect on all the rest of his life. If he had any guts he would tell Felicity what he thought of her; and he would break with her right where they were.

"I wish you were a man!" he growled ineffectively. "I'd just beat the living hell out of you. You're not . . . you're a woman . . . and that's why you do such dirty things. You know you're safe. Anyway, far as getting a punch in the jaw is concerned."

She was all smiles. Alluringly fresh in her spotted linen. And provocative as she could make herself.

"Hop in, my sweet, I adore you.'

"Oh, go to hell."

Nevertheless, he got in. As he shoved the car into gear and they turned slowly out of that yellow square, he looked back regretfully. "There goes a friend," he said. "Poor Jesus. I've got an idea you and I are going to leave a trail of my friends in our wake."

"He won't blame you, my darling. And he *is* such a little fool."

"Doesn't matter. He's wretched. I can't bear to think of him . . . standing that way . . . his hand on his face. We're a couple of lice, we are."

"Absolutely, my darling."

* * *

There was something oddly proper about Flick. For all her boasted indifference as to whom she slept with—and Lynd wondered at times: was this so devastatingly important? thinking, to cheer himself up, of the great artists, actresses and women of the world who had had a panorama of *affaires* before they married into the Peerage. Flick at times, he knew now, positively hungered for propriety. And simplicity. That night, at Ujue, he caught her darning socks. And very skilfully. He loved the sight of her little hands moving so quickly as she shoved the needle back and forth over the wooden egg. And she had grandly used up most of their small allowance of water to wash his handkerchiefs (an unappetising job, he thought, to do for any man). She had them pressed against the small window-pane. She had one beautiful bare leg thrown over her knee and was singing to herself in that strange, sad, hoarse voice that had such a rasp of regret. Blissfully contented.

He moved towards her. Then, afraid that some chance remark or gesture would set her off again, he moved as unostentatiously as he could to the window. He leaned there, smoking, watching the lights go out in the little *pueblos* that hung like clusters of grapes on the mountain sides. He heard Flick say "There!" She had finished the socks and stood up, brushing the ends of wool from her. She came over and put

F1

her hand on his back, her mouth once more lifted up in that ironic grin of hers: "Well, my sweet?"

"Nothing," he said. "I do love you, you wretch!"

*   *   *

The next day she followed him like a poodle around Ujue. In that remote *pueblo*, perched on its solitary mountain tip, they felt they were both above and free from this world. There was no hotel in this village of stone. No written word on its cobbled, climbing, twisting streets. They had put up with the same Spanish family which had housed him four years before on his lonely mule ride across Spain. When they entered its iron-studded door, Tony showed Flick, with some fear that she would laugh, the same hot, smelly lower quarters where his two mules had slept; the room directly below the one they were given. Nothing had changed in Ujue, not even the memory of his stay there. Old José and his wife received him like the Prodigal Son. They had been a little awed by Felicity at first. But this was where her easy manners came in. His first fears that she would hurt these people were unnecessary. She said she loved roast rabbit, and ate it uncomplainingly. José, taking heart, even insisted she drink the red wine out of the *porron*, squirting it into her open mouth, without touching it with her lips. Lynd saw that she ruined her spotted linen dress without even so much as a glance at it. She was, he thought, trying to be decent for his sake. He was sure of it afterwards when he saw her trying to soak out the spots of wine with salt and hot water. She was more careful about her clothes than her morals, he thought.

The priests, in the little fighting church whose tower crowned the mountain *pueblo*, awoke them at dawn with their chanting. Flick and he leaned out the window and watched the day strike Navarre. The pink tiles of Ujue's roofs shoaled like scales into the pool of morning mist below them. Then the sun burned through and they looked down into the terraces of olives and ploughed fields, the Spaniards and their cattle going out to the day's work on the mountain slopes. They went down to breakfast and sat on stools around the little acacia fire while they ate a leathery sausage and *migas*, that peasant staple of bread shavings, garlic and mutton fat. And Flick ate it.

"Perhaps a little wine," said Tony, understandingly, "would help to wash that down?"

"Well . . . it might help."

They drove back to Pampeluna in a beatific mood.

*   *   *

But it passed. Perhaps it was the white sherry. It might have been, Lynd was afraid, that Felicity felt she had been good long enough. It may have been his own inflamed jealousy when he was drinking . . . his thought that he would so soon be parted from her . . . that made him fling a lot of nasty remarks at her about her past life. They had the hell of a row.

This was in the hotel of the bullfighters, their own room, to which Augusto had climbed so hopefully to invite them to his village. Augusto was the doyen of Tony's Spanish friends. His village was in the high Pyrenees, high up at the head of the valley of Roncal where there is no pass into contaminating France. Augusto, who turned into a goat once he was in his beloved mountains, spent eight months of his year in Paris. There, in the Quartier Latin, he had grown the beard that made him look so much like a faun himself. Lynd and he had enjoyed each other's companionship in both places.

"Feelicity . . ." implored Augusto when she began to weep with rage. "*Vous êtes très ironique !*"

"Let her be," said Lynd. "Have another drink."

Augusto drank, pounded his knees, and tried to get a smile out of Felicity. She wouldn't leave Tony alone.

"I'm through," she said.

"All right; you're through. Come on, Augusto, have another drink."

He filled Augusto's glass without offering any to Felicity.

"Give me some of that."

He gave her a glass.

"I'm through."

"I know it. Say something new for a change."

"You . . . and your damn' Spanish friends!"

"What have they done to you? Merely tried to be nice to you."

"You Cook's tourist!"

"Shut up. Cook's tourist! I'd like to see you get on in Spain the way that I do. I'd . . ." It did seem damn' foolish, what he was saying.

"Oh, yes—'When I get you to Ujue . . .' 'You should see Augusto's village, my *darling* . . .' You cheap edition of Ernest Hemingway!"

"Go on. Go to hell; I told you to. You and your damn' artist friends . . . fornicating each other around Spain. That's the only kind of Spain you know. What the ceilings looked like!"

Felicity threw the sherry in Tony's face. He jumped up, took her by the throat and shook her. "You talk that way to me, you little bitch. . . . I'll damn' well kill you."

Augusto leapt to his feet. He sprang to them. He hovered. . . . His hands reached out to touch them . . . then they drew back again. . . . Felicity felt her throat. She was silent. Just a few gurks inside her showing her fight to master herself.

"Tony? . . . Feelicity? . . ." Augusto looked helplessly from one to the other. In his rage Lynd had flung Felicity back across the bed. She now wiped her eyes with the end of a sheet; and, taking advantage of this momentary blindness, Augusto seized her hand and tried to force it into Tony's. She scratched Augusto.

"Leave her alone. To hell with all of it. Come on, Augusto, let's you and I go downstairs and have another drink."

"No, Tony. . . . We must all be friends."

"To hell with you, then. No, sorry, Augusto—you mustn't get in between us when we fight. You'll lose an ear. You'd better push off. Leave us alone to our sorrows."

"I won't! I . . . Tony, *amigo*"—Augusto looked imploringly towards Felicity—"for my sake . . ."

Now Augusto was crying. He seized the bottle of sherry and spilled half a glass. Tony snatched it away from him. "I'll ring for another bottle," said Augusto. Quickly, he pulled the bell-cord.

"I'm sorry, Augusto, you should see such a row."

"*You damned prig!*"

"Oh, for God's sake, Felicity, can't you forget that word?"

"No, I can't." She was suddenly laughing. Augusto saw it and seized her hand. He jerked Tony and shoved his hand in Felicity's. He gave a great sob himself. Through a veil of tears Flick and Augusto smilingly watched the maid enter.

"Jerez! *Jerez!*" cried Augusto.

"My God!" said Tony. "We ought to stop!"

"Prig," laughed Felicity.

"All right. Maybe you're right. Here, my sweet, have some of this. Have a lot. Then we'll all go across to the Café Suiza."

* * *

When he walked into the office in London he thought that Marjory seemed a bit strange. She seemed to be avoiding him. Finally, as she was putting down some papers on his desk, she said awkwardly: "Miss Luba Power has rung up."

"What did she want? When did she call?"

"She just wanted to know where you were?"

"Did she leave any address, any telephone number? Where can I get hold of her?"

Marjory said she didn't know. Lynd had the impression she was not telling the truth, but then it would be impossible to press her to answer. When she had gone back to the other room he dialled Luba's old number. The Exchange girl said it had been disconnected. Putting down the receiver, he was glad. Life had enough complications these days. And Luba would meet more than her match in this situation!

The Spanish trip had left a bad taste in his mouth. If he and Flick were going to go on, it certainly could not be like this. A couple of Bloomsbury intellectuals, perhaps, going off on an affair might have thought that they had grasped a lot of the colour of life out of their Spanish fandango. But he and Flick knew that it was headaches, a lot of drunken arguments that never led anywhere, and a lot of the real Spain, the colour of its streams and mountains, that they had missed. He was, he knew, no longer an *amigo* at the Bullfighters' Club—they had left a trail of wreckage even on those narrow little stairs.

In the melancholic mornings—when neither of them had felt kind enough to admit this they had simply continued the fight. But now the time had come for him and Flick to call a truce, to face the fact that their feelings towards each other were too intense to be continued as an affair of any sort. They would either be the making or the breaking of each other. There was no escape from that.

When he looked around him he saw a great many of his friends leading very irregular lives. In fact, of the early crowd that Chris and he had first come into when he entered journalism, there was hardly a pair at this day which remained together. They had, in various degrees, drifted apart from each other. Either it was open, cynical cold-blooded divorce, or one side or the other was stomaching the fact that the other person had another lover. The lives of foreign journalists seemed to lead to this, the unorthodox way they trooped around the world, the opportunities that were offered to them, the betrayals of all standards of life that they saw every day all around them. They had to report too much daily treachery to have much faith any longer in man's ideals. They soon acquired the Bohemian's contempt for any of the irksome obligations of conventional married life. They were artists, in their way.

The love between him and Flick, he thought savagely, was a great deal more beautiful and held a lot more truth in it than that of half a dozen of his divorced friends. The very people who, he knew, were every day criticising his conduct, and very likely to Christina. He was furious with them for that, for these things never matter until they strike home; and by their complacent sympathy and advice they were making Christina suffer for the very things they had done themselves. He had often tried to point this out to her, and without success. He could understand that; she felt too deeply about it. And he didn't blame her. On the other hand, it was essential that he saw clearly this example of his kind friends, before he took to a sadistic contemplation of himself.

"The trouble with me is," he said to himself, "I'm chicken-hearted. I'm too fond of Chris to leave her, and I'm too addicted to Flick to let her go. As a result I am being called a perfect monster all around London."

It wasn't fair, he knew. But what was there that he could do about it? He was disgusted with the easy advice that one of his best friends voluntarily offered him:

"I wouldn't stand it for five minutes, Tony. A man's got to live. And he lives in his pants, you know."

Tony shuddered. "My God," he said, "do you mean to say you can treat a woman like that—a girl who's been decent to you for over ten years: You're crazy! A thing like this is a hell of a problem to answer!"

And so it went. More and more of his friends, Tony knew,

were coming to Christina with their solicitations. Not that she invited them, or even let them talk. And more and more the anger flamed within him at this unjust estimate all these people were making so glibly of his life. To hell with all of them, became almost his daily slogan. He began to shun some of them.

*   *   *

Felicity herself had said to him, undermining his sense of values he suspected: "You were wrong to be so faithful for such a long time to Christina. It is your fault that she expects such dog-like faithfulness. You are the person who is really to blame. Not she."

But then, when he admitted sourly one night that perhaps he had been foolish to have been so true to Christina, it was Flick who murmured: "Oh, why? . . ." As if she herself, behind the façade, appreciated such a love.

It was because he knew that both he and Flick valued just this straightforward faithfulness, that he was so furious with outward criticism. They weren't rotten in their own hearts, no matter what anybody might care to think.

They did not know what was going to happen. But the one effect of all this criticism, simply because of its injustice, was that it drew them together in a common self-defence.

*   *   *

Senator Hancock came to town. One morning when Tony was dejectedly running through the London newspapers the great man stalked into the office. Lynd was surprised to see him up so early and looking so fit.

"Love," said Senator Hancock, when Lynd mentioned this. "That's what makes the world go round. Miss Svenson and I flew over yesterday in the Paris plane. Here, get Marjory to see about our mountain of trunks, will yer—they're coming by boat. We've been shopping. Tony, I'm enjoying life!"

"How the devil do you manage to keep away so long from the Senate?" asked Lynd.

"Makes no difference. I've got all the money I want. Only wanted to be a Senator—once. Y'know; just to show I could do it. Matter fact, I've been doing a little political work on the side—gonna go back an' tell 'em all what the hell's the matter with Yurrup. Trouble with these Englishmen is—they won't work."

"What's the use of working . . . piling up goods on the dock," asked Lynd, "when you can't find somebody to buy them?"

"When I was in Rome," said the Senator, "I wouldn't even speak to Mussolini."

Lynd escaped from answering that by looking at the pile of letters on his desk.

"Say, Tony," said Mr. Hancock, "I'd sure like to have my little girl meet your missis."

"Oh—all right. What about to-morrow night? Have dinner at our house." Tony thought. "And look here, if you're investigating politics—how would you like to meet a real Bolshie?"

This new Russian secretary, anxious to know about *bourgeois* life, was now about to learn something.

"Say, that'd be swell. I'd like to talk to one of those guys."

"Okay," said Lynd. When the Senator went out he called up Christina, explained what was up, and was lucky enough to find that the new secretary at the Soviet Embassy was free for to-morrow night.

"I say, Mr. Lynd!" said Marjory. "You *are* a one. Coo! Think of puttin' those two men together."

* * *

The Lynds were very proud of their drawing-room in Cheyne Walk. Christina had brought back some pussy-willows from the country and a bough of young green leaves.

Their reflections shimmered in the light of the dancing fire as they stood in a glass battery-jar against the wall. Senator Hancock, in a dinner jacket with sparkling diamond shirt studs, leaned against the Adams fireplace. He spoke through his cigar:

"Why, I've got a *wine*-cellar in my house that's twice the size of this—and it's full from top to bottom! Lemme tell you about that house, Mrs. Lynd."

Christina came down with Miss Salome Svenson at the same time that the maid announced dinner. Miss Svenson was a beautiful greyhound Dane, with ropes of plaited blonde hair twisted around her head to form a crown. She was about six inches taller than the Senator.

"Lemme tell you about that house," insisted Mr. Hancock as they sat down at the long, polished refectory table. "Y'oughter see that house! Isn't another like it in the whole wide world. Nossir. I got one of the finest architects in New York—and I says to him: 'I'm gonna send you to Yurrup. I don't want you to feel hampered. I want the best of everything that is. What you see in Tudor—well, I want you to pick the best that you can get out of all that. What you see in the Elizabeth period—take that. Go to Italy and see what the old Greeks did. And then I want you to go to Egypt . . . some of those baths like Cleopatra had. Copy them to a dot. When you're going through France—stop on your way, make some good drawings of those chatoos on the Loire. Those turrets.' I didn't think Germany had much to offer—so I told him he needn't bother about wasting time there. 'And then,' I says to him, 'come back and build me that house—expense is no object—y'unnerstan'?'

"Well," said Mr. Hancock, tucking his napkin in his shirt front, "y'ought to see that house."

"I'd love to," said Christina. "It must be amazing."

"I'll say so. Why, I got *pheasants* on my place—I let my chauffeurs shoot 'em."

Miss Salome Svenson did not say very much, except to answer, "Yes" or "No" or "I guess that's okay!"

And for some reason, Christina, who could be relied on to make an immense success of any such occasion, seemed strangely preoccupied.

When the women had gone, Lynd left the Russian and the American Senator together while he went down into the cellar for another bottle of brandy. He could see that the small amount in the decanter was a mere moistener for Mr. Hancock.

When he returned he found the dark-browed secretary backed into a corner, with the Senator tapping him on the chest. "The trouble with you Russians is," said the Senator —giving another jab—"is that you ain't got no *culture*. Y'unnerstan' what I mean—no culture. . . ."

The scowling Russian, who had marched a division from Nijni Novgorod to half way across Siberia in the Red and White Russian wars, who had sat on the ice outside a besieged city of Whites—and captured it by sending skilful propagandists into the town, so that it fell from within—held his tongue although the veins on his flushed forehead were standing out like thick cords. Almost immediately they rejoined the ladies he announced that he was sorry, but he had to get back to the Embassy for some special work.

As Lynd was helping him on with his coat at the door, the big Russian hissed: "Lynd—how *could* you work for such a man?"

"I don't know," said Lynd. "Maybe I won't be much longer. I've got a hunch that lightning's about to strike. I don't know from where."

"Well, when the Embassy car comes," said the Russian, "I've ordered it for eleven o'clock, will you tell the driver I've gone?"

*   *   *

When they had all gone, Christina, very pale, sank back on the couch beside the fire.

"Peter," she said desperately, "you've been in Spain with Felicity Correl?"

Lynd bit his lip; "Yes," he said.

"Oh, Peter!"

"I'm sorry. . . . I'm sorry. . . . How did you find out?"

"Luba told us."

"*Luba ?*"

He jumped to his feet. "How in God's——"

"She came over to Mother's this afternoon. And, oh, Peter, she said such beastly, beastly things . . ."

Lynd, a bit shakenly, poured himself out a drink. "Well . . . let's have it," he said.

Christina, of course, knew the Russian story of Luba—but not the London side. She did not even know that Tony and Luba had ever met again. Not until now.

"I haven't seen Luba for months," he said.

"I know it. Oh, Tony, Tony . . . you must forgive me . . . but you don't know what a ridiculous position you've placed me in. That one of your mistresses should come to me and complain about another mistress . . ."

"But she came to your mother's?"

"Yes, but she came here first, for me . . . and when Gudrun said I was over at Mother's she came over there. Oh, Tony—it was *horrible*. . . ."

"Well, how did *she* find out?"

"Marjory told her."

"Now that's a lie. I know Marjory. She would no more betray me than be skinned alive. There's something wrong here."

"There's lots wrong, Peter. But apparently she had been trying to get hold of you for days. She rang up Marjory and she told Luba you were in Spain. How she found out about you and that other beastly woman, I don't know. But she called up Felicity Correl's office and found she was also in Spain. Then she rang up Marjory and told her the whole thing."

"Spain's a big country."

"But it's all true, isn't it?"

"Yes."

"Well, what do you want me to do? I'm all at sea. I still don't know what to think about anything. I've believed you so implicitly all along. I knew about Felicity, of course. But I had begun to see that I had been a little hard-hearted and un-understanding about certain things. I've often felt sorry for you. I feel sorry for Luba now. And many a time when I've seen you looking wretched I was on the point of saying why didn't you have a mistress. But, Peter, Peter . . . you couldn't be faithful—even to Luba!"

Lynd felt his brain escaping him. Talk about emotional Russians! He gripped his head. He had all he could do to repress an unholy desire to laugh.

"It's monstrous!" said Christina. "Why, you couldn't even be faithful to the girl you were once in love with!"

"Of all the nonsense I've ever heard in my life," he said; "to-night I've heard some of it. Not from you. But just this unbelievable situation. Now, Christina, do just listen to me. . . ."

As accurately as he could, he gave a complete, unsparing history of the whole situation. How he had been secretly living with Luba for some time, been quite happy—that physical need of his life had been satisfied, at least—and that he did not feel any shame in doing it. "You've seen Luba," he said. "You know what she's like—there's no evil there. None." He explained the fantastic way that he and Luba had parted. He explained the mood he was in when he met Flick.

"And with Felicity," he said, "I know I am hurting you. You're quite right there, this is something different. But I can't understand why Luba should have made such a scene. If she hadn't been such a bloody little fool I would have been with her still. And, as a matter of fact, I did have one short break with Felicity. . . ."

In a rush to purify himself by making a complete confession, he even told Christina about his stormy scene with Felicity in this very room. He felt reckless to-night—or was it hope? At any rate, it was a relief to sweep away the false scenery of this double life he had been leading. It all sounded a little childish to him as he said it; but before he was through he had told her all there was to tell.

His own intimate story, he did not stress. The physical starvation that had driven him to do these things, he did not talk about. It was the one thing that really counted. Yet he could not bring himself, even now, to fling that in Christina's face. She had enough to bear. She had touched on it to-night, theoretically, about her acquiescence to his having a mistress. But the mere cold fact itself—Spain with Felicity Correl—had already crumpled Christina up. It was odd, but even in that agitated afternoon, Chris had seen enough of Luba not to regard her as a danger to their household. And with unerring instinct, she knew that Flick was. Therefore, this talk to-night must be solely on the basis that he was someone who had done all the wrong.

This, of course, put him in an entirely false position—Christina, blissfully untroubled by physical passion, did not appreciate the way it mastered other people's lives—and his efforts to defend himself under the circumstances made him appear guiltier than ever. It placed upon him the full stigma of being sordid and shallow. "You seem actually to be proud of it!" Christina declared.

"Oh no, for heaven's sake, do listen to what I am trying to say. I know I've done wrong; I know that it is probably wrong for me to look at any other woman than you. I'm not going to try to exonerate myself by pointing out the number of our friends who are no better than I am—or the ones who callously take it to the divorce courts. You do know the feeling I have in my heart for you. And for your own sake I do want to point out to you that we are not the only two people whose lives get a little complicated at times."

"A little complicated! . . . My God, Tony. . . . At times you can talk such rot."

"Well, there it is," he said.

*   *   *

Christina dragged herself up to bed. He went into the other room and fetched the decanter. He knew that smothering cotton-wool of sympathy Lady Mallard had tried to wrap her wounded daughter in that afternoon. He knew what Lady Mallard would say to him; looked pained—and say that he must be prepared to make the great sacrifice. Lady Mallard was a Theosophist! Sometimes, he wondered if these respectable people were really flesh and blood. And what on earth had possessed Luba to come to Christina?

When he tiptoed upstairs after the decanter was empty he saw that Christina had taken the dachshund to bed. Zeppelin's long brown nose and flapping ear lay on the pillow beside her.

THE STORM BREAKS

On the night of June 5th that year, an earthquake struck England. Lynd and Christina were sleeping in an old four-poster bed down at "Jacobs," the old Elizabethan house of some cousins of Christina's outside Canterbury. The shock was the first that was recorded for over one hundred years. When Lynd and Christina felt the bed swaying under them, they sat up. In the dim glow of the dying wood-fire in their room, Lynd saw a picture opposite him swing like a pendulum on the wall.

"Did you see *that*?" he asked Christina.

"I did."

"Well, that's good. If I'd been here alone I would have said it's high time for me to stop drinking."

"You can do that, too, Peter," sighed Christina, and, turning over, immediately went to sleep.

Other guests over the week-end at "Jacobs" had had similar eerie experiences. All were afraid to speak about it at breakfast the next morning, until the *Sunday Observer* came. And there it was: "EARTHQUAKE TREMORS BRITAIN."

It was a ten-day sensation. But that day another quake was to shake Britain; and it was to go on shaking those islands for years and years. On that day a quiet, monk-like little person was received by Ramsay MacDonald at a railway station, named of all places, Waterloo. It was Bruening, the German Chancellor, whispering in MacDonald's ear: "Germany cannot pay." Words so soon to be changed to: "GERMANY WILL NOT PAY!"

A month before that the Credit-Anstalt in Vienna called to France and asked for the big promised loan which would save it from bankruptcy. The French replied the Credit-Anstalt could not have the money—unless Austria publicly renounced the proposed Austro-German Customs Pact. Sir

Robert Kindersley of the Bank of England rushed into the breach, and tried to save the Credit-Anstalt, Austria, Europe —with £5,000,000. It was too late. On May 13th the Credit-Anstalt closed its doors. A crack started in the financial façade of Europe; in a few days it was a crevasse. The world's economic blizzard had begun.

In the next months Tony and his colleagues underwent a journalistic embarrassment of riches. Early familiarity with the people who were supposed to be "at the helm," as the expression was, of the world's affairs had long ago imbued them with an angry scepticism concerning the capabilities, intentions, as well as the political morals of the men in high places. But even that warning of cynicism had not prepared them for this. In the rout that followed the collapse of the Credit-Anstalt they saw Britain's greatest economists publicly denounce each other as incompetents in the frantic suggestions that they were individually putting forth to solve the financial crisis and to save—or do away with—the gold standard.

"Good Lord!" said Tony with great glee to their luncheon table in Soho. "This is all duck soup to me! I always suspected in college that the hackneyed phrases of Labour and Capital, demand and supply, and so forth—you remember the catchwords our professors used to flunk us on at our examinations? . . . I always felt in my heart of hearts that that was all sheer bunk . . . and now we know! *It was!* Those boobs did not know the meaning of the catchwords they were flunking us on. They don't know to-day! It's a perfectly gorgeous retribution."

London! citadel of the world's finance, centre of the world's foreign exchange transactions, "Guardian of the world's financial honour!"—as Ramsay MacDonald was orating, when he was speechifying why England would never leave the gold standard, and disinherit her creditors— mighty and omniscient London City was caught out on the worst loan racket of modern history. Her bankers who had been borrowing short on low terms of interest and lending long on high found that they had £450,000,000 obligations to meet—and only £250,000,000 to meet them with. Their excuse for the vast sums that they now discovered were frozen in Germany, and could not be retrieved to repay their other borrowing, was—of all things!—that they had not known collectively what each London banker was loaning individually to the Continent!

"It iss unbelievable!" cried the little Galician stock-broker at the Soho gathering, "but it is true. I should have laughed if you had told me last week—but now, I shake your hand, if you say the Bank of England is not the Rock of Gibraltar any more. The Old Lady of Threadneedle Street is a whore!"

"She's worse," laughed Tony one day, after being closeted for hours at a time with the secret delegates Hoover had hastily dispatched to Europe over his ill-fated Moratorium: "Do you know that the entire gold reserve of the Bank of England is pledged against the eighty and fifty million pound loans the British have got from the French and the Americans in their crazy effort to save the British pound from going off the gold standard, and that, as we sit here to-day—there is not one penny of gold behind the British currency? Not a damn' cent!"

At that table talk now became so tense that it often threatened to break up their happy family. When Lynd declared that the strong and predominant Francophile section of the British Foreign Office were fools to let clever French statesmen lead them along by the nose to support the futile French attempt to keep Germany second-rate Power in Europe, the French journalist got up and left the table.

"I won't stand such talk," said he.

"I'm sorry," said Tony. "But sit down, and tell us just how you are going to keep sixty million lusty Germans down —unless someone helps you."

The cynical French delay accepting the Hoover Moratorium, a financial peace overture which at that time might have stayed the financial crisis a bit, caused two weeks bitter wrangling at that table. Henty, the London Left-wing journalist, who had criticised Tony for his interpretative dispatches supporting British policy on the India question, came into his own in days of *débâcle*, and guyed the French correspondent unmercifully for his country's narrow diehardism.

"It's you, the damn' French," he said frankly, "who are holding back any chance of making peace in Europe or recovering from the world slump. You're the old kill-joys. You started this racket when you refused to come through with the promised loan you were offering to save the Credit-Anstalt—unless the Austrians dropped the Austro-German Customs Pact. You killed the Hoover War Debt Moratorium by the way you stalled around before accepting it . . . snooping around to see if your fears were right, that it might in some way bring back the breath of life to suffering Germany. You've just killed the Danubian Conference because your nasty, mean-hearted little Prime Minister rushed across and saw our Boob-in-Office, and made Ramsay accept before the conference six of your cynical seven points—so that now the chance of giving any economic respite to the Central European states is gone. They'll have to trust to Mother France now—heh? And for what?"

Henty laughed derisively: "You French! My God! Didn't you know you lost your last chance to make peace in Europe in 1923—when you marched into the Ruhr? To examine German ledgers with bayonets, as Lloyd George put it. Well, you've borne the Revenger . . . if it isn't Hitler, then it's going to be some other German who will turn and fall upon you. . . . I learned a lot about German resentment and intentions in the Ruhr. . . ."

Even the doughty little French correspondent fell silent at that. For it was known to all at the table that during the time Dick Henty had been writing from the Ruhr, hiding in a cellar with telephonic connections with Berlin, the French had put a price on his head. And it was tacitly admitted that the reward would be paid whether Richard Henty were alive or dead.

The dismaying bewilderment of every statesman in office during the early months of the slump incited responsible journalists to a keener interest than ever in their reporting. The crisis had produced an international mêlée in which all forms of voices, unofficial and unorthodox, were shouting. Tony's outer office saw often these days some wild-eyed private "crank," with his own solution of the financial problem that he wanted to see in print. After a long study of the MacMillan Report and a careful survey of Britain's foreign investments, Lynd came to the conclusion early in July that for the first time within modern memory Great Britain was going to finish the year in the red—have a debit in her balance of international payments.

"Well, this one ought to make them sit up!" he exclaimed to Christina one morning. It was his custom to read two leading and opposite London journals while he drank his coffee in bed, and then begin his telephone calls which exchanged opinions with the Pole and other correspondents he was working with, during which they planned each day's work. "Here's an item in the financial columns of *The Times*. . . . Diminished returns from the Argentine . . . which gives me just the peg I want to hang my story on. I've been collecting information for this for weeks. Now, I'm going to let her go. This story to-day will cause a sensation in New York!"

But not a ripple was stirred. His barometer on these occasions was usually one of the London offices of the big American Press agencies. These always overworked men, almost distracted by reporting the fire-cracker explosions of Europe's calamities and minor crises every day now, were too pressed by the exigencies of split-second news-flashing to have time for the long distance, interpretative stories. These men were his friends; they would beat him to any story they could, and usually did; but every so often he would touch off one of these long distance bombs—and they would get frantic cables from New York: "WHERE WERE WE ON THIS?"

Pippet, head of the biggest agency, grinned when Lynd came to him. "Not a word, old soak. Guess they threw yours in the waste-paper basket. What were the gory details, anyway?"

"Go to hell," laughed Tony.

When that day's paper came from New York, and Tony saw that his story had not been used, he went along to the American Ambassador. That distinguished diplomat spat twice, expertly, and hit the same pattern on the carpet of 4 Grosvenor Gardens; then he said: "Look here, Mr. Lynd—I don't blame you for writing that sort of stuff." He tapped the stem of his famous pipe against Lynd's copy of his cable, lying on the official desk. "But I don't blame the American papers for not printing it. Your paper was right not to send that out to its syndicate."

"Why? It's the truth. Haven't I proved that?"

"Ummmm. . . . Well, you've no business writing that sort of stuff . . . not at times like these. England will pull through."

"Very likely," said Tony, holding on to himself. "But you're thinking of London, and comfortable 10 Downing Street. I'm thinking of the Rhondda Valley in Wales . . . with all the unemployed miners standing along the kerbs with their hands in their pockets . . . of the dead textile towns in the Midlands . . . the shipyards where you won't hear a solitary riveter working nowadays. . . . Just about one man out of every five potential working men in this country is without a job. It would be a damn' good thing if some of the American delegates to these cock-eyed conferences left their swell hotels in London and went up to

Manchester for a few days . . . or Ashton-under-Lyne. . . .
Then they would lose some of their idiotic, criminal
optimism. . . ."

The American Ambassador was the type of man before
whom a journalist, if the diplomat had any respect for
him, could speak his mind. Journalists knew him as an
intensely practical, hard-boiled gentleman, not overgiven
to soft-soaping the British. He nodded now at Lynd's
picture of the stricken Midlands and Britain's four major
industries.

"Go on and write it," he said. "But remember one thing:
just scare journalism does no good. There are too damn'
many good reasons for panic these days."

"No," said Lynd. "And I agree with you. I don't believe
that the British are going to 'muddle through,' either—I've
got too much healthy respect for this country's genius for
compromise. . . . I think they are going to *think* their way
out of it. But that's got nothing to do with my story that the
British are in the hole . . . that they are a long way into the
red, right now!"

The Ambassador hit another rose on the carpet's design.
"My sneaking opinion is that you're right," he said.
"Officially, I am making investigations into the matter. . . ."

He gave Tony a quick smile and picked up some correspondence on his desk to indicate that the interview was
ended.

* * *

That evening when Tony came home he said to Christina:
"Look here, my love, you and I are going down to Wales.
Would you like to?"

At dinner, he explained: "It won't be much fun. We'll
have to put up at Pontypridd . . . and the scenes you'll see
will fair break your heart. But I've been talking with the
Ambassador this morning. . . . I think the conditions in the
Welsh valleys need an airing just now . . . in the American

GL

newspapers. A few cold, realistic stories to let the ordinary American know—*and feel !*—just what it is like to live on the 'dole.' There's a spate of damn' diehard propaganda, not only in this country, but over in the States, about the joys of life on the unemployment insurance pay. The American end had a very dirty purpose to it. The Republicans and the American bankers are in a state of jitters that something like the British unemployment insurance scheme will have to be introduced into the United States. They are afraid they will face something very like a revolution, if they don't. Result . . . they want to discredit the 'dole' system in England. The chief point that the American bankers are making, while they are holding out on making another loan to the British to save the pound, is that this maudlin British Labour Government must cut the 'dole.' . . . Superficially this dirty, mean measure will show England's goodwill and serious intention to put her house in economic order. . . . Fundamentally, it will give the American die-hards all the ammunition they want to say: 'See . . . even the British had to cut their own dole. . . . It doesn't work, you see!'"

"Why, good heavens!" said the overjoyed Christina; "that is just the one kind of story that I would love to work with you on! When do we start?"

"To-morrow," said Tony. "I'll get the car greased and in order to-night. Pack the bags. . . . We'll go over to the coast and get a swim while we're at it. And we'll show Zeppelin some holes in the ground bigger than even she can dig."

The morning they woke up in Pontypridd, Tony asked Christina to look out their window. The street kerb was lined with men, all standing with their hands in their pockets. They looked as if they were waiting for a procession of some sort to come along.

"Miners," said Tony; "at least, they were, or might have been. But not a man there who's over forty will ever go down a mine-shaft again. Know what they're waiting for? The Old Age Pension to come along."

Along the kerb were some wooden barrows. A few Welsh housewives, with baskets on their arms, were carefully bargaining for pieces of meat and bits of fish that even from the hotel window looked in an almost uneatable state.

"Miners' wives," said Tony, "buying their Lucullian dinner on the 'dole.' To-day, my sweet, you and I go shopping."

Christina's entrance always provoked a moment or so of uncomfortableness in the shops. The butcher looked ashamed of his meats; and one automatically apologised: "Inteet to goodness, madam, it's not even Argentine. This is scraps." He explained that what the Welsh miners were eating was meat that they would not have considered fit for their whippets in the good old days.

Christina saw what Tony couldn't see, the tawdry quality of all the clothes in the stricken shops. He saw her, with a look of poignant regret in her eyes, holding up some of the tiny woollen substitutes meant for children. "It's ghastly!" she said in almost a whisper.

For two days they drove around with an insurance agent whom Tony was lucky enough to encounter in the bar. The man was collecting threepence a week from the miners' families for their burial expenses.

"So that they can have a decent funeral," he said. "You wouldn't think, would you, in times like these, that people would care about such things? That they will put aside the money to bury them—when they haven't got enough to eat! Look you . . . did you notice the way all the brasses were polished, and how they had blackened their hearths? That is decent, isn't it?"

"Decent!" Christina made no attempt to dab away the tears that filled her eyes. "I have never seen anything so heroic in my life. That last house we were in . . . that woman was only too right when she called her husband a hero."

In that tiny dwelling, with the invariable aspidistra placed in its closed parlour window, they had found a Welsh woman in the very act of polishing the brasses of her kitchen fire. She brushed aside a wisp of black hair from her brow and said to them defiantly: "My man's a hero, he is. He won't have the dole. He happens to know a foreman over in the other valley. He's got a job over there...over that...."

Without realising its drama, she drew them to the window and pointed to the bleak, scarred hillside behind her house. "Every morning," she said proudly, "my man climbs the mountain. He has to start before it is light, and he never gets home until it is dark. In the winter, when there is ice on it, he climbs up that mountain on his hands and knees. . . ."

They drove along streams that ran black as ink with the mines' refuse, where gaunt piles at the pitheads reared against the empty sky, where trees and vegetation itself had died in despair over so much ugliness. The children were playing tops, but in Tonypandy, Tony pointed out that not a single wheel was turning.

"When I was here in 1926," he reminded Christina, "when I went with these Welsh miners through the whole General Strike, Tonypandy was a perfect furnace of Communism. There was another mining town above here they used to call 'Little Moscow.' Now there is not an 'ism' left in any of them. Did you ever look upon such a scene of silent despair?"

Christina shook her head: "That's what you should call your articles," she said—"'The Valley of Despair!'"

That night, when they returned to their hotel, a young miner was waiting for Tony, and begged him to think if there was not some way he could suggest of helping the young miner find a job in London. "I've been up twice," he exclaimed. "Walked there. Last time I got a job . . . but

I could not make enough money on it to bring my wife there. We're trapped, I tell you. We can't get out of this valley. I've got two kiddies. My God, man . . . can't you see what I fear for them? Have you got a kiddy?"

Tony looked at Chris and hoped she had not heard the last question. Then in a low voice he said, "My dear fellow, I wish to Christ there was something I could tell you. But I can't think of anything. I just can't. Won't you have a drink with us?"

The dark-browed Welshman nodded and sat down at the table where Chris was waiting. "I'm not used to this," he said with a shy smile when Tony put the tot of whiskey down before him. "It will make me drunk, if I take much of it." He began on Christina, his sorrowful lament about his children's future. Wasn't there anything that she could suggest? He declared that one of the reasons why so many of the miners never went home during the day and "just stand around with our hands in our pockets," was because they were afraid that if they did go home they would eat all the food in the house. With pencil and paper he and Chris took the "dole"—and then tried to figure out how his family could live on it. More than Tony, Christina saw the stark desperation of the scale.

When the young miner had said his polite good-bye, Tony went to the bar and brought back a double whiskey for himself. "I feel like getting damn' good and drunk to-night!" he growled.

"Peter . . . I don't blame you," said Christina. "I'd like something to drown my own imagination. It makes me furious. Wild!"

"Now . . . you see why I hate them so? These damned lousy politicians . . . all the world over. I wanted us to come down here and see this scene once again . . . because Ramsay MacDonald & Co. are going to cut the 'dole.' That's what they're headed for . . . in England; it is always the poor who are hit first.

"And in my own damned country," he growled, staring at his empty glass, "if the rich and the damned politicians don't lay off all this bunk about 'rugged individualism'— and give the poor rugged individual something to live upon . . . then it is the stinking rich who are going to get it in the neck. You can understand now . . . how I feel . . . when I have to listen to one of our 'ambassadors at large' . . . shooting off his face in a Park Lane hotel. . . ."

"It makes you want to kill them!" said Christina.

*   *   *

The Labour Cabinet did cut the "dole." Lynd stood with the crowd of amazed journalists in the street between the genteel door of 10 Downing Street and the gloomy façade of the British Foreign Office while they waited for the Cabinet wrangle to end. The Americans wanted the British to cut it by twenty per cent., a thing that meant practically starvation, instead of mere undernourishment, to its hundreds of thousands of unemployed recipients. The British Cabinet persists in the genteel subterfuge that no vote is ever taken on a question: decisions are merely reached by "an expression of opinion."

Tony learned from a faithful Labour member of that Cabinet how the "expression of opinion" came about— how during the days of bitter argument that were to split the British Labour Party and drive it into the wilderness, a representative of the British Conservatives and a representative of the almost defunct Liberal Party sat in a middle room in Downing Street, waiting for the cut to be announced—how a representative of the Bank of England sat in another room, with his hand ready to pick up the transAtlantic telephone and call the United States.

Finally, "an expression of opinion" decided that the dole should be cut by ten per cent. Ramsay MacDonald arose and said he would take this decision into the next room to put it before the representatives of the two other British political parties: "Is that enough?" he was alleged to have asked.

"Wait a second," they were supposed to have replied. "We have to ask them."

They went into the final room and told the Bank of England man that the Cabinet had decided to cut the dole by ten per cent. "Is that enough?" they asked.

"Wait a minute," he replied. "We must ask them."

Tony then wrote the scene which will be debated by realistic historians for generations to come, of the fatal call on the trans-Atlantic telephone to Governor Harrisson of the New York Federal Reserve Bank:

"Is ten per cent. enough?"

London was asked to wait a minute—until the Governor consulted Washington.

* * *

This eye-witness account that Lynd cabled his Washington paper did not see the light of the news-stands. To Patrick Byron, who he found in a suicidal mood in the Café Royal that night, Tony expressed the philosophical way he had now taught himself to receive cuts in his cabled dispatches. Showing Pat the truncated dispatch as it appeared, he smiled:

"So, you see, some of me lived—but most of me died."

He then gave Patrick the final passionate disclosure made by the distressed loyal Labour minister: "Brother . . . when Ramsay went to the Palace that night to see the King . . . Arthur (Arthur Henderson) and I thought he was coming back to go out with us . . . to go out into the wilderness and reform the Labour Party to make another struggle to hold office . . . instead he came back leading this so-called National Government! Ramsay and Snowden have sold the pass. . . ."

Lynd made a hasty and unorthodox trip up to Lossie-mouth to see MacDonald at the "Hillocks," and forced that rhetorical Scot to admit that the ten per cent. cut in the dole only meant a saving of £12,500,000—a mere drop in the bucket in the astronomical figures of Britain's expenditures . . . that, as an authentic economy, it did not mean anything. Why, he asked with apparent carelessness, had MacDonald then agreed to this paltry cut which meant the virtual annihilation, for a time, of the British Labour Party in office?

"Because that expansion had to stop," said MacDonald testily.

"The social services, you mean?"

"Yes."

When Tony returned to London he gave this story to Patrick Byron to use in his Liberal newspaper. "Here's a sensation for you," he said; "right on the eve of the November elections!" But Patrick wouldn't use it. He shook his head.

"My paper's just a gang of damned, thrifty sentimental-ists, when it comes to the showdown. They'd never print that. The lousy bastards . . . they only talk Liberalism as a theoretical class-room subject. . . . You watch them run for cover when it begins to rain! Anyway, Liberalism is dead. I've decided to quit."

Booboo, it seemed, had done the unthinkable and suddenly gone off on a trip to South Africa on her own. Not, as before, to allow Patrick the free run of London to work through another infatuation with some new girl. To Patrick, this was the sign that his wife was leaving him for good, and all the world looked distasteful.

*   *   *

When, for weeks, Tony tried to get his paper to print his predictions that England was going to leave gold—only to receive a couple of admonishing cables from his new boss as a consequence—he gave the information he had been collecting to the luncheon table in Soho. He described a conversation he had just had with a prominent London stockbroker, who said:

"Tony, my lad, I don't know whether it will be of any use to you. But we just had orders to-day to sell large blocks of British securities . . . and the order came from someone who was in a position to know what England was going to do about the gold standard. I wouldn't tell you this . . . if it didn't make me furious to see an Englishman doing a thing like that. I'm buying dollars to protect my own position."

"When did he tell you that?" quickly asked the little Galician.

"Last night," said Tony, "at dinner. He was explaining why he would not take any time off for shooting this season. To my mind, if you knew this fellow, you would say that's a pretty significant sign. I've acted. I've sold my wife's War Loan, which is all our life savings, and bought dollars. I've also wired my paper that if they don't want to print it, they can at least place on record my own personal opinion that within a week England will be off gold."

The table looked solemn.

"A bit unpatriotic, isn't it," put forth the upright Henty. "You live in this country, you know. Why desert the sinking ship?"

Tony nodded. "I quite agree with you. When I spoke to my wife she wanted to let it ride . . . our few thousands, with the British pound. But look you, as the Welsh would say—what about this big chap who sold his British securities? . . . He stepped out. Didn't he? It is only the little fellows who will be left holding the bag. This is the first time in my entire career in journalism that I have used any advance information, or even a hunch, if you want to call this that, to make money. This time, I'm only saving it, as it happens.

G1

"There's a lot of personal anger in it, too," said Tony. "It infuriates me to hear Ramsay going on to make speech after speech about England being the guardian of the world's financial honour—when they know they're going off gold. You can't feel any altruistic patriotism . . . not when you know things like that."

This was at a Thursday luncheon. On Monday, Tony found his hand clenched by the little Galician. "Thank you, thank you," he almost sobbed. "My friends wouldn't take my advice . . . but I'd have been ruined if I hadn't done what you said."

"Oh, that." Tony felt embarrassed by this gratitude. He had been down himself in Throgmorton Street that morning, and had just written a lengthy dispatch about the admirable way the sturdy British had taken this momentous jump from gold. No panic, no wild rush to buy commodities, no lascivious eagerness apparent on the part of these average Englishmen to see how they could profit by it. In times of stress, he once again felt his amazing admiration for the way these people could face disaster. He apologised to the Galician.

"It's funny," he soliloquised. "We always speak of England in terms of its politicians. It's a Labour Government in power, or a Conservative gang . . . but, sitting up here in the West End, and hanging around Whitehall . . . we almost forget the stubborn, steady British business man. Politicians are charlatans and liars by trade. I guess they have to be. But I felt downright ashamed of myself to-day, when I stood in that crowd in Throgmorton Street and watched the conduct of those ordinary Englishmen who were left holding the bag. They are the real England."

* * *

During these months Flick was in Canada. Her father, with that astuteness that had enriched him enough to buy a British peerage (an honour that was all arranged now), had had no qualms about deserting the sinking ship. He began to unload his British securities the day he read the advanced proof of the May Report—that sinister document with which the artful Liberals and Conservatives hoped to break the Labour Government, but, instead, broke foreign confidence in the British pound sterling. The patriotic old financier was now over in Montreal protecting his Canadian investments from the world blizzard on that side of the Atlantic.

Flick had gone with him. Her Australian papers no longer wanted any personality notes about British high life these days; they saw enough prominent names in the casualty lists every morning of the financial crack-ups.

It was the first time that Felicity had been in Canada. Tony wondered, with an amused smile, how she would find the up-and-at-'em Canadians—especially, how the Canadians would find her. Flick's sense of humour, to say the least, was not Colonial. Still, there was a set out along Shelbourne Avenue, or whatever the name of the street was, that thought itself very English, and Felicity Correl would probably find some soul-mates among them. He hoped not.

He was too busy these days, watching and reporting how England rode the world slump, to have much time for his personal problems. In his conning tower of an office as a foreign newspaper correspondent he saw crisis followed so swiftly by catastrophe that the two terms soon became synonymous.

For some time he had been aware that his Washington paper had a distinct "policy" these days—and that the prominence given to his carefully produced cables had little connection with the importance he was reporting of the British events. The political group in Washington behind his paper were using English happenings as material for a lesson they were trying to impress upon the American public.

The May Report was a drastic recommendation of cuts

in all of England's essential services, the pay of the postman, the school-master, the soldier, the sailor—in fact every Englishman who worked for the Government, and could not hit back. With the Labour Party hurled into the outer darkness there was nobody left in Parliament strong enough to protect them. They were, therefore, but logical victims. Tony found that he had been selected as another one. Marjory handed him a cable as he came in one morning announcing that his salary had been cut by twenty per cent., and that London office expenditures and entertainment allowance must be held down to below £10 a month. The millionaire Washington newspaper proprietor also added, philanthropically, that Lynd would be expected, along with other members of the staff, to contribute to Washington's fund for poor relief.

"I am now," he told the bewildered Marjory, "more personally interested than ever in seeing that the United States adopts unemployment insurance."

He said to Christina that night: "Well, my sweet, this means that I will have to live a proper life in spite of myself. On ten pounds a month even I can't be dissolute. Any luncheons I give visiting firemen now will have to be out of my own pocket. And my salary now will be just about enough to keep this house above water."

As Tony had at that moment an expensive, but very useful luncheon planned for several foreign delegates who were in London on conference, he decided to go through with that entertainment anyway—and not at his own expense. Luncheon was at the Berkeley, where he ordered the most delicate food and rare wines that that distinguished restaurant could provide. Then, explaining his predicament, he asked each one of his guests to sign the cheque. In a happy mood over the cognac they all wrote their flourishing and distinguished signatures. Tony then paid the bill and sent the autographed cheque to Washington along with his expense account.

There was an awed silence from the cheese-paring accounting department.

*   *   *

Lynd wrote the Invergordon "mutiny" of the British Navy over the pay-cuts, when the crew of the battle-cruiser *Hood*, largest and proudest warship in the world, refused to obey orders and weigh anchor, but sat on her anchor cables instead, and sang the "Red Flag." It gave him a grim pleasure when the Tooting Bec school-teachers suspended all sports activities as their part of the 2,500 London school-teachers who had pledged themselves "to restrain from all extraneous activities," until the National Government replaced the so-called economy cuts it had just ruthlessly made in their meagre pay. It was a sardonic comment on a British Government's morals when the Navy and the school-teachers feel they have a just cause for strike. He went up to Seaham Harbour to hear Ramsay MacDonald play upon every instrument in the emotional orchestra to persuade that stricken community to return him to office. He witnessed Philip Snowden turn with scorpion-like vindictiveness and quote his infamous "three home truths," in his election speeches, of what had gone on in the ill-fated Labour Cabinet—and had the satisfaction of showing in his cables to America that the Iron Chancellor had told merely three half-truths.

Such inside knowledge could do but little more than confirm the already low opinion that Tony and his colleagues held of Europe's and even England's politicians. Then Tony went down and sat with the one good man he had met in world politics, George Lansbury, and sat with that honest Labour leader all during the fatal morning when the election returns were announcing that the British Labour Party had been almost annihilated in the November panic elections. As the telephone jingled in Lansbury's little home in Bow

Road, and it was announced that one impregnable Labour stronghold after another had been swept by the Conservatives, the so-called National Government Front, the white-haired old statesman's hand trembled as he lifted the mouthpiece. . . .

"It's an avalanche!" gasped Lansbury. "Brother . . . we are hurled into the outer darkness. . . ."

On that morning Lynd knew that MacDonald and Snowden might continue to call themselves Labour leaders, if it pleased them; but the working masses of Great Britain, and the world, would never trust them any more. They had sold the pass. And there before him sat the man who, by the sheer goodness of his character, would give dignity and power to the little rump of the Labour Party that remained in Parliament. It was a sad thought, for just simple goodness, he could easily foresee, was to count for very little in the sordid days to come.

It was the fate of honest men like George Lansbury that they should be ineffective against the opportunists, that made him loathe the politicians of this world.

*   *   *

That night, weary, Lynd was sunk in an armchair beside Christina before their fire, when Patrick Byron rushed in.

"I've done it!" he cried. "I've done it! I've found the straight road. . . . There is just one road ahead of me now!"

Shocked to see sophisticated Pat in such a state of sheer earnestness, Tony tried to joke: "Gone Bolshie?"

"Yes! That's precisely what I have done."

He had thrown up his £1,000 a year job with his so-called Liberal paper to get a maximum salary on the *Daily Worker* of £2 10*s*. a week.

It was characteristic of British hypocrisy, declared Pat, that when economies had to be made—the people who could not hit back should be the ones the Government would hit first: the poor, the unemployed, the army, navy, postmen, police.

"You're damn' right!" said Tony; but then, his sense of fairness aroused: "What about the income tax and the death duties? . . . ."

"*Bourgeois!*" sneered Pat, and then laughed: "The rich can stand those. The others can't. Can you answer that argument?"

Tony shook his head.

The so-called National Government's economy cuts in the essential services were immediately followed by wholesale wage reductions in all British industry. The Government had set a safe example.

* * *

"And now," said Lynd to Christina, "I'm through. We're going down to Somerset. I'm going to take a week. I'll take it whether the paper gives it to me or not. We're going to get into tweeds, you and I—we'll roam the moors. And I'll get some rough shooting, some cock pheasants— and perhaps a woodcock."

They set off the next morning, the rear of the old Lea-Francis full of bags, his gun, and a big fat duffle full of rough tweeds and heavy boots.

They climbed through the red and dying ferns, waded through rough gorse, watched a pack of staghounds hunt the red deer of Exmoor, walked home at night, exhausted and happy, through the grey and ghostly beech woods. Christina's eyes brightened, her fair hair took back its sheen; she looked ten years younger. But, after dinner, in his slippers around the fire, they had very little to say to each other. Lynd, making various excuses, usually sought the tap-room.

One sunset, sipping a pint of soft local beer, he listened to a London "gentleman" being odiously man-to-man with the local rabbit-trapper. The rabbit-trapper, ex-gunner in the R.F.A., had just driven him back from a rough shoot. "Well," said the sportsman, frightfully pleased by the way he could talk to a countryman (because a British yokel always knows a gentleman when he sees one, you know), "we'll just have the other half of this one—and then I'll toodle up to my bath."

"Thank'y, ser—don't mind if I do."

When the gentleman had gone, the local water bailiff put down his pipe: "Get anything, Jarge?"

"'E? Why the likes o' he couldn't hit a flock of barn doors coming over."

* * *

"That's one of the worst dangers for England these days," said Lynd, as he and Christina were eating a dinner of roast pheasant and a sweet with rich Devonshire cream. "Too many 'gentlemen'—in quotation marks. Complacent dumb-bells—who love to talk about 'democracy.'"

His exciting bag on that cold October day had been three cock pheasants, a blackcock—shot in the roots!—and a woodcock he got going down a long row of dying red beech just at sunset.

They took Zeppelin, their dachshund, with them, and she dug almost all the way through to China—as she always did on the occasion of such rambling walks. Then she said, *Woof!*—stamped her funny front feet, staring at them with her alert, intelligent brown eyes.

"Zeppelin knows more than most dogs," said Tony, as they watched her digging at lunch, "because her ears are so close to the ground!"

"Well, anyway," said Christina, "she expects to see something drop every time you shoot—so don't let her down!"

In Somerset, he and Chris had a few of the happiest days they had ever known together. Even she spoke about it, thanking him, much to his shame, for the days they had had.

"I begin to have hope," she said. "I don't want to have ever to feel not in love with you. But sometimes, lately, I've almost felt you wanted me to? It would kill me, I know— but do you want to be free?"

He was thankful that, for once, he did not have to lie to her when he affectionately patted her leg, and exclaimed: "Why, of course not! Good God, Chris! You and I are together for life. I'll never leave you."

This last, he knew, had always been true—even when he was suffering most. He would never leave Chris.

*   *   *

A few days after Luba's inexplicable scene with Christina and her mother, she had rung him up at the club. She had, according to the porter, been ringing him there every day for the past two weeks. He felt nothing against her for her incredible act of coming to make such a scene before Chris and Lady Mallard. Neither did he feel anything for her, one way or the other. Everything was dead now in that direction. But he felt his heart jerk when he saw her pale face at Zappi's where they had agreed to meet. She was telling the entire Zappi family about the latest Power disaster.

"Yes, we had the bailiffs in . . . going to dispossess us . . . father's very ill, you know. . . . I smuggled most of the *valuable* things out into the backyard and over the fence to the woman next door. . . . The bailiff never thought of that . . . wasn't that funny? . . ." Luba gave a bright little laugh. "But we had no beds to sleep on! Wasn't that simply *frightful*? . . . Daddy made an awful fuss. . . ."

"*Can* the bailiffs take beds?" said Tony.

She stopped long enough to put up her insolent little pug nose towards him, which he kissed obediently; and then she continued her recital to the sympathetic Zappi family. It made his blood go cold. What that girl could endure! And now she could talk to every outsider about it.

"Are you angry with me, Fofoiser?" she asked, when the Zappi *ménage* had left them and he could pin her mind down to what she would like to have for dinner. "I'm afraid I lost my head."

"I should say you did. I wish you weren't so damned communicative. You let me in for a hell of a mess. Not only that, but you've needlessly hurt Christina."

"But how, Fofoiser?"

He looked at her. "Really, Luba——" he began; then he turned to the menu. "Where are you living now?"

"Well, for a couple of nights we all lived here. Didn't we, Miss Zappi?" The Zappi girl, who was now a waitress, nodded. Lynd waited until she had taken the order and left, then he asked: "And now?"

"We have a flat off King's Road. I told Daddy I'd bring you around there to-night. He is very low and depressed."

* * *

In what had once been a semi-studio, the Powers were living in what, in that one room, looked like royal splendour. Every solitary trinket they had was either along the long mantelpiece or on the top of an ancient sideboard. Ronald was gone. But Mrs. Power now had a *salon*. This was supplied by a Russian baroness, with a wilted skin powdered the colour of pale violet and a tight mesh collar around her sagging neck, and an ancient English major, who said at intervals, "Really, by Jove! . . . You do surprise me, Roderick!" Roderick had become thin and colourless; only the lids of his eyes were red. He stared at Lynd and breathed heavily before he could get enough breath to say, "Hello." Mrs. Power had shrunk until her face was like those shrunken heads the South American Indians make. It seemed little larger than an orange. And from beneath her mane of greying hair she stared at Lynd as malevolently as ever.

Tony tried not to see any of this. But when he drove Luba out to the Ace of Spades for a late cup of coffee and a toasted cheese sandwich, a thing she adored, he said, "My dear, a few days ago I was ready to murder you. I was. But I do want to tell you one thing; you are a blasted little idiot— but I also think you are, without any reservation, the bravest person I have ever known!"

"Oh . . . Fofoiser! how nice. . . ." She was trembling. "But I can't keep it up, you know. Not always."

"I know," he said.

What was going to happen to her?

*   *   *

They made no attempt to return to their former status. Only once. One Saturday afternoon in late summer, when he met her, he was so dead beat that he could hardly talk to her. He left the car where it was and dragged her to the nearest pub. "For Christ's sake," he said, "just let's sit still for a minute. Don't talk." He spilt the whiskey as he lifted the glass.

"You look dreadful!" she said. "You're in a terrible state. What's the matter?"

"I don't know," he said. "I'm all shot to bits. . . . The Paris office has an extra man, so has Berlin, so has Rome— only London, in all this business, the centre of it all—I've just myself. And I've got that damn' cable to beat out before two o'clock every day. Then . . . I've been drinking too much. I take about three double whiskeys now every day after my cable goes. And I don't stop there!"

She gave her bird-like laugh. "Do you know what you're going to do? We are going across to Calais to-night. There's just time—if we act fast. Got some money?"

"No. But I can get some at my club. It's only a few streets off."

Luba nearly knocked him out with the pace she drove that ancient Lea-Francis for Dover. They just caught the last Calais boat. They stayed in the station hotel, their window overlooking the painted funnels and masts in the harbour. They opened their windows and looked at them as they were having *croissants* and honey and big bowls of French coffee for breakfast. They stayed there all day. "Oh, I'm so happy," she said.

Then a whistle blew. He happened to have his arm around her at the time. And she nearly jumped out of her skin.

"It's you," he said, "who need the help—not a big lump like me."

"I'm so tired, darling."

*   *   *

A week later, after he had left his office, Marjory came running after him down the street. A hospital, she said, had just telephoned and said that Miss Luba Power was there. Could Mr. Lynd come at once? Marjory handed him a slip of paper with the name and address written on it, and Tony jumped into a passing cab. At the end of a long ward, full of mute and twisted bodies under their white sheets, he saw some screens around a bed. Harrowed by the faces of pain that followed him, he almost ran to it. Luba lay with her heavy hair splashed across a pillow, her lips open and puffed, her dark eyes beseeching his. He leaned down and kissed her dry lips. "Fofoiser!" she whispered.

When she tried to smile he felt that he could bear it no longer. "Just a minute!" he pled, "I'm coming right back."

He was frantic. He located the doctor on duty and said:

"But she can't lie here . . . not when I can help her. Can't I move her?"

The doctor shook his head.

"Is it as bad as all that?"

"Yes—her heart. It is simply run down. It doesn't want to work any more. Do you know anything about her?"

Lynd saw the doctor eyeing him, and knew the thoughts that must be running through his mind; here is her man, he was thinking coldly—a man who did not take care of her. He was desperate with self-reproach. He summoned all his will, and said: "She simply must get well! I'll do anything you like, I . . . we can afford it. Just tell me what you want me to do."

"Just a second," said the doctor, "I'll go back with you." He went there, and Tony saw him looking down into Luba's eyes. What he saw there made him smile; he nodded to Tony to follow him. "It's all right," he said. "If she lies here for a week or two—perfectly quiet—and you can take some worry off her mind, I think we could move her in a few weeks. Then I must tell you, I think it's nothing but Switzerland. . . ." He tapped his chest. "It isn't only her heart. She is just at the end of her vitality. Give her all the strength you've got."

*   *   *

They were happy afternoons. One day when the Sister smiled and said: "I know all about you, Mr. Lynd," Tony knew that Luba was becoming her old self again—he could imagine her gossiping with the hospital staff. The screens had been removed, and always when he came into the ward, he saw her talking earnestly to the emaciated old woman in the bed next to hers. "We both share the flowers, Fofoiser!" Luba chirped happily.

It was an experience that filled him with the most punishing self-accusations. Which made him feel cheap and ashamed of his own easy life. Which, if things had not been the way they were, might have been the making of him. He had told Christina about these visits on the first Sunday, when he explained why he would have to leave the Mallards' at once after lunch. Chris had been upset, but had quickly agreed with his anxiety. She had even got several places, with their prices, in Switzerland.

But as Luba became stronger the idea of Switzerland was refused. She shook her head stubbornly. The day before she was ready to leave she said to him:

"Take me away, Fofoiser. Take me some place into the country, where we have been before. Spend the night with me, as we used to do."

They decided upon the same hotel overhanging the weir at Maidenhead, and he drove her down there that afternoon from the hospital in his car. They had tea at the far end of the lawn, under the cherry tree, Luba lying in a deck-chair. There she said:

"I've given up, Fofoiser. I'm going back. Yes . . . India. So you won't see me any more, Fofoiser."

He sat silent, staring at the river. "Perhaps it is just as well," he said finally.

"Oh . . . Fofoiser!" He could not meet her eyes, but he heard her saying: "I've always loved you. Always. I've lied to you so, Fofoiser . . . told you such fibs . . . just because I love you. That time when you came back from Berlin . . . and you ran into Bumby . . ."

"Yes?"

"Well . . . he was paying for that flat. Fofoiser—look at me. . . ."

"Yes, dear."

"Bumby wrote me by the next boat, the one after you and I came back, and asked me not to try and get a divorce. He said I couldn't, and there'd only be such a fuss that both he and Edward would have to resign their commissions. Edward wrote too . . . the most amazing letter, Fofoiser . . . and said that whenever I wanted to I could always come back. I had a letter from him only last week, and he still feels the same way. He's an amazing man!"

"He must be," said Tony slowly.

"I don't love him."

Tony knew that Luba was wanting him to look at her. She wanted him to give the answer to that last prompting sentence. But he shook his head.

"Is it Miss Correl?" she asked.

"It's everything, Luba. Flick . . . Christina. . . . It's no use. No use at all. It's—it's too late."

"I know. I've been lying to you even here, Fofoiser. Bumby didn't write—I did. I wrote to both of them from Nice. I knew on the boat that you and I would never, never get married. Up until then I had always been foolish enough to hope. . . ."

"You see," she said, her voice changing slightly—"I had always remembered you as you were. Silly, wasn't it? But when I remembered how fierce and determined you used to be, I always thought that, Oh! if I could ever find my Fofoiser again, he would put *everything* right! I thought you just could do anything! And then I found out."

"What?"

"Oh, that you didn't want to, Fofoiser. That's part."

"And the rest?"

"That Life doesn't want to—it doesn't want us to marry. And so we never shall. You tell Christina, Fofoiser."

"Oh, she knows that already. My dear, I don't know why Christina does stick to me, but she does—and as long as she does, I'll stick to Christina. Perhaps, after I get burnt out a bit more, I'll become a decent husband again?"

She laughed. "You'll always be a rogue, Fofoiser. That's why you're so nice. But I don't think you're happy."

They talked surprisingly easily from then on. With her patient soul, she bore him no grudge for his obvious relief that she was going back to her husband again, and that

India was such a long way off. Her chief concern was what her mother and father would do if Roderick lost his present job. And when the conversation took that turn Lynd discovered that her principal reason for lingering on in England was because she wanted to be with her parents. It was only with them, it seemed, that she could ever feel carefree and happy. But even so, she could not stand the strain of living with them now, the way they had become. She told Tony she felt like deserting, "to go off like this!" But here, he saw, Luba only wanted strengthening of her purpose from him. And he gave it to her.

"Tell me the truth," he said. "You aren't lying to me about your husband?"

"Why should I, Fofoiser? I—I told you about Bumby, didn't I? I don't know what to think of Edward. He really must be a remarkable man!"

Tony thought of India, of poor old Budgin blowing his brains out over a girl in the Delhi hotel. He looked at Luba lying there, so fresh and lovely now. Heavens . . . there was a lot of life for those two people yet! He thought of that ghastly, despairing ménage out at Hammersmith, full of Pomeranians; life was horrible, but——

"Get back to India just as quick as you can!" he said.

*   *   *

When Flick came back from Canada she found Tony in a reckless mood. "I see you have been drinking again," she said.

"Of course. And you've been having another affair."

"Well, what business is that of yours?" She stared at him.

"Damn you," he said.

"Look here—if we're going to go on at each other like this there is no use going out this evening, is there?"

"Not much."

They were sitting in a Strand pub. "I'm fed up with myself," said Tony. He told her the story of Luba's departure. "There's the story of what was once a perfectly decent love . . . and look at the end of it." His hand trembled as he squirted the soda into another glass. "My God . . . when I think of the muck that we make of our lives. Or is it just that life is built that way—that the rather harmless love such as Luba and I might have had just doesn't exist in this world? I know that I was an utter sweep not to go off with her . . . but she knew from the first that I wouldn't. I told her so. Yet . . . I took what I could get. The trouble with Luba was—she wasn't scheming enough—like you."

"Thank you," said Flick.

"Well, you know what I mean. You go into life as people went into battle, prepared to come back with your shield, or on it. You give no quarter. You don't expect any. The hell of it all is . . . that you do look upon life as if every man was your enemy. You are always on guard with him. You are on guard with me. You won't let yourself be yourself . . . for fear something might hit you. You're like a damned little lobster, with a shell on it . . . and I'd like to put you in a pot."

Flick laughed at this, a welcome note of gaiety in her usual hoarse rasp. He was quite prepared for the invariable "Of course!" she made.

"You *like* being called hard," he said. "You *love* being a cynic. You *adore* being told that if any man opens his heart to you he is playing with certain death."

"Of course!" gurgled Flick.

"Sure you do. All because you're sure in your own mind that you're really a soft, sentimental little woman. Well, you're not. You're a swine, Flick."

She was in ecstasy over this attack. So much so that he ceased to make it. Flick had gone around so long, with her sword in hand in this world, that he wasn't going to play up to that side of her character any more. There could be a certain tartness in these semi-playful recriminations with Flick that were as exhilarating as a rough towel, or a stiff drink of neat Navy rum, anything that makes you throw your head back.

But the thing he had really wanted to tell Flick as he waited for her to stride in through the door to-night was that he was bored with the over-use of his own emotions. He wanted to give them a rest. He wanted peace. He didn't even want the renewed nerve-strain that the continuation with Flick would mean. He was not tired with Flick. Far from it. He would like to keep on seeing her. Why not?

"That's just the point," he said, suddenly speaking aloud his moody soliloquy. "If you and I keep on seeing each other we are simply bound to have a succession of rows . . . not necessarily rows with each other . . . just rows that the situation will bring. And it's not worth it. See my point?"

"Well . . . if you feel that way," said Flick. "Well and good." She looked around the room, as if to see if there could possibly be anything interesting in the other people present, yawned, and said: "*Good* night."

He walked along to his club. This had been probably the most unsatisfactory quarrel they had ever had. There had been no meaning to it. As he walked slowly up St. James's he thought of how often he had let his impatience bungle this thing called love, the unbelievable amount of trouble he had willingly let himself in for to get it, the substitutes he had usually accepted for love itself. In the early days he had danced like a crazy Harlequin to the joy from the mere *newness* of his sensations. Just excitement. Then, a bit more critical, it had been the search for the exotic, the romance of its setting. Moscow, for instance, with its Asiatic horizon of the painted church domes against the green midnight sky; and New York, the adventure of coming out into its

silent, empty streets, when you could hear your own footsteps, and only the highest windows caught the morning
sun. The apparitions that moved about London after the
darkness had long been down, and the philosophy of the
midnight coffee stalls; the ecstatic security of his own cabin
on the P. & O. boat, when he had snapped the lock
behind him . . . and turned to take the triumph he had been
planning for fourteen years. Yes, but even as that victory
turned to ashes as he took it, he knew that he had been
shown a mockery—Luba was just a lovely frivolity.

That was why he had urged her to return to India. That
was why he had lied to Flick to-night. Flick meant peace.
But he could not have it with her, not with the tenderness
he still felt for Christina in his heart. There could be no
peace. Therefore the only thing to do was to steel himself
into renouncing Felicity, and win back to that comparative
rest of his emotions he had known during his ten years'
former faithfulness to Christina.

It had been a strange sensation, that conscious tran-
quillity. Looking back, he saw now that the mere physical
side had never been the major reef that had done so much
to wreck his and Christina's life. He had only imagined it
was. And imaginations in things like that, of course, were as
tangible and destructive as rocks. With a good half of his
mind always absorbed with vain regrets about Luba it was
a miracle that Christina had lived with him as long as she
had. That she had not quarrelled more about inconsequential things. That her straightforward spirit had managed to survive. But the harm had been done. He knew
now, in Christina's subdued manner, the lack of any
spontaneity in her laugh, that he had taken the edge off
her spirit. It was one of those things, he knew, that could
not be replaced. Christina had been marred.

That was the thing that he could not say to Flick to-night
—because he never discussed Christina with her—and that
was the situation that he must make the best of now. He

would miss the "rough-towel massage" of Felicity's sardonic companionship. He would miss the physical side. But what he gained by continuing with Felicity was not enough to justify his punishing faithful Christina any longer.

"My God!" he said to himself as he walked up his club's steps. "I must be getting what people call a healthy mind!"

But, immediately, the sight of the womanless men sitting in the Club bar threw him into a panic. There was no more terrifying sight in the world than these lonely men, trying to keep up a languid and lack-lustre conversation with each other as they sat in bored companionship over their wine in the almost empty dining-room. Or that of the Club habitués, leaning against the bar. He was terrified that he was already jettisoning most of his recent encouraging philosophy. With dismay he followed the others' hungry glances as they watched a clubmate come in and pick up six bottles of hock at the bar that he was taking on to an after-theatre supper. Good God, he hoped he would never have to feel the way they looked! He looked so solemn, himself, and lonely, drinking double whiskeys in the corner, that he was asked what he was thinking of. "What's on your mind, old boy?"

"Oh, nothing . . ." Tony smiled. "I was just thinking that it is only the rich who can be philosophic about the joys of poverty."

Leaving them to puzzle out this cryptic remark, he went down to the desk and tried to telephone Felicity. She was not at home. He tried two places where he thought she might have gone. He could not think of any other. What on earth, he wondered, is she doing with herself now? Damn it, if I hadn't been such a fool we would already be in bed together.

He went back upstairs, pulled his chair up to join the group, and finally accepted their hilarious invitation to make a night of it with a snooker party. He played sadly, angered by the fleshy interest his partner took in every shot.

*   *   *

At the coffee stall in Sloane Square he ate two saveloys, and listened to a man tell him that his father had worked for thirty-eight years in a mine—and then gone blind; his mother had died of cancer; and he had gone to Canada— where the Manitoba farmers made him eat porridge for breakfast.

"They *made* me eat it!" he whispered.

"Good God," said Tony. "'S'tragedy!"

"My sister took gas," said the man.

"Good night," said Tony. "You're breaking my heart!"

He walked over to the Embankment and made himself sick.

*   *   *

There was a chill in the dawn air, and when he softly let himself into the house, he saw that Christina had been sitting that night with her chair before the fire. The drawing-room was just as she had left it. The embers of the wood fire had died. But Christina's sewing lay on the arm of the deep chair and a novel she had been reading—she always read when she was doing anything with her hands—lay on the old Indian carpet. That was a bad omen. Chris always read herself to sleep. She must have been unhappy when she went to bed.

Upstairs, on their treasured worm-drilled bed-table, he saw a tube of Phanadorm tablets. Chris had taken these to put herself to sleep. He was always afraid she would take an overdose—perhaps on purpose. He must warn her again about that in the morning. He stood there, staring down at her face.

In sleep, Christina's high-cheeked little face had a stubborn look. And all the sadness he had put her through showed in her mouth—the corners of her lips were slightly drawn down. As if she were dreaming of some unhappy incident. Yes, he thought, she had plenty to dream of there. But—could he help it, could he help it . . . ? Wasn't it just too damned unlucky that life had trapped them like this? He wondered what Chris would have been like with another —a different man? Her eyes opened.

"It's you, Peter?" she said sleepily.

"Yes."

She was fighting to get back into the oblivion of sleep. "Listen, Chris," he said, "I want to talk to you." He sat down on the edge of the bed and reached for her hand. It humiliated him to see how quickly she sat up and removed the net from her hair. She wanted to look attractive.

"Don't sit on Zeppelin," she said. "She's somewhere in the bed." A stir from below Christina's feet at the sound of the word "Zeppelin" showed the dachshund's whereabouts. That was an added blow to Lynd's disordered mind.

"Yes," he told Chris, "I have got a disordered mind. I can't *think* straight these days. I'm so damned muddled up. You know I love you—and yet, look what I do to you."

"Were you with her again?"

"For a little while. Only at the beginning of the evening."

"Oh, Peter. . . ."

"I know. It's hell."

He patted her hand and stood up. There was nothing to say. There never was. As he was sitting on his bed, taking off his trousers, the phone on the bed-table rang. He grabbed it. He knew it would be Flick. And it was. She was very drunk. "You little! . . ." she said.

"Listen," he said. "You shut up. Can you hear me? Well, go to hell!" He jammed the receiver back on the hook. In a few minutes the phone rang again. This time he took off the receiver and let it stand. For a second or so both of them could hear Flick's rasping voice. Then there was silence.

"There is one thing, at least, that you could do," he heard Christina's cold voice saying: "You could prevent your mistress calling up before breakfast to have a drunken scene with you when I am still in bed."

"I know it," he moaned. "I'll stop that."

But what he was really thinking about was: Where did Flick get so drunk? Who was she with? Had she been sleeping with someone? Where?

*   *   *

The scene slid on.

Cracks in the world façade widened into crevasses. Public figures, one-time idols, toppled into them. Reporting the London end of European conferences, Lynd searched through the speeches of the statesmen and delegates, and knowing what was being kept hidden from the public— knew that all he was sending in expensive cables to the United States was just blah, blah, blah. . . . He got his head cracked the night the police charged the "hunger marchers" in Trafalgar Square. He and another correspondent were standing below the horse-statue of King Charles the Martyr. Behind them a jam of Bloomsbury intellectuals and Café Royal "Communists" were packed on the pedestal of Nelson's Column. "Get out of our way!" an infuriated police inspector yelled at them. "An' let us get at those bloody barstards!" When they charged, one of the foot police took a passing swipe at Lynd's head that knocked him over. It did not hurt; but he was stunned by the blow— and when the mounted police swept past he saw several tousled figures squirming on the asphalt. One man was dragged past him with the blood shining black in his matted hair. A man had been knocked by a police horse through the window of a raincoat shop by the tube entrance. He was still impaled there—stuck on a thick sliver of plate-glass. When Lynd forced his way to him he was moaning: "I was only looking! . . . Only looking! . . ."

A "gentleman" was pulled from his horse in Hyde Park!

"Now this *is* revolution!" exulted Patrick Byron.

Byron was seldom shaved these days. His clothes seemed never pressed. Lynd wondered whether Byron ever combed his hair. At any rate, Patrick was always shoving his long fingers through it. But he was wildly, deliriously happy!

"I'm doing something!" he said. "With my job on the paper I really am in the thick of it. Taking part, by Heaven! It's grand!"

*   *   *

"Wish I had even the fool faith that Patrick's got!" said Lynd, as Christina sopped some of the blood out of his hair the night of Trafalgar Square. "I'm having to send an awful bunch of tripe to the paper these days." He laughed: "But I'll put some heart into to-night's. This is one of the few events where I have not been altogether on the side-lines!"

He wrote an ironic description of the scene that night; how the real "hunger marchers" had been blockaded by the police from reaching Parliament to present their petition. Later, he sent a cable full of bitterness about the vicious sentences given to the hunger-march leaders—several of whom were not even on the scene that gory night.

He was surprised at the big play the American papers gave them. Perhaps, he thought, it is because misery loves company; and they wanted to show that things are just as bad over in England as they were in police riots at home. "But if we had had Chicago or New York police in Trafalgar

Square that night," he told Christina, "there'd been a lot of deaders instead of merely wounded men."

* * *

With the advent of Roosevelt several of the London correspondents lost their jobs. One of them, a man who loved England, and thought himself ensconced for ever in that gentle land, shot himself. Another vanished into the oblivion and, Lynd hoped, the peace of the English countryside. Another buried himself in a Spanish village on the Mediterranean coast and wrote a book about what he called his "episodic life." It was a bitter book, called, *To Reign in Hell*! Strangely enough, it made a hit and became a best-seller on both sides of the Atlantic. Although its author was very funny about it.

"Look at 'em!" he cried, shoving a pile of U.S. newspaper clippings under Lynd's nose. "Look what those Goddam Jew-boy New York book critics say about me—that I haven't *felt* anything! Jessus H. Christ! . . . After all *I've* been through! . . ."

* * *

1932, 1933 came and went, with their succession of futile international conferences leaving a trail like an earthquake behind them. At the 1932 World Economic Conference, Lynd, for the first time, met his other boss. The ex-Senator from Georgia stepped out of the train on to Victoria railway platform accompanied by an egg-headed college economist carrying an enormous golf-bag with about a hundred clubs in it. Things, from the very start, did not look too good. The Senator from Georgia was a neat, dapper little man (Lynd had been told he was quite an "element" in Washington's social life) with a tight, mean little face. He did nothing to belittle that first impression. He began to "pan" the conference before he even asked what it was all about—which,

HL

in this fiasco of all fiascos, was just the right line to adopt. Lynd had ordered him his suite of rooms at Claridge's; some of the London personages whom the British Ambassador in Washington had subtly given him a letter to (with, Lynd judged, warning letters and instructions sent on ahead) found the Senator from Georgia a genu-*ine* English Lord to play golf with! And Lynd forgot all about him. The Senator seldom came out to the Geological Museum where the conference was being held, and that kindly old gentleman, Secretary Cordell Hull, spoke to empty houses on the abolition of quotas, high tariffs, etc. (the wise British, on the eve of the conference, having hastily concluded trade treaties with Denmark and seven other countries—all of them including the very things the conference was in session to abolish)—yes, dear old Cordell Hull, looking as extinct as the map of dead volcanoes which hung outside the committee-room's wall. And Tony, with a hundred or so other bored correspondents, dutifully cabled their paper weeks of more official hypocrisy, subterfuge and just plain lies, and voted the Geological Museum bar the best non-restricted club in Europe.

"Well, it's been a great conference," said the Senator from Georgia, pump-handling Lynd's hand as Tony saw him off on the boat-train for Paris. "I just reckon this ought to show that maniac, Roosevelt, where he gets off!"

The Senator seemed genial enough. But, like the toneless flash of heat lightning in a calm summer sky, Lynd several times noticed what he took to be a flash of positive hatred in the Senator's eyes. He was a tricky politician, who prided himself on keeping a poker-face; so Lynd was not sure. "Nevertheless," he said to Christina, after he had driven back for luncheon when he had seen the Senator off, "I think he'd fire me . . . were it not for old Hancock. And I wonder where the hell he—*and* Sweetie—are these days?"

He looked out into the little paved back garden, shaded by overhanging summer leaves, and thought secretly what a blow it would be to Christina if they ever had to leave this little house. So much of it was just *her*!

* * *

But things were not static for Lynd. Quite the opposite. He had been drinking secretly lately. Some time back their little wine cellar under the foot of the stairs had always had a couple of bottles of whiskey in it. Now, he noticed, Chris had taken them out. Only the wine remained. She said she did it because of the servants; she didn't want either of the fresh young Norwegian girls to give it to their young men. But he knew the real reason. Christina had pled with him about it.

"You've got such a fine body, Peter, and such a future. Why let it all go down the drain?"

"I'm nervous," he said irritably. "Nervous as hell!"

He tried playing more tennis at his club. It was a wholesome environment. The people out there were as different from those he was flung with in his work as if they had come from another race. Many of them were the usual type of retired English Army or naval officer; some of the younger ones were stockbrokers, bankers, or in the Civil Service. The girls were pretty—but too healthy, Lynd thought. "Trouble with me," he thought one day, as he sipped a whiskey and soda in his white flannels on the cool veranda, "I'm just depraved." He wanted Flick's sneering, scarlet lips. . . .

* * *

The thing happened without warning. Flick was to meet him at an hotel off Leicester Square. When she was already a quarter of an hour late she telephoned him there saying she would be another fifteen minutes. Without thinking, he walked along to the hotel opposite to see if there was any ticker news. He found two other correspondents there and accepted their invitation to have a drink. Then he bought a round. Flick could now wait for him. It soon came to his turn to buy another round of drinks. When an English correspondent who he knew was an old friend of Flick's came in, Tony also bought him a drink. "I'm becoming a real sadist," he thought.

He saw the boy from the pub across the street come in and look around. The boy came over and said the police wanted him to move his car.

Lynd took his car from the side street and drove it around to a parking place. As he turned around the corner, he scraped a standing car. He parked his own car along the kerb and was on his way back to apologise and offer to pay the damages, when a helmeted policeman seized him.

"Did you 'it that there car?" he demanded.

"I did," said Lynd. "And I was just going back to it. Why?"

"I'm going to charge you, sir."

"What for?"

"For being under the h'influence of alcohol while in charge of a motor car."

"Go on—you're joking. Take your hand off my arm."

Lynd jerked his arm away from him and tried to walk on.

"'Ere, 'ere, sir—nonna that!"

"What the hell are you trying to do?" Lynd was angry now. He gave his arm another jerk to free it.

The next instant Lynd was seized. The officer who was holding him was beckoning to another policeman who appeared at the end of the street. They both seized him and began to frog-march him. Filled with fury at his own actions, the indignity of his position, he made a last frantic effort to fling the Bobbies off. "You idiots!" he hissed. "You damn' pair of fools! Lemme go. . . ." Now, he realised, he *was* getting drunk.

And just at that instant the fat figure of Freddy Wayson swung the corner, heading for his old drinking place.

"Hello, hello, hello, old boy!" cheerily piped Freddy. "Just come back from India to find you in this position. What is it, officer?"

"Drunk, sir . . . 'it that there motor car."

With a wit that never left him, Freddy laughed. "You're absolutely right, officer—take him up. But, I say—let's find a taxi. Can't walk him this way, you know—not all the way to whatever prison bars you're taking him to!"

"Well . . ." The policeman hesitated. But Freddy had already hailed a passing taxi. "Well," he grinned, when Lynd, he, and one of the officers sat down inside, "this is damn' bad luck. Do you have to take him up, officer?" He told the cab to stop.

The officer told the driver to go on. There was no use trying to argue about it, he said. This here gentleman was going up before a magistrate. "Tried to 'it me, 'e did."

"Now that's a bloody lie!" said Lynd.

"Shut up," said Freddy, giving Tony's hand a hard clutch.

"Well, it is a damn' lie! You get up there and say that, officer, and I'll call you a bloody liar right before the whole court. Wish to God I had hit you—you big stiff."

In the charge-room the sergeant on the desk perfunctorily asked Lynd did he want his own doctor. Lynd, still fuming under what he felt was a monstrous injustice, said they could bring any doctor they liked. He glared at the officer who had arrested him. When the police-station doctor finally came he flashed a light in Lynd's eyes, asked him to walk a straight line—seemed to hesitate—and then nodded.

"You're a Canadian, aren't you?" he asked Lynd.

"No. American. Now I suppose that means you will try and give me the limit. Yes?"

"No, sir—we don't do things like that. Not in England."

"Oh—don't you!" said Lynd.

* * *

His watch, money, and other trinkets were taken away from him and he was led into a stone corridor stinking of disinfectant, where a smudged green door was opened, and he found himself in a cell. Later he learned that it was the same one occupied for a time by a famous poisoner. Freddy Wayson told him that. And he took one evening before a crowd at the Café Royal to do it. There was a long, bare plank bench stretching the length of this human coop with hole at the far end to be used with a lavatory bucket. Grinning grimly, Lynd lay down with his feet towards the lavatory end. Then he reached for his cigarettes. When he found that a treasured old Russian copper cigarette case had also been taken away from him, he set up a row. Through the aperture in the heavy board door he sent along a few shouts. After a time a policeman came along outside and asked him what he wanted. "You can't have them," he said when Lynd asked for his case back.

"Even steal those from me!" jeered Lynd. "You're a hell of a fine lot, you are—you London policemen. 'Oh, don't you think our policemen are splendid?'" he mimicked.

The police officer grinned at him. "I will see what I can do, sir." He came back with the cigarettes.

* * *

It had taken fat Freddy some time to locate Christina. When he did locate her by telephone in the country, Tony's wife was all for rushing up to Town at once. "But it wouldn't do any good, I told her," said Freddy through the door peep-hole. "We don't want her to see you in here, do we?"

"Should say not," said Lynd.

"I can bail you out," said Freddy. "I'm broke myself. But if you'll sign a chit I'll go over and get it cashed at your club."

"What's the use—all you have to do is fill out a form

anyway," said Lynd. "Might as well spend the night here. And thanks, Freddy—get me a couple of packets of Gold Flakes sent in. I'll probably not sleep well to-night. This isn't a comfortable spot."

"Toodaloo," chirped Freddy. "I'll just bugger off down to Fleet Street now. . . . See that this damn' thing doesn't get into the papers: American Correspondent in police cell—Ha-cha!"

*   *   *

Christina's face met him as he was led into the courtroom the next morning. It said, "All right," and her smile was loyal—if wan. She had, as it happened, raced home that night; but the police told her he had refused bail and was already sound asleep. Which was true; he had slept until wakened in the morning. So she had had to go through all of that night with her thoughts. Christina, with her upbringing—in spite of her association with him— could not take things like this lightly. Try as hard as she loyally would.

He had to sit in a row with the other "offenders" and see two minor criminals given a few days for an attempted theft of articles from a parked motor car. A flashy young Italian with wing-shaped shoulders was given twenty-one days for pimping in Soho. Two girls were turned over to the Matron on some charge that Lynd didn't listen to. And then the sight of the officer, the original one who had laid hands on him, sent him into a tremble of rage again. He had to stand in the dock while the officer read from his note-book. Lynd waited, hoping he would not shout out, if the officer attempted to say Lynd had hit him; but all the officer said in his high sing-song voice was "he resisted arrest."

Lynd admired the Magistrate's sense of justice when he made the officer admit that he had placed his hands on Lynd before Tony made any fuss. The officer also had to admit that he had found Lynd's car, parked precisely and in a narrow space. "That shows," said the Magistrate, "that he was not incapable of driving a car?" The officer had to agree with that. Then Lynd took the stand, and, still trembling, stated his case. It all seemed to be going very well; the Magistrate made an occasional note. Then he nodded and Lynd stepped down.

"I shall fine you £30 and suspend your driving licence for one year," said the Magistrate, calmly placing his finger tips together.

"Wha——" Lynd bit down on his lip.

*   *   *

"Perfectly outrageous!" burst out Christina as soon as he joined her outside the court. She said it before a body of waiting policemen, while Lynd was writing out a cheque to pay for his fine. "You—you dare to call this British justice! What about that Guards officer who kicked one of you in the wrist the other night and said, 'Take your hands off me, you swine! Can't you see I'm a member of the ruling class!' . . . You only fined him ten shillings! *British* police!"

"Well, madam, I——"

"I don't want to hear any more from you. Where is my husband's car?"

As they had left the light on all night—although the car was in the police-yard—the battery had run down. And one of the policemen, smitten by Christina's attack, insisted upon cranking it for them. Christina thanked him, a bit mollified. Then she took the wheel.

"Funny . . ." mused Tony as they were going out to Chelsea; "to think that I don't dare touch that driving wheel!"

"Well, you never did like my driving," said Christina. "Now you've got to."

*   *   *

The Mallard family were very sympathetic and clannish about it. Christina had not said a word of reproach to Tony. She was too furious with the police. But, at their regular Sunday lunch with the Mallards, something that the General had probably said to her aside, made her explode at the table. She repeated again the incident of the ten-shilling fine against the Guards officer who had kicked a policeman on the wrist. "They did it," insisted Christina, "just because Tony is an American. I know it. I could see it in that Magistrate's complacent, mincing face."

"Oh, I say!" protested the General. "I wouldn't say that. That's not British, you know."

"British be damned!" said Christina.

"Now, Chris . . ." said her mother, looking pained.

Magistrate! Lynd needed no explanation to see how that name shocked the Mallards. They were horrified. But they were with him—all of them. Even Christina's uncle came around after lunch to show how he felt. "Sorry, old chap—they certainly do come on you these days. Motoring offences. Have to use Chris as a chauffeur—what?"

* * *

For a week Tony was so disgusted with himself that he even refused to see Flick. He was fed up with everything. During this time Lady Mallard got hold of him. She coughed:

"Tony," she said, "don't you think that you really ought to try a cure?"

"I do," said Tony.

"I don't like to interfere," said Lady Mallard, "but you don't know how distressed Christina is about all this. She hasn't *said* anything—not one thing. But I know that little face, and when I see it like it is now I—I simply can't stand it. Christina is a one-man dog, you know—and her whole life is centred around you. Won't you pull up?"

H1

Here, again, was this reserved decency of the Mallards. "For a mother-in-law," smiled Tony, taking her hand, "I must say you are a wonder. Why didn't you preach at me? Why be so decent? I know I'm a sweep. . . ."

"I don't think so—not yet. I've been talking to Dr. Sundersen—the Swedes are very realistic about such things, you know—and he said that with a man like you, so full of life and—and lustiness, as he put it—that it is terribly hard not to have the excitement you get from alcohol. And then —you began so late, you know. Drinking, I mean. Why, when you married Chris—why, up until *the two last years*!— we none of us ever gave a thought about it. I know that sometimes you got a bit too much . . . but then we all have done that."

Lady Mallard was progressing towards some definite suggestion. Tony could see that. "Now just what is it," he said, anticipating things, "that you want me to do?"

"Dr. Harbrace!" said Lady Mallard.

"Who's he?"

"Well . . . it's pretty awful. But he stopped Charley Portley."

Charles Portley, now Lord Swivvle, had been the outstanding scandal of the Mallard set. It was estimated, people said fairly, that he drank £50 worth of wine and whiskey every week. He was now a teetotaller—but seemed to have lost all interest in life.

"Not a good example," said Lynd. "He acts as if he had all the life taken out of him."

Lady Mallard stiffened. "Well, *something* must be done."

"All right," said Lynd, angry now. "I'll do it. Bring on your Dr. Firebrace."

* * *

As it turned out, the doctor's name was Laybrush (Lady Mallard could never get a name right, and always forwarded his mail to unknown addresses); but she had already been to Dr. Laybrush, who knew all about Lynd when he and Christina drove there the next evening. "So you're the culprit?" he said cheerily.

Lynd did not like this opening and stared at him coldly. "If you put it that way," he said. It was humiliating, this experience; but, he said to himself, it must be worse for Chris. They both sat down and stared at the mousy, unkempt little man before them. He might be a genius. . . . His hair, and his study, and his whole house certainly looked untidy enough; a man who lived for science. Certainly, he had no bedroom manner.

"Well, if you want to take it," sniggered Laybrush.

"What is it?" asked Lynd.

Laybrush explained that experimenting over twenty years with a drug that made people vomit, he had discovered that by a succession of over-doses he could make people stop drinking. One of his patients, a woman whom he had dragged back from death after an almost successful gas-oven suicide, had offered her unwanted body to the experiment. This was to see how much he could increase the dose without killing people. He now knew its limits. And—Lord Swivvle was one result.

"But he's so *dead*," said Lynd. "I don't want something that's going to leave me a walking corpse afterwards."

"Indeed not!" said Christina. "Don't you take it, Peter—if you feel that is what it is going to do."

Laybrush sniggered. "Lord Swiffle," he said, blurring his v's like a German, "was always dead. It was a shame to stop him drinking. I would undo it if I could. But—with him—it seems to have worked marvels!"

This was more like it. Lynd looked at Dr. Laybrush with interest—even hope. "And with me?" he asked.

"You'll think you're going to die. No—don't smile," said Dr. Laybrush, suddenly very serious: "You *will* think you are dying. And you will be very near it. That's why you will see—if you are willing to undergo this cure—that you will never be left alone for an instant. A nurse will always be with you."

Lynd felt a little clutch grasp his stomach. This did sound drastic. Also, it sounded as if there might be something to it. If it was as bad as all that. . . . "All right, I'll take it," he said.

* * *

The next afternoon, a very sunny and bright one, Lynd was admitted by one of those chalky, flat-breasted women who always seem to become matrons of London nursing homes, into a dark and dismal former private house in Knollington Place. He was standing there in his top-floor room, gazing out at a skyline of nothing but chimney-pots when Dr. Laybrush tripped into the room.

"I suppose I'd better get undressed and get into bed?" said Lynd.

"Yes. You'll be there several days. Nurse will put away your clothes for you. You'll have nothing to eat or drink, you know—except straight whiskey—and you won't hold *that* down very long. Not much. It is very unpleasant. But you can smoke, you know. All you want to. I stuck this into a feller's behind once, you know—and he hopped straight out of bed and went to Paris. He had been posing as a Buddha, naked, before his wife. You won't do that, will you?"

"Which? What?" asked Lynd.

"Why, go to Paris."

"No, I shan't go to Paris. Where do you want me to take it—arm—or behind?"

"Arm will do. *There*. Now I'll sit here for a minute—I've given you the limit. You begin to heat up in a minute. I don't want a corner. . . ."

Lynd lay back and felt nothing at first. Then it seemed as if someone had turned on an electric light bulb inside him.

He began to burn. "It's here," he said, gazing inquisitively at Dr. Laybrush. Dr. Laybrush had jumped up and now put a half glass of neat whiskey in his hand: "Drink it," he ordered.

Lynd did.

In a few seconds he felt gripes reaching up to him from the soles of his very feet. The pains bent him forward like a hoop. Furies were tearing at his intestines. He seized the big kidney-basin which stood ready on the table beside him. Writhe, writhe, writhe . . . he could not squirm away from these fingers tearing away inside him. He could not empty himself. . . . Finally, he fell back exhausted. Though still burning.

Dr. Laybrush, who had been watching him—almost too closely, Lynd thought—sighed and took his pulse.

"Splendid," he said, as if vastly relieved. "Now I'll leave you. You're a big man—and I did give you the limit. The rest will be slightly smaller—but you will feel much worse . . . Oh, much worse. You must be prepared for that. You have three or four days of sheer hell ahead of you. There's the whiskey—drink as much as you can of it."

"Thanks, I will," grinned Lynd. He reached for the bottle and poured himself out another half glass. Maybe, he thought secretly, it will kill this pain. But Dr. Laybrush already knew what Lynd was hoping. "No," he said, "you will not get drunk—and that is just the hell of it. Here's Sister—Mr. Lynd, Sister—*Good*-bye."

Lynd was sick again.

*   *   *

"Ah," said the little Irish nurse sitting on his bed. "What a waste of the grand stuff!"

"Have some yourself," said Lynd.

"Not me!"

"Go on, it will do you good."

"The same way it's doin' you, I suppose?"

Lynd smiled weakly. This was the third night. He did not know how long he could hold out on this. How long before something would snap inside him. It had been a vortex of horror. But he had got on top of it. That bitter sullenness that had stood him in good stead once or twice before was with him now. As nobody except one of the two nurses could see him he was not forced to face any weakening sympathy. He was alone. The Irish girl was pretty; he wondered what she would be like in bed. Why not, he thought. Then he said:

"Come on, Sister—you've forgotten; it's time you gave me another shot in the arm." He had these all day and all night at regular three-hour intervals; and he knew that for the next hour he would be writhing like a snake with a broken back.

They watched the dawn come. Sister had become sentimental. "When I tuk up nursin'," she said, "I said to myself, 'Now, you are going to be a noble woman—a noble woman, mind you.' But the ithers—they just laughed. 'You wait,' they said; 'you wait—in a couple of months you'll be just as hard as the rest of us!' Noble woman . . . be damned. . . ."

He had no memory whatever of the next day—just a blur of vomits, whiskey, vomits, whiskey . . . and a feeling of sinking. . . .

On the fourth morning he woke up to find the two nurses, the Matron and Dr. Laybrush standing beside his bed. Laybrush was saying angrily: "Well, you should have called me before. It's all right in this case, but . . ."

Lynd lay with his face pressed so that his nose was down between the bed-clothes and the wall. He could not rise up. "Hello," he croaked—to attract their attention.

The Irish nurse put her arm around him and deftly pulled him so that he lay face-upwards on his pillows.

"It's all over," said the Doctor. "Now you are going to have a cup of strong tea."

"Graaand," Lynd said slowly, then tried to sit up. He had beaten it!—He hadn't cracked. And now tea! He did not know that this first moisture that was to enter his system—and was meant to stay there and soak into him—was the worst torture of the whole villainous ordeal. He spouted tea like a fire-hydrant. Then he collapsed.

* * *

It was around noon when the room began to take shape again. Dr. Laybrush was speaking to him. "Lie still," he said. "Sleep. Sleep. You must lie quiet for several days."

That night the Irish Sister said: "Well, you were a bloody little hero. You took it foine! Now, seein' that you didn't finish that bottle—and you're never, never again going to touch the stuff in your grand life . . . I will have a nip."

"Noble woman!" smiled Lynd.

He patted her leg, but she jumped up. "Look at 'im!" she said. "One foot in the grave—and him trying to seduche me already. I'll be leavin' here, Mr. Lynd, before you get well!"

When he did get out, Dr. Laybrush's parting injunction was: "For two weeks you'll be as weak as a rag. Don't try to do anything."

* * *

Late that autumn he and Christina went down to the old rough shoot in Somerset again. They tramped the hills, and wore their way through the dying red ferns, and sat on the open slopes and watched the blue shadows of the far hills darken at sunset. Zeppelin thought herself quite a shooting dog now and whined and tugged whenever Lynd went forward to pick up a bird.

It was a hunting hotel, with several vast bath-tubs on every floor; and they both revelled in the warm soak at nights before they got into old clothes and went down to dinner. For a few days everything ran smoothly between them—then the tension set in again.

It began with a call from Flick on the telephone. Chris heard him speaking. That night when they went up to their room she said: "What do you want me to do, Peter? Things can't go on this way."

"What way?"

"You know what I mean—*her*."

"I don't know." He felt helpless and shrugged his shoulders. "What do you want me to do—become a monk or something? I *am* made of flesh. And look here, Chris, I give nothing to Flick that I take from you. Do I?"

"How could you?" she gasped.

"Well—let's just be truthful about it. I don't sleep with you. You know you don't like it—although you'll say you do now . . . just to please me . . . but that's *awful* . . . to do it like that. So what do you want *me* to do?"

"Anybody," said Christina desperately. "Anybody else but her. Oh, if only Luba was here!"

Tony paused. Often, lately, he had been wishing that himself. There was something feverish about Felicity, an eroticism that never left her in peace. It drove her on and on. It had affected him that way too. He was never restful now. Always racing up and down a jagged skyline of emotions . . . a giddy happiness, when he was with her . . . the first few minutes, anyway . . . then either anger or gloom. And lately she had taken quite a new line of country. At first she had purposely boasted of how free she was with men. Would he ever forget it, that sentence? "When I feel that I can talk to a man better in bed—I get into bed with him."

Now she was trying to retract all that she had said. She had, she insisted, said such things because he made her angry when he tried to criticise her. Now—she would rub all of that out. Now—she wanted him to leave Christina. He shook his head.

"Chris," he said, sitting on her bed. "We ought to have an understanding, you and I. There is more than a façade in you and I sticking together. You've been the best woman I've ever met in my life. Now, now," he smiled; "don't get angry and say you don't want to be called a 'good' woman . . . but you *are* good. That is just the very point. And I—at least something in me—well, I am held by that goodness. Don't belittle it. You've often said you wish you could behave like a tart—I often wish you could—but that's not you. So . . . let's keep trying the way we are . . . maybe I'll see the light and pull around."

"Peter . . . would you mind if I slept with someone?"

"I guess so," he said. He wished she would. It would make things so much easier. But did he wish that?

"Well, listen, Peter—I think it is better if we live apart. For a time, you know. The Ackworths have asked me to go out to Egypt with them. He's stationed there this winter. I think I'll go. I have no spunk just now."

He put his arm around her. That sturdy, gallant little back. But he breathed more freely now. The strain would be lifted.

* * *

"Well, I wouldn't stand it not for five minutes," said Patrick Byron. "Not five minutes."

"You mean you would coldly leave a woman who had been faithful to you all these years? Don't be idiotic."

"Well, I've left mine."

"You mean she's left *you*."

"Well, don't go jawing that in my face. I don't like you."

"Go to the devil—with your lousy ideas."

* * *

"Listen, old boy, you've been hitting it up lately. No cure can beat you."

"I know it, Freddy. The whole damn' thing was based on merely scare-psychology—half kill you and then think you'll be afraid to drink."

"Well, I would—the way you are."

"Why, how can you say that? I haven't been tight since Christina went away."

"No. But you haven't ever been strictly sober, either. And that's the worst kind, old chap. I've seen one or two of the lads go that way . . . just sort of slide out. . . ."

"Yes, you're right."

"And then your nerves, old boy, your *nerves*—you're like a bundle of worms these days. Christ, it makes me nervous just sitting here with you."

"Well, then, get up. To hell with the whole thing."

*   *   *

"Mr. Lynd," said Marjory, "here's a cable for you. I don't think you will like it."

Lynd read:

"YOUR CABLE TO-DAY ABSOLUTE NONSENSE STOP RELIABLY INFORMED CIRCLES CLOSEST WHITEHOUSE MY PRIVATE CABLE YOU ACCURATE STATEMENT TRUE SITUATION STOP GET BUSY AND SHOOT US THE REAL DOPE"

It was signed by the Georgia Senator. "Not nice, is it?" said Marjory, looking at him anxiously.

"Nice! The little twerp. God! What is he trying to do—turn this office into a propaganda bureau?"

Lynd sat down and called up a man he knew in the City. "Fine," he said. "Swell. Yes—that is *just* what I sent! But this information is supposed to come from close to the President. Doesn't matter? It's only what the Americans

would *like* to have happen—eh? Well, that's been my story
—and now I sticks to it. . . .

"Marjory," he said, sitting down at his typewriter. "I'm
sending a cable 'urgent,' and it's probably going to get me
fired. Senator Twerp, I think, is bucketing in foreign
exchange—or else he's just a damn' fool. Probably both."

Whistling slightly, he began to tap the keys.

"Why this is the same thing that you sent this morning!"
exclaimed Marjory as she read the long "urgent" cable.
"Three times the ordinary rate!"

"I know it," said Lynd. "Only this one's a hell of a lot
stronger, isn't it?"

"I'll say it is!" breathed Marjory apprehensively, proud
of her American slang. "Coo! Mr. Lynd, you are a one!
Do you think they really will let you go?"

"Ha-ha. . . . *Let* me go? Marjory, unless Senator Abner P.
Hancock sticks by me I am already out on my ear."

"Mr. *Lynd*—that's just what I wanted to tell you. Senator
Hancock is in *Paris*! He telephoned just after you went out
for lunch."

Lynd jumped. "Well, buzz off that wire—and then you
sit firm in your seat, Marjory—and watch the fireworks go
off. That cable is the straight dope. But it might be my
last."

* * *

"Paris wants you."

Lynd held the telephone by his bed. "Yes, yes—hullo,
Senator."

"Tony, issat you?"

"Yes—go ahead."

"Well, I just got cable fr'm Anson an' he's sore as hell
at you. . . ."

"I know, I know—go on. . . ."

There was a pause and then Lynd heard Miss Salome
Svenson speaking: "Good evening, Mr. Lynd. Percival"—

so that was what the P. was for!—"wants me to read you a wire he has just got from Washington. Shall I begin?"

"Go ahead. . . ." Lynd reached for a pencil and his pad, but a few words after Miss Salome Svenson started to read the cable told him that he had no need to bother; he had no need to bother ever any more about what the Senator from Georgia sent to Senator Hancock.

"Thank you," said Lynd to Miss Svenson, "that's all plain enough—although it took him a couple of hundred words to say it—I'm fired."

"Just a minute, Mr. Lynd. Percival has been listening on the other ear-piece. He wants to say something to you."

"You're fired hell!" yelled Senator Abner P. Hancock from Paris. "You just sit where you are and leave this to Papa. I like you, Tony—you're the only one in the whole Goddam outfit that hasn't tried to kiss my tail. It's been covered with blisters. Good night!"

*   *   *

Two days later Senator Hancock strutted into Lynd's office like a fighting cock. "Got in last night," he said. "But I had to eat a meal with some friends at Simpson's. Business. Say, Tony, you're not only childish—you're worse than childish—to get excited by that wire."

"I wasn't excited," said Lynd. "Didn't have time enough. But it said plain as day that I am fired."

"You? Hell! Listen, Tony, I know what he's doing— he thinks he sees a flutter in a stabilisation between the dollar and the pound—yeah? Thought so. Well—I happen to be bucking it just the other way. Get me? You stick straight to the dope—that's all I want. One of the flimsies I got of your cables in Paris saved me from busting my neck. Anson's gonna bust his—an' let him. Say, Tony—don't let him bother you—I can make him cry."

It was cheerful news and Lynd asked about the health of Miss Salome Svenson. "Never better," said the Senator. He suggested that he and Tony go back to his rooms in the hotel and have a drink. Miss Svenson was out shopping with some friends.

"S'pose you wonder why I'm always skippin' off over here to Yurrup? Yeah? Well, Tony, it's like this—it's no use sitting on my fanny in the Senate—Roosevelt's got all of 'em with their ears batted down flat. I've got all the money I want—but I can't live easy, like I want to, with Miss Svenson . . . not in the States. Understand? Folks are so Goddam narrow-minded there. Don't know whether I've ever told you I've got a wife? No? Well, perhaps the less said about her the better—yes, the less said about that fat bitch the better for everybody. . . . Anybody . . . What was I saying, Tony?"

"Oh, I don't know. You were just talking about things. Life, in general, I suppose."

"That's it—Life! Tony—I want to live! Live! Understand? Sixty years old and worked every Goddam year of it—even when I had the millions pourin' in. I never lived. Well, Miss Svenson has taught me how to live. Now if you say she loves me for myself alone—I'll fire you for it. That is what I used to say myself. But I know better now.

"But I'll tell you what we are, Tony—we're friends now. Real friends. Let me tell you what she did. Bought her a diamond necklace in Paris—paid twenty-five thousand dollars for it. . . . That makes you gasp, doesn't it? Well, I did. And what did Miss Svenson do? She took it back. She wouldn't have it! I spent two whole days and nights trying to make her accept that gift. Nope! Wouldn't have it! Now what do you think?"

Lynd hated to say; Miss Salome Svenson was cleverer and playing for bigger game than he thought. But he couldn't say that. He just nodded.

A queer smile came over the Senator's face—a sort of leer at all life. "I know damn' well what you're thinking," he said; "she's playing for the big shot. And *now* I'll tell you something. She doesn't have to play for the big shot. She's already got it. I'm making over to her while I am in London now enough sound stocks and investments to leave her without a worry for the rest of her life—and I hope it will be a long and happy one. I told her that in Paris when I was fightin' like hell to make her keep that diamond necklace— and *still* she wouldn't have it. She said there was something wrong—it would cut in on our happiness. And she would never feel comfortable in it. Now what do you think?"

"Well, it's by me," said Tony. "She must like you."

"Well, there's nothing so Goddam extraordinary about *that*, is there?" burst the Senator, heated for a moment; then he gave a fat chuckle. "Old man's love, Tony. May and December—that's what that fat bitch, my wife's, always trying to jab into me. Sugar-daddy. . . . Go on. . . ."

Lynd felt ashamed. He laughed. "Well, you *have* got a certain amount of charm," he said honestly. "I feel it myself."

"Atta boy! Atta boy! You wait till you and I get off in the *Ultimate Objective*—then we'll show 'em what life is like. I've a hankering for warm weather . . . and palms. Looka here," he said, holding up a little piece of painted wood he unlocked carefully from his small bag. "That's a Le-o-nar-do de Vinkey. . . . That cost twelve thousand dollars."

In a few minutes the Senator's charm had passed. The bottle of Courvoisier '65 was sinking low. "If Miss Svenson don't come in soon," said the Senator, "then you and me'll go off to that other place—where we had the lobsters that night. 'Member—Grand Duke Dmitri . . . Haw-haw-haw! . . ." He was still slapping his leg when Miss Svenson came in. She wore a fortune in furs, and the crisp wind had reddened her healthy cheeks. She had only a minute, she said, as some friends were waiting for her downstairs. "I thought it would be chummy if you and Percival had this first lunch together." The Senator pinched her cheek: "All right, Baby. Okay by me."

"You go into that bathroom for a moment," Miss Svenson ordered the Senator. "I want to ask Mr. Lynd's advice about something."

"Maybe it's a present?" said the Senator.

"Perhaps," said Sweetie.

When the Senator had gone and loudly slammed the door, Miss Svenson nodded for Lynd to follow her out into the hall.

"Don't let Percival drink to-day," she whispered urgently. "I'll tell you why later—but don't let him drink!"

"I can't *put* him on the wagon."

"No—but hold him down. It's very important!"

* * *

"That place we went to," said Lynd—not wishing to face that head waiter again—"that's not what it was. Come along to my club."

"Okay," said the Senator as he crawled into Lynd's car. "You can't frighten me!"

"I've got a lot of work to do this afternoon," said Lynd, testing him, "so I'm going to drink nothing but beer. We have some good country brew there. Like that?"

"W-e-ll," said Senator Hancock, "if I can have a good dry Martini first. Come to think of it, Tony—I've got a job on hand too. A big one. Drive on, Cæsar."

When Lynd dropped him back at the hotel, the Senator slapped his back. "We're going to live, Tony—live! Remember what I told you—right before all that gang at the Club—get that schooner, I'll give you the money while I'm here—and we'll call her the *Ultimate Objective*. Sixty years —and now I start to live."

Tony leaned out of the car to shake hands with him. "Well, Senator, if I'm as full of beans as you are at sixty years I'll think myself lucky. See you to-morrow." He drove off in the Strand traffic.

* * *

It was about six o'clock when the bedside phone rang the next morning. When Tony took off the receiver he thought there was something wrong with it; it was making screaming sounds. Then the words came through: *"He's dead! He's dead! He's dead! . . ."*

* * *

At the hotel Lynd found the Swiss manager already dressed in his neat morning suit and waiting for him. "My God! What happened to him?" said Lynd. The manager put up a pair of soft white hands.

"It is very embarrassing."

"Yes—but what? What happened to him? Was he run over, or what? When did he die?"

"It was a letter, I think," said the manager. "He seemed very upset." The manager was in such a state of jitters that there was nothing to be gained by talking to him. Lynd jumped in the elevator and went up.

"Dead . . . dead . . . *dead!* . . ." Miss Svenson, lying on the bed with her nightdress torn open, could do nothing but moan. Looking for the Senator, Tony found him dead on the bathroom floor. His legs were cocked, one over the other, like a Russian ballet dancer's in mid-air, and he wore an idiotic expression of contentment on his face. Lynd closed the door, came back and sat down on the edge of Miss Svenson's bed. She clutched his hand. "Dead? . . ."

Lynd nodded.

He was sitting like that when there was a knock on the door and the man standing there said: "I'm the doctor who was attending the Senator. May I come in?"

"Couldn't we talk in the hall?" said Lynd.

"Yes. Perhaps that would be better. I can come back," said the doctor nervously to Miss Svenson.

*   *   *

"He had a prostate gland," the doctor was saying, "but that was not really the cause of his death. As far as I could make out—he was very drunk when they sent for me—he got a letter yesterday when he came home from lunch——"

"Yes, I dropped him here," said Lynd. "He hadn't been drinking then . . . only a Martini and a couple of pints of mild beer."

"Yes, I know—that's what his—Miss Svenson told me. But this letter—that's what did the trick—apparently he found that an old friend he had been doing business with for years had been cheating him all along. It was an awful shock to him. He seems to have been a very sentimental man. Miss Svenson kept telling me he had a heart as big as the Atlantic Ocean. Anyway . . . when he got that letter . . . he went into the bar here and got drunk before he even went upstairs. Bartender told me that. Then he drank a full bottle of brandy in his room. Somewhere about that time Miss Svenson came back. She said she couldn't do anything with him—he was quite demented. They had dinner in their room. The amazing man seems to have eaten a whole broiled lobster. Then he was seen downstairs—in his pyjamas—trying to find the chef and give him five pounds for cooking the lobster. Then he began to get in pain—and they sent for me. I gave him a sedative, saw him in bed, and thought he was all right when I left him."

"Could you have saved him?"

"I might," said the doctor, and then quickly retracted that. "No. He was for it with that prostate gland."

*   *   *

In the next few days Lynd knew he was breaking law after law of strict England. And making the manager break them.

Upon the death of the Senator a flock of human vultures descended upon the hotel. Lynd came on them perched on chairs in the foyer; they tried to go up with him in the same lift; he found them on the floor of the dead Senator, with a maid or a floor-waiter backed down a corridor, desperately trying to disown they knew anything about the Senator's death. At Lynd's request there had been a re-shuffle of the hotel's domestics; all the servants on the Senator's floor had been transferred temporarily to the top floor. The new ones had been told they would lose their jobs if they gave any information about anything to any-one. The hotel was so vast that Lynd learned, with surprise, these top-floor servants did not even know of the tragedy on the second floor.

"But they're not the Press," said Lynd to the frightened manager; "nor are they like the rest of those buzzards sitting out in the foyer now. You know what bad publicity it will be for you, don't you, if the sensational newspapers here come out with: 'DEATH IN THE ——. U.S. Senator found dead in bed with a woman who was not his wife.' . . ."

"Oh, don't, Mr. Lynd! . . ."

Foreseeing complications, Lynd had had Sweetie change her room a few minutes after he reached the hotel. In a dressing-gown, Miss Svenson went up a backstairs and into a room directly overhead. All her things were moved up. There, moaning on her bed, ripping open one silk nightgown after another, she might have been in another world—so far as the questing vultures down below were concerned. Lynd found he could lie blandly, right and left. He had to. He never went through a period of such tense evasion, deceit and sheer invention in his life. "Baron Munchausen won't be in it!" he told Freddy Wayson afterwards.

Freddy, reading the announcement in the newspapers, had dropped in to offer his condolences. "That's a hot piece," he said, poking at the paper with his pipe; "sailor before the mast stuff out in China . . . never been to school . . . sixty million dollars . . . did you give them that?"

"Certainly," said Lynd, "and it's true."

"That doesn't cut any ice. I might as well tell you, old boy, that there's *another* story going the rounds of Fleet Street—your angel Senator died with a tart in bed . . ."

"Ha! . . . Tripe!" said Tony.

"Honest?"

"Abso-lutely!"

"Well . . . I can kill that story if you want me to. . . . You know how I killed the one about you . . . that police court stuff?"

"Indeed I do. But you needn't bother about this one. There's nothing in it."

Lynd knew Freddy. He would be drinking in the Fleet Street pubs around noon, urging the reporters there to write the story, laughing, saying: "What of it, old boy—it doesn't make any difference if it isn't true . . . you can always deny it." It would be the surest way to make libel-frightened Fleet Street editors throw the story out.

A cable from California advised him that the Senator's lawyer was on the way to London to settle Mr. Hancock's affairs. He was flying to New York to take the first ship. This was precisely what Tony most wanted. Before the story got into the afternoon newspapers that first day, Lynd had made Sweetie dress, come down and give him a hurried account of what she knew about the Senator's clothes, valuables and correspondence. "Where's he carry his money —the big money?"

"Wallet—back pocket," said Sweetie.

"Right," said Lynd. "You take that."

"There's his diamond shirt studs and everything!" screamed Sweetie.

"Leave them alone!" said Lynd.

"You take them," said Sweetie. "He liked you—he'd like you to have them."

"Listen," said Lynd. "I'm not taking even so much as a *match* out of this room. I'm going to break the law now—badly. Every damn' law in England before I'm through. We'll leave some change in his pockets—so that it doesn't look as if somebody had rifled him. But you take every pound you find in that wallet—all of it—I don't care how much it is. *That's* what the Senator would have liked." Lynd stared desperately at the wardrobe trunks full of new, unworn suits, shoes, drawers packed with silk underwear and the $140 pyjamas.

"Do take some pyjamas," moaned Miss Svenson. "They're so sweet!"

*   *   *

"Mr. Lynd, you are lying to me," said a bird-nosed young woman who had come across from Paris. "I *know* there was a woman with Senator Hancock when he died."

"Then why ask me about it?"

"Mr. Lynd, it will do you no good to keep up this pretence with me."

"Yes? Mrs. . . . what is *your* name? . . . Well, it will do you no good to act the way you have been doing around this hotel. You'll get the London Coroner on the job before you're through. You say you're a great personal friend of Mrs. Hancock's? Well, if you don't stop trying to bribe the *concierge* and the servants in this hotel, *I* am going to cable Mrs. Hancock that you are deliberately—after being fully warned by me—attempting to create a scandal. Good morning."

*   *   *

"I would like to see Senator Hancock's things."

"You can't see Senator Hancock's things. They are all sealed up or under lock and key. Why do you want to see them?"

"*Signor* . . . I cannot speak such things in public. Will you come over there? Yes? So kind, thank you, I was with Mr. Hancock in Italy; we buy a Leonardo da Vinci pedella —yes? Ah . . . you have seen it? Yes. Also we buy one veree fine old master. But Mr. Hancock 'e iss afraid of the United States Customs—also our own laws against exportation—so we paint another picture over it. But I know Mr. Hancock . . . he drink tereebly all time Rome. So I don't give him real picture; I get some artist friend mine paint me another one. There! Upstairs . . . Senator Hancock he got that. Here is real picture." The sleek young man tapped an innocent looking roll of paper.

"Fine!" jeered Lynd. "Leave it with me, leave it with the hotel manager—we'll put it with his things."

"No. I want that other one."

"Wait a minute," said Lynd. "I'm going to call a policeman."

He went over and sat down in the bar and drank a Whipley's cider. "Nothing for me yet, Charley," he said. "Not until that man I told you about leaves Town."

When he returned to the lobby the Italian with the bell trousers was gone.

* * *

"Mr. Lynd, Trans-Atlantic Telephone Service say your call for the Senator in Washington is coming through at three o'clock."

"American or English time?"

"English. Mr. Lynd, Mr. Upjohn of the U.P. was in. He says you're a damn' liar about Senator Hancock. He says he *knows* there is something fishy about the story you are handing out. He says he is going to find it out—if you won't tell him. Maybe, he says, he will keep it a secret."

"Ha—good old Upjohn. Watch him like a hawk, Marjory. That man is *good*! I wish he weren't on the trail."

* * *

"Hello, Senator . . . this is Lynd speaking; yes . . . Anthony Lynd . . . your London correspondent. Yes. You know the news. Know all of it? Yes—that's right—he did *not* die alone. (Weak voice from Washington: "Oh, my God!") What I'm calling you for is this—I want *carte blanche*. . . . What's that . . . well, a free hand . . . a free hand to do anything, pay anything, and that the vouchers will be sent to you personally—and you will pay for them. (Voice from Washington: "Do you . . . do you think you can keep this thing out of the newspapers? . . .") Yes, if you'll give me a free hand. One voucher will be for a first-class fare on the *Olympic* sailing next Wednesday and a compartment to Los Angeles—with unlimited hotel and food bills all along the way. Just the way a certain young person came to Europe. That sounds too much? Let me tell you, Senator—it's for your own and the paper's good. It's what Hancock would have wanted—and that's the only way I'll go through with it —I've already promised all of that. Is that Okay—all of it? (Voice from Washington: "Oh, yes, yes, yes. . . . Anything you like. . . .")"

"The dirty little skunk!" said Lynd to Marjory. "He's absolutely wetting his pants, he's in such a funk. I'll bet he's got a couple of cuties, too, and doesn't want the spotlight turned his way. Buy a ticket, promenade deck, for Miss Svenson on the *Olympic*—get a letter of credit, better get it in U.S. dollars, for two thousand dollars for Miss Salome Svenson, Passport No. 1996342. Go over to the hotel . . . no, don't do that, because now that damn' Upjohn will spot you. I was going to ask you to go over and sit with Miss

Svenson . . . she's in a hell of a state. I think she really did love the old boy. Funny—but there you are. Now he's dead I think I've been fond of him all along myself—he was such a roughneck!"

"Where is he, Mr. Lynd?"

"He's over in the London Mortuary Parlour—or something like that. Wouldn't keep otherwise. Carried him down the backstairs last night in a box—with a purple cloth draped over it. Regular Roman Emperor! Man representing this mortuary wanted to bury him here . . . tried to sell *me* a plot; 'We bury lots of Americans,' he said."

"Coo! Mr. *Lynd*!"

"What time does the *Berengaria* get here with that lawyer crook from the U.S.? Victoria Station—around two o'clock next Wednesday. Splendid."

"You're not getting much sleep, Mr. Lynd."

"No. But I'm feeling fine—haven't had a drink for days. Now for Mr. Upjohn."

* * *

"It's no use," said Upjohn of the U.P. the next day. "You can't kid me, Tony—I *know*."

"Well, then, if you do—shoot. Send your story. Same time I'll send a wire to Washington, to a certain Senator— and tell him to get into touch with your boss in New York. I'm going to tell him that I have warned you *not* to send out a story that will do so much damage to so many people in the newspaper world."

"A story's a story," grinned Upjohn. "Come on, Lynd— kick through. It cost me five pounds . . . but I do know that there was a woman in the Senator's room when he died."

"Of course there was a woman," said Lynd suddenly. "Why the hell shouldn't there be? Do you think everybody's a bloody little celibate? Are you a bloody little celibate? Am I? Hell, no. Now . . ." Lynd looked toward a far corner.

"If you must know the truth . . . and by God, you are the only one who got on to it . . . Senator Hancock did have a floosie over in Paris. He picked her up in that hairdressing parlour by the Café de la Paix. She came over that last night to join him. But when she got here the Senator was so drunk he was no good to her. They had dinner in his room—Senator ate a whole lobster. Imagine that—with a bottle of brandy inside you? And then he passed out and she got so alarmed she came down and they got a doctor and the Senator died— so what have you? So there you are, you weasel; send the story. Blacken the old man's end—you ghoul."

"Go on, Tony—you know damn' well I've got my own reputation to keep up. And my job."

"Course I do. But I'm going to wire Washington as I promised you. Maybe—if you're too free and easy—you won't have a job."

"Blackmail!"

"No. Just a word to the wise. Is it sufficient?"

"No," said Upjohn.

Tony gave him a cigarette and shrugged his shoulders. He watched Upjohn push out through the swinging doors. By the time he got back to his office and sat down to write his cable, Lynd realised, Mr. Stanley Upjohn would realise that that story of a Paris floosie was not *news*—not, considering the antics of the usual American innocents abroad.

* * *

But what a story Miss Salome Svenson would have made! With the American end! . . .

* * *

"No, Sweetie," said Lynd, "I don't want anything. Not me! How much was there in the wallet—one hundred and fifty-three pounds! Well, I'm glad you've got that. Here's a cabin for you on the *Olympic*—hope it isn't the same one you two came over in. Goddam it, it is bad luck, isn't it! And here's a letter of credit for two thousand dollars. That will see you back to Hollywood. God—but you've had a tough break of luck! I'm out of luck about my schooner—but I always looked on that as just a pipe dream. . . ."

"No, it *wasn't*!" sobbed Miss Svenson.

"And my job's up the spout. Don't care much now. . . . Wouldn't like to work for that other son-of-a-bitch, anyway —no soul to him. You know, old Hancock *did have* a soul!"

"Oh, Mr. Lynd, Mr. Lynd! . . . I'll never see him again. Won't you let me go over and just look at him? Please!"

"Absolutely not—it's the worst way to remember him. Think of him in Paris, London, Rome . . . wherever you've been . . . having fun with him. He was a good old boy. Think of him that way. But . . . my God . . . if he'd only lived a few more days you would have been fixed for life. . . . I saw the sketch of his will on the back of an envelope. . . ."

"And that necklace!" shrieked Sweetie.

"Yes, he told me that. Tell me—it just makes no difference now—why did you take that back?"

"Because I loved him. I really did love him. He was so good to me. And I just couldn't stand seeing him make a fool of himself. Somehow . . . I felt it wouldn't be *normal* . . . do you see? I didn't want *him* to have doubts about me."

"Yes . . . he'd have had them—if you'd taken it.

"There's a bill here," said Lynd, "for twenty men's suits from Lanvin's. . . . I thought that was a woman's shop?"

"Yes, but Percival always had his clothes made there. . . . Oh my God! My God! . . . I'll never see him again! . . ."

*   *   *

"About this wallet," said Lynd to the hotel manager in his office, "I want to put it back in Mr. Hancock's satchel."

IL

"But you can't, Mr. Lynd. It's sealed. It will be breaking the law."

"We've already broken the law enough as it is," said Lynd. "What about that second doctor who was called in to swear to the circumstances of Mr. Hancock's death—so that we could dodge a coroner's investigation? What about that? And just look at the lies you've told."

"You made me!"

"Well, open that safe and we'll stick this wallet back. You sealed it. Put on a new seal."

"Mr. Lynd . . . there was a woman here this morning with what she says is a power of attorney from Mr. Hancock's wife. What shall I do about that?"

"What was it? Oh, a mere cable. Well, anyone could send that to anyone—anyone who wanted to get at Mr. Hancock's private effects. The woman is outside, you say? Bring her in."

It was the woman from Paris.

"Ho-ho! *You*," said Lynd. The woman had not expected to see Lynd there and started to back out.

"Now," said Lynd, "I'm going to act. That cable in your hand means just nothing—abso-lutely nothing. Mr. Hancock's lawyer is half-way across the Atlantic on the *Berengaria*—gets here Wednesday. Now"—to the manager—"before you let anyone tamper with Mr. Hancock's affairs—telephone Mr. Gustaf Leil on the *Berengaria*. I'm sending him a radio right here and now to that effect." Lynd reached for a pad on the manager's desk and began to write it. The manager looked at the furious woman; her bird-beak was white at the tip from rage. "You see," he said, raising his white, Swiss hotel-keeper's hand. "I am helpless."

"What is it you're after?" said Lynd suddenly to the woman. "Why all this flock of vultures—trying to get at Mr. Hancock's papers? There's something shady about this —I know somebody, somewhere, has rooked the old man out of a lot of money. Someone he had trusted. Who *are* you, anyway?"

"I refuse to speak to you!" said the woman.

* * *

"Marjory," said Lynd, "it's all over."

He sat there and stared at his typewriter. "Leil got in. I met him at Victoria. First thing he said was: 'Where is that lousy broad? I'm going to break her so-and-so neck!' 'Mr. Leil,' I said, 'did you pass a big ship as you came up Southampton Water?' He thought a minute, and then said: 'Sure—we passed the *Olympic*, going out.' 'Well— she's on that,' I said. 'Senator Hancock awaits you in the London Mortuary Parlour.'"

Lynd got up and fetched a packet of Gold Flakes from his overcoat pocket. "I'm only telling you this, Marjory— because you've been in on it all—and you've been very good. Mr. Gustaf Leil was as drunk as a coot when he slid out of the carriage at Victoria. Worse than old Hancock ever was. I got him drunker. I had to do everything I could to keep him away from that crowd at the hotel. . . . They're still sitting there . . . bloody vultures.

"Well, I took him out to my house and got him thoroughly plastered. Then, like a fool, I took him to a revue. He was sitting with his arm around my shoulder, asleep through most of it—and then I noticed that the girl sitting next to me was giving me some nasty looks. Finally, the man with her—Regular Army officer bloke—leaned across her and hissed: 'You will oblige me if you will act like a gentle-man!' I didn't know what to say—and then I saw that that old wreck, Leil! with his arm around my back, had been *pinching* that girl's back! . . ."

"Mr. Lynd! Mr. Leil was a one!"

"So then I got him out . . . stepping on about a dozen people's toes . . . and took him to a bar across the street. I told him it was just beer—but what he was drinking was half beer and half gin. . . . I gave him two pints of it. That settled him. The night porter and I put him to bed.

"This morning," said Lynd, "when I went down to see him—where do you think he was? Sitting in a stock-broker's office across from the hotel—waiting for the New York Exchange quotations. At ten o'clock! 'Do you know what time it is in New York now?' I asked him. He didn't know. 'Well, it's just 5 a.m.,' I said. . . .

"But look here, Marjory—here's the funniest, strangest part of all of it. You know, when Mr. Hancock was here before, and you went over to his hotel to take some dictation —you remember the vast wardrobe he had of things . . . and how he was hung with gold chains and elk's teeth . . . like a Christmas tree . . .? Well, it was even worse this time. And when I told Sweetie—that's Miss Svenson—to take anything she liked from his wardrobe . . . silk scarves . . . anything—what do you think she took?

"She took six boiled shirts," said Lynd. "Six shirts for evening dress. And that was all."

"Coo!" said Marjory. "For someone else?"

*   *   *

The late winter of 1933–34 brought Christina back from Egypt, looking bronzed and fit, but with a few grey hairs starting. Tony, who had gone out to Croydon to meet the Paris plane, had too many drinks while he was waiting for it. Their meeting was not too pleasant. It was not a reunion.

In fact, he blessed the existence these days of the fat, very unreliable Freddy Wayson—he was always around the house. "I like him," said Christina, "because he can make me laugh." Freddy, whose uncontrollable wit had killed any chance of ever getting another permanent job along Fleet Street, was free-lancing and corresponding for some Indian newspapers. Many a night when Lynd came home late—after an evening with Flick—he saw the ashes of Freddy's pipe knocked out against the fireplace. Christina, he learned, had been talking to Freddy about things.

"What would you say if Chris slept with *me*?" asked Freddy.

Lynd stared at him. He stared at Freddy Wayson a long time. "By rights," said Tony, "I suppose I ought to knock you down—which, as you know, I can do."

"Not now, old boy," laughed Freddy. "I'm too fat.

"What I mean is," said Freddy, jabbing his pipe at Lynd—"How would *you* feel?"

"Well," said Lynd, "in the first place, I don't think you could make the grade—Christina's too particular. Next, secondly, and finally—I don't think Christina could do it— not with anyone. She's just not built that way.

"So the question you're asking," Lynd continued, "just has no sense in it. But why do you ask it?"

"Because, old boy, I don't think that if you left Christina she would be half as much cut up about it as you think she would."

RETURN JOURNEY

As they went past that ironic statue of Liberty, Tony faced New York with the peculiar sensation of a man who, twenty years the wiser, is starting to live over again. Not to waste money, he had come over tourist; and a German Hitler-refugee who stood beside him along the rail, gasped as he saw the man-made cliffs, with their millions of office windows peering at them from Manhattan Island. "*Mein Gott!* It's Babylon!" he cried. "Well," said Tony; "it may be reward for you?"

The German was a playwright, with a new manuscript in his arms; and Lynd wondered what would be his fate—a Broadway success, with all the glittering enchantment that can bring; or the sheer physical pain of merely trying to buy comfort in this most luxurious and cruel city in the world.

"New York always scares me," he told the Jew—"every time I come back to it."

He was glad that no one would meet him, and he could have the week-end to consolidate himself before he took the train to Washington. No one from the paper, as in the old days, would be there; it would be a brave man indeed, under the new Cæsar, who would identify himself with Lynd before it was known how he and the new boss would get on. Lynd was waiting patiently, like any humble citizen, for his bags to be passed when he felt a strong grip on his arm. It was Bill Draper, his oldest friend in the States. They had gone to the same university, played in the same teams, had a hearty tolerance towards all their contemporaries; and Bill's eyes as they looked into Tony's now had an understanding grin. "Well, you old roughneck," he said quietly.

"How did you know I was on the *Olympic*?" said Tony equally quiet.

I1

"My secret service. Don't think I'm a politician for nothing, do you? Wait a minute."

Bill went over to the head Customs shed and came back with an official. "Which are your trunks?" he asked Lynd. In a few minutes everything was in the back of Bill Draper's Packard.

"That all you got?" said Bill.

"You know me," laughed Tony. "That's me entire worldly wealth!"

They drove up the Hudson and over the sky-circling new Washington Bridge into New Jersey, where Bill Draper had his home. It was a white wooden house, Colonial style, on the crest of an empty green hill. Janet, gardening gloves still on her freckled hands, for Bill's wife was a blazing red-head, came out as she heard the wheels crunching the gravelled drive: "Tony! Tony! My beloved! . . . ." After he had submitted to being kissed, Janet's face lighted up with a new thought: "Bill—do you really have to drive back into town? Couldn't you change your mind and have lunch?"

"Nope. Just drove out here to deliver this load of horse-meat. Now I'm off. Say, Tony, have you any particular fashion in cigarettes? Will Camels do? Don't tell Jan the whole story before I get back."

Bill had asked him no questions on the way out. Neither did Janet when she drove him out to the Country Club for lunch.

At the Country Club Janet introduced him to a bevy of young fashionably dressed women who, in their flowered hats and dresses of gossamer tissue looked brazenly cool when Tony thought of their husbands sweating in New York—the heat of those dirty dock streets still stank in his nostrils—but then, as he reflected, most of their men were probably on the New York Stock Exchange and were even now sitting down to an unbelievably good lunch in some smart, gay eating place up-town for a two hour chat about golf, sailing, tennis, whatever their favourite pastimes were, and he found himself envying them. The Americans had learned how to live since he had worked in New York. Bill had met him in a cool "seersucker" suit, an untidy costume it would have been as much as an American business man's life was worth to wear to the office only a few years back. New York was being at last recognised for what it was in summer, a sweltering tropic city, where the nearest to the original Indian nakedness was the only possible attire. And any time after five these tired business men would begin to be met by their lovely wives in the glistening motor cars that now crunched the Country Club drive as he and Janet drank several Barcardi cocktails before they sat down to lunch. The men, out here in New Jersey, would have time enough for at least nine holes of golf, a cool shower bath and a change into a fresh linen suit before they began to mix cocktails in their own homes or drove off to a noisy party somewhere else and another excellent meal. In all truth, he thought, the New Yorkers certainly had learned how to live since the War.

Janet led him around, practically on exhibition—"Bill's old boy friend, Tony Lynd, who's just got in from London" —and cut short conversations with one or two of the prettiest women by saying, "Leave that for to-night. You'll see him there." He was, he knew then, headed for a dinner party himself, and moaned to the cool Janet, "I'm going to die in that heavy black dinner jacket!"

"You can wear one of Bill's white ones," she said, eyeing him with a slow smile. "I shouldn't imagine there was very much difference between you in your birthday suits?"

He realised the luxury she was permitting herself, this little game of talking so intimately with Bill's oldest friend, and he caught himself looking at her with a similar picture in his mind. She must look very neat in a bathing suit . . . and particularly without one. He wondered what their relations were. The picture bothered him and kept coming up before him during lunch. Her talk, too, led him along this line. "You're a bad one, Tony Lynd," she said. "The life you've led! . . ." She did not mention Christina's name, but he could sense at once that she knew he and Chris were no longer living together, and she suspected, quite naturally, another woman in the case. She did say Christina had wired he was on that boat.

On that cool porch he could have put the situation. It might have done a lot of good to clear the air in his own mind. But, even with Janet, he knew that he could not go into the analysis of his own years of frenzy during which he had been faithful to Chris. There was no reason to discuss Chris. Better let Janet think what she thought. And he could not contemplate discussing Flick. Poor Flick! After all was said and done, she, too, had a lot to bear from him. It was true that in the beginning, during those days when she used to boast deliberately of her relations with other men, to crucify him, she had purposely wrecked his sense of values because she was jealous of his propriety, his home, his life with Chris, even of poor Zeppelin the dachshund, whom Flick had once deliberately tried to kick. But then, when she had seen him going down the drain, the wreck he was making of himself by the way he drank in London, she had tried to save him. Save him for herself, yes. But no woman could do anything fairer than that—dirty as it would be to Chris. At the last talk on the subject he had had with Flick —an entire week-end of exhausting, bitter argument—she had done her level best to make him go off with her right there and then. She would have thrown up everything, run the absolute certainty of her crotchety father's disinheritance —the old *parvenu* was determined to marry Felicity into the old established English aristocracy. She had not said so, because that was not Flick's way; but she would have gone off with him if he had not one red cent and had had to begin a new life where he would not even be free to make her his wife. She would incur any stigma. Her courage was absolute, without any reservations or fear for the consequences; and, despite the wreck he had made of his own life since he had touched and fallen in love with her, he no longer felt angry with Flick for the things she, because of this love, had made him do to himself. He had to feel respect for her. It was a good feeling. He wanted it. It somehow made things right that he should feel this admiration for Flick.

After all, he was the loser all around. He had protected Chris, because on that fevered week-end he had not let Flick, using all her cleverness, make him do the thing that would smash Christina's life. Christina would fret and feel wretched the way things were—he could not help that—but she would at least not get the blow in the face that his going off with Felicity would have given her. It was a hopelessly unsatisfactory situation. This seemed another one of those problems to which there was no answer.

And to Felicity he had played one of the dirtiest tricks he had played on any woman. He had made all his plans with a sullen secrecy. The first thing she knew about his going to the States was when he had written her from the boat. It had been a necessarily stubborn letter; and he did not want to remember any of it, except that he told her he intended to be alone. It would be a fake to leave Christina, and then use Flick as a consolation. Their relations, his and Flick's, were not like that. Flick was not consolation; Flick was a positive offering in herself. He had refused to let people tear them apart, up to this, simply because he liked being with Flick. He admired her. But to separate from honest Christina also meant a separation from Flick. Flick was no substitute. He must go alone on this effort he was making. He had done things that way, deliberately played this filthy trick on Flick because, after all, there had always been a certain amount of savageness in their relationship—she could take it; and he counted on her pride. He knew Flick. This was probably the end of her.

Looking at Bill's wife now, Janet seemed only an amateur about life. The thoughts that had heated his blood a few moments back no longer troubled him. He felt cool, unemotional; and decided he would wear his black dinner jacket that night.

*   *   *

The day had, in many ways, been a reproach. The kindness of Bill and Janet he had expected—although he had had no intention of seeing them just yet; and he was not surprised by the spontaneous hospitality of the other people they had taken him to. One had a new Herreschoff sloop at Watch Hill, in which he and his wife were now going off on a summer cruise. They at once asked Tony to help them bring her down to Barnegat, if he liked. Another had a farm in Tidewater, Virginia; and, when he heard Tony and Bill talking about former duck-shoots at dinner, he asked them down for a week's quail-shooting in the fall. An invitation which Bill firmly clinched; although Tony said—"I have no idea where I'll be."

"Oh, I'll see he's there all right," said Bill.

Bill's book, *American Wildfowl*, Tony knew could not have been laid by his bed by mistake; for the last time he had been with the Drapers was when he and Chris had spent a glorious November week at Bill's duck lodge on Currituck Sound. And he recalled now the continuous boom of the Atlantic rollers swishing up the golden Carolina sands, as he and Bill and a "native" had stood on Draper's wharf over in the Sound after a sunny windless day (thoroughly enjoyed by the girls, who went swimming; hated by the men as the sound was too full of water for the ducks to come near the blinds) and they had watched the windy evening sky flame into clouds of burning salmon red; and the native had said, "I reckon to-morrow'll be a purty day!"

A "pretty day," in the vernacular of a Carolina duck-shooter, means a cold north wind, blowing like hell down the Sound—blowing most of the water out of it, in fact—so that the shallow flats are exposed and the ducks have to come out of the sanctuary of reeds and, following the courses of water, fly close enough to the blinds to see the decoys and come down. Yes . . . a terrific day . . . with only the pintail whistling down the leaden sky . . . great strings of Canada geese, flying high over the Atlantic surf, going down to Florida . . . and, in a gale that fairly blew the hair off his head . . . Tony had got his limit of four geese and ten ducks before ten o'clock.

The reproach of this first American day had been in the healthy propriety of this type of American life. Tony knew enough not to think the men and women were all angels. In fact, Bill, seeing him up to bed, had made a remark about what a bloody brute one of the men was to his lovely wife. But they did not boast about infidelities, or try to talk like Aldous Huxley's books. They were, in fact, what the London Bright Young Things of the 'twenties would have called "*hearties.*" Yet Lynd knew enough from Bill's life; the courageous way now, as a District Attorney, he was trying to clean up State politics; that stubborn jaw of Bill's he had often seen sticking out beneath a football helmet; the way, for that matter, that Bill could bring down a goose, and his bit of War service, that Bill had a lot to recommend him. And although Bill's impulsive frankness, when he was on a pet subject, might not have soothed a consciously reserved Englishman, Tony knew that Bill Draper was one of the quietest, most humble and modest men he knew.

It was the integrity of these home lives that so upset Tony. These orthodox American homes, with the children playing around the grounds in rompers, the nurse, the wives driving off to their country clubs and harmless (but were they so ineffective now?) political lectures. They may have Community Plate instead of Georgian silver on the dinner table; the furniture was obviously not antique; and, with the inevitable *Saturday Evening Post* and *National Geographic* on the library tables and reams of contemporary books, there might be even an irritating youthfulness about the average American home of this class. But they were homes, places that were lived in. Bill's eldest son, Tad, had gone to Andover, where Tony went to school—the only place in his so-called education that he cared about; and Tony knew that Wellington, in England, was the exchange-school for Andover, and that if he and Christina had had a son that was where he would have liked him to go. This thought brought him back to the comparisons he had been making all that day and at dinner between the two more or less parallel sets of people in the English and American life. The outstanding difference was that, in England, the majority of the men, very nearly all of them, in fact, would have been in one of the Services; Army, Navy, the new Air Force, Civil or overseas. This inevitably contained a certain air of snobbishness. Here, as Government service, synonymous with corruption in American life before Roosevelt, held out prizes that most of his kind did not want, Tony's friends, or these people who might have been his friends, had gone into business, law, or the scientific professions.

The man who owned the farm in Tidewater, Virginia, a professional dirt farmer, of the gentleman class, was such an anachronism in American life that he had been a curiosity at dinner. He was a dozen times asked the question: "But who do you find to talk to?"

What had upset Tony the most had been his secret thoughts of the happiness that the women were getting out of these American country homes. With their gardens, some place where she could dig—for Christina was just as fervent as Zeppelin that way—a home such as these would have been the one thing that Chris would have loved. He ached at the thought of how easily it could have happened. He and Chris might have had a very contented and sweet existence, if—well, there was still this question of the flesh. . . .

The dinner party depressed him. He felt like crying out when these pleasant people expressed their envy of his "interesting life," how eventful and exciting they thought it all had been. He felt like apologising to these men, whose integrity and orthodoxy he respected, when they started to apologise to him for their daily round of coming home every night on the 5.15. He did stop them talking like that. "Don't be silly!" he protested, trying seriously to show them what it meant to live continually out of bags, in foreign hotels and *wagon-lits*, fighting with Customs, *concierges*, censors and railway porters around the world. "The only thing that ever catches up," he laughed, "is my bills!"

One of the wives said coyly: "Why, you're a world gipsy, Mr. Lynd!"

He could have killed her. As he was talking he had become conscious that what he was really doing was telling them indirectly what a grand life it all was!

* * *

Bill Draper could not stand the muzzle that he and Janet had apparently agreed to put upon themselves; and after he had said good night to Tony, Bill came back, and said:

"Tell me, Tony—what about Chris?"

"I don't know, Bill. I think the best way to look at it is to say that Chris and I have declared a moratorium. She still has the house. . . . She's living in it. . . ."

"For how long, Tony? This moratorium business?"

"I don't know that either. Until I get straightened out with myself, I think. It's hard to say. . . . We didn't fix any act or ultimatum. . . . She's happy. . . . I suppose so. I hope so."

"Sounds pretty trying for both of you?"

"Yes, I think we're both going to find it so. But she's a stout-hearted little devil. . . . You know Chris. She hasn't any material worries, anyway—not yet. There's no enmity, you know. . . .

"You know, Bill, you're funny," Tony said suddenly. "You aren't much different from the rest. All my friends seem to think that they—or their other friends—can do anything: divorce, keep a mistress openly, have some damn' foolish affairs. . . . But they all act—you too—just as if Christina and I had no right to part!"

"You haven't," said Bill. "You haven't. Jan and I have always said, 'Now, there's a pair that will never come unstuck!' So there!"

"Sorry to disappoint you," smiled Tony, opening the carton of Camels that Bill had placed by his bed.

"Well, I'm not going to let you."

* * *

It pleased Tony to think that most of his friends would take Christina's side instead of his; and most of them would not leave either her or him—they would always be a bridge.

* * *

In the locker-room of the Country Club the next day, when he and Bill came in from a round of golf, he immediately learned that Roosevelt had supplanted Prohibition in the conversation—and that it would be more politic to keep his political opinions to himself. Bill, driving home, was actually angry with him. "It's all right for you," said Bill. "You're a goldarned 'foreigner' and not supposed to know anything. But I live in this community. And let

me tell you—I disagree with every damn' thing you
said!"

Tony was hot. "It just gives me a pain in the tail," he
retorted, "to see a man like Roosevelt giving a spiritual
reformation to this country—which was the one damn'
thing we needed—and to hear every Goddam man who's
got a few dollars he's afraid of losing calling Roosevelt a
bloody swine. Christ! it doesn't look to me as if Roosevelt's
reforms are wrong. . . . I listened to half a dozen men at
that club brag how they were breaking them! Answer me
this now: How the hell can Roosevelt be blamed—if he
can't find enough honest people in the United States to
live up to his programme? I mean people who've accepted
the Blue Eagle—and brag, like that bunch, how they're
pulling the tail feathers out the bird. . . . You big mutt!
He serves us right!"

"'We'" snorted Bill Draper contemptuously. "Who
the hell are you to talk of we? What do you know about the
United States? Where the deuce have *you* been all these
years? What country have you bettered? Even your own
li——"

Bill stopped, jammed the car viciously back into second
as he took their winding hill drive.

"Yes," said Tony. "You're right. You're right. So go
plump straight to hell!"

*   *   *

The feud had been patched up by the fiery Janet, who
almost made a war between Tony and herself by bringing
in the Oxford Group to settle things. Tony was conscious
when he went into New York to catch the Washington
Pullman on Sunday night that Janet Draper's feathers were
still ruffled. Bill turned out to be the final peacemaker.
That was usually Bill's part.

*   *   *

In Washington he knew he would find an entirely different kettle of fish. An unspiritual man, self-made, spectacularly successful, who had taken hold of the dignified, independent old paper that Huntingdon Ridley and Senator Hancock's death had let drop in his hands, and was making a national name for it. He was a go-getter, with every connotation that that term implied. Ruthless, heartless—his first acts had been the terrible chopping of what he called the "dead wood" from the office; throwing on the market dozens of loyal newspaper men who were too old to begin again. Bill Draper knew about him, said he was fast becoming a personage in Washington politics, and that if Anson P. Ricket could not kick a hole in Roosevelt's slats—he would like to know who could. He had the confidence of all the big business men.

"A sinister recommendation," said Lynd.

* * *

Lynd had seen the new Cæsar in London, and was not put off by the face he met. It had the mouth of a wolf-trap.

"Well?" said Mr. Ricket.

"Good morning," said Tony.

He was expected, he saw, to say something. But he thought he would let Mr. Ricket wait. Then he said innocently: "It's marvellous in this air-cooled office!" The remark had point, for Mr. Ricket's cathedral-like room was the only air-cooled office in the five floors the paper had in the skyscraper; the rest of its staff suffocated in Washington's fiery furnace. "Do you mind if I smoke?" said Tony.

This was more than the great man could bear. He looked at Tony suspiciously. Finally he managed to say: "Er . . . thanks for what you did in London. You know what I mean?" Without thinking, Mr. Ricket looked over his shoulder as he said this.

Tony nodded his gratitude for this acknowledgment of the week of anxiety, and luck, he had had keeping the circumstances of Senator Hancock's unsavoury death out of the world press. Mr. Ricket was a generous man!

"What do you propose to do, Mr. Lynd?"

"I was just going to ask that question of you."

"Hmmmmm . . . I see, I see. . . . Well, what is the exact position, Mr. Lynd? I haven't got your file before me. Didn't know you were going to pop in on us like this. What is the position with regard to your—eh—work?"

It was not a very able lie, from an astute man like Anson Ricket; but Lynd accepted the opening gambit: "I wrote Merrill," he said, "that I thought I'd had enough of Europe." This was the way he had decided to leave Chris and the whole London scene. "It was time I saw something of my own country for a change. Apparently, you agreed with that proposal whole-heartedly. At any rate, you have appointed my successor."

"So I have. Ah—Mr. Merrill!" Mr. Ricket frowned, and Lynd wondered if he had let his old assistant in for anything. He didn't care much; Merrill had been scared of his life ever since he had rushed back to Washington and bowed his knee to this man. "Well, that's fine, Mr. Lynd," Mr. Ricket was saying. "As soon as I get through these letters, I'll send for Mr. Merrill and talk it over with him. If I'm not mistaken, he already has some idea about an assignment for you. Meantime, make yourself at home, make yourself at home. Glad to have you back with us. Good idea for the men in the foreign field to come back to the home base. Get filled with good old Americanism again. You're inclined to forget that, you people abroad—especially in London. Bring Mrs. Lynd with you?"

"No. She's in London."

*   *   *

It was amusing to watch the people outside. They did not know whether it was safe to be friendly with him or not. There had been no sign yet from the air-cooled room. The reek of the dictator was all over the place. "Well, if you cut *his* throat only water would run out," said Lynd to try one of them. The man went grey.

As he was walking through the offices a little dark-haired man came up and spoke to him. "Good morning, Mr. Lynd," he said. "You don't remember me. My name's Netley." Then, as Lynd tried to place him: "I came over to the Brussels Third International Conference. Say, Mr. Lynd, have you got time enough to come outside with me and have a drink?"

"I'm not drinking."

Lynd saw a couple of the men at near-by desks look up, and then raise their eyebrows at each other. Apparently, he had a reputation. Perhaps Merrill? . . .

"I was just going along to see Mr. Merrill," he said. He looked toward where he had seen Merrill sitting, but he was gone. "Gone down to the presses," said someone. "All right," said Lynd to the little man, "I'll go with you."

*   *   *

It was the paper's old bootleg rendezvous; and almost as soon as they had sat down half a dozen of the men came in. "Hello, Tony! How's the boy?" He shook hands with all of them. They all tried to buy him drinks; they all expressed their dismay that a good old trooper had gone on the wagon. One of them even suggested an ignoble reason. Lynd laughed the loudest at that. It was good to be back with them again. He did not blame them if they wanted to protect their homes and families by not flaunting their friendship for him before the present boss. It wasn't they who were to blame; it was the new Cæsar. Finally Merrill came in. He clenched Lynd's hand.

"Well, well, well! . . ." he said.

"Well, well, well? . . ." said Tony.

"Sing it," said someone.

"What'll you have?" said Merrill.

"I'm not drinking," said Lynd.

"Well, *well*, WELL!" chorused the rest.

Merrill glared at them. To Tony he said: "When you get through come on up. The Chief has got a grand idea for you."

* * *

The idea, as Merrill outlined it effusively, was that Lynd should go out and cover the United States. "Tell us what labour is thinking! Tell us what the farmers think! Tell us what the good old U.S.A. looks like after twenty years in crazy Europe! Boy! You can just write your name all over the map!"

Lynd stuck a rude thumb over his shoulder: "Did *he* really think of that? All by himself?"

Merrill looked uncomfortable. "Well, I did help him a bit. Sort of suggest it to him."

Lynd thought. "Ask him if I can see him for a minute, just for a minute."

Mr. Anson P. Ricket was smiling and held out a presidential hand. "Well, Mr. Lynd—how do you like *that*? How's that for an assignment? Pretty broad—eh?"

"It's marvellous," said Lynd. "I couldn't have asked better. I want to thank you very much."

"Don't mention it, Tony."

"The only point is, I suppose you want me to write things just as I see them—no yes-man business? Nothing like that, of course."

"Certainly not! Don't you know the reputation of this paper! Ruggedly independent! Get out there—out there in the field—tell 'em what American labour thinks! I know that the American worker doesn't want to join any of these Goddam *unions*! Just browbeaten into 'em. And now Roosevelt's encouraging 'em—making class warfare. Tell 'em what labour really thinks! And I don't mean Labour either—not with a capital L. There isn't any Labour Party in U.S. politics—I mean the honest, ruggedly independent U.S. working man. The kind you see, all around us, who come from stricken Europe and rise to the top all around us every day. For we're all just folks together, Mr. Lynd—just plain honest people, like you and me. And, Mr. Lynd, I want to give you one last injunction—you can do a lot for yourself as well as the paper on this assignment. You can make a name. Remember, the Home Office is watching. And here's my parting promise, Tony—this paper never forgets!"

Tony, who was glad that the advent of Franklin Roosevelt had put a stop to "just plain folks" in the White House, looked at this man and saw that the President had an enemy who would use every weapon in the arsenal. He said:

"Well, you want me to give you all the information I get, don't you—on what the American working man *really* thinks? It might be a good idea, you know? Something new."

"Sure I do! Er—but be careful where you get your information from."

*   *   *

*   *   *

Tony's pilgrimage helped him more than he believed possible in his efforts not to think about Christina during the next weeks. In many ways this was also a personal quest; for he was rediscovering his own country with the eyes of someone who might live in it again. That was where the benefit of twenty years in other parts of the world came in. He was shocked in his first major interview, and so consistently shocked by the childish stubbornness of the big men he met, that he soon came to the conclusion he had come up against a wall of stone minds which refused to believe social evolution outside the United States.

"It will take the American Federation of Labour longer to get recognition from us," boasted a steel king to him out in Gary, "than it took Soviet Russia to get it from the United States!"

The question they were discussing was the tardy right, just given to the American working man by President Roosevelt under his famous Section 7A—the right to organise and have his trade union represent him in collective bargaining with his employers. It was a right which the British workman has had for over forty years; and, when Tony pointed this out, the big steel magnate said: "Ah, but the American workman is not the British workman, my dear sir."

"Neither," said Tony, "seems the American boss. Is this the reason why you steel men here have imported one hundred and fifty-four armed private thugs from New York? As you undoubtedly know, they are occupying the entire fifth floor of my hotel; and as you probably also know they had one thousand six hundred dollars worth of rifles, automatics, sawed-off shotguns, black-jacks—the English call those life-preservers for some strange reason—taken up to them by the back stairs yesterday afternoon. And yet you tell me that the American workman does not want to join an American Federation of Labour trade union?"

"He doesn't."

"Then why all the shotguns?"

"Because the workers have threatened to strike. We must protect our plant."

"But the workers are not striking for higher wages, strangely enough—they are striking because you refuse to let them join the trade unions. They're striking for that all over the United States. So I don't see your argument. Incidentally, why did you have to import the one hundred and fifty-four private killers, from the company that supplies such industrial assassins in New York? Aren't there enough legal policemen in Gary, and the hundred or so private police you have behind these gates, to protect your plant?"

"No! And look here, young man——"

"Gary is the largest steel town in the world, isn't it? Does the Mayor of Gary, or whatever you call him, know that you have imported private American citizens from New York—and a more sinister bunch of thugs I've never seen —and given them shotguns and revolvers to use on the citizens of Gary who work in your plants? Have they been sworn in as police and given the right to carry firearms?"

The big man chewed his cigar.

"It's interesting," said Lynd. "Roosevelt legally gave the steel workers the right to organise and join the A.F. of L. under Section 7A—the United States Steel Corporation says they cannot have it. How long are you going to keep it away from them?"

"You heard what I said when you first came in."

"Yes, I remember that—about recognition and the Soviets. The one hundred and fifty-four thugs moved their quarters this afternoon; they are living in Pullman cars, with negro porters, which were run in on the railway tracks beside the blast furnaces of the big plant next to yours. One of them offered to shoot me this afternoon. We met in a saloon, where I was having a coca-cola with one of the A.F. of L. organisers."

"*Which one?*" the big man could not prevent himself saying.

Tony laughed. "It strikes me that your attitude towards your workers can be called, to say the least, inhumane."

*   *   *

Tony knew that Bill Draper would have agreed with everything that the steel magnate said. He would have justified the President of the other big steel company in importing the private killers from New York. But he wondered if honest Bill would have been so cocksure and callous if he had been with him on those Gary nights. He believed that Anson P. Ricket really believed it, when he said that the American workman did not want to join a trade union—it was even possible of the man he had just been talking with to-day. That was precisely the trouble; the bull-headed ignorance of the American employer concerning what the workers thought within his very gates. Or concerning what the workers thought as a class. The Republican Party, with all its astute and slippery politicians, did not know enough not to side with Big Business in holding back from U.S. labour the right that Roosevelt had given it to organise—they would find that out at election time. Meanwhile, these big American industrialists were almost rupturing themselves trying to hold back the wheels of time. Or were they? Perhaps, in the long run, they were stronger than Roosevelt? And progress? The edicts of the United States Steel were like "the unwritten and immovable laws of heaven." Gary, steel's stronghold, was a fortress of invested privilege within the United States.

Behind the board fence of the Illinois Steel Company lies the largest manufacturing plant behind any single enclosure in the world. It stretches for three miles along Lake Michigan. It is a town in itself, well-planned, with a population of 15,000, and its own police. This population works there—but lives outside.

Surrounding this steel-town is the Calumet River—steelworkers call it "the Moat." It is forty feet across. Twenty years before it had been over quarter of a mile wide.

On the other side of "the Moat" lies Gary, Indiana, where the steel-workers live. This small city did not grow up: it was built to plan. Viewed from an aeroplane, its checker-board of wide cement streets, squares and grassy parks present the most modern industrial layout in the world. Certainly, of its size, there is no equal to it, not in England, not in Europe. Twenty-two years before, all this had been a barren waste of sand-dunes.

These two towns cannot live without each other. Gary, Indiana, has a population of 85,000. According to good or bad times, anywhere from 10,000 to 15,000 of them work in the town of the United States Steel Corporation.

Three times every twenty-four hours the gates of "steel-town" open: 2,000 workers pass in, 2,000 pass out. They have a pay-day every fortnight. On the money they bring out in their pay-checks lives the whole town of Gary, Indiana. The whole 85,000. There is practically no other industry.

If there is a strike, if there is a war—because strike means war in the United States—the gates of the town of the Illinois Steel Company close. As many of the ten, twelve, fifteen thousand men who are employed at the time can hurry inside its gates from the other town. "The Moat," the barbed-wire wooden palisade with its armed police behind it, the Illinois Steel Company, and the imported killers will protect them. Across the waters of Lake Michigan will rush steamers bringing strike-breakers from across the lake to complete the complement and man the machines.

But, for those other people who stay in Gary, the strikers —the pay-checks have stopped. Giant Steel is sick; so is Gary, Indiana; the butcher and the baker and the grocer stop giving credit; shoe shops take out the good and put cheaper pairs in their windows; dentists, doctors ask for their money first, before they will treat a case. . . .

Three steamers lay at the company's waterfront, behind the barricades, waiting to bring the strike-breakers during the days that Lynd was there; half the day shifts slept inside the gates for fear a strike would break. With the monstrous silhouette of domes and tubes and towers black against the hearth flames, Lynd wandered along the streets of Gary, talking in saloons and on the sidewalks with Germans, Czechs, Italians, Poles—all the races of Europe that had poured into the Melting Pot.

They were afraid.

In the dark and stifling night, an old Ruthenian said to Lynd: "Mister—United States Steel has never lost a strike! The women are afraid. In 1919 they turned the soldiers on to us."

A dejected man sitting before the idle pumps of a glistening filling station spat and remarked: "Mister—last Sunday was the worst since this station started. Didn't sell a gallon of gas to a Goddam Gary car. None came in. Usually I got to have a couple of helpers, Sundays. All of Gary drives out to the sand-dunes to picnic and swim. But did they last Sunday? Like hell! They saved their money and stayed at home. Everybody's scared. Mister—the Amalgamated Association of Iron, Steel and Tin Workers of America has never won a strike against United States Steel!"

The taxi-driver Lynd ordered to take him to the cabaret said: "I might as well take the wheels off this cab—you're the first fare I've had to-day." At the cabaret, where an imitation Mae West took off her scarlet dress and brassiere and waved her odious sweaty breasts before his face, Lynd talked with the two A.F. of L. organisers in Gary. They said:

"Mister—do you know the worst thing we're up against? —the American workers ain't got no class consciousness. Those Polaks and Bohunks you see out in the street, the black labour, they've got the idea they're workers, all right. But they're dumb. But the men who man the machines, the men who might do us some good—*they* don't think they belong to the labouring class! No—they're all going to own a business for themselves some day! *They* won't side with

the Bohunks! That's what's the real trouble with American
labour, Mister—no class consciousness."

Lynd thought of the recent foreigners, the Bohunks, he
had been talking with in the cheap beer-parlours—men
who even yet could hardly talk "United States"; if their
dream was that they did not belong to the labouring class,
because, in this Land of Opportunity, they would one day
become proprietors—then that was the real American
tragedy. . . .

*   *   *

"During the War they told us: Fight or Work! . . .
Either you've got to fight or you've got to work. . . . Ten
million dead. Millions maimed. . . . *Now we got to fight to
work!* . . ."

It was the Fourth of July picnic of the United Rubber
Workers of North America at Springfield Lake. A few miles
from Akron, Ohio, where 5,000 of them were on strike. The
speaker stood in an open glade beneath the trees in his
shirt sleeves. He tore his collar off. . . . His words were
carried by a sound-truck to hundreds of children bathing
in the lake, to scores of middle-aged families opening lunch
baskets in the wooden pavilion, to hundreds of young men
and women doing a square dance on the wooden pier's
dancing floor, to kids stuffing popcorn, sliding down chutes,
watching a silver-spangled girl on the flying trapeze, to ten
girls in the scantiest of bathing suits parading before three
leering judges to win a beauty prize. . . .

". . . and what happened when this Goddam capitalist
system crashed to atoms in 1929? . . . People took gas,
whole families took gas . . people jumped out of windows
. . . people jumped off bridges. . . ."

The lips of the few hundred people surrounding the speaker
became grim.

". . . and that same state of affairs is going on right now
. . . even under the New Deal! . . . The bosses won't obey the

law. . . . They won't give us Section 7A, which gives us the right to collective bargaining . . . which gives us the right to demand some of the stuff that the bosses have taken away. . . . It's not us, it's the bosses who are defying the law. . . ."

Somebody shouted. A hundred heads nodded.

"The boss still has the same selfish idea: What God has joined together let no man put asunder—let no man, not even President Roosevelt, part the boss from his profit! . . ."

The crowd cheered and then laughed at his joke. The speaker was thought by nearly every rubber worker to be a Swede, named Olsen. He wasn't; he was John Olchen, son of a Hungarian, born by a German mother in the suburbs of Budapest. . . . A brave American. One of the 200 "organisers" the American Federation of Labour sent against the United States Steel Corporation in the bloody 1919 Youngstown strikes. Olchen was one of the fourteen "organisers" who did not quit—or get killed.

"Roosevelt's got vision," he said to Tony over his beer. "That guy Hoover couldn't see no further than Wall Street. . . ."

*   *   *

In Chicago Lynd was asked to a dinner party at which there were two millionaire packers, two European opera-singers, two of Chicago's most brilliant and beautiful hostesses, a dilettante explorer and his well-dressed, well-publicised wife (her reputation was that she never wore the same dress twice) and a distinguished university vice-president—to give them in the order of their social strata. The conversation was so venomous that his hostess leaned across and whispered in Tony's ear:

"You know—sometimes I wonder if I really believe the things I hear myself saying against Roosevelt. I wake up in the night and shudder about it. It's his attack on the nickel; he hits our pocket-books—that's why we hate him so."

As they were going home one man telephoned a public garage to come and fetch his motor car which he would leave before his house. His wife removed a diamond bracelet from her arm, two pearl ear-rings, and lifting up her dress, calmly shoved them down inside her stocking.

"Why all these precautions?" asked Tony.

"Because," said the man heatedly, "our own garage is behind the house, down a dark alley. . . ."

"And we don't want to get knocked on the head," said his wife.

"What price American Constitution now?" said Lynd.

The remark was pertinent, because all through dinner the talk had swung back to the American Constitution: how it reached down through every stratum of American life to protect even the humblest citizen. Lynd had already brought the vials of wrath on his head by pointing out that a former Governor of the state had stolen $2,000,000—and got away with it!—that in 1928, Chicago had had 369 murders—and not one execution (London, city of 8,000,000, had twenty murders that year, of which seven murderers committed suicide and eleven were hanged) and said: "I've always heard that Chicago has the best judges that money can buy—if you have the money!"

* * *

Detroit was an unintended circus of 10,000 Rotarians marching down its boulevards, dressed in tropic pseudo-helmets, behind brass, busbied bands of both sexes, whose drum-majors cake-walked down the streets saluting with their batons banners welcoming the world conference of Rotarians from New York, Battle Creek, Galway and the Malay States. The night Lynd walked into this, 10,000 hilarious wearers of the cog-wheeled badge sat down to twenty-two State banquets in Detroit's Masonic Temples and hotels.

The Detroit Chamber of Commerce booster's sheet said that the city manufactured 3,000,000 automobiles a year, 75 per cent. of production in the United States; in the first five months of this year production had risen 89 per cent. over the same period of last; Detroit's individual bank accounts had increased by 134 per cent.; building contracts by 524 per cent.; Stock Exchange dealings by 176 per cent.; power consumption by 71 per cent.; employment had increased by 126 per cent., etc., etc., etc.

It said nothing about the fact that, before Roosevelt, there had never been a trade union in the Detroit motor industry —and that in the last eight months the A.F. of L. had organised 130 unions in their auto and body works! All of which the Detroit Chamber of Commerce had fought tooth and nail.

"Brother boosters!" said the automobile man who had dragooned Lynd to their table and forced on him a paper hat. "Mr. Lynd is one of those there crazy Americans who lives in little old Yurrup! He's just been having a look-see at the United States—investigating recovery in God's country —in spite of Roosevelt. Tell us, Brother Lynd—what are your impressions?"

"Hate," said Tony. "Just plain hate."

"There you are, gentlemen—you see how they hate him!"

"Not him," said Tony. "*You.*"

* * *

His long-suffering paper, because its Washington editors must have squirmed, did not cut his dispatches. Mr. Anson P. Ricket was too big and wise a man for that. He had evidently announced the edict not to cut one word. On the contrary, Lynd found himself advertised as the show-piece in the paper's window of traditional independence, giving both sides of the case. But he had a difficult time in finding

K L

his stuff. For one thing, he saw that, beginning with his first Gary story, not one of his stories was ever sent out to the paper's syndicate. New York, Pittsburgh, Chicago . . . none of the readers in these cities would ever know his tale. He was being buried in the unimportant Washington mausoleum. And even in his own paper he had to search; his stories were always changing from place and page; killed by unarresting leads; lost among the want ads., where the people who read them might have been uncommonly interested—but did not count.

Two harmless colour stories; a farm labourers' strike in the world's largest onion patch; and an hour's talk with Henry Ford, who made the interesting social comment: "I never use the words 'working man'—we are all just folks together," made the front page.

*   *   *

He bought a second-hand car and drove down through the drought-stricken corn belt; and here, in the pitiless middle day, when the parched cattle hunched together under the shady trees, he sat with desperate, thankful farmers who told him how Roosevelt (they said him and not the Government) had loaned them 40 cents a bushel against their corn, stored in their cribs, when the market price was 12 cents; and now they were taking it out and selling it at 60 cents.

"There's enough to pay his money back—and twenty-cents a bushel, brother, for ourselves—and that's the first time in the history of the United States that those damn' sharks on the Chicago wheat-pit didn't get the difference!"

To Tony's delight, when he got his own paper with this story, he read an extraordinary, acrobatic leader written by the Editor—trying to prove that *the farmers did not want this 20 cents*!

"That," he said, showing the editorial to the Governor of Iowa, "is the last straw! From now on I am prepared to believe that the great gullible American public will believe anything. At least, my Editor seems to think so."

*　　*　　*

He discovered early on that all the sinning was not on the side of Big Business or the enemies of the Government. At Freeport, Illinois, he found a frantic Farmers' Committee scratching their heads at 8.30 in the morning—to see that 15,672 little pigs did NOT go to market.

The reason, a bit complicated, was that the local farmers had some time back lied to the Government's income-tax assessors about how many pigs they had—giving a lower number. And, now that Roosevelt was going to pay them a bonus of $5 for every pig they didn't raise—they had turned in figures, lying again, showing thousands of purely mythical pigs they had—and were not going to raise, to get the bonus.

It was all very Alice in Wonderland—in which these solid, stolid tillers of the soil—"backbone of the nation," the political orators called them at election times—showed a capacity to thieve and lie better than any Cabinet Minister under the Harding Administration.

If these 15,672 little pigs—which had never been born—went to market now, there would be hell to pay.

*　　*　　*

Lynd found that half the farming land in the great corn-and-hog state of Iowa was mortgaged, most of it to the insurance companies; the farmers could not pay their loans; and in Omaha, Nebraska, he entered the nine-storey office building where 1,600 U.S. Government employees and officials were working night and day trying to transform these loans, with Government grants—so that the farmers would not lose their land; and—"Uncle Sam's gone into the farming business now!" said the harassed director of this relief work. Here, too, Lynd found that much of the wretched farmers' plight was due to their mortgaging one safe farm to buy another—just as venal and unwise as any speculator on the New York Stock Exchange.

Omaha was in a local prohibition area. Its cement streets were lined two rows deep with the motor cars of country people who had come in for a drink. A local lawyer had just bet the Mayor $2,000 he could show him 400 speakeasies openly selling liquor in the town. In the Fox-Hunt Bar, run by Mr. Fox, a polite negro was so alarmed by Tony's persistent statement that all he wanted was lemonade, that he brought him an "Old-Fashioned" Bourbon whiskey cocktail, anyhow: "Ah's thinkin' you'll really want this!"

Owing to the ruthless deforestation of its basin, this section of the once-populous Missouri River had dried up. With melancholy memories of Mark Twain in his mind, Lynd asked the negro if there was not still some steamboat traffic on the old Missouri.

"Yassuh. Las' year dese people had a boat—but she done got away from 'em. So dis year we ain't got no boat!"

*   *   *

Doing his steady one article a day, driving and collecting information, and typing at night after he had reached an hotel—Lynd approached the Badlands.

The proprietor of the hotel he had dragged himself into in Sioux City said: "Mister, do you know what's the matter with this damn' country? There's too many of us working for somebody else—*somebody we'll never see*! These chain-store proprietors take the legitimate profits that would come to us—and pay us a salary. . . .

"This whole damn' country [grows up in fear of its

livelihood. . . . Absolutely. . . . Land of rugged individualism. . . ."

He declaimed: "Take this drug-store on the corner.
Who's it owned by? A Wall Street group on New York!
They have chain drug-stores all over the country . . . where
the proprietors are only clerks. Same thing with the grocer's
shop—there's a big New York tea company owns that.
Butcher—a damn' nice little German—he's just been
crowded to the wall by the Chicago packers. . . . Made
him sell out. . . . He couldn't sell their 'quota'. . . . Fired
him and put in a new man from out of town. . . . German
shot himself. Haberdashers? . . . Everyone in it working
for a gang of speculators in Chicago. Me? I'm part of a
hotel system . . . only a paid manager. I used to own this
hotel. But I'm too fond of fishing. . . . It takes the guts out
of you. Always scared of being fired. . . . Mister, what
happens when all these happy little bits of individual
enterprise are blotted out all over America? . . . I'll tell
you: courage and contentment goes with them . . . passes
right out of American life! Mister, half the Americans in
the United States live all their lives in a constant state of
fear they will get fired. . . .

"And the farmers?" said the little man. "Why, whole
towns have been bought up here in the Middle West, and
cleared to the ground. . . . Make way for the tractors and
the big farming combines. . . . Make way for Wall Street
profit. . . . Men as well as houses are disappearing from the
land. . . . There's a farm out in Montana of one hundred
thousand acres that boasts one of its men, with their mechan-
ism, can till one hundred and twenty acres. . . . Swell!
But turn that around: One man on one hundred and twenty
acres!—*What's happened to the other families that that land
should be giving a life? to Breadlines.* . . . And where's that
swell blue grass of Montana now?"

"Yes," said Lynd wearily, "a lot of wise men have long
been pointing it out that life on the land should be a mode

life—rather than just a mere means of making a living. But I don't see what will come of it. . . . Not when Big Business goes into farming."

The reason why the proprietor himself had come up to his room was because Tony had sent down a grey flannel suit, stiff as cardboard with the mud that had come in as dust from the roads and dried with his body-sweat, to see what could be done with it. He was typing now, in one pair of pyjamas, while he had another drying from a coat-hanger in the open window. The manager said he hadn't seen any travelling salesman turn up in a state like this. Lynd ate a salad of tinned crab-flakes as he worked. . . .

"What makes me so damn' mad," he said over his shoulder, "is that this isn't America. I love my country— what Big Business has left of it. But I hate like hell the people who are running it . . . and I don't see how we will ever get it away from them. . . . Do you?"

"Me, mister? No, I've long ago given up. Once I wanted to own a big house, bigger than the Jones's next door, and the biggest auto in town. But I don't want that any more. I want a small decent life, rather than a large indecent life. —and even that I can't get. You can't live that way in America. The tide's dead set against you. . . ."

The man's talk about fishing offered a more enjoyable subject, and Lynd turned to that. It was good, for a few minutes, to forget the selfish scene he was reporting. But even here it came in: "I'm a Virginian by birth," said the man. "And last year I took my car and thought I'd drive down to the old Blue Ridge Mountains again and get myself some spring trout. . . . 'N'what did I find—my old river had become a sewer! . . . It was floating with yellow scum from a pulp mill. . . .

"'What the hell!' I said to a local. 'Are you going to stand for this? Can you stand this stink?' And what do you think he said? 'Don't talk like that, mister—that there damn' timber company owns every politician in the state!'"

"Yet that's not America, is it?" said Tony. "Not the kind that you and I have liked. I've been driving now for weeks—and I've talked to hundreds of men and women who think like you do. But the minute one of them gets a political job he acts like that. How do you account for it? The moment there's a slight boom on the stock market every one of you will get in on it, risk what you've got on it, mortgage your farms and your houses. . . . You won't *stay* small— that's the trouble. . . ."

Tony looked thoughtfully at his half-finished story. "The thing that has been dawning on me—as a *practical* suggestion, mind you—is that we ought to establish *examples*. Dot this country with small, secure and contented lives. We can do it. It won't be easy. Our Army and Navy officers provide an example wherever you see them—lack of the money urge. And they're a fine type. We ought to create a huge Civil Service . . . with office-holders in every American community. That would do two things: It would take most of the graft of the political patronage out of the politicians' hand—and encourage decent young men to take up service in the State as their life's work; and it would create a fearless body of small, independent people in our national life that would encourage others not to break their necks trying to make money all day long. . . . It would improve U.S. morals!"

"You're dead right there, mister—the opportunity to make good in this damn' country is too often changed into the *obligation* to make good—make money. You have to try, anyway."

* * *

It was with talks like these in his resentful head that Tony left the stifling cities, the red barns and blazing cornfields of the Middle West, and drove out into the empty Badlands of the Dakotas. Former prairies where the Cheyenne and the Sioux used to live on the flanks of the great buffalo herds. The land of the Great Drought. These grassy prairies, once covered with flowers in the spring, should never have been ploughed, But they had been made victim of the "railway racket." Not many years back, with the cesspool of corruption at Washington, these lands had been hilariously thrown open for the last American homestead rush; people raced at a signal on horses from a starting line to stake out free farms. If they lived there three years the land was theirs. An epic of generosity in print. In reality, the railways, wanting local freights to pay for their mileage towards the west coast had imported thousands of immigrants from Central Europe. In blazing Dante, South Dakota, Lynd found an entire colony of Bohemians, only two of whom could talk English, gazing mournfully at ploughed land from which a sirocco had blown all the top-soil away. . . . "They've blown away, mister—our farms!"

* * *

On the Cheyenne Indian Reservation he found the old squaws reviving a lost art—they were "jerking" meat. Cattle and horses were dying by the thousands, as they had neither grass nor water. In the Missouri River bottoms, beside a miasma of spladder-docks stinking in the sun, he came on an Indian who had a mare and a foal which had to travel ten miles between that muddy water and their munching of parched pasture every day. Soon, wept the Indian, the mare would die. "She can't keep it up, mister. . . . She ain't very strong. . . . " At Mobridge, South Dakota, he saw train-loads of cattle being evacuated, hundreds of them dropping dead in the freight cars: "And when they cut 'em open, mister," the two telegraph operators in the railway station told him, "they find their stomachs are full of mud. They eat the grass that close down to the earth. . . ."

The old squaws were given the cattle which died, or some of those the Government had paid for and shot; and, squatting on their hunkers in the scant shade of bushes, these women took a fat slab of red meat, cutting always in the same direction with a knife—and turned it into a red rag, like a dish cloth, which they hung on bushes to dry in the blazing sun. In a few hours it was dry and as stiff as a wafer.

"You got to cut it down so thin you can see through it, mister," an ancient squaw cackled to him. "But . . . he-he . . . de young girls can't do it—dey cut deir hands! He-he-he. . . ."

She was nearly a hundred years old, and had "jerked" meat like that in the days of the buffalo.

* * *

Rain, rain, rain? . . . It was a question everybody asked him as he drove along. When will it rain? . . . Their eyes were blood-red from staring at the burning sky. . . . As he turned on to the absolute Badlands themselves, a tornado funnelled towards him in a maelstrom of black dust. The corn bent and roared like waves of the open sea. Farmers rushed out and stopped their windmills. . . . The world became black as if passing through an eclipse. . . .

Next day he saw great dun-coloured mists rising above the scorched plains. The Great Main Range of the Dakotas was being evacuated for the first time in all its history. Cattle cars crawled like caterpillars along the railway tracks across the plains. . . . Cowboys came toward him at the back of maddened animals. . . .

"Get away, mister!" a foreman advised, riding up to Tony's halted Ford. "They might break any minute. Drive off over yonder and let us drive 'em past."

The cowboys wore goggles to protect their eyes; they looked like owls as they sat on the fence of the railway corrals, waiting for the relief trains to come along. . . .

K1

"The Great Arabian Desert! That's what it is, mister.
We're all washed up. Some of these steers are being taken
all the way down to Mexico in search of grass. . . ."

That night he reached Winner, South Dakota—and his
pilgrimage ended.

*   *   *

Winner was a typical western prairie town, with all the
bleak ugliness and stark manhood that that implies. Standing
at the junction of its two main cement streets, it was possible
to look four ways out of the town on to the blazing prairie
and red hills beyond. The houses were mostly board, one-
storey, with a false raised front. Behind the huge plate-glass
window of its main hotel, cattle owners, with silver spurs
dangling from their effeminate high-heeled boots, sat in
rocking chairs with their feet on the brass window-rail;
smoked, spat, took occasional swigs from a passing flask—
and philosophically opined they had all gone broke and
would have to start life, somewhere, all over again.

They were discussing where. . . .

The reason why, they said, they were finished in this part
of the Dakotas was because the land had been blown clean
away. Years of ploughing had broken the grip of the rich
black "gumbo" soil; it had powdered in the drought; the
last sirocco had blown it actually over steamships entering
New York Harbour. Lynd saw one German farmer trying
to dig his house and his farm implements out of black
"gumbo" drifts that were eight feet high. Most of the
Dakota Badlands lay like a skeleton of a horse, after the
vultures have picked its bones. . . .

*   *   *

Shots rang out from the railway station, where the
Government was shooting cattle. A red-eyed rancher told
Lynd that even in Winner, with its artesian wells, water

was being bought by the bucket. "I've got a pet horse," he said. "Riding animal—and that horse ain't going to die! Not while I can buy gasoline. I've got a barrel in my car, and all I am doing now, mister, is driving back and forth from here to my ranch to give my horse, and a couple of other animals I am trying to save, a decent drink. Have one yourself? What'll you have? Not drinking? No! Well, I'm damned: if it wasn't for the whiskey, I don't know what I'd do. Shoot myself, I guess." But these South Dakota men and women did not whine. They still had the spirit that had brought them to the Badlands—and they were *free* men.

The next day Tony sat with the cowboys in the octagon wooden shed of the Winner sale pavilion, and watched the desperate ranchers auctioning off their horses to other, more optimistic and gambling men who thought they could beat the drought. He read this sign:

HORSES
Bringing less than $25
are not Guaranteed.
Others are Guaranteed as
to Wind and Eye unless
they are called in the Ring.
EXAMINE
YOUR   HORSES
Before you
take them out!

Before the sale the cowboys and a few cattle owners stood in knots outside the wooden pavilion or wandered glumly among the cattle-pens, joking cynically about any buyer who was fool enough to come and bid for this remnant of dying stock. One or two were obviously having a last-minute battle with their own judgments as to whether they would withdraw their own offerings and make a last try to stick out the drought. Most of them were dressed in leather chaps, high-peaked "ten-gallon" hats, with silver spurs, and coloured handkerchiefs tied around their leathery necks in the true cowboy fashion that Lynd had never expected to see off a magazine cover. And among this Western throng was a man in tropical pith helmet, Harris tweed coat, and flannel trousers; an obvious Englishman.

He did not join the groups, although several men knew him, Lynd could see, from the friendly way they nodded to him; and he heard one say, after the tropical helmet had passed: "All washed up. He's out of it!" With the Englishman was a frail woman in white in a fashionable little Panama, who with a firm grip on his arm, seemed to be leading him through the crowd. "Yeah!" said another cowboy; "and he's sure taking it hard!"

The cattle-men at Winner were totally different from any others Lynd had seen on his tour of the States; chiefly because he heard no whine from them. The grim jokes they were making outside the sale pavilion came from men who had lost, most of them, every penny they had. And their sense of humour now was to beat the other man in telling the most gruesome catastrophe story. With the ordinary cowboys this did not seem a major calamity, as, it was obvious, they considered all their worldly goods lay beneath their hats and in their skill with horse and cattle. They could always find, they seemed to think, another cattle range. But Lynd heard even one of the biggest cattle-owners in the state, who was stopping at the hotel, exclaim: "Well, the joke's on us, boys! This is the reward for what they call 'rugged individualism' . . . the great Main Range is finished. When this is over the Packers back in Chicago will own all of us!"

"Well, the Government's trying to stop 'em," said someone. "But it can't work miracles."

"Can if you give it a chance," said the cattle-owner. "Conservation—and in five or ten years you'd have grazing land back on this soil."

"Five or ten years! Say, mister—what are you going to eat during that time?"

* * *

In the shed Lynd got a seat on the octagon benches near the Englishman, and watched him as his two private saddle-horses were led in to be sold. He saw him shrink in his clothes when the bidding stopped at $38. "Want-'im-at-forty? . . . want-'im-at-forty? . . ." pattered the auctioneer. He stopped to take a drink. "Say, boys—you're not paying attention! These are real *horses*. Saddle-broken; owner guarantees 'em sound in wind and limb. . . . Owner's pride and joy. . . . Now, boys. . . . Sold—thirty-eight . . . to that gentleman in the corner."

An attendant came in and squirted some water on the dusty ring. Someone said, awed by such prodigality: "Now, don't that beat hell!" Lynd saw the Englishman tottering as his frail wife helped him down the rows of benches and he went out with them.

"That's bad luck," he said, hoping to get a story from them.

The woman started, like a frightened person who has been touched, and then asked: "Are you a buyer?"

Lynd felt slightly ashamed of himself when he had to say, "No, I'm merely writing about the scene."

"*Writing about it?* Ha-ha! . . . " The woman's laugh was close to hysteria. "Do you think it is so amusing? Local colour?"

Tony knew he was reddening. The Englishman, a heavy, freckled-faced man, was staring at him belligerently, so angrily that Tony felt unable now to make the sympathetic statement he had on his tongue. He turned away, but the woman called: "I'm so sorry. Won't you come somewhere and sit down for a few minutes? We have to go back later for some other stock." In the empty dining-room of the hotel Tony became aware that the woman was now very anxious that he should remain with them, as if she wanted help with her husband in some way. She said: "You must come out to our place. It was lovely once. We'll show you what a fine place we had." It was all in the past tense.

That afternoon, when a prize dairy bull of the Englishman's had been sold, Lynd followed them in his car across the red, scarred prairies until they came to the banks of a dried up river. Here, in a patch of mottled cottonwoods, stood a ranch house, with high French windows opening on to a withered lawn, and all the shrivelled remains of what had once been a lovely rose garden. The woman sighed as she nodded at the waste, and said to Tony, "We have had some happy years here." She turned into the kitchen door and gave some directions to a fat Indian cook about dinner; and the Englishman, waking up to his duties as a host, walked Lynd around to a chair on the veranda and said: "I'll get the whiskey."

The wife came out first, seemed very embarrassed, then said: "Don't drink too much, will you? You see, my——" Tony nodded.

"I'm on the wagon myself," he said.

"Oh, bless you!" She gave a nervous laugh. She smiled at her red-faced husband's amazement when he found that Tony would not drink; and then she could not conceal her agitation when the English rancher said: "Well, all the more for me, then. I feel I need this to-day."

* * *

They were not the usual combination of distinguished impecunious Englishman and wealthy American wife; he had been the English Vice-Consul at Lobito, she a schoolteacher tourist whose attempts to travel about Angola unescorted had landed her in trouble with the amorous Portuguese.

"Ye-es," drawled the freckled Englishman, "I had to acquaint her with the customs of the country."

"You mean you kicked a Mr. Da Costa where he sat down."

"M'ye-es. . . . Damn' nice place, Lobito. If you've got a good head. Know Lobito?"

Tony shook his head. He felt that he was going to be embarrassed by this stricken family's reminiscences.

"We-ell, it's got its compensations. . . . It's a jolly long way from the Home Office—I was in the shipping business, you know—the Consul part is only honorary. But there was too much of this, though," drawled the Englishman, stroking the bottle lovingly. "I've buried a lot of good men in my time. . . ."

His wife shuddered.

"So here we are," she said quickly. "You see, Albert didn't like cities any more than I did. And when my brother left me this land we came all the way from Angola to settle here!"

"Quite a change," said the ex-Consul. "Quite a change. . . . Ye-es. . . . We're what the boys around here call 'washed up.' . . . Funny term, isn't it . . . when you consider it's all due to a two-year drought? . . . I don't think we can get anybody to *buy* this land. . . ."

He had an acute case of acne and his nose, bulging like an over-ripe strawberry, seemed about to burst. His blue eyes had been washed out by the tropics until they appeared too faded to be of use. But suddenly Tony saw that these milky discs were fixed on him with a peculiar indefinite expression, as if Tony's face had moved out of focus, and he heard the Englishman begin to speak of him in the third person:

"What's this man doing?" the Englishman asked his wife. "Writing about *us*?"

"Now, Albert . . ." The woman looked at Lynd helplessly.

"Does he think it's funny?"

"Don't talk like that, Albert; he won't understand."

"Won't understand? What won't he understand? That we've lost this place? . . . That you and I are washed up? . . ." The old worn tongue seemed hardly able to drawl the words. Then the mouth was filled with whiskey again, and the Englishman shook his head. "I won't let 'em come on here . . . not on our land. . . . No . . . I'm going to do what that old German did . . . the old Hun, God bless him. . . ."

"It's the mortgage," the Englishman's wife hastily cut in to explain. "You see, we had a chattel mortgage on all our stock. All the ranchers around here have that. And up until a month ago the insurance company wanted to try and make us sell our land. There had been a certain amount of trouble around here . . . with some of the ranchers."

"Trouble? Ha-ha. . . ." The Englishman sniffed and rubbed his roseate nose. "No-o . . . there's no trouble. . . ." He waved a flaccid hand at Tony. "Old German didn't have any fuss. . . . He just took a shotgun and sat there with it across his knees . . . and the Sheriff—that's a good man, that Sheriff—he told the insurance vulture he'd just better flap off and come back to dun the old German another day. . . . Edith . . . that's what I'm going to do. . . ."

He got up unsteadily and went in.

"He's been drinking like this for a month," said the woman hastily. "He's looking for his revolver now—I've hidden it. You'll stay the night, won't you? . . . You must stay. He'll be all right in the morning; the Sheriff's coming out, with the insurance man. I know my husband can talk him out of it."

It was an ordeal that required more self-control than Tony cared to use. The Englishman, who, in a dim way, knew his wife had hidden the revolver, made a quarrel out of every statement. It was all Tony could do not to get up and walk off—or say something. But the woman's face held him to his promise. They were both relieved when the

Englishman began to blur his words and talk about the old days in Africa.

". . . Ye-es . . . first day I landed at Lobito had to be honorary pall bearer....N'man wasn't dead....I saw him lying there'n coffin full of blood....Tha's fact....But then undertaker came along and threw the lime in before I could stop 'im....Could a saved that man....P'raps.... Not against that bloody lime, though—that finished him! Portuguese unto dust . . . hunh? . . . N'well . . . that's kinda things I've been seeing. . . . Life full of shadows and black people. . . . Always threw the lime in, in Lobito. . . ."

With the moon coming up behind the scraggly burnt limbs of the cottonwoods, Tony felt that he could not have wanted a more macabre conversation. Finally the rancher began to snore. . . .

"I don't blame him," said his wife. "He just loved this place. It was completely our own. . . . Wherever we looked, for almost as far as you can see—because the low hills are our boundary—we own this land. In this last ten years here we haven't built a thing, or hung a picture, that we did not stand there and discuss it together . . . telling each other how it would look twenty years after. It's pretty sad to lose that."

Lying there that night, as the moon slanted through his window, Tony watched its moving beam illume a solitary picture hanging on the smooth clay wall. He thought of a night years and years ago in Spain, hot and silent as this, when he lay alone in the white room of an Andalusian hacienda and watched the silver beam move towards a shining crucifix on the wall. He felt again the aching loneliness of that bright night.

* * *

The night in the ranch gave a queer, introspective turn to his thoughts, partly about his own selfishness—for the plight of the ranchers had not moved him. He felt utterly unconcerned as he watched their tragedy. He was bored with disaster; he had seen wholesale catastrophes that made their mountain look like a valley. Even the Sheriff spoke of Tony's unconcern, when he said: "I guess you're used to these kind of things?"

That was when, to give the English rancher a chance to have a last haggle with the insurance agent, the Sheriff had driven Tony over to see the old German's place. They reached it after driving straight across country that was as threadbare as a worn rug; its very ribs seemed to show, as were those of several freshly-dead cattle on the plains which the buzzards swooped over. The German they found patiently trying to dig himself and some of his farming implements out of head-high drifts of what looked like black snow. This was the rich black "gumbo" soil that the sirocco had blown away from the grazing range. The old German had hidden his two horses that the insurance company wanted to seize.

"Oh, dey's somvere," he said mysteriously. "Sheriff—it ain't my fault."

"I know, Dirksen—you've always been straight."

"Vell den—you tell *him* to lay off!"

"*Him*" was the insurance agent who was even now *en route* to the German, after he had finished with the English rancher.

The Sheriff grinned. "Can't have no gun-play, Dirksen. I'll have to arrest you. But hell—you'll have a good time. I'm not rough with prisoners. Why, damn it, some of 'em actually cries when I turn 'em loose!"

"Now, Sheriff . . . dis isn't funny. . . . You can tell him what to do—tell 'em to go to hell." When Tony asked him when he thought he could start farming again, the old German looked around at what had once been his land. Some tumble-weed was rolling in wraith-like skeletons across the pebble-dotted soil. "Maybe I can. In two years? . . ." he said. He was black as a chimney sweep.

The Sheriff nudged Tony and pointed to one of the German's cows that was standing, like an upright carcase, dejectedly by the dried rim of what had once been a mud-pond.

"Now all you see there," said the Sheriff, "is just bones and hide. Can you see anything there to can? Now, that cow is a-longing for a little grass. She ain't going to get it. She ain't got no hopes of getting anything to eat to-day."

*   *   *

Driving his own car back to Winner, Tony reflected upon his own hardness to both these scenes. They simply had not moved him at all. He had lost the capacity to be disturbed, just as much as he had lost his enthusiasms. Life simply did not stir him any more; he was satiated with sensations. He had watched the Englishman tamely lose his ranch without any other feeling than wonderment that he did not resort to direct action the way the old German had. The English-man, characteristically, had submitted to the law; when the agent informed him that the insurance company had decided to foreclose, he had simply nodded his head and told the insurance man to go ahead. He would have thought it vulgar to threaten to shoot people, the way the wretched German had. It would have been far better, thought Tony, if the Englishman had met the agent when he was drinking. Because then he might have threatened to shoot anybody who dared to cross his land—the way he had said he would do, the previous evening. A frightened agent, reporting to the head office in New York that the English-man had promised to shoot their representative, might have made them afraid of outraged public opinion. Hun-dreds of the Iowa farmers had saved their farms that way....
It should have meant something to the Englishman, to

notice that the agent was so nervous that he took the
Sheriff with him these days. The old German had temporarily saved his ranch simply because he had become an ugly
customer. He was dangerous. The Englishman's ranch was
worth seizing, and his very respectability had made him
easy prey. . . .

The Englishman had bowed his head to the law, a complex codification bound in calf, evaded by every big business in the country, laughed at by the trusts, cheated by
every millionaire who thought of the expedient of employ-
ing an attorney to show him the legal holes through which
he could escape paying any income tax. The Englishman
illustrated another conviction that Lynd was acquiring in
his rediscovery of the United States; that only the little
people feel that they need obey the law.

And that the old German had perhaps the logical answer.

*   *   *

In Winner he found that two weeks' mail had caught
up with him. Among the pile was an envelope whose
genteel enamelled lettering showed that it was from
the inner sanctum of his paper's office, from Mr. Anson
P. Ricket himself. He ripped that one open immediately,
and read:

". . . Your reportage on the formation of the Company
Unions at Gary and Detroit is a gross, biased, and most
superficial survey of this very important industrial
situation. . . . It reads as though you had been listening
to common gossip. . . . We cannot print such material as
this. . . . I have already had a letter from the Vice-
President of the Independent Steel Company you attack
at Gary . . . and, as he very rightly points out, there is no
reason why the American working man—*and the American
employer*—should not combine in a company union to

mutually co-operate to try and solve the industry's problems. . . ."

"You old bastard—you split your infinitives," said Tony as he eyed the letter. He remembered the pursy-faced Vice-President at Gary, how furious he had been when he repeated to him what dozens of his own workers had told him about the company unions: "Well, mister, when you strike—it doesn't give you strike pay; when you strike—you're no longer a member of the Union. So, if you ask us, when is a union not a union, we'll say—when it's a company union!" Tony remembered how he had enjoyed telling the Vice-President he was going to quote this in his Gary story—unless the steel baron could refute it. The postscript on the letter from the Inner Sanctum also made Tony laugh, and then take the lid off his typewriter with an oath. It said:

"I am glad to see that in hard times like these our correspondents feel they can stop at such expensive hotels as the Drake in Chicago, and the Book-Cadillac in Detroit, from where you sent us this highly misinformative last article."

Tony jammed down the shift key to block letters and typed: "PLEASE ACCEPT MY RESIGNATION HEREWITH."

"If he's not printing my stuff," said Tony aloud, pressing the button for a bell-hop, "he can't complain I'm letting him down on the job. Also, there's no use staying on on that paper."

It was with a dim feeling of sorrow that he sat down to read the rest of his mail. It was no fun, leaving the paper—even if it had changed hands. Another letter from the paper contained his blue-pencilled expense account, with an annotation by Merrill opposite the bills at the estimable Drake and Book-Cadillac, and a letter from him, written obviously after a talk in the inner sanctum, also saying the Company Union story was unpublishable, and ending: "Don't think you are writing editorials—just give us the news." "Well, you know where you can put that one," smiled Tony, consigning it to the waste-paper basket. He felt better now. As he expected, there was a very decent letter from Christina, saying she hoped he wasn't finding it too difficult, working so close to his new boss, asking him how he stood the heat, and saying that she hoped he was not too lonely. It ended, as a letter from her was sure to do, wishing him good luck in all he did. It was neither cold nor asking for sympathy itself, just carefully impersonal. Knowing her, he could read behind every expression the loneliness she herself felt. He suddenly felt very sad, and close to her once more. He sat there, staring at her writing, and then sat down to tell what had happened to him up to date, ending with his resignation from the paper. He wrote:

". . . . I don't know exactly what I will do now. Not another newspaper job, I think. Not in the U.S. The old bastard will have his knife in me—and everything over here is all on the side I don't want to join. There's not a living on the Left-wing weeklies . . . the only ones who ever try to tell what's going on. The New York *World-Telegram* and the *Times* are good, of course . . . but I know they're full up. . . .

"I've a terribly strong desire to try something else. . . . I can't tell you what it is just now. . . . If I were younger, felt more enthusiastic, I'd get a job under the Administration. . . . But I'm fed up with politics. . . . If you were here we could talk things over, but don't worry—I'm thirty-nine, sober, and coming back to my right mind. . . . I may do a Phœnix yet. . . . I'm giving myself a vacation to begin with—phoning Bill Draper to-night to see if he can sneak off from the law business and the highly possessive Janet (she's smarter, by the way, and has gone

Oxford Group)—to see if he can spend a couple of weeks down Chesapeake Bay with me. . . . How'd you like a farm on the Eastern Shore? . . . Remember? . . ."

One letter looked hopeful, and amazingly opportune at the moment. It was from a radio corporation asking him would he care to do a series of talks on the United States. They would like to see him on the question. It was addressed to the paper and was now over a week old. He would see them in New York.

When he was throwing the envelopes into the waste-basket he found himself automatically looking around for another one. He knew what it was, the gap in this first correspondence he had had since leaving England. There was nothing from Flick.

He looked at his watch, saw that it was now seven o'clock in New Jersey, and put through his call. . . .

* * *

As time was of no importance, Tony made Chicago in two days. He held the car at eighty-five miles an hour on the empty western highways whose perspective opened through racing swamps and hours of sun-scorched plains. He fretted as other cars blocked his way in the towns and cities that lay between. His mood was the driving combination of anxiety and desire. For he had never yet overcome his early terror of New York, that modern Monitor, waiting at the end of his schoolhood days to take away his youth. He never had believed that man could be born to spend fifty weeks every year of his life in an office of some sort; he did not believe that now: but he knew enough now to know the man-trap that New York could be, and that what man could make of himself, those glorious possibilities, and what the average American actually did content himself that life should be were two entirely different things.

And very tragic it was, too: the fatalistic way the average New Yorker accepted his shuttle-existence in the ceaseless interaction of roaring subways, elevated railroads, trolleys, and the final express elevators that shot him vertically upward to begin his task. More unpardonable, because, instead of admitting that life had forced him to accept this fractional, microbe existence on the revolving belt, the average New Yorker usually boasted of it: Gotham, he told you angrily, if you dared to criticise it, was the finest city in the world.

Christina had had only one summer in this madhouse of seven million people on narrow Manhattan Island. But it had been a terrifying one for a person with her comfortable South Kensington life. On those suffocating summer nights, as they panted for air on some bench along Riverside Drive—fleeing from the obscenity of their narrow little slit of an apartment—they had vowed that once they could escape, starvation itself could not bring them back to this slave-mill again. New York held no prizes that they wanted to win—or that they could not gain more leisurely and in a civilised climate. New York, Chris insisted—after she had become thoroughly frightened and angry with its senseless rush—was not the inevitability that all eager Americans, even Tony, accepted it to be.

Chris, being English, a woman, and someone who did not have to work, had had the average English tourist's idea of New York for the first few weeks. That it was the most exhilarating, beautiful, and luxurious city in the world. She had had no way of knowing that it could also be the most cruel. She never saw, with her Londoner's idea of comfortable city life, the most glittering ghetto in the world. And Tony was determined, if he could make a success of things, never to let her see the meaning of the city's crowded streets.

Chris, at first, had not understood the significance of the book-like thickness of the New York Sunday newspapers—

why they were so big that it would take a whole day to read them; nor the convenience of the soda-fountain beneath their wretched kennel called an apartment house, whose awful actuality, as one of the chief compensations of New York life, did not dawn on her until she got the full meaning of a New York Sunday. It was when she was reduced to reading the comic strips, the pages that most New Yorkers usually began with, and she realised that you can't get out into the real country from New York, not unless you have plenty of money, and that their proprietors expect you to lie around and read their book-like newspapers all day; that an apathetic walk in Central Park and a repair to the soda-fountain afterwards, with a movie to top it off, are the most that any such city dweller can expect from any day of the week, that Chris broke out into alarmed and open rebellion.

Tony, always of a practical mind when adversity had him in a corner, took a pencil and paper and sketched out an amusing, because it was so terrifying, chronology of their lives. "Here you are, my sweet. Here's my morning battle in the subway to get down to work. . . . Here's the hour I usually manage to snatch for lunch . . . and here's my subway battle to get back to you at night. Here we are going to a movie or a show. . . . And there, my love, is our pet soda-fountain . . . in the drug-store which sells *Sex*, *True Confessions*, *Hollywood*, ham sandwiches . . . all, very correctly, included under the list of American drugs.

"For six days a week shalt thou labour . . . and do nothing else except this. Sunday, you know about. Unless we get out we shall be expected to do this for fifty out of every fifty-two weeks in the year. That means that in twenty-six years we shall have had one whole year to our very selves. . . . Now, do you see any way to get around this argument? Aren't my mathematics indisputable? I know New Yorkers won't admit it—but there it is in cold black and white."

Well, they had made their escape. They had seen their dawn at Astrakhan: they had witnessed the sensible lives the Germans live—the athletic Sunday crowds out on Wansee, the *gemütlich* little beer gardens for those elderly ones who stay in town; they had stood, thrilled, in its main railway station and watched all able-bodied Munich, with skis and rucksacks, going out to the mountains; they knew the peace of a Paris Sunday, the week-end cottages and shoals of bicyclists by which all Londoners who care to can quickly escape into the country from the indescribable Sunday boredom of that great city's West End. For the last ten years they had lived large periods of their lives far beyond the reach of any city at all: in the Balkan villages, in remote parts of Russia, in the gentle English countryside, in the snowy mountains of Slovenia, far beyond where the pavement ends. . . . Like the physical pain it actually was, they had quickly forgotten their feverish frustration in New York.

And now he was deliberately driving back to it. Driving just as fast as he could go. Quickly, he told himself: I must make the beginning, and get it over with.

He had made this decision automatically. In London, that dreadful night when his drunken argument had led to the decision to live apart from Christina, he had thought of returning to the States as the one way of making a complete break with the European scene. He had not been aware of the full purport of his action then. But in the Dakotas, even as he typed out his brief resignation from the paper, the skyline of New York rose like a mechanical silhouette in his mind. After all these years he was, at heart, still an American. And a hundred percenter, at that. It was New York, when the cards fell for a new start in life, that he saw as the one and only place to begin. In his mind's eye, its man-made cliffs again rose up, staring at him with their millions of office windows—that challenge of towering masonry which he had faced with so much uneasiness every time he

returned to it since before the War. He had always known
that one day New York would get him. And now it had.

The chief reason, he knew, why he was deliberately going
to the one place he feared most was just because he wanted
to tackle the most frightening enemy at the start. The reason
why New York had trapped him was just because of the
failure he had made of his own life. Not something that had
happened to him, a turn of bad luck: but a thing which
he had deliberately brought on himself. The first years with
Chris—when he had felt, perhaps foolishly, that he must
protect and guard her from many of the ugly facts of trying
to make a new start in post-War American life—his very
thoughtfulness for her had made, or kept him a decent man.
Then, when life suddenly became easy for them, even
glamorous, so exciting was his work, he had let himself go
to pieces. He had satiated himself so with vicarious sensations that he had acquired a craving to gorge his own
physical senses as well—and he had acquired the cynicism
and looseness of thinking which impelled him to gratify
them. That was why he was like a wide-open gate when
Flick came along. He was ready for her. So ready that his
headlong gallop for gratification could not be reined up
even after Flick, when she saw the wildness she had aroused
in him, tried to tame him again. He had ridden for a fall.
He had had it. Now he was starting with a cool head again.

Well, here it was. As he drove across town through the
desolate Sunday streets he thought of Bill Draper and himself coming into town the next morning. Bill had shouted
his jubilation over the telephone all the way from New
Jersey to the Dakotas, that Tony had decided to settle down
and at last become a good American, as Bill phrased it. He
had at once declared that he knew at least a couple of good
jobs in New York that Tony could create for himself with
all his experience: and the beginning of Tony's dismayed
protests that he may not want to settle down in New York
for all the rest of his life was buried under Bill's shouted

exhortations to cut the cackle and come east at once, and to leave it to him about fixing up the boat for the Chesapeake Bay trip. As he swung left to go out upon that beautiful aerial ribbon of the Washington Bridge overhanging the Hudson, Tony reflected that it was just twenty-one years since he and Bill had been down that old bay together . . . planning so eagerly in the cockpit of the little *Spindrift* the lives they would lead.

He had not let Bill know that he would get to his place this afternoon, and he was glad that it was raining, which would drive Bill home from the golf-course. He did not want to get there and have the anti-climax of having to pursue Bill around the grounds of the Country Club. Bill's car was parked before the porch steps and Tony jumped from his and entered the house without ringing. Bill and Janet were sprawling in Morris chairs in the library, surrounded by a litter of Sunday newspapers. He thought they were having a quarrel at first: there was something so restrained in their greeting. And then Bill, still holding his hand, said: "Tony—come out on the porch a minute. I want to speak to you."

Out there Bill put his arm around him. "I'm afraid, old boy, I've got some bad news for you. It's about Chris."

"Dead?"

Bill nodded and placed a newspaper clipping in his hand. Bill went in and Tony heard Janet say to him, "You brute! How could you do it to him like that!" and Bill's reply: "Well . . . he had to know it sooner or later. . . ." And the words boomed like a gong in his head as he read:

9 DIE—GERMAN AIR CRASH

Seven passengers and both pilots were instantly killed to-day when the London plane crashed immediately after taking off from Cologne Aerodrome.

. . . Only one American was among the victims of the

accident: Mrs. Anthony Lynd, wife of the American newspaper correspondent. . . .

Other names are: Frederick Wayson, English journalist. . . .

Tony took a pencil from his pocket, and began to cross out the last lines.

INTERMISSION

In Hamburg, aside from its famous Tropical Institute, he knew there was a famous scientist whose *Klinic*, if rumour was right, was a voluntary prison. Once you place yourself in that great specialist's hands, you do not leave his locked walls until he tells you to. Tony went to him. He went after three nights alone in Cheyne Walk, in that haunted little house, where every step that he took, every door that he opened struck him blow after blow with the memory of Christina, until his mind gave under it. The next day he gave the keys to Harrods, directed that they should pack every solitary thing they saw inside the house and store it somewhere, and took the night boat from Harwich.

As the lights of England fell behind him he intended never to see them again.

He knew when the white-coiffed nuns silently admitted him and locked the double row of doors behind him that he had voluntarily surrendered his liberty to another man. It was time. The old gentleman made him undress completely and lie on a sofa while he twisted his legs, tapped him with a rubber hammer, and then with the faintest of brushes lightly touched him, making him keep his eyes tightly closed and say *"Ja!"* when he felt this gossamer touch. At the end when Tony stood there in the indignity of his nakedness, and all that it implied, the old man said:

"Monsieur, vous ne pouvez pas aller à Londres—vous resterez ici!"

The old German's macabre French was a sinister part of this humiliating examination. He knew that the gay white trellis over the window of his room was really made of steel. He knew that in his narrow room, and in a carpeted corridor thirty paces long by three paces across, he, and the eight men whose doors opened on to that walking space, were as

LL

isolated from the outside world as the mutilated dogs he had seen in Pavlov's Petrograd laboratory.

Some of these men were also disfigured. On the day the two nuns had locked the doors behind him he saw a figure walking at him. It was a man dressed in plus-fours and carpet slippers, wearing a Tyrolean jacket with an Iron Cross in its button-hole, with two eyes set in a scarred face that were as opaque as blue marbles. He never turned his eyes. When he wanted to look in another direction, he turned his whole body. He was a German major, a "shocker," who had been blown up by a land mine during the World War, and, Tony learned, this was the third time he had been in there.

That day, as this automaton figure approached him, Tony stepped out of his direct path, and watched him march until he came face to face with the oak door. Then the major did an about turn and marched back again. He kept his arms straight down, pressed against his sides, as he marched.

Another man came up, grinning loosely and dressed in a green bath-robe, who giggled in American-German: "Do you know Graf von Eckstein? . . . *I* know Graf von Eckstein. . . ." This man never did anything except lie on a sofa in the corridor all day, never picked up a book or a newspaper, and always arose and tried to look gay and careless when the little scientist strode through. The great specialist never said more than ten words to any of them: he did not believe in attracting a case's attentions to his own symptoms. . . . But Tony knew that every request that he made, the amount of food that he ate, the names of the Tauchnitz books that he asked them to send out for, and the hours he spent writing magazine articles on his typewriter, were all noted down meticulously in his dossier. One of the most depressing spectacles he was forced to witness in life was the daily evening effort of the man who knew Graf von Eckstein trying to appear happy—and normal— when the little specialist hurried through. The man did so want to get out, to run, anywhere outside those closed doors, out into the free streets with the people moving about in them, into the green fields, where even a tramp could lie, before the doctor nodded his head finally, and they sent him off to some place where he would be locked up for the rest of his life, and he would never get out into the world again.

And there were so many people walking freely about the streets, they knew, who were more mad than they were.

In some incredible fashion Flick learned where he was and sent a carefully worded wire to him that she was coming to Hamburg and must see him on important business. By a mistake which never should have been allowed to happen—because the assistant doctor had been told to humour him—Tony was led to believe that he would be allowed out the next morning to go down and meet her. With a surge of joy that matters no longer rested in his hands (she must be already on the boat by the time this cable was handed to him) he had shown it to the young surgeon, who nodded sympathetically and patted him on the back. It was all he could do to feign sleep that night, so that the night-sister would not report that he had been "emotional." A very dangerous symptom to have noted in your book. He was already dressed the next morning when his cubicle door opened, and the great scientist stood there.

"*Monsieur . . . vous voulez aller dehors?*"

"*Oui!*" smiled Tony, trying not to look like the man who knew Graf von Eckstein.

"No," said the specialist. Then, in phonetic English: "*M'sieu*—your brain is in grave peril. No!"

Tony sat down on the edge of his bed. It was vital now not to show any emotion—not even to fake a congenial acquiescence. He must be absolute in his action. "Very well," he said, shrugging his shoulders, "I must do what you say."

"*C'est juste!*" said the scientist.

"Now," said Tony, "I shall stay here until you, your-self, send me out—I shall never ask you to let me go again."

The little old man came over and put a hand on Tony's shoulder. "*Monsieur*," he said, in his execrable French, "there is no use fighting a war that can't be won. But you can win this war. You can be saved. Therefore you must fight."

Tony nodded and, standing up, took off the coat of his grey suit. He hung it back on its hanger. In the "looney-bin," as he always called this place to himself, he never wore anything but slippers, an old blue flannel shirt, a pair of fairly presentable flannel trousers and a battered tweed coat that he had fished, shot and slept in. The peaty smell of that old Harris was a comfortable reminder of days on bleak Shetland moors, and utter loneliness. . . .

*   *   *

There was singing above him at nights, so hoarse and loud that he wondered that it was permitted in such a scientific establishment. Then he learned that they were split-mentality cases, lying in hot chemical baths, where they lay from six to midnight every day, and were then given a powerful injection to knock them out until some time the next day. Some of them would have to have these injections every day of their lives. Their illusions had become the real world they lived in; and this world was illusion—it frightened them. There were thuds of feet some nights on the floor above him, the heavy clunk as booted internes rushed to the case, a sharp squeak as an injection was forcibly given . . . and then silence. In the morning he would see straps of white canvas webbing, drying from the steel lattice above. There was one little figure who never got out of his night shirt, who trotted back and forth, back and forth, from the corridor door to his lattice window all day. Then he would clutch hold and peer through the lattice . . . like a mouse. . . .

Once or twice Tony heard himself cautioning his own self: "Steady . . . hang on . . . blast you!" It would be so easy to let these shrieks and things get on your nerves, or you might get impatient. There were men behind glazed doors who roared like lions, and where there was an inside lattice . . . far away from the glass. His profession made every experience in life interesting, and he found he was able to take an unemotional interest in his own progress. For instance, a few days later, he knew that the doctor would have been mad to have let him go outside that day. That morning he had been nothing but a jungle of emotions, with no pattern; and he thanked God that Flick had not seen him. He smiled as he thought of the pressure the highly intelligent and forceful Flick must have put on the old scientist—the old man looked positively grim when he told Tony that he would not discuss that scene. And, he thought, as he could always depend upon Flick's intelligence, she would be wise enough not to worry if she did not hear from him. Flick, in fact, probably knew more about him than he did himself.

The man on the left of him died, so did the one on the other side of him. The first one had been a walking mummy who, in a camel's-hair bathrobe, stood in one spot for half an hour before he could send a nerve-message along to his foot to take him a step further in the direction of the toilet. Tony, reading a book in the corridor, noticed that it took him nearly an hour to go ten feet. One morning he saw a slight woman, all in black, talking with the nun before his door, and he knew what had happened.

One of the worst scenes to face was the incoming cases. They were brought in on a grim little pram with rubber wheels and a long horizontal hood of red canvas, with a celluloid window in its side. Through that peep-hole he saw their twisted faces as they passed, and, what remained of the men they once were, being unstrapped, pulled out and lifted into a bed in the cubicles.

And not one of these interesting, perplexing cases in the corridor was the victim of an accident, a man who had been run over by a trolley or a car; they had just been under the wheels of Life. The distinguished Hanover surgeon, for instance, who knew too well how morphia can deaden pain, or make one forget, whose forearm was dotted with punctures, and who was considered one of the most hopeless cases. The inmates of the *Klinic's* poor wards walked the cement courtyard in striped hospital suits, with the torn and bleeding faces that they had scratched at nights. . . . Tony, looking down, counted thirty-four of them. There were a hundred or so more locked up, or strapped to their beds, the howlers at nights. He was allowed, after a time, to go out in the yard and walk with the thirty-four—and watch them try to catch the pigeons with their hands. He wanted the fresh air.

He was told that there were certain hours when the poor patients could not use the yard, and he and the Iron Cross Major, and the man who knew Graf von Eckstein, could have the yard alone to themselves if they wanted it. But he preferred to walk with the others; it was a good test for him. And he knew that it was noted down in his dossier. The nuns always smiled at him peacefully when he came in from these walks.

It was these nuns who were his greatest adventure in this prison of his—the long, interesting, thought-provoking talks that he soon came to have with them. When he searched for the secret of their undoubted happiness. Swathed in black woollen skirts, with their breasts lashed flat with stiff white aprons pinned so as to conceal every outline of the woman in them, these placid creatures brought the very essence of contentment into his thoughts. The head nun had a gay sense of humour, although she had never been outside this corridor for twenty-seven years (except two weeks every year when she went straight from the *Klinic* to a train for her convent), and after she was off duty this light-hearted woman would pay an unofficial visit to him every night. She would stand there and chat. He wondered at her absolute happiness. She looked down, wondering perhaps what he was thinking, who had seen so much of the world. And the thought made them both laugh. She made it plain that she thought him rather a sinner, but there was hope. . . .

And he, with his smattering of German, and his lexicon, managed to tell her that, although he had always been sceptical, she was making him think that there was something after all to be said for the good life. He did not say this facetiously, although he tried not to be too solemn about it—he didn't want Sister Theresa to think that he was a case of "when the Devil is sick the Devil a saint would be." But he wanted her to know that he appreciated her sheer goodness—and he did.

Just plain goodness. . . . He pondered on that. When he looked at Sister Theresa now as she came into his room—to bring him his coffee for breakfast or straighten up his books and papers, after he had been writing all day, he saw her with understanding. He began to feel that he was seeing life itself that way. One afternoon, when he was reading in the corridor, he felt as if someone had reached inside and untied a knot in his brain . . . it was a consciously physical sensation . . . he put his hand up to feel his head. . . .

He woke up half an hour later in the same chair. His book lay beside him on the floor where it had fallen. He felt a drowsy contentment such as he had not remembered since he was a boy. When the specialist came into the corridor that night he felt that this was so remarkable that he must speak about it. The great doctor nodded towards his room and followed him into it.

"Something *must* have happened," said Tony incredulously.

"It has," said the scientist. "Look at your face."

Tony stared at himself in the mirror. Where there had been lines in his forehead cut deep as if gouged with a carpenter's steel marker there was now a smooth brow. Three weeks later the *Deutschland* came up Southampton Water, but Tony did not get off her. No one knew he was on board. He felt his heart tug as he heard her cable clunking in through the hawse-pipes, and he clutched the rail until his knuckles were white as he watched the green shores he knew so well drop behind him. In the dusk the coast of England dropped below the horizon and the *Deutschland* rolled in the slate September seas. Then there was just the cold wind and the lighthouses flashing. . . . He went below to his cabin and sat there, and stared at the little steamer trunk he had taken from Cheyne Walk to Germany, at his suitcases splattered with the hotel labels of Europe's capitals, at his shotgun and the cases of trout rods that he and Christina had so often packed together.

And at that moment, as the door was locked, he dropped his head in his hands and wept bitterly.

THE LAKE

"What's he like?" asked Virgie.

"How can I tell?" answered Ken. "Ain't much chance for conversation, driving that truck up the trail. Seems all right."

"Now I know everything. Thanks."

"Well . . . if you must have details: He's an American, somewhere around forty, doesn't drink—least he didn't want it when I offered him a shot—six feet, sandy hair, white and unmarried, far as I can tell. Doesn't look like a grouch, but looks to me like a man that'll keep to himself. Like the Hun."

"Well, that's not much of an addition."

"Nope. Wouldn't call him an addition. And if he does get feeling matey, I'd say it will be with the other people up the lake. The Debenhams. Their sort."

"I *thought* he looked nice."

"You did, did you? Well, you won't see much of him except on mail days. It's a seven-mile row from his place to here. I asked him if he wasn't going to get an outboard motor, and he said he didn't think so—not yet. That's what made me say I thought he'd keep himself to himself. Same as you ought to do."

Virgie had watched her husband and Swanson, the big Swede, helping the newcomer with his things down to Swanson's launch. There had been a whole motor-lorry full of stuff; but Swanson had borrowed a couple of skiffs and was towing the whole damned interesting outfit up to Mead's place right away.

"People on this lake," she said angrily, "act as if it was a damn' crime to talk to each other!"

* * *

"You had some bad luck!" Swanson yelled in Tony's ear. (His boat-engine was just an ordinary Buick motor with its muffler taken off.) "Tree fell and knocked off one end of your place since you seen it two weeks ago."

"How about a place to sleep?"

"Oh—you can get in the door all right . . . just knocked off one end. Big fir. Chop it up and you got enough firewood to last the whole winter!" Swanson grinned; it was, evidently, his idea of a joke.

*   *   *

The tree was both a bad and a good start. It was a terrific object, seen lying on the ground, about two hundred feet long and a good ten feet thick at its base by the up-turned roots. Its branched tip had crashed through the kitchen end of Mead's old cabin. "You'll need a hand with this," said Swanson profoundly.

"Just what I was thinking. Want the job?"

The big Swede started to accept, and then said: "I'd give it to the Count. That's an old German lives up above you—that's his smoke up there. He'd like a job. Want me to speak to him? He won't ask much. He's broke."

*   *   *

In the morning, when Tony was unpacking his stuff, he saw a bluff red rowboat being pulled up on the beach. A fantastic figure came towards the cabin, a German Falstaff wearing a kilt, with a French *béret* on its head. It stopped at the door and bowed.

"Captain Heinrich von Hauptmann," it said, hands pressed politely against its side.

"Anthony Lynd," said Tony, trying not to smile. "Won't you sit down? I don't know where."

"I am told you require my services?"

"Oh, yes, the tree—you've seen it, of course?"

"The tree—yes. That I shall cut with you without pay-ment—such is the custom here. In return, if you will be so kind, you will come up to my place and assist me with a tree of my own. It takes two men to handle a cross-cut saw. But these other things"—the Count looked around the cabin; at the hole in the far end of the cedar-shingled roof; at the floor boards, shrivelled with the rain and snows of twenty years; at the broken windows—"I shall make you an estimate for these."

"Oh, I'll do a lot of this myself," said Lynd firmly.

"We shall see," said the Count.

*   *   *

The German was not a bad helpmate, not at first. As they toiled with the cruel cross-cut saw during the last of the sunny days Tony found his philosophy quite invigorat-ing. Captain von Hauptmann said that the only way to live in the woods was to keep entirely to yourself. In that way you permitted yourself to get in tune with the forest. If the forest meant nothing to you then you would find it very difficult indeed to reconcile yourself to life out here. It would be far better to live in some big city, even if you were so poor that you had to live in the ugly parts. It was not easy to live in the woods. You had to find a philosophy.

While at first that sounded rather pompous, Lynd soon came to think that the Count was right. If you permitted yourself to associate with the people down at the store, said the Count, you were neither one thing nor the other; you merely had a cheap, crude life. That, he said, had been the trouble with old Mead; Mead was not a real gentleman; he had not had sufficient pride, or courage, to live alone. He wanted company, no matter what it was. And they had laughed at him, those people around the store. . . .

They knew he was not the real thing. A man must watch himself.

The Count asked Tony no questions; where he had come from, or why. He volunteered no essential information about himself. When Tony rowed up to return the Count's assistance by helping him with his tree, the old German was obviously pleased to show him around his unbelievable house. He called attention to the staring heads of game, saying he had shot them in German East Africa. He agreed with Tony that his German combination shotgun and rifle was a beautiful and handy weapon. He conducted him with pride through his imposing private carpenter's shop. "As for the rest," he said modestly, "it is very much what you would expect, is it not?"

It was not. The last thing Lynd could have expected was to find a Bavarian *Schloss* in B.C. During his tour of the strange house he was conscious of a figure that moved about silently, and when the Count said, "We shall now have some coffee and cakes," what had obviously once been a very pretty girl came in and quietly took her place at a table that had already been laid. She was not old now, but she was very thin, and the peculiar yellow of her waxlike skin made her vast head of auburn hair seem, somehow, most unpleasant. As if she was conscious that she did not please, she made painful efforts not to be brought into the conversation. The Count did not seem to notice this, as he was doing most of the talking. His topic was the ruthlessness of the Allies in the Treaty of Versailles.

In that, as it happened, he had a willing listener in Tony, who was able to tell him many of the recent scandals of the Geneva fiasco. But so successful was the arrogant German in provoking a retort, that before they had finished the excellent coffee and cakes, Lynd found himself heatedly defending the French.

*   *   *

Work around the cabin kept Tony busy most of that first winter. The largest object on the landscape needing attention was the fallen fir. The weight of wood on the ground, its brute immobility, instead of its airy gracefulness became apparent to Lynd when he and the Count cut off the top and tried to move it from the cabin. They had to cut it into little sections. "Ha-ha-ha! . . ." the Count laughed triumphantly in his beard in the sunshine as he saw Tony stand up after vainly trying to move a slab; "you learn these things. . . ." It was as if he had just assisted in giving Lynd a lesson of the woods. It looked a woefully long time before they would have finished sawing that long trunk into discs, about a foot thick, a size that would go in his kitchen range; and then split all the wood circles into kindling wood, and have to stack it. The Count encouraged Tony to be practical. "In the vinter," he gutturalled, for he still was awkward with his "w's"—"you vill appreciate this" (he sometimes said "abbreziate"). "You will be thankful that you do not out in the cold snow have to go in search of firewood. And ven the drifts are big—you do not get it. You use bark—and *pouf*! The bark is up the chimney. . . . No, it is always better, my friend, to have a big supply of firewood well on hand. It is your friend!"

But they had not got half-way through the fir, largely owing to the German's conversation, before the rainy season hit them. For six weeks the rain rattled like lead shot on the cedar roof. Lynd thought he would go mad at times. Then he turned to work inside the cabin. He became so interested in his handicraft that he often discovered he had let his last cup of coffee stand untouched upon the table. It was a table he had made by splitting off a thick board slab from the fallen fir. It had never occurred to him at first; but, in a place where he saw nothing but forests all around him, he could not get a sawn plank.

He had to split the great slab off with wedges, and then plane it smooth. He collected a painful array of blisters, which, after he had pin-pricked the water out of them, became red and then soon turned into callouses. But when he had finished, using peeled ash trunks for legs, he had a long refectory table such as the old monks would have made.

On this he ate and read beside the oil lamp on long and silent nights. And there were nights that frightened him when he could not drive that sickening feeling from his heart that if he had remained in London poor Chris would not have been driven to this desperate experiment—of—of whatever her relations were with Freddy Wayson—he would never know. It did not matter. But it was he who had driven Chris to her end.

*   *   *

It was with no feeling of adventure that he faced this wilderness. He despised himself. If he struggled out of it, this self-disgust, it was because this life would make him strong again. He had made the one great mistake of all his life, and he would ever pay for it. He wanted to. For that way, only, lay his absolution.

*   *   *

During the rainy season, Lynd learned another reality of the lake; and that was what it was to row seven miles down to the store. With the head winds that he often had to meet, such a thing as a raincoat was an impossibility. And he did not have one; he always lost them. An ordinary "seaman's" slicker that he had bought in Seattle fairly steamed him when he wore it. So he soon learned the physical despair of being out in that relentless weather, when the rain even finally came through his felt hat—unless he wore it Montana fashion—blew into his eyes, and ran in a trickle off his nose. Like any logger, when he reached it, he steamed the moisture out of himself by standing as close as he could get through the throng around the red iron stove in Smedley's store.

He did a lot of thinking on these dreary rows, often about a low, green little skiff, with a most unseaworthy cabin built atop of it, which *tump-tump-tumped* morosely out from the further shore, just where he turned around the arm of Bald Mountain to get into the main lake. This was the Tread boat, as steady, and reliable, and slow as that old dyspeptic settler himself. Lynd usually saw him only at a distance, as Tread went down, hugging the lee of the shore himself. But one gale of a day, when Tony was hardly making any headway against the howling winds that swept over the mountains from the Pacific as he fought his way back from the store, the green launch came alongside him and old Tread threw out a line. "Make her fast!" the old man shouted above the wind. "Then climb aboard."

Lynd threw his home-made waterproof canvas bag into Tread's cockpit and negotiated the exchange from boat to boat. The old settler, who had picked up the habit of chewing tobacco somewhere in the mist of his early American days, shoved things off a seat on the other side of the little one-cylinder engine, and gave Tony a watery grin.

"All hell and get out, ain't it?" said the old man, nodding towards a slate lake, frothing with racing white caps. "I kinda thought you'd welcome a tow to-day?"

He tried to make Lynd let him tow him out to the mouth of North Arm, from which Tony would have the gale behind him on his way home. When Tony would not hear of it, Tread then insisted that Lynd come into his place for tea. Maybe, by that time, he said, the wind would drop. "No use ruining yourself!" said the old man.

*   *   *

The Tread home was a museum of evolution on the lake. A side room, made of grey weathered logs, was only a store-house now, but it had been the original cabin Tread had built forty years ago. Built on to it was the long main room in which they now sat down to tea. This room was also made of logs, but polished on the inside, with their crevices chinked with grey moss. The huge flat-topped stove that stood at the far end was the latest thing of its kind on the lake, with a hood for warming dishes and keeping food hot, and a deep section on one side with a hot-water tap. With its various rings and ovens it offered enough cooking combinations to keep old Mrs. Tread happily employed all the day. The tea biscuits that she put down before them were excellent; so was their own blackberry jam, made from the wild berries of their own clearing, which were also greatly favoured by the bears.

In fact, when he was having tea with the Treads one day, Billy came racing in and snatched his rifle, yelling to Lynd that he had seen a black bear eating blackberries down at the end of the forest clearing where he was ploughing. Lynd, who had shot plenty of deer in his life, but had never seen a live wild bear, ran as fast as his legs would permit him through the woods, just in time to see the excited Billy taking aim. He felt sorry for the poor bear, standing up there on his hind legs and pulling the bushes down to him with both paws—it was such a lovable, childish action. Then the bear crumpled up and began to roll over and over on the ground.

"Hi!" said Billy, shouting the first thought of the woods —"There's some fresh meat!"

*   *   *

The life of the two Tread boys was also shown in this log-walled living-room. Two glass-covered cases of birds' eggs and butterflies they had collected as children. The prongs of the first deer he had shot, now used to hold Matt's Winchester rifle. A library containing *With Clive in India*, *Pike and Dyke*, nearly all the G. A. Henty books, *Midshipman Easy*, *The Rover Boys*, Oliver Optic's canoe club stories;

David Copperfield, Ivanhoe, Kenilworth, Marmion, Tom Sawyer, Huckleberry Finn, the stories of Bret Harte; and a corner rack of histories, geographies, almanacs and a three-volume encyclopædia.

Old Tread, who had been watching Tony with eager eyes as he saw him reading nearly every title of this shelf, finally said: "Want any of 'em? I like to read them over myself. Mrs. Tread and I got a lot of pleasure out of reading those books there to the boys . . . when they were growing up."

Neither of the two Tread boys had been to an elementary school, but had learned their early lessons in the cabin, where both old Tread and his wife divided up the work they thought each was best suited to teach. They had sent both boys down to Quamicot, twenty miles below, to live there during the three years they went to grammar school. Then the War came, and adventurous Matthew, two years older than Billy, vanished from Quamicot and enlisted in Princess Pat's, coming out after the Armistice as a sergeant; and Billy had grown big enough to help his father keep open some of the fields.

Mrs. Tread deplored this cabin-schooling that was all they could give the boys; but the old man shook his head and said that what he had been taught at school in England hadn't helped him very much, and that he thought most education was "just stuffing." To both their surprise, Tony said heartily: "I absolutely agree with you! There's a tremendous amount of talk about all that now . . . the foolishness of all the importance formerly attached to examinations, and all that nonsense that made life such a hell when I was a boy. . . . But it came too late for me, I'm afraid! . . . ."

The men laughed, and as they did so Tony realised how very, very little old Mrs. Tread knew of what had happened in the world during the last forty years. She obviously thought it wicked of him to jeer at such a sacred, hard-come-by thing as education, and sneer at "examinations."

She was a sea-captain's daughter whom Tread had gone down and brought up from Victoria some thirty-five years before, and she was wearing a black woollen dress that she had made herself. Old Tread, Lynd learned, was the only person present when his two sons had been born; and it was he who had taken them away from their mother, and cut the cords. . . .

It made him think of Gorky's first story in *Through Russia*, where he tells of how, as a wandering vagabond, he assisted at the birth of a child on the Caucasian shore of the Black Sea. And, with the exception of old Dr. Feather, who had probably forgotten all he knew, there was no doctor on Scaup Lake now. None until Quamicot.

Even at that first tea, the Treads took Lynd enough into their confidence to tell him of their worries about Matthew. He had been very queer, they said, after he came back from the War. Gloomy and silent. They did not know what to make of him. But Billy, they both said, was a very happy boy. "He hasn't had much to disturb him," said old Tread.

This unexpected tea was turned into a welcome to Lynd on Scaup Lake. The Treads insisted that he stay to dinner with them. "You won't have anybody at home, waiting for you!" laughed old Tread. And Lynd met Matthew and Billy. Two amazingly different types. Matthew almost resented Lynd's polite questions about France, and tried to answer everything with merely "Yes" or "No." Billy, the cub, was full of questions, chiefly as to why Lynd had decided to settle on the lake. And how had he heard of it? Until his father shut him up. . . .

It was obvious that there was some sort of perpetual argument going on between his father and Matt. And part of it came out at the dinner that night. It was about a donkey-engine. The boys apparently saw no use in wasting their strength and lives in keeping open the back clearings in the forest and trying to cultivate land on Scaup Lake, when there was no way to get their produce to any market. This came out when old Tread, reminiscing about his forty years on the lake, said philosophically: "During that time I guess I've grown everything that could sprout, flap or walk—and lost money on all of them!" To which Matt said sullenly: "You certainly did." And Billy burst in: "Well, one of these days, Dad, you'll just have to be sensible and let Matt and me go into the logging business. Old James says he'll give us a standing order *any* time we buy that donkey-engine!"

The old man said: "No—you're not going to fell those trees . . . not while I'm alive. There's a lot in those trees, and I'm not going to have them cut down. What's the use of it all?"

"Only the money we can make," Matthew growled.

"Money? . . . Why're you always talking about money? Haven't we always been able to make a decent living on this land? Now, you cut down those trees, and——"

Matthew made a gesture and scowled at Lynd. It was obviously meant to tell his father not to discuss family affairs in public.

"Oh, all right," he said. "You have things your own way. It's your land."

"Now listen——" began Tread.

But Matt, to end the topic, stood up and began to stack the dishes on the table. And on this awkward note Lynd made his excuses and went home.

* * *

Scaup Lake was so far from Victoria, and the impotent or corrupt Forest Department, that the big timber magnate who was at that time logging the lake felt free to outrage every law of the Province and human decency in the way he was cutting down its forests to sell to England and Japan. The lake had sixty miles of shoreline, nearly all of it virgin forest. The stand of gigantic cedar at its head was said to be the largest in all Canada. James owned the *War Eagle* and the big No. 1 logging camp. The Swede, Swanson, with a few other Scandinavians, was working a small hand-logging outfit cutting around the edges of the lake, and pitching the easiest trees, which fell into the water. These were made into booms and towed down to the foot of the lake and sold to Jesse James. But the big timber man would buy anything, providing he could get it cheaply enough; and, when he came up to the lake, he had been encouraging the two Tread boys to log the big stands of cedar and fir that still stood untouched on the long shoreline of land which belonged to Henry Tread. A shoreline which the old settler stubbornly refused to have touched.

Having dinner with them that stormy night, Tony was unaware of the blasting effect this Tread donkey-engine would have on his life.

*   *   *

When the alders turned yellow Lynd took his Mannlicher and climbed to the ridge of Bald Mountain where he could look down upon the lake. It spread out before him like a large, irregular Y, with its base resting against the grey ridge of rocky mountains that shut it off from the Pacific, and his own cabin lying below at the foot of a broken arm. Beyond the narrow lake, on either side, rolled the impenetrable forest as far as the eye could see. From this height the green mat looked smooth as velvet, with only here and there the grey gap showing off some curving ravine. Except for a few optimistic and veteran prospectors who never would give up their search for "colour" in its pouring streams, most of the country had not been troubled by a white man. The Siwash Indians who once lived around Scaup Lake had been herded nicely by a kind Government on some Indian lands down by the mouth of the Scaup

River beside a shallow reach thirty miles below where they
could spear the salmon coming up from the Inland Passage.
A few of the more industrious among them still came up
to Scaup Lake and trapped over in the Nitinat country;
a wilderness so dangerous, because of trees which had been
falling over each other, rotting, and making pits ever since
the retreating Ice Cap, that they only went in there in pairs.
There were some Indians over on the Pacific side, a village
of Haida, who sat in their stone towers, watching for the
almost mythical sea otter whose skins sometimes brought a
thousand dollars a pelt. Otherwise this long fifteen-mile
stretch of upper lake was uninhabited, except for Lynd,
and von Hauptmann, and the remote logging camp on its
very head.

The mountains at the head of the lake played with colours
in the dying lights of day. On calm, sultry sunsets, they
seemed floating in mid-air; they were dark humps in the
mist; when there was neither rain nor heat-haze they
seemed to disintegrate, to powder into intangible shapes of
gold and rose. . . . It was on evenings like these that Lynd
missed Christina most. She would have loved this changing
scene. And when he let himself think about this he sat with
his chin resting in his cupped hands, and forgot the deer
he had come up there to kill. But if he stayed there long
enough his sorrows seemed to drowse and he felt that the
spirit of Christina was in this land he looked upon. He felt
tempted to call to her. He had no need of von Hauptmann
to warn him of the danger of breaking such a spell.

* * *

Towards the last of the rainy season the lake rose so high
with the swelling waters that the bushes on his foreshore
vanished beneath the waves and he began to wonder if the
lake was coming into his cabin. It was when he was laughing about this with Smedley down at the store that a clear

young voice said behind him: "Well—it has come into our
drawing-room! This time it actually lifted the rugs!"

He turned, and saw a young girl in whip-cord riding
breeches and rubber boots. She had blue eyes and fair hair.
"I'm Aline Debenham," she said. "I was just going to
bring a note across to you. We want you to come to dinner?"

"That's very nice. I'd love to." The Debenham place was
only four miles across the lake from him, but up until now
he had never seen this girl. From Swanson's gossip, he had
heard that both of the Tread boys were sick with love for
her. There was no other girl on the lake.

"Well—if you come to-morrow—you can row right in
our front door! No, I'm only joking. But just come as you
are. We all go like that."

To row four miles and back in the darkness, for a dinner
he did not want to eat, was not Tony's idea of what he would
have preferred. But he had accepted, and, leaving the lamp
burning on the table to locate his cabin on the way back, he
pulled rubber boots over his grey flannels, hauled the
stiff sticky yellow slicker over his tweed jacket, and set out
to row four miles on a misty night. If there had been
a telephone on Scaup Lake he would have made an excuse.

The Debenham ranch-house, as they called it, was about
the only part of their estate that was above the racing waves
at this time of the year. Two miles down across lake from
the mouth of the North Arm, he saw the row of lights from
its windows. It was an imposing place, for that part of the
world; and, as Aline had said, he very nearly could have
rowed in the front door. Instead he tied his rowboat to its
front steps and banged on the door. The laughter with
which Cecie and Copey Debenham greeted his wet entrance
showed at once the happy-go-lucky way these exiled English
people had accepted their misfortune. A morose little man,
who had not shaved that day, was introduced as the Growler,
and immediately said to Tony: "If you leave your boat
where it is, you'll scratch our paint."

He said nothing about the fact that, the waves banging it against the porch stairs as they would, they would also chip all the paint off Tony's rowboat. On the other hand, without waiting to let Tony do it, he went out and pulled up the skiff on the porch. He was already wearing a pair of knee-high white rubber boots. And he did not take them off for dinner.

With the Debenhams Tony had no need to worry about making conversation. Growler said nothing. But Cecie and Aline merely took turns asking questions—all of them about changing London. The smiling Copey managed to get in a word here and there, confined to the club that, as it turned out, both he and Lynd belonged to. Copey had not been in it for fourteen years. And the dinner surprised Lynd with what could be done, if one had enough persistence, in these parts. They had an excellent mushroom soup (tinned); but after that was a cold salmon that the Growler had been down to the salt Inlet to catch, one of the Debenham geese, with some home-grown potatoes, roasted; and a *compôte* (also tinned), but with cream so thick that Lynd had to use a spoon to get it from the jug.

"Our c-cow!" said Cecie Debenham, with her attractive stammer. "M-my dear, I don't see how she does it without a bull."

The Debenhams became positively feudal after dinner over the forthcoming marriage of the Duke of Kent with Princess Marina. Cecie Debenham's father had been a general, and it was strange, Lynd reflected, how a certain type of Englishwoman, born in a Service family, consciously feels as if she has a domestic interest in the Royal Family's life. Cecie's chances of seeing England again were very slim; Copey had three elder brothers who must die before he would come into the peerage, and enough money to allow him to return home. "Just my luck," he grinned philosophically, "to have three healthy brothers and not one of them even get wounded in the World War!"

On £600 a year, they said, they could not live in England, "So," said Aline, "we're pigging it out here."

She did not mean that. She had been five when the Debenhams came to Canada, and not until this year had she thought of the possibility of getting back. But Cecie had been planning; and now that Aline was eighteen they had decided to send her back. They had saved enough money to buy her tickets and give her a year to do what she liked.

Her one ambition was to dance with the Prince of Wales.

*　　*　　*

Christmas Tony spent with the Debenhams; he couldn't very well refuse their insistent invitation; but, he felt, he had been rather a wet blanket. When Christina was alive he had spent several Christmasses away from her in different parts of the world. But on this particular one he could not get out of his mind the pictures he was drawing of the wretched Christmas he had given her four years before, and what a cheerless companion he had been on that trip to Garmish. It was the heavy snow, perhaps, that brought that last German Christmas back so poignantly. Scaup Lake had suddenly become unbelievably beautiful with every tree in the tall forest encased in snow. He could not believe it when he climbed laboriously up to the ridge of Bald Mountain and saw that the green forests were now a glittering field of white sparkling under the intense blue sky. As this cold meant nasty work in an open rowboat if a snowstorm should start on Christmas night, the Debenhams had had their roast goose for lunch, so that, if necessary, he could row back to his own cabin before dark. It did not snow, but he made an excuse and left before sunset. The lake seemed unnaturally black and inhospitable across the red streaks of the dying sun; and for several minutes after he had rowed out beyond the lee of the Debenham point he sat there, letting his oars trail, debating if he wouldn't row down to Digger Bean's and spend the night. There would be some riotous doings down there. He would not have much time to think about himself after he got in *that* company!

But he did not want to test himself too far on this Christmas night; if he started in to drink in the woods, then he would completely go to bits. His only way was to persevere in the life that he had decided to live from now on.

* * *

The actual composition of this life he had determined to live came to him only in fragments. He could not see the entire scene. Its quality was to be just plain uprightness, if he had that in him—and from that to become something useful. Whatever that could be on this lake? For he had decided to remain here. As he made things for his cabin he did so with the feeling that they were for a permanent home. It was something unheard-of from his friends' point of view, and even from his own, to bury himself out here in the woods like this. And it amused him to get their occasional letters, Pat Byron's in particular, and read their amazement that he should be where he was.

They did not know the actual locality. When he had reached Seattle, which place he had used as a base while he looked about for a place to live, he had placed his affairs in the hands of a young lawyer he had been given a letter to there, a friend of Bill Draper's. And, since he had begun having his mail forwarded there, he had seen no reason for change. It meant only the loss of one day or so. And days on Scaup Lake, he soon came to believe, did not count at all.

Bill Draper had written him several letters, pleading with him "not to take things so hard," to come back to the States, "because, feeling the way you do, I don't see how you can stay out there and *not* be in the thick of things. I won't call you a quitter; I just think you're crazy. That's all. Anyway, I'm with you, so's Janet, and if there is anything we can do, why just let me know. . . ."

He felt that he simply had to answer that letter convincingly; first, to head off any more of them; finally, to clarify things with himself. He spent a long time drafting the letter, throwing away just-begun sheets, as he always did when he tried to write a short story; and, as always, he found himself hunting around the cabin to see if he couldn't find the first draft—because that was what he had wanted to say. The finished product he did not think convincing. Part of it said:

". . . You, I, all of our friends have always accepted it as axiomatic that we should live in a city. The farthest we have ever dared let our miserable imaginations roam was that we might have a home in the country—and commute. Isn't that so? Just try and think it over. . . . Now I know that you call me an Anglo-maniac. . . . Nevertheless, there's a community about thirty miles below here that's nothing else but Englishmen . . . retired Army and Navy officers . . . and things like that. One is a business man, retired after twenty years in China, where he made a pile. . . . So just to live somewhere on pensions isn't the sole reason. . . . Far from it; these people are living damn' good *interesting* lives. . . . You and I have always thought of shooting and fishing as something we did on vacation. . . ."

"No," said Tony to himself as he wrote that last: "I've got to be honest with myself in this letter! Therefore I've got to admit that I can already see the day coming when shooting and fishing are going to bore me, just as they do the Growler, and even Copey—who was brought up to that sort of thing—so I'll just point this out to Bill. Makes what I am going to say stronger, somehow."

". . . The point is, if I don't *want* to live in a city, why should I? Because I'm either just being a sheep, not thinking and following the rut—or else it's because I'm afraid of what my friends say. Can you give me another reason? And what you say about my owing a duty to the United States *is pure nuts*! To whom?—the political pimps? . . . to provide another hopeful but futile reformer? I'm not such a prig as to think the U.S. needs me. And if I did——"

"Now *here*!" grunted Tony to himself—"is just the main point."

"Bill, if I did think that, that I could be of any use—look what I would be up against! You know the way they buried my stuff on the paper when I said anything that knocked Big Business. Yes, and you know what your friend, the president of the broadcasting firm, said to you when, without my permission, you went to him and said that they ought to get hold of me—'Anthony Lynd's a radical,' he told you: 'We won't touch him.' So what am I to come back to do? Write social books? Yes, before Chris died I had thought of that. As long as she was alive I thought I had to take care of her, make money—you know, I talked it over with you even before I went out to Chicago—that book I was going to call *Created Equal*. I remember how sore you were when I said that was a good snotty title . . . because the one thing people weren't in the U.S. was equal. You said I was a Bolshie! Well, when I sent in my resignation out in the Dakotas that was the thing I was thinking of at the time—but on the drive back to New York I saw it wasn't a good idea—conditions under Roosevelt were changing so fast that the book would become obsolete while it was being printed. . . .

"I don't think Americans would have wanted to read it anyway. They'd think it unpatriotic!

"As it is out here—answering your last question—I'm doing nothing but just marking time. . . . Just living. . . . I'm not even trying to write! Now, if that isn't a break with my past life, I'd like to know what is? Another, Bill—I'm strictly on the wagon, and it looks as if I'm going to stay there. . . . This is my last word on the subject of coming back, so please don't get me stirred up by bully-ragging me about that. One of these days maybe you and Janet can visit me here. The . . ."

He added:

"And if you're worrying about my finances, how I am going to live, the capital I turned over to Chris before I left London, poor Chris turned over to me in her will. . . . *That might be the worst thing that has ever happened to me*—because without *something* to keep me going out here, I would have to get out—there is no way that I could make money out here, not with my dud leg. . . . So, by using very little capital, living chiefly on interest, and a bit of writing now and then—I can live here for life. . . . How's that for security?"

"Hmmm . . ." he thought, as he read the letter, "there are slews of Englishmen doing this all over the world! But I couldn't explain that to Bill. And the hell of it is, I can't even convince myself!"

He had shaved that morning by the log fire he had made in the main room of the cabin, and the mirror was still on the table he had pulled near the fireplace. He turned it around and studied his reflection in the glass. The pouches under his eyes had long since disappeared; for on the awful night when he had begun that final argument with Christina in London he had been drinking (it was a Sunday and he had just driven up after a week-end with Flick), and in the agony of that discussion that led to his sudden decision to live alone he had realised that some of the wild statements he was making came from a disordered mind. And at the sight of Christina's stricken face he had declared that same night, that he would stop drinking on the spot. It was on this basis—that he should really try to win back to his old self—that Christina had assented that perhaps the best thing for them both was for him to get out.

That was why, when he reached the States, he had plunged into his work with so much determination and taken all his pilgrimage as only the road which would lead back to himself. During the time he was writing the strike series he had never thought of a drink. In fact, he had rejoiced at the way his mind had come back to him. And with it, every day, had come a conscious return of old values. His mind was no longer heated and subject to fits of despondency when he saw another man with a pretty woman. He was, in fact, considering whether he would dare write Christina and report these miracles—for such they were—a happy letter that he knew would bring great relief to her—whether they came together or not—when Bill Draper had given the news of her death. Then, when the world came down round his head, he felt that the only thing to do was to keep on with this promise to find himself.

He was always paying Chris tributes she never knew about. He felt that he needed full command of his mind to face the fact of her death. He was one of the men to whom drink never gave "Dutch courage"; it always took it away from him. And out here, facing life without her, he did not grieve so much for her sake that she was dead—in her queer, fretful soul Chris had never had a great hankering for this world, neither of them had; it was just that in this scene they might possibly have had a splendid partnership. They would be living the existence in which she had always been her best.

Writing Bill had been difficult, because Bill had never had the true *Wanderlust* and been tortured by all that it meant.

Bill was essentially modern, a man who adopted contrivances. Bill would never know the ecstasy that drives some Austrians to attempt unscalable rock faces, nor the silent satisfaction of watching sunset on the empty peaks from the door of a mountain hut that you could reach only by risking your neck. Not that Bill wouldn't risk his neck; or that he would not make the climb; he just would not get the absolute soul-satisfaction from it. It was when they got to the parts which other people did not think worth getting to that Tony and Christina had so often begun to live. . . .

The appreciation of grey rock, and Alpine meadows blue with spring gentians, and just plain loneliness, Tony meditated, is a thing which you must consciously defend. Life will take it away from you, this ability to enjoy.

"Yes," he said, falling naturally now into the habit he was forming of holding imaginary conversations with himself, "you have to guard your values in this bleeding world. Your sense of appreciation rots, just like your wretched teeth. Stupid people are the first to get dulled. They see a little of life and become blasé, think they know the rest. That's the true *parvenu*. A great character won't stop growing no matter where it is put—not even in prison. You should find something each day that will widen your view of life. And I should be able to find that right here."

He was reasoning, he knew, along the lines that old von Hauptmann must have followed. It was the conscious adjustment of a man trying to live inside his own experiences. It was the intelligent man's answer to isolation. The vast difference, out here in B.C., compared to climbing somewhere in the Tyrol or the Dolomites, was that you always knew there that in a few hours you could climb down again to a rich civilisation. There would be the square in Bolzano or the fine life of the Alpine Austrians. You had both the pleasure of just your own company, or of others', in Europe. Here, in this real loneliness—you must find your civilisation inside your own self. You could accomplish this in either of two ways; you could concentrate on your immediate life, consciously creating an interest in each small task—and try to forget the rest of the world. The thing that very likely old Tread did without thinking. Or you could be more self-reliant than that; and that was to realise that this lake could not chain your mind . . . you could live more intensely your mental life on this quiet lake than you could in London. In that way, instead of becoming deadened, your mind would grow in stature.

It surprised him, to make a candid analysis of one of his usual London days—his meals, his work, his progress to the office, and possibly the entertainment of a theatre—and then contrast it with these days. He had not done so much thinking in London, he realised, or been always interested. What he was really missing most out here was just the movement of people. And he was not "living" any more when he was riding on the top of a No. 14 bus than when he was merely chopping wood out here. That was a truth he must impress upon himself constantly.

The danger, as the old Count had pointed out, was the life around the store. Once become involved with the vanguard of suburbia and no will-power he possessed could give his imagination the wings to escape. In the one or two casual talks Lynd had with Brinsley Greville he had seen enough to be aware of how that Englishman suffered, the contacts that he had to put up with, the privilege of his own personality that he had compromised with even on this far-off lake. He had no privacy. His wife, Zonia, was pretty, but an affected, frustrated little thing, always tackling Lynd in the store to come down and have dinner with them. Virgie Cullen, a hard-boiled blonde, also got into conversation while he waited at the store for mail. From the haughty dignity with which these two women met, Tony caught a few pictures of what a small hell social squabbles among the eight lower Scaup Lake families could be during the lonely, shut-in winter.

Solitude, Lynd learned, could become a habit. He was

ML

annoyed when he saw the Debenham skiff rowing around his point, even though it was always manned by the ingenuous Aline. Whether she used them as an excuse, he was not sure; but her appearance always meant an almost unavoidable invitation from Cecie to come over for some occasion. To refuse was to admit plainly that he did not want to come; he could not find the excuse of having something else to do. It was some time before he discovered the obvious escape; and that was merely to absent himself when he saw the skiff round the point. . . . .

Then one day when he was making for the woods he turned and saw that Aline was trailing him.

"Not this time!" she laughed. "I saw your tracks in the snow. Matter of fact, I saw you cut out of your house and make for Bald Mountain when I was half-way down the arm. You did, didn't you? 'Fess up!"

He opened his mouth to deny that, but then he laughed. "I did," he said. "Is that bad of me?"

"Not very," she said. Aline was the type of blonde, with white eye-lashes, whose blue eyes always look as excited and impersonal as your own sister's, whose mass of wavy hair is always blowing about and getting in those eyes, who makes you think "What a nice girl she is"—with never a thought of kissing her. Tony, looking at her, wondered why this was with some women. Luba had had this same expression of healthy innocence; yet she was so seductive you could hardly keep your hands off her. Aline, he knew, could wander with him through all the woods of Canada, and he would never once turn to hold her hand. He felt sorry as he thought this, and for fear that he might have shown the lack of interest she aroused in him, he hastily made the suggestion that they go back to his cabin and have some tea: "Now that you've caught me," he laughed.

Her face fell. "So you were running?" she said. "I wasn't quite sure."

"Now look here——"

"It doesn't matter, it doesn't matter." She waved a mittened hand. "I'm only coming over here to dodge Matt."

"Matt?"

"Yes. He's bothering me."

Tony moved along, going back in their own footsteps, kicking down the drifts that might be high for her. The vain courtship of the two Tread boys was common property on Scaup Lake. Cecie, at different times, had said that she was annoyed by it. "You know what kids are at her age," she said, looking up from her invariable knitting. "That's one of the reasons why I want to pack her off to England. Billy's just a St. Bernard puppy. But that Matt . . ." Even on that day Lynd had thought it queer, the way everybody on the lake always alluded to the elder Tread boy as "that Matt." Never just plain "Matt." Now, when Aline used his name, it sounded weirdly like a stage cue—and that Matt had now stepped from the wings to do his part.

Courtship in winter-time on Scaup Lake was, as Lynd easily realised, an almost impossible thing to conduct secretly, and he thought he understood most of the implications when Aline said: "Our boat-house. He asked me to come down and sit there with him while . . . while he tried to get our engine to work. Then he acted so silly. I don't see what fun people get out of always trying to kiss each other. It's so stuffy!"

Lynd sighed. "If you'll fetch the cups, I'll get the primus lighted."

She followed him into the kitchen. It was obvious that she wanted to talk about Matt Tread, to clear some question in her mind. "And when I made him stop, he got angry," she said. "I don't like it."

"What do you think of my store?"

Tony forced her attention to his shelves full of tins. The seven-mile row down to the store in dead winter had, after a couple of trips, lost its first charm; and in the last two trips he had brought up enough tinned foods to make him independent of it. With the pride of a housewife, he made Aline admire his larder. "I aimed at variety, but there the store failed me," he said. "But wait till you see the menus I've ordered from the Hudson Bay Company. I bought everything on the list. Going to give myself some grand dinners. This mouse-cheese Smedley stocks is only good for cooking —want a Welsh rarebit?"

"Are all boys like that?" persisted Aline.

"Usually . . . if you don't know how to handle them. This the first time you've been kissed?"

"Gracious, no! I've let Billy kiss me, and Matt. But now Matt's different."

"Always Matt——"

"What did you say?"

"Oh, nothing. Well, if you don't like it, say so—make him see it. He'll stop. He must."

"That's what I told him. But he didn't. I had to run out of the boat-house."

"Umm, you did that, did you? After this you keep out of the boat-house when Matt's around. That's my advice. I don't know any other instructions I can give you. This is a situation you must handle yourself; no need to bother your mother about it. After all, Matt's only being human."

"But I don't like it!"

"Then do what I tell you—keep out of the boat-house. And when spring rolls along, don't accept any of Matt's invitations to take a walk in the woods."

"But . . . it's awful . . . to have to feel like that about him."

"It is how you feel, isn't it?" Something suddenly gave him the idea that she was lying. She was not telling the whole truth about her feelings. "You make me feel rather embarrassed," he said bluntly, "with your maidenly confidences. You're nearly eighteen, Aline. Snap out of it. The worst thing in the world is for you to try and tell yourself that Matt has been trying to maltreat you. He is doing what every man of his age in the world would do. Matt is just in love with you. And you know it! So is Billy—the chump. So stop this nonsense. If you love him, kiss him. If you don't, don't."

He went into the kitchen and poured the boiling water into the teapot. "This matter of whether you ought or ought not to marry one of the Tread boys is another question. Personally, if I were in your boots, I'd give myself the chance of seeing England first. That's nothing against the Treads, mark you. But you might as well look around a bit first. Most girls do. So I'd keep out of that boat-house until you come back. Understand what I mean?"

He was furious with Aline after she had left. That she had dared to upset his equanimity by making him party to this passion that was operating across the lake. He had just about been able to forget such things, for days on end. And he certainly was not cut out for the part of fairy godmother. He hoped that the way he had put his advice would have its effect. It was dismayingly awkward, this attempt to warn a young girl of the facts of life, as they call them. A long, long way from certain conversations he had had with Flick. . . .

*   *   *

As he lay now beside his open window at night he heard the snow falling from the trees. It dropped from the high branches of the fir forest with dull slushy thuds. The earth and the trees began to smell slightly. The forest was lighter at nights with a rising, ghost-like mist. Streams appeared among the rocks and began to gurgle down the sides of Bald Mountain. He had cleared some alder bushes of the snow by his water-edge that had been bent over all winter under heavy drifts. And these were the first to reward him with their light, trembling green against the blue lake.

The lake was freshened by morning winds. It changed overnight from the black, sullen loneliness of winter to this

windy vista of dancing blue. The jays began to scream around
his cabin, and one morning he heard a strange, unearthly
humming and found a flock of cross-bills outside his window.
The whiskey-jacks, which had been his only companions
through the winter—they would fly down from the trees and
light on his hand—became bolder and walked into his cabin
to see what it was like inside. One morning when he came
back, naked from his first dip in the icy lake, he found a jay
eating the strips of bacon he had cut to cook. He always lit
the primus the first thing every morning before he attempted
to get dressed. If he was having them boiled, he put the three
eggs in the coffee-pot to cook while he washed. But fried, he
always cooked them in the hot bacon fat, when he was
ready to sit down and eat. He bought eggs by the gross from
the Hudson Bay Company, was at first puzzled how they
kept fresh, then gave it up; they just did not go bad, that was
all. When he could manage to get a fresh loaf he pressed a
large slab of bread against the hot frying-pan full of bacon
fat in the mornings and made himself the B.C. equivalent
of French toast.

He enjoyed those meals. He greeted spring by drying his
black-and-red checked mackinaw thoroughly in the sun
and then stowing it away in a deep chest he had made. He
went about now in just soft, blue flannel shirts. The chest he
had made from lengths split off a long cedar trunk that he
and the Count had left cut for house purposes the previous
autumn. He had also made rows of shelves which now held
an interesting library of books. For solid enjoyment, and
perhaps to bolster up his philosophy, he had started re-
reading all the Russians: Turgenev, Chekov, Gogol and
Gorky were all there in strangely assorted bindings and
volumes, so was *The House of the Dead*; Joseph Conrad and
all of Somerset Maugham—he had read *The Painted Veil*
twice that winter, marvelling at the simplicity Maugham
achieved with his delicate, ivory-carver's skill; he had tried
again and again to finish Olive Schreiner's story of the

African farm, but was put off every effort by Lyndall's interminable diatribes about life—Lyndall, whom he thought he understood so well; that girl did "date." She should not have been allowed to talk so much. It wasn't her character at all! He was downright angry with Lyndall. Reading was entirely different on the lake from what it had been anywhere else, even in hospital. Here the vicarious adventure was not menaced. He could live for days with one of his characters—*as* one of them. He had the feeling he was deepening as he read these tales. Anyway, they gave him at least the illusion of growing strength. He had subscribed to the Book of the Month Club and the Literary Guild; and when he rowed down to the store he was always expectant for the contemporary book he would find there. He kept pace with books and the outside word by reading every word of the *New York Times Book Magazine*; and, for what was wrong with the world, he had faithfully subscribed to the weekly edition of the *Manchester Guardian*; that old bible of his journalistic days. That, with the prodigiously fat Sunday *New York Times* complete, was enough to give him breakfast reading for every week. He had started, like the hero of Somerset Maugham's Malayan story, reading the daily edition of the *New York Times* every morning while he ate, keeping them stacked in order and cutting their wrappers in sequence of dates; but that, he found, was affected and a bother. He had too many other things to do around the cabin. But he cancelled that daily subscription chiefly because he preferred the world he continued to live in by reading books. Gradually he let more and more of the Sunday papers lie unread; and a whole reddish pile of the weekly *Guardians* stood, uncut, by his fireplace.

He did not care. The world was fading out.

His rows down to the store were chiefly to get the latest books. He kept enough food now and lamp-oil in his cabin to last for months. The more he kept away from everybody else, the less lonely he felt. He got used to going without people. In many ways he felt that he was consciously undergoing a mental convalescence. Just as he had often lain in wheel-chairs or in deck-chairs on hospital lawns, or on that Nasrieh balcony in fetid Cairo, and felt day by day a strength he had almost forgotten come back to him. It was complete repose. It was idyllic. Perfect. He wanted nothing to break it.

*   *   *

He had not seen anyone for days when he heard the roar of Swanson's muffler-less Buick engine coming down the lake. He often heard it. It was by their exhausts that people were known on Scaup Lake. When the wind was blowing from their direction he sometimes had the steady tump-tump-tump of the Tread boat wafted down into his pocket of clearing from over Bald Mountain. Except when he was chopping there was always complete silence there. He often wondered what he must look like to the fishing eagle that sat most of the day on its nest of thick branches on top of the cedar by the mouth of the river beside him. A puzzling figure he must present, appearing in the mornings to break the silence with his splashings in the lake, then vanishing for an hour into his cabin; and then the bird would watch him sardonically as he made feeble noises with his axe in the clearing. Watching the bird, he often saw it hop awkwardly up into the air, spread its great wings so that the white under-feathers blazed in the sun, and circle, peering down. . . . Then it would return with a fish, like an aeroplane's torpedo, held in its talons. Examining the ground around the base of the cedar, he found it littered with the backbones of trout and salmon. They lived well, those eagles. . . .

At the roar of Swanson's engine Tony saw the eagles hop into the air and soar off down wind. He left his brush-hook in the apple orchard, which he had started to clear in earnest, and went down to the lake.

Swanson was one of the two men on the lake whose presence he did not resent. They had a sort of mutual understanding that allowed them to talk in monosyllables, or say nothing, when they wanted. The other man was "Digger" Bean, who, as a professional cougar-hunter, had once or twice dropped in on Lynd when he was up-lake with his tiny mongrel dogs, and with whom Tony occasionally passed the time of day while he was waiting for mail at the store. The Digger was a sophisticate, a battered merchant marine engineer, with a lewd knowledge of the North African cities. He had, years ago, come out to the lake with the idea of investing his savings in a fishing hotel, but he had found bootlegging for the logging camps a much more profitable and less tiring enterprise.

The Digger, when Tony admitted he had once been a heavy drinker, said discouragingly: "Well, one of these days, I guess I'll get you for a steady customer. It's always there, when you want it!"

Swanson ran his boat hard on the beach, jumped nimbly on to the tops of her cabin, and from there sprang on to Tony's pebbled strand.

"How's things?" he asked. He handed Tony a pair of pine grouse. "They was just making love," he said cruelly, "down by the water. So I knocked 'em over. Couldn't help it!"

One of the noises now in the woods of spring nights was a peculiar grunting sound that Tony had at first thought must be two trees rubbing together. Then one morning he had seen the cock grouse doing his love-dance before his blasée mate. To Tony's amazement, and delight at witnessing this secret courtship, he saw the cock grouse blow out his neck until balloons of flesh like two pineapples appeared before his breast. Then this grunting noise was boomed. The female bird sat on a log and seemed to yawn. Tony walked up to within ten feet of the fool birds before they took any notice of him. Now here were two dead ones.

M1

"You bloody murderer," he said to Swanson.

"Well," the Swede patted his hairy chest. "How you finding things? Good? Damn' cold winter? Yeah? Count just told me you ain't one for company. What do you think he's doing now? Setting in this spring to build a stone fireplace . . . he'll burn his damned self up some day."

"I haven't seen him for two months. We had a row over one of his carpentering jobs. He got on my nerves. Have some coffee?"

Swanson flung off his hat and sprawled in a chair. He was not his usual monosyllabic self this morning. He had several things on his mind. "Well—lake's looking up," he began. "Treads are going to buy that donkey-engine. Yeah! Old Jesse's talked 'em into it! She's second-hand. He's advancing half the money. Gonna take it out of their first booms; 'n Matt and Billy are going over to Vancouver to take a look at it. I tried to warn 'em."

"Against James? He's an old crook, isn't he?"

"Yeah. Ever see a big logger that wasn't? That ain't the point; he's putting some of his own money into it. Point is, there's a rush just now; Yapan's in the market again— had an earthquake or something. Anyway, the damn' Yaps are buying all they can get. Good for us, 'cause old James hasn't wanted any booms since last September. Now he wants everything he can get—rush business. Take anything. So he's talked the Tread boys into buying a donkey-engine."

Tony nodded.

"And when the Yaps stop buying," went on Swanson, "so does Jesse James. He'll have made back the money he laid out all right. . . . Then what are them Treads going to do with that damn' donkey-engine? That's what I'd like to know. That's why I stick to hand logging. I ain't got no overhead. I don't owe the Tread boys nothing, but I tried to make 'em see that. But that Matt wouldn't listen. He said I was trying to keep them out of the market!"

"He's a funny devil."

"Yeah. He's a bad one, that boy."

Swanson looked around. It was not done on Scaup Lake to ask another man what his business was, how he came to be there, why, or even what he intended to do now that he was here. Lynd, for instance, often wondered what could be the story of Shorty Murdoch. What on earth had brought that pessimistic little Glasgow Scot out here? He wasn't doing anything. And it amused Tony now to see the way the big Swede's roving blue eyes took in every detail of the cabin, lighted on the rows of books, as he tried to read the titles; and then watch Swanson shake his head. The Swede, obviously, had given it up. Tony had enjoyed the same experience with Digger Bean, watching that man's shifty appraisal. Those eyes missed nothing. And the stealth of that silent stare made Tony uncomfortable as he watched it. The Digger made no comment, but the big-hearted Swanson exclaimed: "You sure have made this one nice place! Y'ought to come up some time and take a look at my place. My Missus is a great hand for keeping things ship-shape. When she's spring-cleaning, like she is to-day, I can't find no place to sit down! Drives me out the house! Want a lift down the lake?—that's why I dropped in here. It's a mail day. Saturday.

"Aw, come along!" said Swanson, when Lynd began to refuse. "It'll change your luck!"

*   *   *

The white snow still glistened on the upper mountains, but the forests on their flanks were green, and the lake scudded before them in blue and foamy shingles as Swanson's skiff rocked and roared on her way down to the store. Passing old Dr. Feather's point, Lynd saw that the old gentleman and his grandmotherly wife would soon be in it; he noticed with a grin, Swinton, the game warden, and little Shorty

Murdoch trying to peevy a big stick of fir trunk, that had been left by the fall floods, back into the water. This explained one way by which the little Scot amassed the $85 which, he boasted   all it cost him to live a year on the lake. Swan   poked a thick finger in the direction of the game warden, and yelled:

"First time I've ever seen him work! He talks too damn' much—yeah?"

Both Tony and the Swede knew that Swanson's shout, above the roar of his engine, could be heard by the two men on shore. Tony saw Swinton stand resting on his peevy and stare at their boat as it went on down the lake. It amused Tony because Swinton had annoyed him beyond measure with his affected air of being the English gentleman, in the few times they had met; and Digger Bean had said that Swinton had asked him about Lynd, the newcomer—the American. "Did I think you was the kind of guy who would shoot a deer out of season? I said: 'Sure—we all do'— and you ought to see his face! He knows just as well as I do that the loggers up at No. 1 pit-lamp a deer whenever they feel like it—and he's afraid to try and catch them. He's afraid he might get a bullet in him, sort of accidental-like one dark night. Of course, if they did pot him, there would be no way to prove it."

*   *   *

Smedley's General Store and Post Office was enjoying a spring rush of men and women who were feeling the winter leave their stiff bodies and who were in an expansive mood. Smedley was an enterprising young man, who was continually importing new lines of shirts and boots to catch the logger's or the settler's eye; and Lynd always found his displays interesting and effective. Smedley had no store-window and no show cases; he couldn't have had much room for show cases in that oblong pine box, all that his store was, thirty by twenty feet square. At least one-quarter of it was occupied by the cubicle and boxes of the Canadian Post Office. When the enterprising young Canadian had a new line to display he simply hung it on a hook, well above people's heads, where everybody could see it, with its price tag in full view. To-day's offering was three shirts; red-and-white, blue-and-white, and green-and-white, marked: "GENUINE LINEN—99c. each!"

"You're worse than Broadway!" Tony smiled at Zonia Greville, who helped her brother with the rush on mail days. "Ninety-nine cents!—why don't you just say a dollar? Give me three. Yes, I'll have one of each."

"What size collar do you wear, Mr. Lynd? We don't see much of you these days. Don't you ever get lonely up there?"

"Oh, sometimes. But not much. Give me size 44 chest—I won't button the collar. Here's a list of groceries—mind filling that out? How's your husband?"

Zonia made a face. "Oh, he's down at Quamicot with Major Slattery. He thinks he's caught an Atlantic salmon, and Mr. Greville has gone down there to look. Wouldn't let me go along, the mean old thing. Said it was business. Why don't you ever look in on us some time? How about tea to-day?"

"I can't," said Tony. "I'm going back up with Swanson. I'm only waiting for him." He was thankful to have such a legitimate excuse, because the lower Scaup Lakers, he knew, had their social distinctions—and Mr. Axel Swanson, that lovable Swede, was not considered eligible. Swanson had the boy, who attended to the butcher's department, busy filling a big sack with meats he was taking back to his hungry Scandinavian loggers. Virgie Cullen sauntered in, very attractive in her hard-boiled tartish way, slung out a provocative hip at Tony, and made her usual Mae West remark: "Why don't you come up and see me some time?"

This always amused any of the loggers who happened to be standing about, and they guffawed and winked at Lynd. "Bought some new shirts, have you?" she said, shifting her gum and stepping up to feel the texture of the one Lynd had in his hand. "Guess I'll get a couple of these for myself. I'd look well in them. Okay?" She held one up in front of her.

"Say, Zonia!" she cried—"Got one of these'll fit me? Yeah—perfect 38. I think I'm going to wear pants this spring," she said to Tony. "Ain't that what the girls wear where you come from?"

"Some did," smiled Tony. "Sometimes."

At this remark one of the loggers slapped his leg, yelled "Oh-ho!" and went into a fit of laughter. Virgie raised her eyebrows at Tony.

"Sir!" she said. "It's trousers I'm talking about."

He had complied with the parry that Virgie usually demanded, and now he felt free to go outside and sit in the sun while he waited for the mail. On winter mail days a pot-bellied iron stove stood in the centre of Smedley's store; and you could hardly find standing-room among the packed crowd of loggers steaming around it. Perversely enough, when the stove was removed in the spring, they all sat outside. To-day they were all standing at a respectful distance around a low, red motor car with nickelled headlights, in whose low bucket driving seat sat a petulant little man wearing suède gloves, and gnawing a cigar. A roll of well-fed flesh bulged over his high collar. He was insolently unaware of the bashful loggers staring at him. "Where's that Tread man?" he asked. "Matt?"

Leaping to obey this indirect command, one of the loggers trotted around the side of the store and, shading his eyes with his hand, stared up the lake. "Comin'!" he yelled. "'Bout half a mile."

Virgie came out and stared at the car. "Who owns that boat?" she asked.

"Him?" One of the loggers stared at her in surprise—
"*that's Jesse James!*"

"Do tell," said Virgie. She went over and held out her
hand. "Hello, Mr. James—welcome to our city. You're
putting on weight. Ain't seen you for years."

The little man started, gave her a venomous stare with
his bulging brown eyes, then let his glance rest upon the
shining waves of her luxuriant, but unnaturally blonde hair.
He gave Virgie a slow smile.

"Since when, Baby?"

Lynd caught his breath. He wondered how Mr. Ken
Cullen would have taken that. But Virgie's husband was
down for the mail, and one of her mottoes was obviously
that one about when the cat's away. She returned the smile,
put one hand on her inviting hip and with the other lightly
touched the back of her trim head. "Oh . . . I used to see
you around town," she drawled. "I've met you, socially,
in Vancouver . . . ye-es, indeedy!"

The little man leaned towards her and shut one eye.
"I've got you," he said.

"My husband," said Virgie quickly, "is Mr. Kenneth
Cullen, the man who has the Government mail contract
for this place, and owns that boat down there. He knows
you; I've heard him talk a lot about you. He'd be pleased
to see you again, I'm sure."

"Well, he'd better hurry," said the little man in a
remarkably changed voice. "I'm off soon as those two
damn' Tread people get here. When they come, tell 'em
I'm over in the office." He jammed the car into gear, and
leaving a contemptuous belch of exhaust gas in their faces
drove to where his log booms lay about a quarter of a mile
off. Virgie put a new piece of spearmint gum in her mouth
and said to Tony:

"You know that guy's worth a couple of million dollars?
Fact! Y'ought to see some of the parties he used to throw
over in Vancouver—for the politicians. Bring 'em over from

Victoria . . . where they thought it didn't make any difference what they did. Say, Kid—cast your eyes on Matthew Tread!

The change was startling. Instead of the lanky, loose-jointed youth in boots and mackinaw, a neat, well-built young man now walked through them, wearing a trim double-breasted blue suit. The fretful scowl had given place to an expression of cool composure. Tony admired the ease with which Matt asked the curious crowd where Jesse James was and then walked along to the Company's office. A brown English felt hat sat at a nonchalant angle on his trim head. And Billy, Lynd noticed, had been left to carry their bag. He came up from their boat now, the very picture of a gawkish, self-conscious young man in his "city" clothes.

"Well! . . ." said Virgie, as if she had been holding her breath. "That Matt is a hot one!"

The loggers were also breathing easily again after the close-up view they had had of their fabulously wealthy employer. It made Lynd angry. He did not like the feeling of having stood in a crowd, abject as any group of Balkan peasants facing a policeman. Even less had he liked the way that pompous little king in this part of the world had stared insolently at these people as if he were not even aware they were alive. The scene was worthy of a Moscow cartoonist. And, for a few disgruntled seconds, he knew that he had experienced some of the rage that the intellectuals among Labour must know. He would like to take a fall out of Mr. Jesse James. All he did, however, was to walk across to Billy and say:

"Looks like a pretty slick customer you and Matt are going into business with. If I were you I'd make him put it on paper—get a contract out of him of some sort. So that he doesn't leave you holding the bag."

"Do you think so?" asked Billy, anxiously. "What would you make him sign?"

Lynd remembered what Swanson had told him a few hours before. "Oh, make it simple," he said. "Here, come into the store and I'll jot down two clauses on a piece of paper."

He scribbled them quickly and handed Billy the note. "One of them say," he pointed out, "that Jesse James agrees to take all the logs you cut, regardless of quantity. The other—you'd better ask Matt about this—is that you don't begin to pay James back his advance on the donkey-engine until you have cleared in net profit the money you have paid to get it up here. That last clause means absolutely a tid-bit to him—but it might save your skins. Talk it over with your brother to-night on the Vancouver boat.

"I don't know anything about the logging business," Tony added. "But if you could pin him down to some minimum price, you might have at least the semblance of a contract. And I think you'll need it."

He could see that Billy was in such a state of excitement over his first trip off Vancouver Island that he had probably already forgotten where he had put the paper. Lynd expected nothing to come of it. He had only stepped in because he did not like the looks of Mr. Jesse James. The strutting little Napoleon annoyed him. The man was the epitome of everything he detested; he was an enemy of everything that was decent on the lake. He had come there to ruin it—which he would, with his ruthless logging. His kind were going to do the same thing to Canada that they had been allowed to do to the United States. What Virgie Cullen said about his Vancouver parties for the Victoria politicians had an all too sinister bearing on the subject; for it was notorious how—by paying the politicians and the Forestry Department to close its eyes—the big logging companies were wrecking Canada, obeying none of the paper-laws that were intended to prevent annihilation of the forests. Quoting Attila, Tony growled to himself that night as he ate: "Where I pass not one blade of grass shall remain!"

It was the boast of the Hun.

*   *   *

The trivial incident at the store had so annoyed Lynd that he was unable to regain his composure for days. He felt it cheap of him to try and win back to it. Like a tap on the shoulder, this face of James' had reminded him of a life he was trying to forget—or dodge! The last ugly question kept presenting itself. Trench-dodging, like the escape attributed to Swinton, was a tangible thing. Life-dodging? . . . Well, that was something not so easy to define. Had he cut and run? Had his last winter in solitude been a Rip Van Winkle's dream? . . .

Staring up lake towards the old German's *Schloss*, he suddenly realised that he was acquiring a new respect for that sullen man. Von Hauptmann had been right; don't mix with the people around the store had been his warning. Well, Lynd had not strictly done that—but his petty chit-chat with Zonia Greville and Virgie Cullen had been a much weaker display than the old Hun's dignified aloofness; and while the Treads were definitely the most authentic settlers on the lake—everyone else had only followed them—the two boys had deliberately stepped out of that original frontier life by buying a donkey-engine. They had associated themselves with the second-growth on the lake—the people who came in after the settler; the vanguard of alleged progress. The Tread boys, acting under James' supervision, would wreck their own homestead, leave a wasteland of raw stumps where their great forest now stood. To them, the forests and the jungle against which they had been taught to fight since they could swing an axe were now going to be conquered by their new donkey-engine. That they were destroying something that man cannot create did not occur to them. They would have thought it childish.

It was Swanson, a Scandinavian who thought it was his mission in life to cut down a forest wherever he found one, who said as they passed the Tread point: "Seems a damn' shame, doesn't it—to cut down a purty place like that!"

*   *   *

But the remote position of Lynd's lonely cabin at the foot of the North Arm was so shut off from life on the lake that, in a few days, he ceased to think about it. Before the trout took a fly that spring he had been setting night-lines, which he baited with preserved salmon eggs. When the lake lay perfectly still, as it did most mornings, he could see the spots on the trout that were dangling from the hooks. At the far end of his clearing, where his delta was rimmed by the northern mountains, a crystal clear river ran into the lake. In the spring it had been a frothing torrent, sweeping everything down with it, slides of earth and snow, boulders, whole trees, with branches mangled by its rapids, which it spewed out of its rushing mouth into the lake. It had been intensely alive. He had been fascinated by its activity. Then one morning he noticed that he did not hear its roar any more. The lake at its mouth was no longer full of swirling eddies with remnants of roots and trees carried around in them. When he tramped across he looked down into a clear, bottle green depth in which the grey bank of boulders could be seen going down into the darkness. Lying against this bank, their fins barely working, he saw at least a dozen huge rainbow trout. . . .

He waited for an on-shore wind to give him enough riffle, and his first fish was a six-pound rainbow that took him all over the place. His reel screamed. When he had beached it he found that his heart was beating just as excitedly as over any big fish he had landed in Scotland. He got five more that morning, not one of them under three pounds, and then lost his only Silver Doctor fly to a big trout that took him under a sunken tree. After that he tried Jock Scotts and every fly in the book, but the rainbow would have none of them. When he had cut a withy to carry the fish back he realised that he had caught more than he could do with, and he was now faced with the irksome task of rowing around the lake to give them to someone. The Feathers lay nearest, and, after putting the two smallest fish in the larder for himself, he shoved his skiff into the water and sailed up towards his point.

He had already made some lee-boards, and was going to write to Victoria for some light muslin to make a sprit-sail. As it was, he was using an oar for a mast and one of his old blankets. It made a pocket to catch the wind; and, running before it, he slid beautifully past the on-racing waves down to where the old Doctor's bungalow stood on its sloping point. He had forgotten that it was a mail day and arrived to find the Swintons, old Henry and Mrs. Tread, Shorty Murdoch, the Feathers and their lady-help, Miss Gay, in the middle of lunch. It was too late to back out, so he obeyed the Doctor's insistence to sit in the chair he had pulled up. It saved him from several rows to distribute the other fish as he gave them away there and then. Mrs. Swinton, he noticed with a secret smile, managed, after just enough protests, to get the largest one. He was rather proud of his catch; they looked attractive, laid out side by side on the porch, and he was nettled by the superior way Swinton tried to examine them.

"Ah," said Swinton, "what did you catch them on?"

Lynd was tempted to say "worms," but said that he had caught them all on the same Silver Doctor. "I lost it. And then I did not get another rise. Queer, wasn't it?"

"Ah! . . . I always use a Jock Scott."

It was Swinton's complacent smile that made him do

it. Tony, remembering that his fly-book was still in his pocket, took it out and slid it across to the game warden. "Show me the size Jock Scott you find best?" he asked innocently.

The book was full of Wilkenson's, Thunder-and-Lightnings, Jock Scotts, a beautiful palette of feathers among which the uninitiated fisherman could easily lose himself. Swinton, seeing the trick that had been played on him, fussed about, playing for time himself, passed over the gaily coloured Jock Scotts, and held up an iridescent Alexander.

"That's a nice one," he said evasively.

"That's an Alexander!" said the Doctor.

"Oh, yes, yes . . . I know," said Swinton. "I was just admiring those peacock feathers . . ."

Lynd knew that Swinton's bluff had been called, and that from now on he could count upon the game warden as a mortal enemy. It only made this a certainty when Shorty Murdoch said: "Ye're not allowed to use an Alexander on Loch Leven. It's a murderous fly." Swinton hastily shoved back the book, took out his pipe, and said: "Well, Doctor, what about the mail?"

It was as abrupt a dismissal of the fishing subject as the game warden could make. Mrs. Swinton began to inform Shorty Murdoch about a pamphlet she had received from Washington, the U.S. Department of Agriculture, on edible mushrooms. Mrs. Swinton got more reading matter free than all the rest of the lake paid for. Old Mrs. Feather, who, even with her tin ear-trumpet, could never take more than an irrelevant part in any conversation, was now trying to locate some letters she had written to give to the waiting Doctor to post; and Tony found himself having to listen politely to old Mrs. Tread's anxious account of her two boys' adventure with the donkey-engine.

They had gone across to Vancouver with Mr. Jesse James, who had invited them to lunch and been kind enough to help them with the man who sold second-hand donkey-engines. Mrs. Tread said, "My Matt's a queer boy, and he might be too shy to thank you for your advice." To Lynd's surprise, he heard her saying that the independent surly Matt had been very much impressed with the suggestions Tony had given Billy, and that the two boys had gone to the point of almost offending Mr. Jesse James in their efforts to make him give them some written agreement. Mr. James had become angry and said that if they could not trust his word, there was no use doing any business with him. So Matt had finally bought the donkey-engine merely on the big logger's promises. Verbally, the agreement had been made, and Matt, who had the cheque with him, already signed by old Henry Tread, had drawn out practically every penny they had in the bank to pay for their half-share.

Mr. James had not had much time to spare the boys, as he was busy with other men, and the last thing he told Matt was that he was now trying to get the railroad to run a spur line twenty miles up from Quamicot to Scaup Lake. That, he said, would open out the territory, and they could have the big logs brought down on trucks rather than the present method of shooting them down the rivers. If he could get the B.C. Parliament to pass the railway Bill, then the development of the lake was assured. "And, of course, my boys would be in at the beginning," apprehensively said Mrs. Tread. Perhaps, she concluded in a tired voice, it was better; perhaps she and the boys' father had been wrong to try and make them go on with just the farm. It had always been a struggle.

"Yes," said Tony; "you are probably right. I could see the boys were restless." Privately, he thought that he was himself witnessing the beginning of a very interesting frontier development; he was watching the two Tread boys cross over. By buying a donkey-engine to wreck their own forests they were deliberately leaving their life of the first settler and becoming part of the spreading second-growth of Canada. It was the accepted, the progressive thing to do. But, Spartan as the farm life had been, they were abandoning its security. By going into debt for the donkey-engine and putting themselves in the power of Jesse James (because there was no one else who would buy their timber) they had already started to work for someone else. And when, in four or five years, they had wrecked the virgin forests that now rose like a great woodland cathedral across Tread's extensive holdings, they might have a few thousand dollars in the bank. They might. On the other hand, they would have nothing but a waste land of raw stumps.

But this, he saw, was an argument he could not put before Mrs. Tread. It was an unpopular thesis for a growing country. In fifty or sixty years, perhaps, when enough virgin forests had been cut down to alarm its citizens, Canada, as the United States soon would, might take a lesson from Sweden and Germany and enforce its timber laws—leave enough trees standing for new forests to grow again. In the meantime—his time . . . all their times . . . the country belonged to the wreckers.

It comforted him to think of the story he already knew of the wreckers. How, after they had come in and cut down all the easy, most profitable timber in a district, they moved their men and machinery on to skim the cream off some new territory. They left the wounded land to recover. And there was always a long lull before someone else came. There was a great lake twenty miles below which knew this story. It was now just a great waste of stumps and deserted bunk-houses. He had come to it because, in Vancouver, when he was looking about, he had been offered several hundred acres there for almost nothing. It had in fact been his first lesson in the realities of his new life; for while there was still a spur line of rails leading into this wilderness, no trains were running; he had to hire a motor car to drive him up the vanishing road. And when he had reached the lake, and stared at its desolation, he had turned angrily on the driver for bringing him to such a place.

"What in God's name did you think I was trying to buy?" he asked.

The local man grinned and said he did not know. He took a couple of "suckers" up every season to see the place. When the British Navy had let go a lot of its young officers a few years back, why, a whole committee of them came up and took a look. They very nearly did buy the land, with the idea of starting apple orchards there, fruit farming. But then, some of the Britishers over in the Okanogan Valley had got at them and warned them; an angry admiral wrote a letter of protest to the London *Times*. "And the suckers didn't bite!" grinned the man. "Why, mister, there isn't an acre of land on this here damn' lake that would pay even *interest* on the cost of its stumping! It'll take thirty years or forty before anyone will use this place again." And so Tony had come up to Scaup, which was the last lake up the island with any people on it. It had seemed safe.

Jesse James was like a maggot that had come in to rot it. But even so, with all his machinery, he was only a maggot.

*   *   *

As he hoisted his blanket to try to tack up-lake around the North Arm, Tony reflected that there were still some sixty odd miles of shorelines to defy Mr. Jesse James' hacking. For years the logging camps would make hardly a scar in it. As he abandoned sail and rowed up through the Narrows he stared at Tread's deep forests on the further shore. It was a terrific sight, the high wall of that dark forest towering over the toy blocks of Tread's cabin and his outbuildings. He could understand why the Tread boys saw no beauty in it, merely something that was overawing them, crowding in each spring on the clearings they had once made, literally an adversary . . . something which meant incessant worry and hard work. They would be relieved when they cut the forest down; it would give them more air.

He saw the bay where they were going to have the donkey-engine slid ashore. An old disused bunk-house he had previously noticed floating on its cedar raft down by the store, had been towed up. He saw people moving on it. He thought grimly of the stream which ran into the bay; how, that spring, he had followed it up one whole day, absorbed in the sight of trout in its deep clear pools, and he recalled an open stretch he had found where the stream coursed over a shallow reach of grey boulders, and the grouse had called in the woods as he ate his lunch in the sun. . . . That day, he had wondered if any white man had ever been in that actual spot before. Well, in about another year, that stream wouldn't have any trout. And he wondered what would happen to the salmon who came up there every year to spawn, when they found their beds choked with logs. . . .

All progress! He was delighted when he looked down the North Arm and saw his lonely cabin at its foot. That, they couldn't touch, anyway! Bald Mountain was too steep to make it worth while to log, so were the mountains on the other side of his clearing. His own deep forest that ran up the crotch of the stream beside him was safe, because it was he who owned all the foreshore. Nothing could cross his land. He and the Count could live where they were, on the edge of the uncut forest, for very likely the rest of their lives. The rest of Scaup Lake could be forced to fall in line with the destructive march of progress, but he and the old German could stay behind. It was a comforting thought. It was pleasant to know that there are some places in the world which could be saved from men like Jesse James, just because he could see no way to turn them into money. The Count's place was also safe—safe because an old logging enterprise had been in there years before the German came and had logged all the easily accessible timber between him and

Lynd's river. This logged land was now a light green growth of straggling young saplings shining in the sun, and full of the calls of the grey pine grouse. And the deep forest that stood above where the Count had built his *Schloss* grew on a hillside too steep to tempt cutting until the rest of the lake had been wrecked.

Again, as Lynd rested on his oars and studied from afar that weird Bavarian residence of the Count, he found himself admiring the old German's sense of values. There was a practical dignity in his surly aloofness. No one on the lake had a good word to say for him; yet, in his unpopular fashion, the German recluse seemed to dominate the whole scene. His bearded frame was the figure of it, of his own legend.

Gossip at the store occasionally had a mail-day sensation when some trout fishers would come back and indignantly declare that they had seen a man walking around naked in the brush.

The old Count, caught unawares in one of his sun-baths, had championed the cause of the upper lakers' privacy by striding down to the lake edge, stark naked, and facing a mixed fishing party of two men and their women by bellowing: "What do you there? This is my property. Don't you step on it. Begone!"

One of the men had said at the store that he wished he had "taken a crack at him," whereupon local pride asserted itself, and he was asked why hadn't he tried? Tony smiled as he thought of that, for, although the Count's beard was heavily shot with grey, Tony had learned the great-bear-like toughness of the former German aristocrat as they had worked together on that brutal cross-cut saw. And the Count, of course, with that fetish of his own dignity to live up to, would have died rather than have been physically humbled by what he would have considered an inferior man. There was a reward in such a bitter pride of self. Tony did not like him, but he thought the Count was living a true

life on the lake. He felt himself a weaker character when he
departed from the stiff-necked model which the atrocious
old Hun made.

*   *   *

It was impossible not to be interested in the Tread boys
with their new enterprise. The donkey-engine, like some
prehistoric monster, was being brought up in sections by
Ken Cullen's indefatigable motor-lorry and assembled at
the foot of the lake. To get it up to where the Tread boys
were going to start their cut, a huge cedar raft had to be
built, on which it could be towed up the lake; and then,
with its steel cable made fast to some fir giant on shore, it
would pull itself up with its own power, like a monstrous
steel salamander. Matt and Billy were building this raft.

The lake pool was several hundred yards from the store,
and Tony frequently strolled over there while he was waiting for the mail to sit on a log and smoke in the warm sun
and watch the two Tread boys at their expert work. This
was where both of them showed at their very best. Their
simple, straightforward minds, Billy's in particular, might
obviously have been no match for the gutter-sharpened
shrewdness of Jesse James. But in this work they recognised
no masters. They knew their skill; their axe-work provided
hours of entertainment for the critical loggers who had
come down in the *War Eagle*. They drove themselves without mercy before this audience as they swayed back and
forth, back and forth, on either end of that cruel cross-cut
saw. Their white bodies glistened with coursing sweat and
Tony saw them bronze under the heat-hazy sun. Matt's
lean shoulders seemed alive with playing muscle; and
Virgie Cullen, who apparently spent most of her mornings
watching this scene, making an occasional wisecrack to
cover her embarrassment, said to Tony:

"Ain't it a damn' waste . . . for a man to have a shape like
that Matt . . . and no one to love!"

"You're getting quite romantic," said Tony uneasily. He looked at her, her face flushed in the sun, and at the peculiar intent stare with which she followed Matthew Tread. The elder Tread boy was a man to make any woman envious, particularly if she were the wife of a fat little man like Ken Cullen. Virgie did not look like a tranquil woman.

"I mean it," she said. "I've often thought it out—what it's all about, this living out here in the woods. Where does it get you? Look at Matt there . . . all the fun he's missing. Before he knows it, he'll be a rusty old split like his father. No good."

"Oh, not so bad as all that. The old man was young once."

"Maybe . . . " said Virgie. "But he doesn't look it."

"How are you making out?" Virgie said, indicating that she would like to have some intimate confessions from himself. "Don't you ever want a woman?"

Lynd gasped. Anywhere else he would have known how to answer that question; even here, it was at least an invitation to a very interesting talk—especially with a hard-boiled little blonde like Virgie Cullen. She would probably have some very amusing ideas about life. But on this lake, his one desire was to get up as politely as he could and get away. He did not want to be drawn on this subject of all others. He was aware now, as he thought of it, that every man on the lake must carry this secret of himself. Every one of them faced this problem.

Reds, the foreman up on No. 2 logging camp, had told him of their " high-rigger," a Finn, who had nearly killed a recent English time-keeper they had—simply because he came back from the woods one day and found the little English clerk merely talking with his woman. "You see," explained Reds solemnly—"women are valuable in these parts—it's hard to get them." Tony had noticed that Reds himself looked uncomfortable, and angry, as he discussed this enforced celibacy of the lonely logging camps. "A guy might as well be in prison!" growled Reds. That was why, he said, when a logger hit Victoria or Vancouver his money was gone in less than a week along Railway Street. "They got a perfect right to get drunk and raise hell," Reds insisted—"It's one of the penalties of being broke—that you got to go without a woman for most of your life. And that ain't the way most men are built."

And here was Virgie Cullen, impudently provoking Lynd to have an open discussion on this painful subject. She was flaunting the possibilities of herself in his face.

"You chuck that," he said. "You ought to know better than to go around asking men questions like that. You'll get into trouble."

Virgie looked at him. She lowered her eyelids and gave him a thoroughly appraising stare. The texture of her skin came into focus, and he noticed, with a little catch of his breath, that her cheeks were smooth and still covered with childish down, and that there was a frank invitation in those blue eyes. Then she said softly:

"Why don't you come down here and take a walk sometime? There's no use in you pacing around up there in the woods. Don't be so unsociable."

Involuntarily, his eyes followed hers to where she stared. It was an old path that led off through the woods along a smooth floor of brown pine needles and dappled shadows, to where both of them could see the sun slanting down into the green pool of a glade. His thoughts played for a moment with the picture of two people lying there in the sun on a drowsy sweet day like this, and what it would be like to feel the smooth flesh of a woman's body again, and then he looked at Virgie, and at her bleached hair, and stood up. "Forget it," he said.

*　　　*　　　*

The summer brought its own antidote in a lazy contentment just to sit by his cabin and let his thoughts drift. The soft winds in the trees lulled him into a half-sleep. With a great unfolding motion the lake had opened up into a full growth of life; the impetuous spring sap had reached its fulfilment; and now in the rich greens and blues there was nothing to do but fall in with the rest of Nature and just drowse. The water grew silent in the river beside him, slacked and stood still. Only the faintest trickle now moved between the sun-baked grey rocks. The trout lay in the clear pools, darted, when they saw any movement, below shelving rocks. The eagles spread their hot wings in the sun. Nothing moved.

In this sultry stagnation, the invitation to a farewell week-end party for Aline came like a message from a forgotten world. He was suddenly active again. He was as excited as a débutante going to her first ball when he rowed across in just the lower piece of his bathing suit with his flannels on the stern seat, to obey Cecie's urgent request to a cocktail or so before the crowd came up from Victoria. Cecie and the sun-burned Aline had been in swimming and were lying in their bathing suits in deck-chairs on their wharf when he got there. The cocktail shaker reposed in a bucket they had lowered into the cool water from the deep end of the wharf. It seemed almost affected, not to have one of Cecie's cock-tails under these circumstances.

"Very economical of you, anyway," said Cecie. "You'll probably be the only one around here that's sober by nightfall!"

Aline, who seemed anxious to avoid sprawling so intimately with a man, when she was practically undressed like that, jumped out of her chair and with a nervous run dived off the wharf. Cecie smiled and then shrugged her own pretty shoulders: "She's funny, isn't she? Still thinks these flimsies are indecent. I think they are, too! She's nice, though. Got a good figure."

"Very!" said Tony. "I should think she'd get on well in London. She's pretty enough."

"Ye-es . . . in her puppy-dog way. She's frightfully immature. That's the chief trouble with raising a child out here; the only persons she won't feel gauche with at home will be the older people. She won't know how to talk to people of her own age. She's just as likely as not to fall in love with a man of forty. She told me she thought you might do."

Tony started, and then laughed. "That's nice of her!" he said.

"Yes . . . she says you must have a dark secret . . . ?"

He knew that Cecie's eyes were watching him, and he stared fixedly at the lake, to where Aline was swimming far out, to show them how well she did it. He wondered how Matt Tread was being handled these days. When Cecie held out the tin of cigarettes, he smiled as he took one, and said: "And how's Copey?"

"Sleeping! . . . the beast. That's all he does do these summer days. You'll probably find him still snoring when you go into his room to dress for dinner. He says he has to conserve his energy to go through this evening's gaiety. Actually, I think the poor old duffer is brooding over losing Aline. He's a bit slow, you know—but he has feelings. And it's just occurred to him what it means."

Tony nodded.

"Yes," sighed Cecie, crossing one pretty leg over the other. "Copey insists this is the end. He's made up his mind that we're never going to get home . . . that he will never see England again. And that's really what's the matter with him—he's homesick as hell! So's the Growler—he's absolutely impossible! M-m-my dear . . . that face——" Cecie tried to imitate the Growler's scowl and then stretched her arms. "So that," she said—"is us! Condemned to exile. Let's go in."

The Tread boys were not there that night at dinner; the guests from Victoria were the faithful Mr. Lyon, very smart in a white dinner jacket he had ordered from New York,

and a smouldering dark-haired young matron who was so
determined to be the life and soul of the party that she
made even the Growler promise to come on the picnic they
were going to have the next day. "You dreadful man!"
Tony heard her saying to him, where she had him cornered at
the far end of the high veranda. "What do you mean—
moping about like that up here on this lovely lake? Yes, and
I'm going to make you go swimming, too . . . you see if I
don't!"

"Now that's torn it!" Cecie hissed to Tony. "He'll
come now—just to spite us."

*   *   *

As this was to be Aline's last day on the lake, Tony, so
that everyone could make an early start, heard himself
agreeing to spend the night at the Debenham place. This
madness was also due to the propaganda of the Mrs.
"Jackie" Buggard, who, the anxious Bertie Lyon assured
everybody, was the smartest "hostess" in Victoria. This
did not make up for the fact that Tony spent the night like
an anchovy on a sofa he found just the length of his head or
feet too short for him. It gave him an unexpected insight,
however, into the amenities of the exiled English household; for at seven o'clock sharp old Nanny appeared, the
family retainer who had come out as Aline's nurse fourteen
years before, and the smiling old servant was carrying a
little yellow enamelled tray on which was a Dresden teapot and a crisp little pile of Huntley and Palmer's biscuits.
"Well, Nanny!" laughed Tony, sitting upright, almost
low-neck in Copey's pyjamas, "you do observe all the old
customs, don't you?"

"It's no bother, sir. It's nice not to change your 'abits
too much from home, sir. Mr. Hiscock always helps me.
He's a very kind gentleman."

With a blanket wrapped around him, Tony prowled

cautiously down the long corridor of the ranch's bedrooms, trying to find where the Growler's bathroom was. He wanted to find a razor, but instead he found the Growler, leaning against the wall, talking into a bedroom from which came the cheery tones of Mrs. Buggard: "It's so English of you!"

"I like my tea in the morning," said the Growler. "In Darjeeling—— Hello, there—what are you after?"

The Growler, who was dressed as much as he ever was—in an open-necked khaki shirt, white rubber boots, and canvas trousers thrust into them, which bore a riveted tag, marked PRIDE OF THE WEST on their behind—gave Tony a scowl and led him off to where, in a bathroom full of squashed tubes of toothpaste, two practical harness sponges, he handed Tony an old-fashioned razor and a brush with about five hairs left in it. These were still in a stiff cowlick from the Growler's soap, and as Tony, making no effort to hide the disgust on his face, looked about helplessly for the shaving stick, the Growler handed him the cake of bath soap.

"I must get some new shaving tackle," he said.

"Yes," said Tony. "You certainly must. Who's coming to-day?"

"Just us—and the Tread boys. They always come. I hate picnics."

"Why do you come, then?"

"'Cause Cecie's taken all the food. I don't mind. I can lie under a bush."

"Not if I know Mrs. Buggard."

"Hmmmm. . . . You're right there. Damn' sight more pleasant to sit on our cool porch. It'll be hot as hell out there in all that sun."

"Perhaps you can get Mrs. Buggard to lie under a bush, too?"

"Ha-ha! . . ." The Growler brightened. "I'd like to. You get a little—eh—you know . . . out here? Ummm?

N∟

Out East we handle things differently. Wasn't so bad out there. No, not at all bad." The Growler looked reminiscent for a moment; then a sly grin creased his cheeks. "Think I'll cultivate Mrs. Buggard. Name's peculiar, isn't it? . . . But she might be useful down in Victoria."

The Growler had changed into a pair of uncreased grey flannels when they were loading the big Debenham launch with lunch-baskets and thermos flasks to go up the lake, and looked uncomfortable in a painfully new pair of brown shoes.

"I'm breaking 'em in," he apologised.

*   *   *

The Tread boys had got the launch to start. When Tony came down with his share of the picnic baggage he found Matt and Billy just washing the black engine-grease off their hands. Here again the two Tread boys were at their best; there was an air of alive practicability about their polite cursing of the launch's habits that was most marked after Copey's good-natured helplessness concerning everything on his place. They both looked pale and taut, nervously anxious; and Tony could see from Matt's scowl how enraged he was that Aline was going to leave the lake. It did not promise to be a gay and careless picnic. Even Mrs. Jackie Buggard's twitterings failed.

Now that the Growler had surrendered, by agreeing to come alone, she was exercising her charm on the melancholic Copey. The change in the Growler had not been for the better. There had been a slight touch of the buccaneer quality in his outrageous white rubber boots; in conventional flannels and the new shoes he looked like what he was essentially, a very ordinary lower middle-class Englishman, who would have remained a clerk had he stayed at home. He should have stayed in his uniform. Mrs. Buggard, apparently, had spotted this denouement at once.

The Growler's prospects of a *houri* in Victoria, meditated Tony, were already dead. The Tread boys had thoughtfully brought their launch as well; and Matt made everyone feel uncomfortable by the way he insisted upon taking it up the lake by himself. His childish gruffness was meant to show Aline how damn' little he cared to ride with her, and it left the possible glory of making the Debenham launch run to the embarrassed Billy. After a dozen back-fires, which almost dislocated Tony's arm, it did cough, and work.

* * *

The spot selected for the picnic was the sandy mouth of a mountain stream that had now practically stopped. Matt had found a pool, a hundred yards back in the shadow of the forest, and they lowered all the flasks in it, with the butter, to keep them cool. Meanwhile Cecie, Aline and the beautiful Mrs. Buggard retreated to the bushes and squirmed into bathing suits. Mrs. Buggard, quite well aware that she had a good figure, provokingly oiled her sleek limbs with Suntan before she sat down, and made the feverish Growler rub the parts that she could not reach. It was all very coy and Tony might have been slightly aroused himself—were it not that he kept rejoicing in the thought of what was going to happen when Mrs. Buggard sat down. That sand would never come off! . . .

The two Tread boys were as shy as Aline in the way they bolted straight from the bushes into the water. So fast, in fact, that Tony caught no more than the slightest surprised glance at their home-made bathing suits, and had time to notice the whiteness, the almost unhealthy pallor of their legs. As children, Aline and Billy had often been tubbed together; but those innocent days had gone . . . they were afraid to look at each other. The Debenhams were the only people who bathed as a sport on Scaup Lake. And both Matt and Billy, after an awkward dip, came out at the far end of the sand and disappeared behind the protective screen of bushes to dress. They made Tony think of the pain of youth, and of his own veteran body, lying so brazenly unclad, beside the velvet-limbed lady from Victoria. Emerging from the water, Mrs. Buggard had bounded nymph-like, a few ecstatic leaps up the beach, torn off the aluminium rubber helmet that had imprisoned what she obviously thought of as her rebellious head of brown curls, and had flung herself abandonedly on the hot sands, which, Tony reflected, were already coating that pink skin so that in an hour or so it would be as painful to touch as if rubbed with sandpaper. Mrs. Buggard would not be the life of the party around four o'clock.

"What queer motive," she asked intimately, leaning back on her hands, "brought you to this lovely forest land?"

"To be by myself," said Tony, lying flat, with one knee crossed over the other, blowing a smoke ring in the motionless heat.

"How lovely!" she sighed.

He lay still. On the way up the lake, while the others were explaining what it was to Mrs. Buggard, he had regarded the red *Schloss* of Captain von Hauptmann. No sign came from it. He had listened to Cecie convulse the Victoria lady and Mr. Lyon by relating how the "Count" had once sent a photograph of himself naked to Chicago and won a beauty contest. He had not defended him. On the contrary, he wondered what the Count was saying to Elsa. For the old German was almost certain to be watching them through his Zeiss glasses. The Count watched everything that passed up or down the lake. There were so few passing events aside from the logging camp's *War Eagle*, or an occasional party of trout-fishers, on this uninhabited part. And he was hoping that von Hauptmann had not noticed him. He would have no chance of explaining to the Count that he was only a spectator in this scene, that he had not joined with glee in a Debenham revel, that he thought all picnics were just hell, anyway. The old German would think he had weakened, given in to this life. He would say to Elsa: "You see; there is another one—without a big enough mind to live alone!"

The Growler, who had been lying like a spent fish, suddenly stood up and produced an amazing flow of conversation, full of quip and jest, gist of which was that it was now high time to eat. He had not gone swimming, having no bathing suit. He marshalled the obedient Billy and the scowling Matt Tread into an expedition to bring back the lunch from the shade of the pool. Copey moved from beside a bush, in whose faint shadow he had been trying to read a Seattle Sunday newspaper Mr. Lyon had brought up, and selfishly placed a launch cushion for himself on the blistering sand. Cecie, after a silent, half-hearted dip, had been lying flat on the beach, staring into the sky as she held Aline's reluctant hand. Aline had wanted to dress, to "get something on!" as she protested; but Cecie had laughed her out of it. "Don't be a little prig," she said. "Mr. Lyon won't mind. You're going to England now."

Lynd heard her telling the attentive Bertie Lyon of a cocktail party somewhere in England which had ended in them all deciding to take a swim, how they had undressed at proper distances on the beach, and of their joyous encounters in the water afterwards. Mr. Lyon responded by asking her had she read *The Green Hat.*

Lynd thought again of the old restaurant in Percy Street that had been made famous by that book, and genial old Stulik sitting down with his customers, with his finger placed against his nose, so gallantly accepting his favourite's dud cheques. . . . He thought of the dazzling Bright Young Things he had seen there, and watched, afterwards, in their inevitable retrogression, becoming habitués of less and less enchanted night places, until finally you became

used to them perched on stools, puffy-faced, already beginning their day's drinking at eleven in the morning in the
bar-of-the-moment off Fitzroy Square. How they would
have shrieked at this banal picnic! He wondered how
Aline would find London life?

Her trunks had already been taken down by Ken Cullen
when he brought Mr. Lyon and the lady from Victoria up
to the Debenham place. Some time late this night, while
there was still enough light to drive through the woods,
she was going back in the car to Victoria. Mrs. Buggard
was giving a little luncheon party for her there; then she
would take the night boat across to Vancouver; the next
day she would be on a train for the Rockies and her four-
day ride across Canada. Then all the excitement of the ship,
the cool swells of the Atlantic; and in less than two
weeks Aline would be leaning over the rail staring at the
low green shores of Southampton Water. England. "Well,
well——"

Tony stood up and said to Mrs. Buggard, "I'd put some
clothes on if I were you. You're going to have a horrible
burn." He helped Cecie spread out the lunch things on a
steamer rug. He noticed Matt go over to Aline and heard
her saying:

"But, I *can't*! What would the others say?"

"Well, I want to have a word with you—alone," came
Matt's impatient words.

Aline jumped up and came over to the luncheon group.
Lynd saw the colour come and go in her young cheeks, the
self-conscious set of her pouting lips, the imperious way she
shook her head. He felt annoyed with her, with all young
women of her age, so completely self-satisfied in the right
they thought they had to be rude to young men. Matthew
Tread was in a furious state; and Tony wondered what, on
this vital last day, the hot-head Matt might have done if he
had had young Aline alone on that beach. That was obviously the situation Matt was trying to create.

"Come on," he said gruffly, while they were munching sandwiches, "let's go out in my boat."

The demand, addressed so openly to Aline before them all, was pathetic in the awkward silence it created. No one spoke. Then Mrs. Buggard, who knew nothing of the situation, saved things by chirping:

"But . . . Aline! . . . such a gorgeous afternoon!"

Aline nodded. Lynd saw Billy go white, and heard Cecie's diplomatic laugh. When Aline turned invitingly to him, Tony said:

"I'm not going to be gooseberry! You two go along." He saw that Cecie was scowling at him, but he knew that he was suddenly angry with the whole scene—the vapid people, this footling effort to be gay on the blistering beach, the stupid physical agony of poor Matt. The whole boring business was disturbing; and why should he be in it? Yes, by God, the old German had been right; live alone—don't let other people make you part of their tiresome lives.

As he studied Cecie now he saw her as a pretty, but faded and frustrated woman, brave—but neither brave nor intelligent enough to do what all the Debenhams should have done long ago; go back to England. All of them. This ghastly picnic was their idea of what the lake had to offer. They had no place in this part of the world.

He watched the Tread boat and was annoyed when, after what everybody could see was a furious argument in its cockpit, he saw Matt jerk the tiller and head back for the beach. He agreed when Cecie said uncomfortably it would perhaps be better if they packed up now and went back, as there were still a lot of things that Aline must do. He rose and helped pack to speed the departure. He was as petulant as the others when the bulky Debenham launch absolutely refused to be started, and Matt, up ahead in the Tread boat, towed them sullenly back down the lake. He resolved that with the rainy season of the autumn approaching, he could easily make this the last time he would visit the Debenhams.

He was aware that he had done very little himself to make the picnic party a success, and, in compensation, he went into the Debenham drawing-room and wrote a letter of introduction to Patrick Byron.

"Here's one of my oldest friends in London," he told Aline. "Perhaps he'll show you some sides of it that your more respectable relatives don't know. He's amusing."

He wondered, as he rowed back in the late green sunset that night, what Pat Byron would think of Aline. Perhaps he should have warned her against Pat's philandering. When he got home he pulled his skiff far up on the grey pebbled beach and turned it over. He probably wouldn't use it again for weeks. It was a chill late-summer midnight, with the mist of autumn already stilling the forest. The mountains at the head of the lake were a waved streak of coal black. No midges formed a nimbus around his lamp as he read that night, making frequent pots of tea, with the kitten that old Mrs. Feather had thrust upon him nestling in his lap.

*   *   *

For the next month he saw no one. An occasional far-off rattling roar announced the passing of the *War Eagle*, and the arrival of a mail day. From a shelf he reached high up on the mountain behind him he looked down on the lake, the yellow block of the store down at its far end, and thought he saw the black bulk of the Treads' donkey-engine. But whether it was still on the shore, or they had got it on to the raft, he could not tell from that distance. The mountain slope he was on was stiff with deer and had probably never been shot over; and he knew that here was plenty of fresh meat when he wanted it. The ducks now began to stream in with the sunsets, coming up from the salt water. So were the spawning salmon; he heard them splashing at nights as they leapt in his bay. He watched them struggling up his river, morose red creatures, covered with white sores. He devoted one

whole day to following them up the stream, actually touched
them as they squirmed and flapped their desperate way
across the shallow reaches. And then he came to a pool
where they lay packed, sullen in their silence as they waited
for the rains of autumn to bring the river to life again and
let them pass up. They were the only sign of life, of movement, in a scene so still that it lay like a painted canvas.

Little nips of raw wind now freshened his face as he
waited for the evening flight of duck on the tip of his point
at sunsets. With his skiff hidden in the bushes, he watched the
lake redden and the mountains at the far end turn into their
soft powder-of-rose. Then would come the whistle of wings.
The fat mallard were already eating the spawning salmon
which had begun to die, and he let them pass. It was no
longer worthwhile to pull back their feathers and smell that
sickening stench of dead fish. It was an occasional widgeon
that he waited for, a fast "baldpate," circling, its wings
cocked to land, that he hoped to bring down. And the occasional flights of teal that dropped in the *bayous* made by the
first rains. When the wind was heavy from the Pacific, the
ducks going up-lake flew close to the waves as they swung up
past his point, and gave him an occasional thrilling shot.
A duck that happened to be fishy was not wasted, because
he gave it to the cat. He was not sure he was right in doing
this. He had raised the kitten on Klim, a milk made from
powder which he mixed with water, and made the kitten
lick from his finger. But when it was still so small, and apparently helpless, that its legs trembled when it stood up, he
came back one evening to find it had eaten half of a fat
widgeon he had laid out to cook. It soon became ferocious
and thrived on the diet of fish-heads and duck insides he
gave it from then on.

The trout, which had simply disappeared during the hot
summer months, appeared again. He noticed a big Rainbow,
working its fins off his point. And one dusk he caught two
within half an hour that weighed two pounds each. He looked

N1

up towards von Hauptmann's place after he had landed the second one, wondering if the old German wouldn't appreciate a nice bit of fresh fish. Then he rowed back and hung it in his own meat-safe that he had built on the shady side of the cabin. He wouldn't make the first move.

He felt that he had won a victory when he saw the German's boat coming into his bay one morning. The old Count seemed to be thinking along those lines, too. He was dressed in nothing but the narrowest pretence of bathing drawers, made from blue flannel, apparently a converted shirt. And he was as browned by the sun as a rotted apple. But his great skin was sleek and shining as he bowed with dignity in the sun.

"Please," he said, "I have come to ask you a favour—my fireplace . . . there is one stone that is too big."

Tony was pleased that morning that the wind happened to be blowing hard up the lake, that the Count was obviously very tired after his struggle against it on the row down, that he could offer him some fresh coffee, and that, with the sprit-sail he had been making, he could actually sail the Count back. This was indeed a demonstration of the way he had adapted himself to the lake. The old German also said:

"I have no cartridges. The birds must know it. My place is full of grouse. Please, bring your gun."

*   *   *

The stone that was too big turned out to be a sheer slab of granite that the Count had unearthed and had been chipping at all summer to fashion into his fireplace mantel. It was no wonder that even with the faithful Elsa the old German could not place it. On rollers he had managed to get it as far as the door. It was from there, and on to the top of the prepared fireplace that he wanted Tony's help. It was a back-breaking job. Tony's first admiration of the ingeniousness with which the Count had used local stone to build his baronial hearth soon turned to hate. He was furious with the Count for inventing such a thing. The brutal granite slid back down the steps and almost broke his leg. They sweated it, foot by foot, across the *Schloss* floor. Then, like Egyptians constructing the mysterious Pyramids, the Count and he, inch by inch, raised it to the required level by prying it up and inserting one block of wood after another atop an increasing pile. It threatened to topple over and destroy them as they made the final effort. "You're crazy!" gasped Lynd, desperately steadying the relentless mass. "You'll kill yourself with this!" But at last, despite the hysterical help of Elsa, they shoved it into place.

"So. . . ." said the Count. "It is correct."

The chimney was stepped back, already built into the brown stained logs of the cabin's wall. It went up through a loft above them, and von Hauptmann made Tony come outside and listen to the description of the castellated chimney that he had begun to build above the cedar shingled roof. "Ah . . . if we only had some storks now! . . ." said the German.

Tony shook his head in reluctant admiration. It was a staggering demonstration of mind over matter. Looking at him, Tony wondered how the huge, hairy Count had ever managed to get up on that roof, how he had managed to stick there, and why he had not fallen through. . . . "And now," said Tony, without thinking, "I suppose you'll do nothing else for the rest of your life but cut logs to feed that damn' thing!"

The Count glared at him. He stepped off and squared his bronze shoulders. "You will not have to help me," he said.

"Oh . . . I didn't mean that," said Tony petulantly. "Where are the bloody grouse?"

The German anxiously led Lynd up a path and into the wasteland of second growth that the old logging camp had left. As often happens, the birds got up in a covey from beneath their very feet. Lynd, taken by surprise, fired into the brown and thought he saw a bird drop. "Over there," he said to the Count, and went after the flushed birds. He got two, which he picked up, and then the grouse circled and went back into the pines. When, after an hour, he came back, he found the old German still down on his knees pulling the undergrowth apart in a desperate effort to find the allegedly fallen bird. Tony was shocked. He tried to stop him. "It was probably a runner," he protested, "and is already miles away from here. Here are two more."

As he gave them over he was humiliated by the joy with which Elsa received them. "Good Lord," he thought, "these people haven't got enough to eat!"

When he was trying to tack down to his place he saw the old German go back into the clearing and start pulling apart the brush again. He was still looking for the other bird.

Then one night, when Tony was returning from an all-day sail up to the logging camp, he put into von Hauptmann's little wharf. Both Germans came down to meet him. That afternoon he had shot two big black duck, not too appetising to eat, and had intended to give them to the von Hauptmanns. Three little fat butterballs he had also knocked over, he intended to keep for himself. They were very succulent. But as he looked at the two old Germans his heart went back on him; he tossed up the three precious butterballs.

"Just got them," he said.

Elsa picked them up. She dangled them in her hand, and then stared down into the skiff where the two big black ducks lay on the floor-boards.

"Humph!" she said. "You only give us the little ones!"

* * *

That he must give a meaning to his own life on the lake was a necessity he had been aware of from the first. He was no Eastern hermit who could live alone in a cave for the glory of God. He was no holy man. And the mere perfection of his own character by his life in this loneliness was an uncertain ambition, unless it led to a use of some sort. No man on the lake had less the right to live a worthless life than he. Yet he could not see how he could make it worth while.

This was the thing that puzzled him, and made the days now not quite so perfect. He pointed out to himself that there were thousands of Englishmen all over the world living lives somewhat like his. But they usually had the excuse that they were growing or raising something to give as a reason—if only to their own consciences—for being where they were. And, knowing Englishmen, he doubted if they ever thought about it much, anyway. He thought of the thousands of other Englishmen who had even less than that excuse to offer. The prodigious number of healthy men in London who had never worked, never would, and whose chief occupation was walking along Piccadilly in a bowler hat and an umbrella of mornings, or discussing how they would run the Government in their clubs—decorative parasites living on the income earned by some adventurous Englishman long ago. Some of them even did not bother to lean down to dress; a valet put on their shoes. He at least had the knowledge that he was keeping himself alive, waiting on himself hand and foot, and that the little money which allowed him to buy whatever provisions he needed had actually been earned by his own brain in former years. He couldn't be more self-contained and justifiably independent if he had deliberately invented this situation—which, in a way, he had by simply coming here. He had earned the right to look any critic in the face and tell him to go to hell.

But, quite naturally in this isolation, his worst critic was to be himself. And he could not placate that. During the first year he had recovered more than he had thought possible from the wreckage of his last years. It had given him back his own mind—an amazing experience—and he found himself capable now of thinking freshly, as he had done twenty or more years before when the great part of this world and its life lay ahead of him, and he was eager for every experience that just sheer living could offer. That very interest in life had now returned to him—seasoned by the critical sense—and that was why now, more than ever before, he wanted a *motif* for his life.

He could not bring back Chris. That existence had been wrecked on the wheel. But a good life now could make atonement and bring its compensation. How could he live that here on the lake?

He was in a peculiar position. The old Count had pointed out the folly of letting himself become involved in the raw life of the people around the store. That, after all, was merely advancing suburbia. Up to a point he could live out of his own personal experiences. Enjoy the spell of his own life.

*　　　*　　　*

In the meantime, he knew, he must just wait. He was part of the lake and its circumstances—just as much as the Tread boys or anyone else. If an occasion arose, and he could not foresee what it could be, he would be here. And this time he hoped that the things he had done, the wreck he had made of a good deal of his life, and the way he was living now, would find him the man to meet it. That was all.

His chief difficulty, of course, was to find an interest in this life.

*　　　*　　　*

Pat Byron had written him two letters in that year. They had been forwarded from the only address Tony had left; the lawyer in Seattle. Pat, trying to blast him out of here, had written:

". . . Well, how are you finding life in the Colonels' delight? From what I can learn the 'frontier' you have selected is a perfect set-up—no snakes to bite you, no angry natives to fight, no possible disasters from Mother Nature . . . in other words, all the thrills—with no dangers at all. . . . It all sounds very nice. I suppose you'll be giving us a book next: *With Rod and Gun up the Alimentary Canal.* I can't see how you stick it. Come back and get a flat at Putney. . . ."

Tony had been furious when he first read that. Just because he did not have the conventional accoutrements of the orthodox hero of an "African" story, because, like some colonial administrator, he did not live in a bungalow where a clap of his hands would bring twenty "boys" leaping to obey his commands, just because there happened to be no lurking black men, eager to shoot or be shot at, this was certainly no "Colonels' delight." He was angry at the parochial quality of Patrick's urban sophistication, how provincial he actually was concerning everything off the road of his own narrow strip of life. He wished he could impress him with some of the realities of this struggle for existence on Scaup Lake. But that would take more than a letter, it would take more than a book. . . .

He had often thought of putting down the saga of these lives. That idea had immediately presented itself. It was an answer to his own dilemma; what to do? It would probably help to clarify his own position in the situation. But when he thought of putting down the story of these shapeless lives some dignity withheld him. He would be guilty of the superficial criticism that Patrick was making. A little more well-informed, perhaps. But essentially he would be putting his own explanation upon the lives he saw around him— not waiting for them to unfold themselves. It needed lurking natives or rapacious Indians to make such a setting tangible to even so recondite a man as Byron. You could not touch him with the mute forces that were working in this scene. You could not get it, the meaning of this lake, across to him. You might make him see it; but you could not make him see what it meant.

For there was a meaning. The resultant of all these forces, emanating from these strangely different people around the lake, was a life. A composite unity—so that if one of them acted irregularly this act would eventually alter the whole. In that way the result of these lives, apparently so purpose-less if only considered individually, was a growth. An evolution. A civilisation. And it was just as real, and as intangible, as the politically-led lives of people who lived where trams clanged in the streets, where rich men need do no more than press a button to have someone even put on their trousers for them, where, despite their desperate will-power to circumvent it, a fair proportion of the poorer population slept on park benches of winter nights, with the day's newspapers as their only coverlets. That anachronistic spectacle that Lynd had so often winced at (and realised he could not change) as he drove home late on foggy London nights up the Mall where these starving, shivering human wrecks lay at the gold-spiked gates of Buckingham Palace itself. . . . It was not a good demonstration for the human race.

Compared to that scene, Scaup Lake could be said to have a very real and authentic civilisation. People could starve here, too. The Count would be really up against life, for example, if Elsa died. If her fingers weren't around to earn money by her ceaseless sewing, the von Hauptmanns would never be able to buy the small essential groceries that they simply must have from the store. Such things as coffee, tea, pepper and salt—even lamp oil, and an occasional side of bacon. Lard, out here, assumed its proper place as an abso-lute necessity of life. The von Hauptmanns could not eat food always boiled. And if they could not run to the expense of lamp oil, then the von Hauptmanns would automatically drop down a couple of pegs in Scaup Lake's life. The old Hun would have to lie on the floor and do his reading by the light of the log fire, as Lincoln did. It was his insatiable craving for books, Tony now saw, that prevented the irascible old German from making an open break with him. He always enquired timidly at the store if Lynd had any books he could spare. And it was with those books that Tony found himself participating in another institution of Scaup Lake's civilisation; its nebulous lending library. It was a thing which had sprung up by itself. Born of the demand. Without seemingly aware of their doing it, the Scaup Lakers had taken to passing on newspapers, magazines, books to some particular person, with the injunction that they be passed on to the next man who would like to read them. With books, a person's name written inside the cover meant that eventually they would one day be handed back to him. This was invariably at the store, which in addition to its twice-weekly function of gossip exchange on mail days was also the centre for this library activity. Lynd always brought down a few of the latest books he had finished, and if the people were not there he intended them for, he merely left them with Smedley's post-office mail.

For the Debenhams, with whom he had resolved to keep on the pleasant relationship of an absent friend, he left the last sophisticated modern novels to come in. Billy Tread, Lynd discovered, always asked for the next reading of them —as that young man was apparently modernising himself on the lake as fast as he could. A distressing thought, mused Tony. Then Zonia Greville and Virgie Cullen got them. From their remarks, their attempts to draw him into literary discussions upon them, Tony tended to regret that he had lent himself to this institution of culture on the lake. Old Dr. Feather read every word of any biography or historical work and patriarchically passed them on to the baffled Swinton. This, Tony liked because he knew that before his own advent the Swintons had considered themselves the *literati* of Scaup Lake . . . and it was sheer poison to them to have to accept cultural manna from his offensive hands. Shorty Murdoch startled him by the hot, awkward manner he thanked him for the opportunity of reading Lytton Strachey's *Eminent Victorians*, and, for a brief second, in these few words they exchanged alone together, Tony saw the offer of friendship in the dour Scot's piggy little blue eyes. But he did not take it up, merely tucking the book under his arm as he said that he was glad Murdoch liked it, and turned to the waiting Zonia to fill out his petty grocery order.

It was the Count who gave him genuine pleasure. For years his arrogant aloofness had made the old German an outsider to the lake library. And he, more than any other man on the lake, was in need of books. Through Tony he came into possession of them again. It amused Tony to pass on to him, before he read them himself, the fat roll of London "society" weeklies the Debenhams occasionally sent down to the store for him. The *Sketch*, *Tatler*, *Bystander*, *Sporting and Dramatic*, *Country Life* . . . all those journals which gave the Debenham drawing-room in B.C. its air of an English country house. The Count's comments were invariably invigorating. All the English upper classes appeared to do, according to the exiled German aristocrat, was jump hedges after foxes, go horseracing, and have themselves incessantly photographed at an unbroken round of sporting events and public banquets . . . when they weren't desecrating the Swiss or Austrian Alps by their amateur ski-ing. . . .

That the Count was well aware of his precarious position, if Elsa should die, was unconsciously expressed by a complaint he made to Lynd in the first week of the rainy season. He had had a touch of croup, and it had been Elsa who had made the eight-mile row down to the store. When the Count next appeared at Smedley's he sought Tony out, and said:

"What do you think almost happened to me? My Elsa almost drowned herself!"

The shrivelled Elsa, who looked pathetically like a starved hare in her woollen winter suit, had tried to catch a salmon on her row down to the store. She had tied one end of the line to her leg and trolled a spoon. A big fifteen-pound dog-salmon had taken it. And when the unseamanlike Elsa had stood up in the row-boat to fight him, he had whipped her over the side. With the salmon, on the end of about sixty yards of line made fast to one leg, and her hands clutching its stern, the wind had finally blown the row-boat ashore, where Elsa had clambered out and beached the big fish. But the way von Hauptmann saw this accident was:

"What do you think almost happened to *me*?"

* * *

The floating bunk-house of the Tread boys' logging venture was a melancholic spot in the rainy season. With the desperate efficiency that characterised all the domestic work of these men in the wilderness, the loggers had got it in living condition again and even tacked up some curtains before its windows. The dirty bunks had been cleaned out and its floor had been scrubbed and almost planed to remove ancient grease spots. But the boards were pitted from the caulked boots of loggers long dead; and the ghosts of these men who had toiled and suffered in this bunk-house could not be eliminated. Its shabbiness was a daily reminder of the small rewards its present occupants could expect from their efforts. It depressed Tony, even to look at it, when he at last complied with Billy Tread's insistent request that he drop in one day on his row home from the store.

The bunk-house had been moored in a little bay made by the mouth of the river that tumbled down from the mountain behind Tread's place and curved through the thick strand of shore forest to the lake. To Tony, the black trunks of the forest expressed a mute and sullen defiance against the death that the ignoble bunk-house meant to them. It seemed a dishonourable end for them, to be the victims of this dirty lodging, the merciless axes, the clattering donkey-engine that was pulling its asthmatic body up from the virgin shore-line.

For the donkey-engine had at last been induced to pull its way up the lake. With sheer-poles to keep its raft from the shore, and a long hemp warp carried ahead and fastened to trees along the waterline, the black monster had been several days winding its warp back on its drum, time after another, until it was finally in the bay. Here its steel cable was fastened to the base of a massive fir and it hauled itself, like an armoured monster, up into the forest.

The jovial Jesse James had shown ugliness over the delay in getting it there, and Matthew Tread had already received a letter intimating that it might be just as well if they began to pay off the half-cost he had advanced them right now. Matt showed the letter to Tony.

"Why, he didn't even have to put up any money," exclaimed Tony. "He merely arranged credit for you with the machinery company. He hasn't risked a cent."

Matt nodded. "Pretty slick—eh?"

Tony stared at the donkey-engine, and then laughed: "Well, it will be just as hard to get that donkey-engine away from you as it was to get it up here—especially, if when they come to repossess it, one of its parts is missing?"

Matt's habitual scowl lifted, and for the first time he had known him Tony heard Matthew Tread laugh. It was more like a growl, but he said: "Ha . . . I could arrange that, all right."

"Then," said Tony, "you're sitting pretty. Don't answer his letter. Let him come to you—as if you were playing poker."

"Ummmm . . ." Matt's face fell instantly. "Not with a big man like that. He holds all the cards."

"Not out here," said Tony quickly, suddenly thinking of the old German who had sat with the shotgun across his knees down in the Dakotas—"It's wonderful how they crumple up . . . if you only stand up to them." He told Matthew Tread, and the other men around the board luncheon table, about the old German farmer, and some of the unorthodox revolts he had witnessed in Iowa. And little Murdoch grinned:

"Ye'll land us all in jug!" he said.

A mule-jawed Swede had appeared from nowhere, and announced that he was a cookie. The Treads had taken him at his word. But from the lunch he put before them that day, Tony had the premonition that the stranger Swede would not last very long even in the Tread boys' Robinson Crusoe adventure. Food, heaps of food, fresh and good, was the one reward, tangible and immediate, that the west-coast loggers demanded for their labours. If a cookie did not please them they ran him down the trail. Neither the old settler nor his sons had ever employed anyone to work for them. The hiring of Shorty Murdoch presented a problem of acute embarrassment. For he was a friend of theirs and, perhaps logically, wanted to be given a superior position of some sort.

"Dey all want to be captain in dat little ship!" chuckled Swanson when Tony saw him at the store. "My gang knows I'm de boss, 'cause I'm de toughest guy in it . . . haw-haw!"

Blue-eyed, gentle Swanson's boast was another expression of the civilisation on Scaup Lake. For, contrary to Tony's expectations, nursed on fiction, he found the loggers as peaceable as lambs. They were too tired to fight, was the way Reds, foreman of No. 1 camp had explained it. "They wait till they get down to Vancouver, and get good and drunk to do that!" Although Reds prophesied that Matthew

Tread would soon be in a mood to kill Jesse James—after he
had found out what it was like to work for him.

*   *   *

Flatly disobeying the Count's warning not to let himself
be dragged into the lives of the other Scaup Lakers, Tony
found himself taking an increasing interest in the progress
of the Tread logging camp. It was action. It was also tre-
mendously interesting to watch the way the two boys were
taking hold of things. The donkey-engine was useful in
hauling the big "sticks" out of the woods, which they
would otherwise have to haul to water over corduroy roads
with horses. But its full mechanical assistance could not be
used until a steel cable was slung between two masts made
from decapitated fir trees. Then the big trunks could be
lifted clear of the brush and rushed to water-edge down this
aerial rope-way.

Cutting the tops off these gigantic towers of fir and rigging
the steel cables between their high tips was the most skilful
and highly paid job in the woods. The "high-riggers," as
they are called, who do this work, make as much as $10 a
day. They are the aristocrats of the woods. Jesse James had
a Finn up at No. 1 camp who was reputed to be the best
high-rigger on the west coast. He was so familiar and contemptuous about danger that he would often stand up on
the tip of a fir he had beheaded, like a tiny statue on a
plinth . . . except that he would be leaning slightly against
any current of air. High-riggers were killed frequently at
their work, either because they cut through their life-belts,
or through some foolhardy trick, boasting, as Pavel would
often show-off before an appreciative camp.

Matt Tread, against his father's furious objections, intended to make himself the high-rigger of the Tread logging
venture. But when Shorty Murdoch and the others made him
see that he did not know how to splice wire cable, he

finally gave in and admitted that the Finn should be employed. Tony went up with Billy Tread to bring him down.

The big camp at the head of the lake was a metropolis compared to the Tread enterprise. Its raw unpainted bunk-houses dotted a hillside made painfully ugly by a wilderness of stumps and broken underbrush. Its cookie was an imposing figure dressed in white, with a chef's hat, and four "flunkies," also dressed in white, to serve him and take his dishes into the loggers. When he jangled on the iron triangle that dangled outside his floating kitchen a hundred men in caulked boots would come leaping like goats down from the woods. At night the bunk-houses, steaming with the sweat of their garments, would be full of the muttered conversation and grumblings of Scandinavians and every tongue in the British Empire, it seemed, including Sikh, a small cluster of which bearded Indians had a small bunk-house for themselves.

The bunk-houses were empty when Lynd and Billy came to them, and they climbed up to where the time-keeper pointed out the high-rigger was getting ready to drop a new top. They had found a pale, blonde girl talking to the little time-keeper when they came off the camp wharf, and Billy explained as they climbed up through the rutted trails:

"That the high-rigger's girl. They're not married, they say."

Lynd remembered what Reds had told him about this "hooker" whom the Finnish high-rigger had found and induced to come up from Railway Street in Vancouver, how he was holding her there against her own will, and of his fiendish jealousy which had driven the last time-keeper, an Englishman, to flee the camp. The present pale-faced little runt of a time-keeper, he reflected, was courting disaster by letting the high-rigger's girl come into his bunk-house office while the Finn was supposed to be at work. When he had looked at him now he remembered Reds' remarks about his doubtful past. Reds had also found him in Vancouver, when he was recruiting along Railway Street for a gang to replace some loggers, and the English time-keeper, who had deserted. Charley Chaplin, as the camp called this present time-keeper, had been playing the piano in a brothel along that street.

"But he's an educated man," said Reds. "Doesn't do nothing but sit around and moon all day. I'll bet you he's read even the advertisements of every damn' magazine in the camp!"

Tony thought now that here indeed was an obvious object for the blessings of the unofficial Scaup Lake lending library. But at the same time he knew that he would never lend the little time-keeper a book. The No. 1 camp was in another world from the real life on the lake. These fifteen uninhabited miles of upper water kept them entirely apart from it. There were no roads, even trails, and as he saw the sordid sore that the loggers were making of these fine forests on the upper lake, Tony thanked the distances that kept him from even knowing they were on the lake. This was one life that he would ignore as long as he could keep it from coming down on him. He thanked God that down his lonely North Arm he was safe.

*   *   *

Pavel, the high-rigger, had just finished a light halyard that he was splicing to take up the high tree and was preparing to go up it when Lynd and Billy got there. His face was wolfish from the sharp wedge that his long jaw made with his high cheek-bones. And he seemed a man who took pleasure in his unpleasant appearance. He spat out the end of a cigarette when Lynd came up, and, aware that he had a fresh audience, went up the tree with the agility of a monkey ascending a palm tree for coco-nuts. The fir was a

good ten feet in diameter at its base, and at first the Finn
looked like a spotted lizard in his checked logger's shirt, as,
with life belt slung around the shaft of trunk he went up-
wards, digging his sharp steel climbing-spikes into its thick
bark, clinging there with hands and feet against its broad
surface. And then, with the slender line of halyard dangling
from his belt, he did look like the monkey-on-a-string that
Billy compared him to.

Well over a hundred and fifty feet above the ground he
came to the first of the lower branches. And here he leaned
out against his belt and began to cut. As the axe bit into the
fresh wood the chips planed out and sailed like falling leaves
down into the brush. His height was immediately shown by
the immense time they took to zigzag down. Reds, staring
upward, said to Tony: "I've seen 'em come out themselves
like that. . . . Just fall out from the tree and turn over and
over until they hit the ground. Humph!" He laughed:
"Wasn't worth while even to pick them up."

"Dead?" asked Billy, awed.

"Well . . . sort of," grinned Reds.

"But I'm not worrying much about this one," said Reds
in a low voice to Tony. "I'm afraid he'll kill my new time-
keeper. That dame of Pavel's is sweet on him . . . and the
little runt can't make her leave off. She's always in there . . .
trying to talk to him."

"Yes," said Tony. "She was there when we came. He
looked rather nervous about something."

"Well, part of it was a strange boat coming in on him;
little Charley Chaplin don't like strangers popping in on
him. And then, he's scared of this Finn here. Pavel's been
making life hell for him."

Reds nodded to one of the logs going across a ravine
which served as a bridge for the loggers. In their caulked
boots they trotted across these slender bridgeways with all
the nonchalance of a city man walking along his pavements.
It was a matter of pride with them not to look down or wave

their arms to keep their balance. But, said Reds, in his rubber boots the time-keeper always found these casual crossings perilous. There was one between the time-keeper's shack and the cook-house, and Pavel had taken to waiting for the little time-keeper to get out on the middle of it before he himself would start to cross it. The result was the poor little time-keeper usually had to jump.

"It's funny," smiled Reds. "But its amusement has wore off . . . and one of these nights Pavel's going to make that poor little devil break his leg."

A yell from overhead warned them that the Finn was about to drop the top. Pavel had worked around the tree; and they watched him dig in his spikes as he prepared to make the undercut. It was a boast of the Finn that he could drop a top so precisely that it would drive a previously-placed peg in the ground. They saw him now wet his finger and hold it up to get the direction from which the slight breeze was blowing; then he leaned back and swung his axe.

Even from the ground Tony could see the slight shiver of the outer branches as the axe hit the tree. It was slightly over a yard wide where Pavel was cutting, and a good-sized branched tree rose from there up. This trembled and began to shake slightly as his heavy two-bladed axe bit into the soft wood. Then it began to topple . . . Lynd heard the cracking as its fibres ripped and snapped apart, and then the roar as the top broke off and left the tree to come shrieking toward the ground. Pillars of dirt, stones and broken branches shot up around its thundering impact. Complete silence. And then they heard the Finn shouting.

He was kneeling on the tip and waving his arms derisively. "Why the hell don't you jump!" someone shouted up at him.

"Yaaaa . . .!" Even at that height the Finn's wordless jeer had a note of malice in it. With a final insolent wave at the surrounding space, he dropped deftly down again along the trunk and began to make fast the pulley to rig the halyard.

"I guess your brother Matt doesn't want a hell of a lot of that, does he!" grinned Reds as he turned to Billy to arrange about the camp's high-rigger going down to the Tread camp.

"Huh!" Billy growled. "You needn't worry about Matt."

Reds laughed as he led them back, short-cut, over a succession of precarious peeled log bridge pieces. "I'm not doing any worrying," he said, a trifle angered by Billy's tone. "Only, the last letter I got from him, James wants to know when you two boys are going to get a boom into the water—now that you got that donkey-engine. He says to tell you it ain't a plaything."

Lynd, in the centre of one of the tricky bridges, heard himself saying: "Oh, you'll get it all right. Tell Jesse James to keep his shirt on. He doesn't own that donkey-engine, or the Treads, either."

"You don't say!" Red's apparent readiness to be offended by Tony's unexpected interjection was turned into a chuckle when Tony told how, over even such a petty affair as the second-hand donkey-engine, the slick Jesse James had avoided risking any of his own money; he had merely arranged credit for his half, which the Tread boys would have to pay the machinery company. "Oh, he's as full of tricks as a basket of monkeys," said Reds, with grudging admiration of his employer's business agility.

Then, as if to show how he stood in this matter, he volunteered to loan the Tread outfit the amazing number of accessory bits of tackle they had not known they would need for a high-rigging operation. "You needn't advertise it," he said. "Only the time-keeper and I know what's what with the camp stores. Just sign a note for them, will you, and let us have them back when you're done."

In this easy fashion the two Tread boys were saved the expenditure of a hundred dollars or so that they simply could not have made. And while Billy, as excited as a child, was being led along the bins of bolts and blocks and drums of steel wire in the camp's pungent store-house, Reds pulled an imitation leather suitcase from beneath his wooden bunk and held out a bottle of whiskey he had bought from Digger Bean. When Tony smilingly refused, saying he had drunk his share for this life, Reds took just a small swig and said:

"You ought to tell that to our cookie—old Hoot Mon MacDonald. There's a character for you. Used to be the manager of a canning company, up in Alaska, once. Had a wife and a home out on Shaughnessy Heights over in Vancouver, and all that. There's two of them. Hoot Mon, and old Champagne Shannon. Champagne is very particular . . . always wears a frock coat when he cooks. They're born buddies, these two—and when they meet they simply tear up the street. They're the two best cookies on the Coast; they get two hundred and fifty dollars a month each; they work about three months steady—and then they quit any job they're on. Figure that out and that means they have something like fifteen hundred dollars between them for one of their regular drinking bouts . . . and it never has lasted them more than a month. Know that, because you can always find them in the market again. And neither of them has any regrets about it—old Hoot Mon tells me the finest nights of his life have been when he's been so boiled he didn't know whether it was a girl or just old Champagne Shannon in bed beside him. They just use the woods as a cure, they tell me; to get sobered up and ready to start all over again. But if you've ever eaten old Hoot Mon's hot-cakes, you'd know why he need never have no fear of ever being without a job . . ."

Reds sighed. "They're a pair of regular artists . . . in their way. A couple of days after you bring one of them, half dead up to a camp, and he settles down with his pots and pans and gets started again . . . why, they fairly make your heart

sing . . . the stuff they put before you. God bless 'em! I says
. . . and so says every girl along Railway Street. They love
those two old men; half that street will be walking behind
them and weeping when they're put to rest. There's something big about them . . . those two drunks. And there's
many a frightened young thing they've given the cash to go
straight. They're genuine old sugar-daddies . . ."

Tony instantly thought of Senator Hancock, and Sweetie,
and death in the big London Hotel—the Senator's exit,
purple-draped, like any Roman senator—and of what had
Sweetie done with the six boiled shirts. April and November.
Old love. The traffic waiting at that corner along Piccadilly
for the green light to let them turn off to go up past the
Berkeley. . . . How often he had sat moodily in that
jam! And it all seemed a million miles away from him
now.

He looked around the little floating bunk-house in which
Reds and the time-keeper lived. They inhabited diagonal
corners. Each had an unpainted wooden bunk built against
the wall, and a table with a chair before it. A little iron stove
held the centre of the room, with another chair before it
now, on which was drying one of the foreman's checked
mackinaws. The floor was full of tiny pit marks from Reds'
caulked boots. A new pair, still unused, stood by the head
of his bunk. Under the time-keeper's table Tony saw a pair
of badly cracked patent-leather shoes.

"He was wearing those," laughed Reds, "when I picked
him up down in number 36. Playing the piano, he was. A
dismal bloke, the Madame said he was, and she asked me to
get rid of him for her. So I took him. Whatever he was . . .
pimp or something. . . . I don't know. He's an educated man.
But he's hell to live with. Never says a bloody word he
doesn't have to. Sometimes I almost wish that that damn'
Finn would kick the stuffing out of him. He gets on my
nerves. Now them other two I was just telling you about . . .
Champagne and old Hoot Mon . . . they're men. You like

'em. This guy's just mean. I always think, somehow . . . that he's plotting . . . just waiting for something, you know . . . to get square with Pavel. I've often felt tempted to speak to the Finn about it."

Tony laughed. "From the look of him, I wouldn't say that god-awful Finn needed much protection."

Reds shook his head. "You don't know. Y'ought to see this mean little bastard's eyes sometimes. That's why I say I'd like to get rid of him. Sometimes, I tell you, this cabin simply *stinks* with hate!"

* * *

* * *

The rainy season usually began with Pacific gales, wet winds that swept in from over the mountains and churned the tips of the fir forest like a green sea. A foam of scudding sud rose like quivering jelly along the grey rocks of Lynd's beach. On these days he gained an exultation from his physical contest with the weather. Coming almost at the beginning of his six weeks' immurement his last trip up to the raucous No. 1 logging camp had brought out completely his own aloofness and self-sufficiency. As he looked out of his cabin windows now on the wild grey mornings he knew that unless he wanted to he need not go out of doors. But he always went out and spent most of the morning working there. A particular stone, placed at the water-edge before he turned in at night, was a water-gauge that gave him a daily small pleasure. He would see it yards out when he came down to it in the morning and several feet under water. It gave him a physical sign of how fast the lake was rising. With the high winds the rising water floated hundreds of dead trees and stumps off the lake shore above him and brought them to his beach. He collected the smaller bits of driftwood for his winter supply of firewood, and, with one or two sizeable trunks, he lopped off their branches with an axe, sawed off the stump and hauled them on rollers far above where the water could reach. In this way each day was filled with purpose and justified by an achievement of some sort. In the crisp days of autumn he could saw and chop up this rising woodpile by himself. And no need to ask the Count's assistance. A broken tip of cedar, greyed and seasoned by years of sun and rains, was an especial gift. He spent two days working this trunk up to a place near the cabin where he could begin to work on it. He split off long slabs with a sledge and wedge and planed them into planks for a chest of drawers he wanted to make. This satisfactory work occupied the whole of afternoons, so much so that he was reluctant to desist and cook dinner when the light began to fail and the lamps had to be lit. He took as much pleasure as an old cabinet-maker in the design of his work.

The river on his right now roared endlessly at nights. The turmoil at its mouth reached far out into the lake. It was a good half-hour's hard climb up into the mountain before he could find a place where it was safe to attempt to cross it. Carrying out his resolve to make himself as self-sufficient as he could contrive, he spent one or two days a week in doing nothing but enlarging his clearing. There was a patch of black soil near the river mouth that was nothing now but a waste of alder bushes. He cut these down, and with a pick-axe he tore up their roots. This was a decision that had come to him late in the year, but, by the next spring, he would have enough land cleared, between the rains and snow, to start a vegetable garden. He wondered if in this shelter of Bald Mountain there would be enough early sun to ripen maize. Anyway, he would have peas and beans, perhaps tomatoes, certainly lettuce and radishes. All of the settlers around the lake had these little gardens, but it was only the Treads who went about it in a businesslike way. It was their fresh vegetables that were sold at Smedley's store to the lower Scaup Lakers, and, when they would guarantee a steady supply, to the big No. 1 logging camp. A supply which the two Tread boys had now proudly announced as stopped, since they had gone into the logging business.

This continuous round of daily work was a justification and provided the physical contest that he had often felt so needful in his life. The urge that he had usually appeased by shooting or fishing expeditions, or mountain climbing with Christina. But whereas those had always been excursions, this grateful physical languor that he felt here, when he reached his cabin tired at nights, was accompanied by the solid satisfaction that that day he had usually done something to earn his right to this freedom. And now, when he picked up his rifle or shotgun to go out for the day, it was with an attitude entirely different from those old pursuits. When he climbed the mountain half a mile back to cross the river over into the second-growth between his cabin and von Hauptmann's place, he knew that it was six pine grouse, at the most, that he wanted to bring back. When he got them, he was done. Because six grouse at one time, he knew, were all that he could have on hand without going bad before he could eat them. And his heart did not give a jump as a bird got up, causing him to shoot long before he was on the bird— as he invariably did shooting partridges in the root-fields of England. Now he was deliberately shooting for the pot, and he felt professional about it. When he climbed up Bald mountain to get a deer, he knew that it was only a small pronged buck that he wanted to bring back. Not the big antlered ones. And even so, he knew that the shooting of a deer meant also a row down to the store to give most of it away. He could not eat it all himself—only the chops and liver. And if he happened to turn up at the store in time, the old German would find the fore-quarters and haunches of a fat little deer awaiting him; if not, it would be understood that Smedley would give them to someone else.

In his isolation Tony had now become so self-sufficient that he did not want to break the spell by again inviting the old German's company. It was during this second rainy season that he realised how utterly contented he was to live completely by himself. He had fallen deeply in love with his unbroken and safe solitude.

He learned the meaning of the sharp rising flight of mallard duck . . . because he saw now that, whenever they could, they fed off back from the main lake, where their sharp upward rise took them up from surrounding under-growth. Rain, to him, coming at him in squalls across the lake, also had a new meaning; the precautions he must immediately take to face it. So had the approaching snows of winter.

The snow meant that for three or four months all the land around his cabin would be so deep with drifts that it would be practically impossible to go out and collect any easy firewood. In his first winter and summer he had burned up the fallen fir that he and the old Count had cut. This autumn, before the rains came, he had merely strolled out into his clearing and collected a handful of dead branches when he wanted them. But, since he had done that, he had created a wide area behind his cabin in which there simply was no available firewood, except standing trees. It was imperative therefore that between the rains and the snow he cut and stack every log that he had beached in the lake's flood.

In those days of the dying, slanting sun therefore, Tony could be seen from dawn to dusk swinging an axe in his clearing. With the small trees it was quite possible for one man to work a big cross-cut saw, once he had mastered the knack of handling it. And Tony, in these matters, was proud of himself by this time. His muscles, he knew, must have stood out like ropes along his shoulders. He was trimmed down so that he felt almost cat-like with the agility with which he could travel the forest. He positively

OL

thrilled with health. He cut the logs wherever he had pulled them up on the beach, and split them there into the same convenient lengths of firewood. These he carried and stacked against the walls of his cabin, as he had so often seen such prudent piles of winter wood under the eaves of châlets in Bavaria, until its walls were lined with them. For immediate use, and to keep a good supply always on hand and dry, he stacked one wall of his kitchen from floor to the cedar shingles. He started dinner and washed while it was cooking, very often taking a quick refreshing dip in the lake. And now when he sat down to the pungent roast grouse or venison (in the various ways he was trying to cook that much over-rated meat) it was with an almost savage hunger. Just living was a highly emotional satisfaction.

His mind was at rest. When he read now he felt that he was bedded-in to this life, and that he was making a success of it. At times the books disturbed him. He would come on some passage . . . some incident or description that would recall his past life. At such times he would often put down his book and stare long and moodily at his typewriter. . . . There, in that black case, lay the answer to his worthlessness. He could do something; he could write, he could create. . . . There wasn't a man on the whole lake who let such an opportunity lie fallow before him. But he could afford to; with the splendid self-sufficiency he had created for himself he had no need to draw at all upon his little capital. The interest on the small sum of money that Christina had willed back to him would not have allowed them to live a quarter of the year back in London. Out here it was more than was necessary. It was piling up in the Seattle bank, and he was taking a pride in seeing how much he could do without it.

As to the other reasons for writing? . . . His answers to these were not so satisfactory, or convincing. But he felt afraid to write. He did not want to awaken his own imagination to the world he was daily trying to leave behind him.

Out here he might be living an illusion of some sort, perhaps? But at any rate, it was just as real and its pleasures were just as tangible as any he had experienced before he came here. They were often more real, in fact.

There was, for instance, a queer power that he seemed to have come into lately. He could spend an entire day in a reverie of some sort. Living as it were in the chrysalis of his own imagination. These day-dreams were unbelievably substantial. They satisfied him just as much as when, as a boy, he had lain on the warm sands of the New Jersey seashore and watched steamers pass at sea, picturing in his own mind the lives aboard them and the fronded tropical isles to which, he hoped, they were bound. And now, as then, they gave him happiness. More than that, the more he got away from all the world in this utter solitude, the nearer he believed he was coming to Christina.

There was not much to divide them now. The disturbance of her leaving the world had died out within his heart. He could think of that now without his first feelings of desperate self-reproach. In a strange way he felt that he had made his peace with her. And sometimes, in this stillness, he felt that he could almost hear her voice.

He would not have been more than moderately surprised if, looking up from his book some night, he had seen her sitting there. She was just as close as that. . . . And he did not want anything to break this peacefulness.

* * *

Of course this was sheer nonsense, these loving reminiscences about Christina, from him, who had made the last three years of her life such a hell for her. But then, there had been ten good years—for her, at any rate—before that. And now, he saw, in Christina's heart, they had always over-balanced the remaining three. That was why she had endured him all during that Flick business. She had said so in so many words. "I've looked after you, Peter. I've given you

medicine when you were sick, I've packed your bags for you,
I married you when you did not have one penny. . . .
Don't think I'm going to let any other woman get away
with you—just because she has taken it into her head you
would be a nice person to own. You are, in a way . . . for
all your wretched unfaithfulness. And I'm not going to
give you up."

The worst blow he had ever been struck was by the sight
of his opened bag the first night he left that Chelsea house.
Nothing was more reproachful than the neat way Christina
had so thoughtfully packed all the things he needed. His
pyjamas and silk dressing-gown, his shaving kit, all on top
where he would first need them. And the clean shirts with
fresh collars in their accustomed place in the top flap. In
this orderliness her last message to him came with everything
that he touched in that bag.

The thing, out here in B.C., that made his thoughts so
hopelessly regretful about Chris was that he was no longer
thinking of her merely in the relationship of a wife. Out
here she had come into focus to him objectively—just as an
individual. A girl, a woman, as he had watched her become;
and he had seen how unbelievably nice she was. He laughed
now and then out here, when a thing recalled one of her
occasional ironic comments about life—that Irish quality of
Christina's wit that he had always found so invigorating.
When Chris laughed her face flushed and she wept with
mirth. So hearty, it was. Not like that hoarse, reminiscently
sad noise of Flick's. But, even now, he could remember how
he had killed that power of enjoyment in Chris. How
the way she always managed to see the grotesque in anything
finally got on his nerves. How, in the tautness of their
relationship, he had fumed with her for what he
claimed was always seeing the "left" side of things; that
if they were going to catch a train—they would miss it;
that if they were driving anywhere—he could not possibly
make the distance in the time he said he could. Petty

things, utterly inconsequential—it wouldn't have made much difference if they *had* missed the train. And now when he looked back on some occasion, he wondered that he had not killed both of them—the furious way he would drive the car, after Chris had made some pessimistic prophecy about not getting some place.

It had been things like that—rotten little, mean little, disgustingly little things that had made them wreck their life. Taken individually, they had meant absolutely nothing; but their cumulative effect had cut a permanent scowl in his brow. His nervous system had become inflammable, so that it needed only the scratch of one of these infinitesimal incidents to set it off. Unless . . . unless, as he had so often done . . . he had damped that powder with alcohol. But then when he, literally, blew up he had no longer the wit to control his sentiments; and he said awful things. And this, as he saw it now, was what he had permitted these little things to make him do to Christina.

All this was too simple; but it was the reason for the wreck. He swept the London scene clear of his mind to look at Chris as he had first seen her; that good-looking young nurse, who always had some amusing, usually snotty remark to make as she brought in his breakfast or did his dressings in the mornings, and who he watched thoughtfully for weeks as he lay on the cool lawn of Chatham Hospital, while Christina captained the nurses' against the doctors' cricket team.

Or Christina in evening dress as they walked back to the hotel one dawn and both of them slightly romantic from the Tokay they had been drinking watched the sun gild the Danube at Budapest. They had had some fine years together.

*　　*　　*

It had been six weeks since he had seen anybody. In the autumn lull between the rains and snow the only movement on the lake had been the changing colours. But there had been something very like a song in their motion. The air seemed washed clear after the prolonged downpour. The heat haze of summer had been driven away. That forest mistiness, for instance, that made beams of light from the sun-shafts through the upper branches. The woods were crisp now. The second-growth between his and the Count's place was a coloured plateau of flaming orange. Its ravines were scarlet with the branches of sumac. Up the steep slope of the mountain behind him the silver birches stood up like yellow feathers. The deep, unchanging green of the fir forest dominated everything, as it had all through the hot, stagnant summer; but the lake was now gentian blue away from the rising sun, and flaked with fresh, racing waves. And across them one morning he saw coming the big grey launch of Ken Cullen. With him was Virgie, who cried as the launch grounded:

"Howdy do, Mr. Lynd. Since you wouldn't come down to see us, we've come up to see you."

Lynd, not at all pleased by this unheard-of visit, heard Ken shouting from its cabin: "That's nonsense. We're going up the lake." When his head appeared above the canvas-covered cabin, Cullen said, "We're on our way up the lake . . . I'm going over into the Nitinat to-night. And Virgie just kept pestering me, as long as we were so close, to drop in. How's things?"

Lynd waded a few steps out into the water and held up his hand for Virgie to alight. "I guess I'll have to carry you," he said.

"Sure, Baby—what do you think I am, a duck?"

He was surprised at how easily he held her, and at his own sensations of suddenly clasping a woman again—even so necessarily remote as Virgie Cullen. He was conscious that he looked a little confused as he put her down. Ken, usually the gayest, most amusing person on the lake, seemed to have very little to say for himself to-day. He walked

behind them to the cabin and appeared to be absorbed in
rolling a cigarette during the first of his wife's gushing comments about how homelike Tony had made his place. He
was highly appreciative of Lynd's cedar chest of drawers.
"Highfalutin!" he smiled.

"I'd have brought your mail and books," he said, "if
I'd have thought about it. If I'd known we were going to
drop in on you."

"I made him come here," giggled Virgie.

She was dressed in what was her idea of a woodland
costume. A dark green tartan skirt of some sort, with a red-
and-black checked mackinaw that had been cut down to
fit her—with the scarlet tam-o'-shanter atop her lemon-
coloured curls she flamed just as fiercely as the leaves
around them.

"But you can't go over into the Nitinat!" Tony said,
without thinking. The Nitinat, which lay beyond the ridge
of mountain above von Hauptmann's place, was so un-
travelled and considered so dangerous, because of the fallen
trees that choked it, that everyone except Ken, who trapped
there, always went in in pairs. That was why, the venture-
some Ken insisted, it was still the best marten country on
the Island. He took five or six hundred dollars worth of
pelts out of there every winter.

"She's not going," he said.

From the frown with which he muttered this, Tony could
see that Ken Cullen would not welcome any more talk on
this subject. After he had introduced Virgie to his larder
and undergone one of her coy whispers (Ken was smoking
in the other room) about the pity of wasting such a comfy
bunk, he ceremonially made some coffee for them and
shoved off their launch. It was Ken who, very unceremoni-
ously, put his arm behind Virgie's knees and lifted her to
the launch. He did this when she was right in the middle of
telling Tony how the Tread boys had finally brought a big
boom of logs down the lake. "Now you let me finish!"

she snapped petulantly as Ken climbed aboard. "Gosh—can't I even talk!"

"There's a lot of mail down there for you," yelled Ken, as the big grey launch backed out to turn. "When I get back I'll tell 'em you're alive and kicking, anyway. So long."

Tony went back to his cabin and sat down on the seat in the sun. He was still trembling slightly from the thoughts that holding Virgie had aroused in him. For almost as far as he could see the launch he saw that red tam-o'-shanter blazing in the sun.

It was two days later, when he reached into the water to seize a wounded widgeon that he had brought down that he realised he had had his left hand under water for some time. His wrist-watch would be ruined. There was nothing to do but send it to a jeweller down in Victoria and have it cleaned before the rust set in. It was an old one that long ago Luba had given him. He felt superstitious about it; it had been with him through so many ups and downs, and survived, that he felt its miraculous working to be an omen of some sort. He would have bad luck if he ever lost that watch or let it stop.

The next day he turned over his skiff, and, after a hard row against the sharp wind, reached the mouth of the North Arm, where he hoisted the sprit-sail. The wind caught him and he fairly bowled along. As he went down through the Narrows he stared across and saw the wreck that the Tread boys were already making of their once-peaceful shoreline. A raw niche had been cut into the deep woods, dotted across which he could clearly see the raw stumps of fallen firs, and whistle-squeaks and puffs of white steam showed him that the donkey-engine was in its destructive operation.

No one would ever catch another trout off the mouth of that river, he reflected.

The old Feathers had gone down for the winter; he saw the blind walls of paper tacked up behind the windows of their bungalow. In a bay farther down he saw the Swinton's house-boat, wisps of blue smoke being blown from its tin-stack showing that very likely the acid little French wife of the game warden was inside. A cluster of four men were sitting on the porch of Digger Bean's shack, with the tawny blur of what looked like a cougar lying on the grass. Bean was, aside from bootlegger, the lake's professional lion-hunter and got forty dollars' bonus for every one of these timid cats that he shot. Above the bridge he saw the wide boom of logs that the Tread boys had delivered and Jesse James' men would shoot down. Hastily stowing his sail, he took to the oars and drove his skiff out from the sucking current into the river pool below Smedley's store.

He trotted lightly up the steep bank swinging the canvas rucksack he always brought down to bring back his mail and supplies. He was constantly delighted, these days, with the almost unbelievable lightness of his own body, how, even with his lame leg, walking through the thick woods was no longer physical pain to him, and the ease with which he could go up a mountainside. Even in the best days, with Chris, he had always been out of puff, and had often wondered at her goat-like agility. He answered Smedley's "Nice weather we're having?" with a cheerful laugh.

"We thought you must have died on us!" smirked Zonia, as he leaned across the counter while she filled his order. "There's a big pile of mail already waiting for you. But you won't get one to-day, because Ken Cullen's up the lake. There's been no one to go down for it."

"I know," grinned Tony. "And he has his wife with him. That's a great spot to take a woman, isn't it? . . . Up by the Nitinat."

"Hump." Zonia's brows darkened. "Well, the big log-ging camp's only just across from her—she'll find plenty of men there."

"Shut up, Zonia!" sang out her brother from inside the post-office cubicle. "Ain't women awful, Mr. Lynd?"

O1

Tony looked at Zonia and laughed. "Some of them," he said over his shoulder. "What's Virgie been doing?" he asked Zonia.

But the wife of Brinsley Greville was apparently still under the domination of her brother, for she made the infuriating reply: "Ask me no questions and I'll tell you no lies," and left Tony to cogitate, if he felt it worth the effort, upon what recent scandal had been disturbing the life round the store during the seven weeks he had been up the lake. Other news items given him by Smedley as he was being handed his mail were that the Tread boys were having **more** trouble with Jesse James because the boom they had **towed down** had been too late to catch the last of the high water, **and** would now have to wait for spring; that the Swedish cookie had left them, taking practically all their available money to pay him his wages, so old Henry Tread was trying to do the cooking now until Jesse James sent the boys a cheque; and that Mr. Hiscock had gone down to Victoria two weeks ago and had not, yet, come back. Ha! the beautiful Mrs. Buggard, thought Tony, remembering that last ghastly picnic.

"Little Aline must be having a grand time over in London," announced Smedley. "Mrs. Debenham told Ken Cullen. But from what I can see in the box here she looks to have been too busy to write more than post-cards. Last one I saw was from Devon . . . photograph of a pack of staghounds. I——"

Tony, shovelling his mail into his sack, slung the cord around its neck and laughed: "You must be in on a lot of this lake life—reading all their mail, Smedley."

"Ho!" The fresh-cheeked little store-keeper coloured. "I don't do *that*, Mr. Lynd! But, gosh! I got to sort 'em, haven't I?"

This was not a mail day, and the store therefore was entirely empty. Lynd had carefully stowed his watch, wrapped in tissue-paper, inside the tin case he had removed from a roll of typewriter ribbon. After pledging Smedley to get it down the quickest way he could to Victoria, he collected the jumble of groceries that Zonia had assembled for him and said his good-byes.

"I'll be down in a week or so," he said. "You'll find that there will be a pile of timber coming up for me, all out and crated. I'm going to build a boat during this winter. A Brook's pattern launch for an outboard motor. Next spring you'll see me simply come whizzing down the lake. I'll take you for a ride," he laughed to Zonia.

In this exhilarating late autumn air he looked forward with delight to this long and interesting task he saw ahead of him during the snow-locked winter. The planks for the pattern he had selected and ordered cut in Victoria, would be accompanied by a keel and stem piece and long sections of straight-grained white oak that he would have to work and bend into ribs over templates. He was already planning how he could make a steam box, filled with wood-shavings, from the monster kettle he now used to heat his bathing or washing water on his kitchen stove. The Evinrude he could order from Vancouver by one mail and have it up by almost the next one. By next spring he would slide a light, fast craft into the water that would take him on fishing or shooting expeditions wherever and whenever he wanted up and down the twenty long miles of lake. All this open country would be his then, more than it had ever been.

If Jesse James could persuade the powers-that-be to throw a spur line of railways up to develop Scaup Lake (i.e. get his timber out cheaply) he could send the *Nimrod* (for that was the name he had decided to give his boat) down by rail and reach the salt water from below Quamicot. There would be nothing to stop him, if he wanted, cruising up the entire Inside Passage. It would be a little wet and risky in wild weather; but he could take his chances on that. He would be alone, and, in exploring that lonely shore-line, he might find some enchanted bay which he would prefer even to Scaup Lake as a place to settle down in for all time. The whole world of this long, forested island would, in all truth, belong to him.

Like the old Count, he developed this day-dream as he rowed. Before he had gone a mile he was already seeing himself in an adventure; a grey day, mist, no wind, with gun-metal humps of sea. He was trying to make an inlet that his chart showed him was forty miles off. He had slowed the motor down to save petrol, because he had lost sight of shore. . . . When the wind came it would blow the sea-fog away—but it might also blow him, too. He would have to put in and beach the boat somewhere before nightfall. Now here was where one of his useless bits of sporting knowledge came in; the wisdom that most of his sophisticated friends considered valueless because it did not lead to making money. This design of light outboard skiff he had selected purposely, because he knew that it must be light enough for one man to beach it whenever he wanted to. Something that, with a roller he would always carry in the boat, he could always pull well above high water over rocks or sand. He also saw now, now that he had pictured such a venture as this Inside Passage expedition, that he would also need a small silk tent. Something that could be easily packed and stowed. He would have to order that. He would also have to make a hooped, canvas hood for his skiff, a thing that he could use as a cabin to sleep under in quiet inlets—that would save him from having to go ashore. And it would have to be long and low enough to act as a shield, to keep waves from coming inboard while he was running. For that, he would also put a much higher combing than the plan ordered for his boat. In fact, he would be as snug as a bug in a rug, unless he got caught off a rocky lee shore in a blow he could not weather. But then, that would be one of the excitements of such a life. . . . He carried on the adventure he was imagining until a freshing wind blew

the sea-fog away and he saw the blue hump of the island to
his left. He ran the Evinrude all out to get there, but the sun
set before he reached it, and it was now too dark to venture
any nearer the shore. He felt slightly frightened and cursed
himself for being such a fool as to leave his last safe anchor-
age, in a mist, when he could not see where he was going.
A compass is absolutely useless in navigating narrow waters.
He no longer knew where he was. He was in real trouble
now because the wind was rising, and this light boat was
not built to withstand heavy seas. Anyone of them might
capsize him. He could do only one thing: head as far out
as he could into the open water while he still had the light.
. . . The land was his danger.

As he thought of a fix like this, he smiled. Well, one night
he might suddenly end up like this. It had to happen sometime. He thought of the lake, and all the solid security of
his cabin. The last of the dying colours still flamed along
the lower shoreline, then came the deep belt of green, densely
silent woods, then a fringe of dead trees and the raw grey
rocks above the timber line. Along the jagged crest of the
ridges there was a thin sugary powder, as if the last of the
rains had turned into snow up there. . . .

He wondered if one day people would come to speak of
him as they had of old Mead? "Oh, that's old Mead's
place . . . that deserted cabin up there. He was a character,
he was. His story was . . . "

"Oh, that's old Lynd's place! There was a queer one,
for you. Now, Lynd . . . "

Would people, one day, come to talk about him like that?
He asked that question of his cabin as he walked up to it.
He had been thinking so intently about the *Nimrod*, with its
Evinrude, that he caught himself glancing quickly behind
for the outboard motor as he sailed his skiff hard up on the
beach—the instinctive fear that he would smash its propeller
on the rocks. And he laughed now as he slipped the waiting
roller under his skiff and jerked it high above water-line,

where he turned it over. Of course, one day, people would say these things about him, with their petty imaginings. And precious little would they ever know of the real story of *his* life. Let them guess what they liked.

*   *   *

The cat came down to the pebbly grey shore to greet him. He took his shotgun and walked back to shoot a couple of blue-bill ducks he had seen coasting along his shore-line. When he came back with the birds he threw one of them into the low grass that he kept cut down before his cabin and went inside to cook his own luncheon. He had brought two rashers of ham down at the store and now started the fire and put one of them in the frying pan. Then he came back into the main room of his cabin and held up the canvas sack to dump his mail out on the table. Two typewritten letters fell out, both bearing London postmarks. Sitting down, he slit one of them. He read:

"DARLING,— . . . Your odious little boy friend, Patrick Byron, brought her over to my table in the Café Royal. He knew damn' well what he was doing, the little ——. She talked about you for half an hour, and, the way things were, I couldn't stop her. I could have wrung her —— neck. . . . So that's how I had to find out exactly what you've been doing with yourself. . . . I haven't bothered before. . . . And look here, you know as well as I do that this damn' thing is not going to work. . . . I'm not going to allow you to make a complete idiot of yourself. . . . What about *me*? . . . You know I haven't been very happy or lucky in life. . . ."

Tony saw the scene as clearly as if he were standing in the Café Royal himself, looking around helplessly to find a table. Flick, probably with some of her artist friends, sitting there with her lips curling while stupid Aline babbled away about British Columbia. He also could wring her —— neck. He smiled as he thought of the casual way, even in pencil, that Flick used the Army adjective. And, of course, Pat Byron had known what he was doing. . . .

*   *   *

So Flick was still free? It was funny, that he had never thought of that—that she might marry. His memory of her had been static; he had tried to leave off thinking about her as he had at last been aware of her, confidently driving off in her car. Not knowing that he was sailing for America. He did not want to imagine her further than that. With his imagination, he knew, he would destroy himself if he pictured Flick's life back in London, the people she was seen going around with, the man who was, very likely, holding her in his arms. As he thought of that now he winced and closed his eyes. The other letter, he saw, had been written on the same typewriter and mailed from W.C.2 a month later, probably from Flick's office in Covent Garden. Without opening it, he walked into his kitchen and thrust it in the fire. Then, after an apprehensive stare at the other letter again, he did the same with that. He speared the cooking ham out of the frying pan with a fork, and, leaning out of the window, thrust it into the meat-safe he had constructed outside his cabin. He decided he would eat later, when he felt hungry again. For the present he wanted something to take his mind off himself. Picking up the shotgun again, he jammed a handful of shells in his pocket and climbed up the stream. It had begun to fall again now. A few hundred yards up it he found a place where he could jump across it from rock to rock. He missed one jump and slipped in, wet up to his waist. The water nearly swept him down. It rushed against him and up his side. Holding his coat up under his arms so as to wet neither his precious cigarettes nor shells, he stumbled ashore. In the clearing he found an old stump among the second-growth and sat there in the warm sun until he was partially dried. Shortly after he got started again there was a whirr under his feet and two pine grouse shot over the painted alders ahead. Ordinarily he would have got at least one of them, but he was slow to-day, and it was with an effort that he brought himself back to that alert instant readiness required for shooting in this brush. It was dusk before he thought of turning back, and, in that darkness that soon fell on him, it was several hours before, working up along the noisy mountain river, he reached a place where he could cross it in the night to the other bank. He was tired when he reached his cabin and did not think it worth the bother to light the stove. He made a large pot of coffee on the primus and put it beside his bed. One of the new books looked interesting, and he began to read. . . .

The woods, chilled with the approach of winter, were unearthly silent. His eyes closed. The rising sun had touched their tips before the wick of his lamp offered up its last moisture of oil, gave a faint pop, and went out. The cat jumped down from the silent bunk.

*   *   *

When the cut sections for his boat came up two weeks later Lynd was down at the store to get them. A letter, which had come up by the previous mail, said that those particular lengths of straight-grained white oak would have to be ordered from Vancouver; would not some other kind of wood do? Tony bought a post-card and told them it wouldn't. "Any other letters?" he asked Smedley.

The little store-keeper shook his head.

"Well . . . so long," said Lynd indecisively. "I'll . . . I'll probably be down on Saturday again."

There was, he quickly answered to Smedley's surprised look, some more timber coming up. But as he said that he had the sickening feeling of what a poor lie it was, even to himself. He knew that he had been hoping to find another letter from Flick. He knew that ever since the minute he had stuffed that second letter in the fire he had been bitterly regretting that he had not read what was in it. There had been a month between dates—enough time for Flick, who was good about such details, to know that he had not cared to answer her first letter that had come to him. Not immediately, anyway. And her second letter might have given some clue to what she felt about things. He had been merely melodramatic to burn that one.

He was annoyed with Zonia for telling him he looked tired—and then her joke that he was probably tired of his own company. She had renewed her invitations that he come down and have dinner, or at least tea with them sometimes. Greville, whom he never saw (that bored Englishman seemed never to leave his beloved hatchery), was in the store this day and added his polite invitation to Zonia's. He knew that he had been boorish to both in the sulky way he had refused. His eyes lighted when he saw Digger Bean come into the crowded store, and he went over and began to talk to him. After a few moments' inconsequential conversation he finally brought the talk around to where he wanted it to go; to get the cougar-hunter to accept a lift back to his place. The Digger pocketed a couple of letters that had come for him, and then pointed to the long and bulky bundle of cut planks that Ken Cullen had brought up in his motor lorry from railhead: "What about this?" he said.

Tony frowned impatiently. "Oh, they can wait until the rest of it comes up," he said. "Come on and I'll give you that lift."

The Digger acted precisely the way Tony hoped he would. He ordinarily walked the quarter mile that separated his place from the store. Now, when Lynd dropped him at his wharf, the Digger expressed his invariable invitation: "Come on in and have a spot with me? It's on the house."

Tony grinned. "Well, not if I drink a bottle, it won't be."

"Ha-ha!" said the Digger. "I told you I'd have you for a customer some day. And, Mr. Lynd—you look like a man who knows how to drink. You got that kind of face. . . . I mean that complimentary, of course; I always say . . ."

*   *   *

When, three days later, the next mail day came along, he realised that he had created a scandal on the lake. He had never been home. Wednesday, Thursday, Friday, he and Digger Bean had been drinking all the time. Once, in a melancholic interval, he had expressed an anxiety for his cat. But "Hell!" the Digger assured him—"there ain't a cat on this here Goddam lake that don't know how to care for itself. And a helluva lot better'n we can look affer'm I tell you. Say—d'you ever know that spot outside Casablanca? . . ."

They went pretty much around the world during those three days and nights. The Digger asserted he hadn't done any steady drinking like this since he'd left the bleeding mercantile marine service, no, not nowhere he hadn't . . . not even along Railway Street. Yes, he knew that place, too. Well, the trouble was that some men just couldn't get along without women, but—hell, he could. Proof was, hadn't he spent twenty years knocking all over this here (Army adjective) world at sea? . . . And look at him now—were there any women in this part of the world? Hell, no! Yeah, Virgie Cullen . . . hot piece, that one. But if anyone knew anything 'bout Ken he'd steer clear of that dame. Trouble! asserted Digger Bean—that's all the hell women was meant for, anyway. "You know, Alex, don't you . . . know the old Rue Ramleh? . . ."

There were intervals when the Digger made tea. There were also intermissions, it did not seem to matter when they came, when the grinning Digger appeared with a platter littered with ham and eggs. He gave Tony a clean bed-room, with fresh sheets, a superior section of his bungalow that he always kept ready for itinerant trout-fishers. Tony learned that the bed had once been slept in by the redoubt-able Jesse James—which occasioned the opening of another bottle, and a wandering dissertation on the general lousiness of commercial ethics. And then he passed clean out. . . .

It was the Digger who, on Saturday morning, informed him about the scandalised store. "It's a small place," said the Digger. "Small-town stuff. . . . You know, everybody else poking their noses into everybody else's business. Who the hell do you think it was come over asking for you?—the Count! Said Zonia sent him over, thought maybe you might be ill . . . ha-ha-haaaa."

Tony did not respond to the Digger's boisterous jeer. He was sick, and felt heartily ashamed of himself. Not quite heartily, for he felt as if the motive power within him was at its low ebb. It was a familiar feeling of weakness; he knew it well . . . when his heart seemed barely able to tick. And it was physical agony to slide his skiff into the water. It seemed at least twice its weight. But when he entered the crowded store there were no tell-tale signs of this inner misery in his manner. Nothing except, perhaps, a peculiar intentness in his stare.

But that apparently seemed enough for the grinning Smedley, who immediately erased his smile and handed Tony the three wrapped newspapers that Ken Cullen had brought up. That was all the mail. And he was particularly obliging when Lynd told him to stow the big bundle of planks in some safe spot, as he would probably hire Ken

Cullen, or Swanson, to take up the lot when all had arrived. Tony saw the old German's eyes fixed on him from a corner of the store; but he did not reply to his nod. He laughed when Zonia asked him if he and Digger Bean had drunk up the whole stock, told her that he wanted two hundred Camel cigarettes, and, when she petulantly wrapped these up and handed him the two cartons, he nodded his thanks and went out.

He had established one thing, at any rate, in those brief minutes he had been in the store—he had made it quite plain to everybody that they could mind their own business. His life was his own. If they wanted to be funny about it, they could do it out of his hearing. He was no old Mead. . . .

It was agony to row those seven miles. He rested frequently. He was drenched with sweat, and the little finger of his left hand had already begun to tingle again. That first warning of the approach of numbness that had been so pronounced when he left London. He felt indecisive in his thoughts. Towards sundown a breeze sprang up and he tacked moodily against it until it stiffened in the Narrows and he turned to run before it down his North Arm. It would be a damn' long while, he decided, before he went down to that store any more.

*   *   *

He woke up one morning to find his cabin filled with an unusual brilliance, and knew that the snow had come. It had fallen silently all night. He felt a sudden surge of happiness and whistled as he stepped into his slippers and went into the kitchen end of his cabin to start his breakfast. He had no idea what time of the day it was, as he had still to go down to fetch his watch from the store, and the sun was hidden somewhere behind the grey clouds over the falling snow. Looking out at the lake, he saw that it had already turned black, as it did in winter, against its rim of white snow. Two of the invariable blue-bills he noticed were coasting along his shore, later, he decided, to be shot for the cat's lunch. In the meantime, it could eat his bacon rinds and sops of toast. The total absence of eggs made it known that he would sooner or later have to go down to the store. He was getting tired of coffee and cold grouse for breakfast, much as that bird would be prized in England. And, with the snow, he knew that his days of shooting for his meals had finished until next spring. He always could, of course, get a deer if he wanted to go to the bother of climbing the side of Bald Mountain.

* * *

He went down twice more that winter. On the second time he found a letter from Flick. This was several days after Christmas, and he found a note from the Debenhams, asking him wouldn't he like to spend it with them. He went outside the store and walked a considerable distance down the snowy road before he opened the thick letter from Felicity. This one was erotic, burning, passionate, and bitterly resentful. As he read it he knew what had happened to him. Even at this distance Flick had burned away the cocoon he had wrapped around himself in his isolation. He was standing there, raw and quivering before her. Like any mollusc taken out of its shell. He was defenceless against her. In this letter she said:

". . . Perhaps I have been a fool to wait as long as I have for you. You can't say I haven't left you in peace. I was wild with you at first when you didn't answer my first two letters—but I have tried to use my brain. I only want to tell you this—I *have* met someone whom I think I can live with. I much prefer you. But if you will have it your own way, that's that. . . . I want you to think it over. I'll be married in the spring. . . . He's in Japan, in the diplomatic service, and I'm going out there to join him. . . ."

Then she added, in an almost illegibly scrawled P.S.:

"For God's sake, Tony, do see what you're chucking away. You know I adore you."

He knew that racing writing, and the tumbled emotions that it meant, even if the whole letter itself had not been a straightforward, complete declaration of her love. He bowed his head.

"I won't," he said aloud, "I won't."

He knew that if he even sat down to answer her letter her resolution would conquer his. He was weak as water against the powerful appeal of Felicity, and the life she wanted him to take up again. He must stay where he was.

*   *   *

To ask the lake for refuge? He tried that during the winter days, with their long empty nights. He felt that if he could stick this out until spring he would really have a chance. He had no compunction now whatever in accepting Digger Bean's offer of the whiskey, with which, he saw, he could almost anæsthetise himself during the long nights. The Digger had dropped in one trip when he was up the lake cougar-hunting. He brought a gift bottle to Tony then. And with that, and the one the Digger had in the launch for himself, he and the Digger had another talkative night. After all, it was company—and the Digger had seen the world.

"Any time you want a drink, Mr. Lynd, all you gotta do's say so. I know how it is with some people. Why once, when I was down off Morocco, we had an English war correspondent climb up the ship's ladder one night. Came right up out of the dark! and begged for a bottle of the real stuff.

"'How the hell'd you get here?' I said.

"'Rowed,' said he.

"I looked and didn't see any boat overside, and the Englishman was all wet, so I said: 'I guess you mean you swum here?'

"'Nope,' says he, 'I rode—take another look and you'll see my horse.'

"'And we've got to give that horse a rest,' says the Englishman. 'He's a damn' good and faithful horse.'"

The Digger guffawed and slapped his knee. "'He can't keep on treading water all night!' I said to the Limey—so we got that there horse up on the damn' gangway. . . . Anyway, we got its forefeet on the gangway. Now, there was another man who knew how to drink. But—damn it, if I didn't have to send that poor Englishman off ship . . . before his horse was drowned!"

With such conversations Tony usually passed the nights when the Digger dropped in on him. He brought the whiskey by cases now. But there were no more letters from Flick.

*   *   *

This, Tony had known all along, would be the worst part of this ordeal—when Flick stopped writing. As long as he had the refusal of her in his hands he could feel on top of this situation, no matter how it hurt. But once Flick broke the tie, and he knew that he had cut her adrift for life, then the final blow would descend. That would be finality.

When the temptation to write, to feel the reassuring tug of Flick on the other end of the line hurt too much, he would deliberately leave the cabin. Even if it was midnight. There was a long semicircle of shore rocks, washed clean of any snow, that he could get along in the night, especially if there was any moon. And, half-crazed with drink and remorse, he would stumble recklessly along this strip. He shouted wild, grandiose threats at the night. . . . At other times he put the mirror before him, and drank the whole night out, arguing with himself. . . . He was aware, in the lulls between these bouts, that he was degenerating physically. It was too much effort now to go out and collect firewood. He watched his supply run out. One night, when he woke up to find himself nearly frozen to death, he smashed up his bookshelves and burnt them in the fireplace. With a grand gesture he swept his larder of tins off the kitchen shelves. When this wood was dying down into just glowing embers he took his axe and chopped two lengths of board out of the kitchen floor. . . .

He was not going to die in his blankets, the way old Mead had died.

*   *   *

He reached the spring. The sabotage of his own cabin had been a good lesson for him. It brought him up short, facing the realities of his position. If he let himself go too far, he *would* end like old Mead. His disgust at such a finish spurred him into looking after himself properly again. He couldn't, in that weather, replace the shelves or boards. But he did not join in the Digger's mirth the next time he dropped in, and saw the wreckage. He was, in fact, a bit stiff with the Digger in that session. After they had had a few drinks together Tony announced that if the Digger was going, he had better be starting to get home. He made it plain that he was not expecting the alleged cougar-hunting Digger to spend the night. "Besides," he said, with a firm laugh. "I can't go on, you know, putting down whiskey like this. My stomach won't stand it—neither will my bank-account. And that's the bloody truth, on both counts. Have another before you go?"

The Digger, he knew, would spread the story about the

vanished bookshelves at the store. His questing eye had, quite naturally, been immediately caught by the unusual stacks of books standing against the walls—and he had at once guessed the rest. So Tony had told him the little part of it that he did not know. It made not the slightest difference. He did not give a good damn what anyone thought. He had already served notice at the store, on his three appearances there, that they could keep their thoughts to themselves, as far as his actions were concerned. He knew that he must have offended the Debenhams by not answering their note, but they could go too. He knew that the Treads had already written him off as just another man who was intending to drink himself to death in the woods. But that, of course, was a thing he was not prepared to un-convince them about. They, too, could think what they ruddy well liked. Only, when the Digger told him that the old Count had fallen off his roof and busted his ankle, trying to put the finishing touches on his fireplace, was he moved to go out from the isolation around his cabin again. But when the Digger added that the bone must have set somehow (or else it had never been really broken), for Elsa had reported that he was on his feet again, down at the store—when the Digger went on to relate that, then Tony dropped the one resolution that might have made him break his loneliness. For some peculiar reason he was aware that he felt a personal responsibility for the unpleasant old exile.

* * *

The very morning after he had burnt up his bookshelves he forced himself to go along the beach and spend all day gathering small bits of firewood. It was really a case of do or die. Another night like the last, and he would have been found stiff in his blankets. It was a brutally cold wind from the north that had suddenly come down upon them. His bay, which had shown so signs of ice whatever the previous winter, froze over solid for about fifty yards out. The Digger, of course, would not venture out in this weather, so Tony spent the next days in sawing up a big log he kicked the snow off, and split that up into fireplace lengths. He cooked over this blaze, scorching that part of him that was towards the fire, and feeling the icy air almost freeze his hinderpart. He saw now that old Mead had been a fool to build such a large main room to his cabin. With the prevailing winds that blew from the Japan Current, even the fall of snow did not make the air uncomfortable. But now, with this cold wind from the Arctic, he could not keep warm in his blankets at night.

He moved his mattress out by the fireplace and made up a bed on the floor before the hearth. He piled most of his clothing on top of the blankets; and, even so, he was always weak with cold when the dawn began to lighten. And he nearly always saw it come. The deer came down and scratched for moss around the cabin. One morning he shot one.

Its blood-stained tracks led to the path up Bald Mountain that he knew so well. It was agony to climb after it. At any other time he would have let it go. But he had suddenly become apprehensive about the state of his larder. He had not reckoned with this ice. He had never considered a situation where, even if he had to, he simply could not get down to the store. He saw that the deer was only slightly wounded; his hands were very shaky these days. There had been two deer. The first had vanished in a few swift bounds. And the other had not been long in jumping to its feet and trailing after it. They split as they entered the woods, and his deer seemed to take the more difficult path, a zigzag straight up the mountain. Cursing his bad shooting, he went after it.

The slotted blood-tracks led under low hanging branches that made him breast the snow to come after it. It had passed through brush that he had to tear apart. He became dizzy with his sudden exhaustion; his breath came in gasps, and his heart felt as if someone's fingers were pinching it. He stared doubtfully back at the lake during one pause for breath. But the sight of the ice made him climb all the more eagerly. Once, for a second or so, he saw the buff body of the deer clearly against the snow above him, but by the time he had swung up his rifle it had vanished. Nevertheless, he chanced a shot into the brush ahead of where he had seen it moving. It was a child's trick, the thing you would expect some sporting store hunter to perform, but he knew that he had at least three or four more shots in the Mannlicher, and there wasn't a chance on earth of hitting anyone else in this part of the world. No one, not even in the summer, came up on Bald Mountain. *Crack!*

As if in answer to this last thought a rifle cracked out right above him. For a moment he thought his hearing had played a trick upon him—that was a snapping tree, perhaps? Then he knew that it had been a rifle shot. The lighter snow up near the crest was criss-crossed with slotted tracks, lanes of them. But the blood stains led straight up to where, on the ridge, he saw a figure bending over the dead deer. It was Ken Cullen.

"Humph," he said sourly, as Tony tried to get enough breath to speak, "so you're the guy that's been shooting deer out of season?"

If Ken had laughed Tony would have thought nothing unusual had happened. But Ken merely turned his back, and with a quick stab and jerk of the knife he was holding ripped open the deer's stomach. He was so excited, or intent upon what he was doing, that he did not even try to save his mackinaw from getting bloody, but merely thrust his arm into the steaming interior of the carcase and ripped out the liver. "That's all I want," he said, standing up.

Lynd watched him hastily stuff the dripping liver into his mackinaw pocket. Then he laughed. It seemed to have the most extraordinary effect upon Ken Cullen, for his eyes fell as they met Lynd's, and the man who was disdainful enough of death to trap the Nitinat alone turned and literally slunk off into the trees on the lake side of Bald Mountain. If he had thrown the liver in Tony's face his action could have been no more uncalled for.

When Tony had paunched the deer he made a hoop of it by thrusting its forefeet through its hind hamstrings and hung it around his neck. Then he walked to the edge of the mountain to see where Ken would come out. Looking down he saw Ken Cullen's big grey launch pulled well into the bushes along the lake shore. In that position it would be practically invisible from anyone on the lake. Ken, on the other hand, could watch everyone either coming up or going down the lake, particularly from the Tread place.

As Digger Bean had remarked, Scaup Lake had that small town mentality where everyone feels a legitimate interest in the affairs of everyone else. It was the reverse side of their communal spirit of helpfulness. And Tony wondered, with a reminiscent grin at Ken's embarrassment, if this was the hide-out where the little trapper had been spending his time during those four or five days' absences from the store when he was supposed to be risking his neck over in the Nitinat country. It would be just like Cullen, who, for all his joviality, was an artful little soul, to be fooling the lake all along as to where he was getting those prize marten pelts.

* * *

The north wind was followed by a three days' snow that changed the activity, and ended the lives of at least two people on the lake. These were two timber-cruisers up at Jesse James' camp who had accepted a Government offer of twenty-five dollars to cross to the Pacific and bring back the sealed ballots of an Indian village on the salt water.

They were not seen again until the snow melted and their bodies were found within two hundred yards of the camp. In the blizzard they had actually worked around and were found below the camp's clearing. The Digger Bean was badly shaken when the weight of snow brought down his roof the second night, and complained that four quarts of whiskey had mysteriously vanished during the heroic work of the next morning's rescue party. Brinsley Greville and Zonia woke up to see the Scaup river flowing through their bedroom, as the lazy Englishman had ignored the warning given to him by older members of the house-boat colony that he should remain awake all the night and scrape snow off his raft.

"In every day, in every way, I'm getting wetter and wetter!" he told Tony when they next met at the store. He pointed to where rugs, bed-clothes, and the contents of all their trunks and bureaux were being frantically hung around their house-boat by Zonia to dry in the spasmodic sunshine. "You'd never think," he declared, as if stunned by the discovery he had made, "that there just isn't one single solitary place out here where you can dry yourself! Smedley won't let us hang our stuff up in the store, damn him. And when the fire's going full out in our place . . . why, it steams like a Turkish bath!"

The point was that the deadly north wind had been the last breath of winter. In a night the gale halted and Tony had wakened the next morning to feel the soft moist winds from the Japan Current over in the Pacific. In less than a week he watched the rains turn the white snow into gurgling grey slush. Bald Mountain was noisy at night with thousands of little waterfalls. He noticed that he was smelling the earth again. So powerful was its presence that he could almost feel the sap begin to move in the trees and thickets and deep roots of the forest around him. He saw its evidence in the green, sticky buds that began to tip the brush by the lake above. He heard the booming of the blue grouse in nights expectant with sounds. . . . And all the while he had the sensations of a suspicious child who is playing a game of "Let's pretend."

He did not believe this any more. Flick's letters had burned the illusions from his life. This was no longer real, for him. For the Treads, yes; for old exiled von Hauptmann, yes—because it was inevitability; there was nothing else the Count could do. But for him—no. He was playing make-believe. Consequently, every evidence of beauty that he was forced to face became an added burden to him. The bright gentian blue of the lake now in the mornings was a reward to the other settlers for having gone through the black winter. The assurance of the green leaves fluttering once again in spring winds might be comfort to the old German, who knew that as long as he lived here he would have this beauty to look forward to. It would always return to him. The long lazy summer days might be looked forward to by the Treads, and even by the unthinking robots up in Jesse James' No. 1 logging camp; for they would be exhilarated by the mere feel of their bodies and the fact that the physical torture of winter work was over for them. But for him all this was just farce.

He was living in a paradise, and yet he felt that he did not belong there. Hastily, he turned to repairing his cabin. He worked now, not with the pleasurable contentment of the previous year, but with the anxiety of someone who wants to set everything ship-shape before a storm should set in. In a setting where everyone else seemed at peace, even exuberant, he was uneasy. He winced at this contrast in the store. In the freshness of a new life (which is literally what every recurrent spring meant to Scaup Lake) even his own problem that he had created had been forgotten—the boat he had been going to build. The last time he had been down there in the winter Smedley had asked meaningly where he had wanted him to put the bulky crates of wood that had come up from Victoria—and when would he take them? The boat, Tony had known, was not at all what the up-and-coming young Canadian was asking about; he had wanted to know what Lynd was going to do—what was happening to Lynd? Tony had told him gruffly to store them any place, and he had known that the young Smedley had repeated this afterward, to all the lower Scaup Lakers—placing his own interpretation upon it.

Now both he and his boat seemed forgotten. Looking around the crowded store, he saw that the crates had been stowed along the wall, turned into a bench, and that half a dozen loggers from the *War Eagle* were now sitting on the potential *Nimrod*. The irony of it all was not lost upon him, and he felt angry with Zonia when, in her rush to serve everybody with their expansive spring orders, she did not even make it a point to try and have a private chat with him. He was being forgotten. Or else, he had established himself that winter as being no longer interesting. In the hustle and bustle of spring, people might not be any longer interested in even the books he had to lend them. He felt that there was something pathetic about that, that he should have sunk so low in his spirits that he could even think of such a thing. In a morose mood he slung his canvas sack, full of mocking groceries and books and newspapers (which he would never bother to read) into his skiff at Smedley's wharf and rowed up to Digger Bean's place.

The Digger was also full of spring, in a lusty mood; and they drank the night out. In the anti-climax of the long row home the next morning, for the lake was as smooth and bland as glass, he realised that he had renewed the arrangement by which the Digger would bring up his mail and supplies, and a certain number of bottles of whiskey every week. He had definitely established the type of life he was going to live on the lake.

He wondered if anything would ever happen to break him

out of it? Could he win back to the old life he had been living here, the illusion, if it must be that, after a time? As he passed he stared across to their camp and saw that the Tread boys had already part of a large log-boom in the water again. He had fallen out of pace, even with that life.

* * *

It was a mail day, he knew, because he had seen the big *War Eagle* go past. And as the Digger had not been up that week he knew that he could expect him some time before sundown. The Digger had been awaiting a couple of trout-fishers from Victoria whom he was going to take up the lake. But as Tony had protested he would not have any strangers dropping in on him, the Digger had agreed to take them up to the stream two miles above the Count's place, where they were going to camp and fish that first night, and that he would come back and have dinner with Lynd. Tony sat there in the sun meditating what a relief it would be when he had some fresh whiskey to kill the gnawing pains in his stomach again.

He had repaired his cabin. The books were now back on their shelves, shelves not quite so neat and smooth of finish, perhaps, but good enough to hold books. And two fresh planks, still unstained, had replaced the ones he had chopped up last winter for firewood from his kitchen floor. A look into the kitchen would show that he had taken to slovenly habits, as far as the dishes were concerned, but the rest of the cabin was in the spick and span order that he always kept the place. With his drinking, he had realised, he must have a daily routine that would save him from himself. The problem of ploughing the garden had provided an enter-prise that took up most of his afternoons, for he had to turn all of the soil over by hand. It was in gripping the iron fork and bashing the big lumps of dirt to pieces that he most felt this growing weakness and deadness in his hands, and it was usually not until well into the day, long after he had been up, that he could work up the resolution to begin his task. For this reason he had temporarily given up his ambition of growing potatoes and Indian maize and had contented himself with the more amenable seeds. Long rows now of bright green showed where he would be gathering lettuce and radishes for his salads soon. He looked forward to these salads, for with his stomach hurting him continually the way it was he had very little ambition to eat meat these days. It was true that there were usually a couple of blue grouse hanging in an auxiliary wire meat-safe, carefully hidden in the woods where Swinton, if he was snooping about, would never think of looking for it. There were, he thought, two hanging there now. It would probably be a good idea to split and grill them for dinner that night. The Digger was unorthodox and would enjoy a couple of fat little grouse out of season. But as he couldn't remember now just quite what day he had shot them he decided that it would probably be better not to take a chance on that, and just throw them away. That was the trouble with these drinking bouts when he passed out at nights; he lost track of time.

To pass the time during the afternoon he cleaned and filled the midge-spattered lamps, shaved, took a swim in the lake and lay naked in the sun to dry himself, and was feeling all ready for the Digger when his launch arrived.

The Digger, who ran his launch on the beach just after darkness came down, was full of an accident that had just happened up at the big No. 1 camp. Pavel, the high-rigger, had cut himself down. Only a Finn, declared the Digger, could fall two hundred feet out of a tree and still be alive. Of course, it had been the branches of a young pine tree that had broken his fall on the way down. But they had

PL

also broken his legs; the sharp climbing-iron on his right foot, declared the Digger, had gone into the Finn's left leg and practically torn it off. He was a hell of a sight. And, if it hadn't been for the No. 1 camp's time-keeper, the Finn would have been dead several hours ago.

"Funny!" said the Digger. "Men up at the camp was telling me that that high-rigger had been making life hell for that little time-keeper all through the winter—and now the little devil turns around and patches him up! That's coals of fire, for you. Ken told me that when he took the high-rigger to the hospital down in Quamicot the doctors there said that no one but a doctor could have rigged up those jury splints on Pavel the way they were —so there's a story for you. They're taking the Finn's leg off to-night."

The Digger, as the level sank in the whiskey bottle, recalled several interesting stories of the mysterious men, with the haunted eyes, Englishmen usually, who seem to live like the shells of men among the lusty crews of the west-coast logging camps. He found a silent, unappreciative audience in Tony, who did not welcome such disturbing reminiscences. They were too near home. When the bottle was empty, and Tony did not offer to open another one, the Digger left.

The wind was strong, and Tony watched his launch butt the waves until it vanished on its four-mile run to where a faint pink glow showed the camp-fire of the two trout-fishers up the lake.

*   *   *

He did not know, but it must have been some time after midnight, when he heard his name being called. "Lynd! Lynd! Mr. Lynd!" In the high wind he knew that someone was shouting to him from the beach. He pulled a pair of trousers on and went out. "Lynd!" The wind hit him a buffet, and down by the shore he saw two white figures. They were the von Hauptmanns. She was practically naked, and sobbing horribly. He had something black thrown over his shoulders and was staggering. Tony gripped his arm and led him towards the cabin.

"It's gone!" moaned von Hauptmann. . . . "All gone. . . ."

In the darkness Tony heard Elsa weeping. In his own dazed, blurred state he went into his room, lighted the lamp, and brought in his blankets, which he threw to Elsa. He stuffed his feet into rubber boots. The Count lay in a chair, trying to cover up his indecency. Tony saw that the black thing was an old opera-cloak. "Excuse me," said the German, "I am not myself."

Elsa screamed: "It's all gone, it's all gone, it's all gone! . . ."

"Desist!" said the Count. He looked up at Lynd. "Our home—it is burned to the ground," he said. "Gone."

Tony went to the door. He saw now what, in his confusion, he had not noticed; the clouds above von Hauptmann's place were billows of red. Low down along the lake he saw the bitter yellow wickedness of fire itself, a high flap of flame itself flicking about in the wind. "My God—all of it?" he cried.

"We don't know!" screamed Elsa.

"Don't—*know*!" Her hysteria was contagious; Tony felt furious with the von Hauptmanns. "Do you mean to say that you don't know . . . that your house . . . *everything you've got in the world is going*! . . ."

"No, no, no! . . ." Elsa pointed and the Count now dumbly held up a hand. Tony saw that what looked like a red rag was a cloth dripping blood. "My guns. . . ." Von Hauptmann muttered that he had tried to carry out his glass gun-cabinet, which had fallen on him. It had been locked, and he could not find the key. "Oh, my God."

Tony, further infuriated by such stupidity, went into his room and pulled his old suitcase from beneath his bunk. In it he remembered was the little tin case of medicine things—prepared for him by the faithful Christina so long ago. And it was of her he was thinking as he came back and dusted the iodoform into the Count's lacerated hand. The thought of Chris sobered him, and he straightened up.

"You've got some sheds up there," he said; "did you make any attempt to save them?"

Elsa shook her head. The Count muttered that it would be impossible to save the sheds; they were too close to the house. The heat would not let you get near them. But the old German seemed too stunned by his loss to be sure of what he was thinking, so Tony left them again and went back to the door.

"Look here," he said, "I'm going up. There might be something that could be saved. Light a fire and make yourself as comfortable as you can."

Without coming back into the room, he went down to his boat. He wished to God that he had not been drinking that night. It was agony to get the skiff down to the water, and it would be torture, he knew, to row against that wind. But von Hauptmann could be no use to him. The two Germans were simply knocked out. They had been literally driven crazy by their grief; they didn't know what they were doing.

He felt that it was up to him to save whatever could be saved, to make the greatest effort he could to save something from that fantastic *Schloss*—it was very important.

*   *   *

Long before he got there he saw that it was hopeless to save anything from the house. Its walls had already fallen in and he could see the black pile of von Hauptmann's

fantastic chimney sticking up through the rose-red flaming
logs. It was this fireplace, Elsa had accused the Count in her
hysterical jabbering, that had set fire to their house; this
had been the first night it was finished, and they had tried
to use it. A thought that again filled Lynd with fury as he
scrambled up from the lake.

He was appalled when he faced the roaring pile. The
pitch in the logs had made the *Schloss* a huge tinder box.
With pops and whistles the logs exploded, every new
opening of fresh wood shooting further flames in the air. He
saw the sheds steaming and beginning to smoke in the heat.
These, at least, he might manage to protect. And in these the
Count, for all his arrogant pig-headedness, would have to
begin his new life.

Shielding his face he ran into the sheds and found some
buckets. It exhausted him to have to run back and forth
down to the lake to fill them. At first it seemed useless; the
water merely turned to steam. But then he saw that he was
gaining on the spreading areas where the sparks were
setting fire. To reach the worst part he had to go almost
within the fire of the house itself to throw the water on the
sheds. He saw that he himself would catch on fire. He
poured both buckets of water over himself before he
attempted this risk. Even so, he felt his face clench—as if
someone's hands had seized it. He was afraid to go back.
But the water, he saw, was still steaming on the boards.
It would save them if he could keep it up. Drenching himself
again he went back and splashed two more buckets as far as
he could up on the sheds. But some cedar shingles of the roofs
were now beginning to smoke. He saw the ladder and
placed that against the sheds. It was lucky that the sheds
were so close to the house that he could not place the ladder
exactly opposite where the fire was most unbearable; its
base would have caught fire. And so he was flung sideways
when the fantastic chimney fell, and one stone, striking his
feet, drove him through the broken ladder against the shed

wall, from which he fell down the slope with the ladder on top of him.

He never knew what had happened.

*   *   *

He heard them saying: "Well, Doctor Feather is the only one . . . but we can't wake *him* up at this time of night." He knew he was mumbling, "I'm all right, oh, I'm all right," and he tried to raise his head. He knew that he was in the cabin of the launch and that its engine was not running, because Billy was talking from the cockpit, and Matt was sitting beside him holding the lantern in his face. They paid no attention to what he was saying, and then he heard Billy swinging the fly-wheel of the motor again. The boat rocked. . . .

*   *   *

" . . . So you have been playing the little *hero* again!"

It was Flick's voice. No, it was just someone that sounded like Flick. No, it *must* be Flick . . . no other person would ever talk to him like that. This was the Treads' best room. . . .

He lay there, staring up at the low ceiling that had been made from squares of Beaver-board. He had never noticed that before. Queer . . . he thought he'd try. "Is that you, Flick?" he asked.

"Hullo, Monster."

"Flick?"

The room darkened as a shadow passed before the window. He knew that someone was pressing against the bed beside him. "Flick," he said, turning his eyes, "how the hell did you get here?"

He heard her rasping laugh. "It's the Flick Service," she said—"Always on time when needed. Does your leg hurt you much?"

He thought a minute. "I don't believe it," he said—
"You're not here at all. You're an impostor."

He knew that he was looking at her skirt; it was a rough
tweed of some sort. He knew that in a few seconds he was
going to look up and see her. "Give me a cigarette," he
said.

He knew what would happen; she would light one for
herself first, which would get all sloppy and wet—then she
would take that out and light one against it for him. And
it would be all covered with lip-stick.

The match flared in the shadowy room as she lighted
hers, and he looked up and saw her face. She was bare-
headed, with her hair done in a new fashion on the top of
her head, and she was obviously wearing a pyjama top
underneath the camel's-hair coat she had on. She had not
changed her taste in pyjamas, anyway, for he remembered
this kind; the white ones with the tiny red polka dots.
He suddenly had to laugh: "You would find me like
this!"

"Yes—you're always doing something silly."

"Ummm . . . what about you?"

"Well, I don't fall off ladders, and . . . and things."

He tried to sit up. "I never fell off a ladder!" he was
beginning to say—but the minute he put pressure on his
right hand to raise himself, the most excruciating pain
lanced his arm. "My God," he exclaimed—"my hand's
busted!"

Flick had caught him and was half-lowering him and
half-shoving him back towards the pillow. He was grateful
to get back there, where his head could feel at rest, and he
raised his right hand now and tried to examine it. It had
given him no pain when he had taken the cigarette. "What
else have I done?" he asked gruffly. He realised that he was
more or less numb now, from head to toe. That was why
he had probably been so slow to do anything when he
realised that Flick was in the room. He was numb, and

he was terribly tired, and half-asleep. He hardly noticed that Flick did not answer when he started speaking again; he was only whispering, anyway, and, nestling his head about until it felt a little more comfortable, he let himself go. . . .

". . . I'm cold," said Tony. He saw that old Dr. Feather was bending over him, and old Henry Tread was standing behind him, looking ridiculously serious. To observe the proprieties, Flick had apparently been removed from the room, for he was lying without any bed-clothes on him, and old Dr. Feather was painting his foot. "What's the matter with that?" asked Tony, trying to raise himself on his elbow.

"No, no . . . lie still. Humph . . ." Dr. Feather dipped the paint brush into the bottle of iodine again and resumed his dabbing at the cut. From where Tony was lying he could not tell whether his entire foot had been coloured or whether what he was looking at was an open wound. He had seen enough of doctors to have his doubts about them, and he did not like Dr. Feather's uncertain attention. "Can't risk infection," said the old gentleman, standing up. "What?"

"Can't you cover me up?" asked Tony—"I'm cold." He tried to bend forward to seize the bed-clothes. He was cold, and he had felt a little shiver run through him. . . . "Have you taken my temperature?" he asked.

The white beard of old Dr. Feather shook as he laughed. "Young man," he said, looking down over his silver-rimmed spectacles, "are you telling me how to do my job?"

It was kind, but derisive, and, Tony felt sure, damnedly stupid. "All right," he said, letting his head drop back; "go ahead."

While old Henry Tread gingerly held up the foot the old doctor bandaged it. Before he had put on the pad of

absorbent cotton, which smelled to Tony dishearteningly like
an antiseptic he had known in his boyhood days, he saw that
his foot had lost its shape. It looked about the size of a
boxing glove. He held up his hand and asked old Dr.
Feather to take a look at that. The old man pressed with
his thumb and finally found a spot that almost made Lynd
shout with pain. "Humph," he said, placing the hand
gently down.

"Broken?" Tony asked.

"Perhaps," said Dr. Feather. "I wouldn't use it, if I were
you."

"I won't," smiled Tony. "Von Hauptmann's over in my
cabin; I think you'd better see him, too. I'm cold; do let
me have those blankets up now."

The old doctor absent-mindedly pulled up the bed-
clothes and said to Tread. "We shall leave him alone
now . . . for the present. You just rest easy, Mr.
Lynd; I'm within easy reach of you. There's nothing
serious."

When they had gone and Flick came back, Tony nodded
towards a big bath-towel that Dr. Feather had been using.
"Let me have it," he asked. When he wound it once around
his neck and then tried to stuff it down the top piece of
someone's pyjamas that had been put on him, Flick tried
to take it away from him. "It's damp," she said. "What on
earth's the matter with you?"

"I'm getting an infection," he said. "I know it . . . I
know what these shivers mean. I'm cold as hell."

She looked worried, and then started to laugh at him:
"My God, Tony—you're a marvel. Now what on earth
makes you think that?"

"Because I know," he said. "Now don't you be stupid,
too."

She took off her camel's-hair coat and placed it over
him, tucking it in around his neck. "Is that better?" she
asked. PI

"Christ, Flick, I'm cold. It doesn't come from the outside. Get that damned old fool to leave his thermometer."

* * *

There were four days and nights when Tony hardly knew whether it was day or lamp-light. It did not matter; in the low room, where the window through the logs was hardly more than a peep-hole, someone was nearly always present. The infection had him. It flushed him at times as if someone had turned on the switch of an electric bulb inside him; he asked for ice, and, when he knew he couldn't get it, smiled wanly at old Mrs. Tread and said they ought to take a tip from the Russians—bury a big cellar of snow in the forest and cover it with sawdust to last them through the summer. He made himself think a lot about Russia, these days, and ice-floes, and the frozen wastes of the Arctic . . . he would like just to stand there, without any clothes on him. Then a chill would race through him, and, even under the pile of blankets, his own flesh would feel so cold and clammy that he did not like to touch it. Unless he guarded against them, the rack of these icy draughts would make him shake, and move his foot, and he would lie there for several minutes simply unable to move from pain. . . . Most of his time was spent trying to get into positions in which he could doze and win back to the oblivion of sleep again. . . . The heat of his blood made a hot-house of his imagination; in sleep, or what went for it, his brain was a jungle of hallucinations . . . he ran, it often seemed, screaming back to consciousness from the horrid adventures that befell him there.

He did this in silence; no one knew what was going on inside him. Not even Flick, who was often sitting in the chair. With her chin in her hands, staring at him. . . . No one must know. The only way he could go through this, he knew, was to take it in sullenness.

To get on top of the situation. Master it. To be brutal about it.

Matt Tread understood this. They were funny boys, the Treads! Billy was worse than a girl, the way he always turned his head away when he had to do certain things for him in the morning. Matt merely grinned. Matt, he knew, didn't like the job. He was quite sure that Matt did not even like him. But he had become interesting to Matt. Matt was watching him . . . to see how he would take it.

"Tough, isn't it?" said Matt in the dusk one morning.

"It's blue hell," smiled Tony.

Matt was dressed in his Pride-of-the-West canvas trousers, pulled over rubber boots, and was on his way to their logging camp. It didn't seem possible, to Tony, that people could walk around so unthinking and easily as all that. Didn't they realise the bliss of their movements? Either Matt or Billy always came in while the other one was cooking their breakfast in the mornings. They let the old people sleep on in bed. Very often he heard Flick talking to them, and, occasionally, her rasping laugh. When they were both in the room at the same time he saw that Matt was upset and distrustful about Felicity; she could always make men feel uneasy. . . .

The old black medicine case of Dr. Feather was left now, permanently, on a table in a corner of the room. And the doctor was somewhere around the Tread place nearly all the day. Tony heard him mumbling to old Henry and Mrs. Tread during luncheon time. Flick always walked across to the Debenham place for this meal. "To give you a rest, you little misery!" she laughed at him. She had brought him a dozen paper-backed books that she had bought on the station at Victoria, to amuse herself on the boat and on the way across Canada—and he could, fortunately, lose himself in these for a time.

Dr. Feather had perversely enough taken a most unreasonable attitude. He had entrenched himself behind his professional mumbo-jumbo, and would not let even Felicity look at the thermometer readings. "He's all right," he kept insisting, "he's all right. . . ."

That he was not all right, Tony needed no one to tell him. Neither did he need anyone to point out the dismay that old Dr. Feather was really feeling over his inability to think of anything that would help him. The familiar-smelling old lotion, he knew now, was arnica; and he knew also that all the instruments and medicines in the doctor's mouldy old satchel also dated from the dark age when the mild antiseptic was in vogue. So did the old Indian Army doctor's medical knowledge. He would, in private life, with his goat-like stubbornness, mused Tony, have probably made a very dangerous general practitioner. He felt helpless, however; after a first flurry of futile suggestions, he submitted to the oatmeal poultices that the old man was hopefully wrapping around his foot, to the doctor's timid probing of a suppurating sore that had opened on its side, to the agony of being made to sit upright, with swathes of blankets wrapped around him, while he let his foot soak in a hot bath of carbolic water that the doctor was trying. . . . When he lowered his swollen foot over the bed, and the blood rushed down, he must have fainted . . . for he came to with his head being held against old Henry Tread's rough trousers. . . .

His foot was swollen smooth, so that it had lost all shape, and the taut skin over the crown was as silky and glistening as the skin of a tomato. . . . It seemed ready to burst if you just put a probe against it.

"Can't you lance that?" begged Tony.

Dr. Feather coughed, and looked uncomfortable. He finally said, "I haven't any local anæsthetics."

"Then give me a shot of morphine. And stick a knife in it. Let some of that stuff out. I can stand it."

He looked around for Matt Tread. If Matt was here he could grab hold of his hands . . . and hang on. He'd like to hurt Matt. He'd make Matt do the yelling. . . . And then he thought of his own right hand which he tried not to use . . .

"I haven't any morphine," said Dr. Feather.

"Well, get some!" Tony suddenly snapped at him. "Do it without—just stick it, quick! . . . That foot must be full of pus. You just can't *stand* there, you know."

He saw the kindly old fellow start and draw back at this insult. He was sorry he had let himself go. He fell back. In the other room he heard old Dr. Feather telling the Treads that they must humour Mr. Lynd as much as they could; his mind was inclined to be a little unsteady now.

* * *

His mind, he knew, was only with him in parts. His thoughts would suddenly go out of focus, and he did not know what he was saying. He could tell that from the expression on Flick's face. As usual, she prided herself on being able to keep a poker countenance—but she could not control her frown when she was thinking deeply—or worried about something. And several times, as they had chatted in low voices at nights, he had seen that unconsciously vexed look on her face that showed she could not make out what he was trying to say. On the fourth morning, after Matt had taken out his bed-chamber, and the obliging Billy had tried to wash his face, he told the younger Tread to lay off trying to jerk a comb through his matted hair and bring Felicity in the room.

Flick, who had wanted to sleep in his room, and had been resolutely prevented by the Tread propriety, came in in her dressing-gown with her hair sticking out like a red halo around her sleepy head. Even then, Tony smiled at the thought of what a shock that must have been to the moody

Matt Tread. When Billy had left them, and Flick, automatically, had reached for the cigarettes and gone through the performance of lighting one for herself and then one for him, he took it, and sighed comfortably: "Flick, we've got to use our heads."

"What is it, Monster?"

"Flick . . . I'm getting delirious at times . . . my mind's slipping. So it's up to you. Old Feather is killing me. I——"

"Of course he is!" said Felicity.

"Well, then, do this. Get the time-keeper up at No. 1 logging camp to come down here and talk to me—Billy Tread will tell you about him. I think he's a doctor. You've got to do it . . . get Feather off the scene, and all that. Try and do it this morning; I'm not feeling too well. Understand?"

Flick's face lighted. He saw at once how she had immediately thrilled at this chance to take full command of him. She had already stood up. There was precious little dramatics about Flick. She moved in secret and, only too often, deeply scheming ways but there was no one in the world, no other person, whom he would have felt content to do this thinking for him. He felt almost escaped from this predicament, now that he had shifted the burden to Flick. And at the same time he was bitterly regretful.

He had been fighting against this complete surrender to Flick. That, perhaps, had been the very worst part of this silent battle he had been fighting in bed. Her presence had brought nearly all of the old world back to him; more, perhaps, because his imagination was super-heated by this fever that inflamed his veins. He had thought a lot of things out. Perhaps, when he was well again, he might change his mind. But at the end of all this, he knew, was a long and heated session with Felicity. He could not tell her now . . . he wasn't up to it. She, in her strange intuitive way, had already seemed to know this; and in these last nights his few muttered talks had nearly all been replies, or chuckles, to the latest and most scandalous bits of gossip she could remember about their mutual friends in London. She had the bitter wit that was just right for this situation. But he knew that she also was waiting. . . .

Flick was frowning. "I want to get this clear—how can a logging camp time-keeper be a doctor? Put me straight on that before I go, will you?"

"Ask Billy. It'll sound crazy . . . he just saved the high-rigger, a Finn, who had cut himself down. . . . He won't admit he's a doctor . . . understand? You'll probably have to use your well-known sex-appeal on him . . . ha-ha . . ."

At that last vicious shot, given even as he was gasping with pain, Tony had to laugh. He grinned as Felicity glared at him and went out to dress. What a lovely thing it was—the delightful way he and Flick could say such snotty things to each other! She was like a man in that. Her retort came when, a few minutes later, she came in to say good-bye for a few hours.

"You little misery!" she said. "I suppose you know that all this is for nothing . . . that that ghastly German's house was burned to the ground?"

"I did not try to save the house," grinned Tony irritatingly. "I was merely trying to acquire merit, my love."

"Fool!"

He had her there; he chuckled as she left; he hadn't told her about the sheds. All the way up the lake she would be wondering what the hell he meant by "acquiring merit"! She would, he knew, think he had some deep meaning in it. Poor Flick—for all her brains, she could be teased in the most childish manner. What a pity, what a bloody shame it was; that they had not met, oh! fifteen or twenty years ago . . . when they both hadn't known so much. . . .

*   *   *

The little time-keeper came. And it was obvious, if anyone could judge from his leering grimaces, that it was in
answer to Felicity's well-known sex-appeal. "You ought
to hear what this young lady has been saying to me!"
were his first words as he came into Tony's room—"The
things she said I was when I said I wouldn't come! You
oughtn't to do that, you know . . . spread it about that I'm
a Doc."

As he was talking he took off his coat and rolled up his
sleeves, waiting for the basin of hot water that Flick had
gone out for. He had spotted Dr. Feather's old satchel, and
with a grin took the bottle of carbolic out of it and shook a
few drops in the basin. Then, before he washed his hands,
he asked Flick to light a lamp and hold it near the foot.
From his coat-pocket he had taken a blunt pair of scissors
with which he deftly clipped the sticky bandages. At once
Tony knew that he was in professional hands. "Ummmm!
. . ." The doctor's grunt showed how serious he at once
thought the foot. He stood up.

"No use touching that," he said. "Don't want to alarm
you, but that ought to be opened right away. I think you'll
have to have a general anæsthetic . . . too much tension
there for a local, anyway. Now we've got to think how we're
going to manage things: (a) you can't be moved, (b)
there's no surgeon nearer than the Quamicot hospital. . . .
Q.E.D. . . . bring him up." He saw the roll of cotton lint,
and, almost carelessly Tony thought, swiftly flung a bandage
around the foot again: then he flapped back the bed-
clothes and sat on the edge of the bed. "That must hurt
like hell," he said.

Tony grinned at this understanding. And Flick smiled.
She held out the case of cigarettes to the doctor. "Know
this man long?" asked the pseudo time-keeper. . . . "He's
quite a character on this lake. Heard you were drinking
yourself blind?" he said to Tony.

"Oh, a bit." Tony growled at this unnecessary weapon

put into Flick's hands. "What are you going to do about things?"

"Go down the lake and telephone to Quamicot. Two or three doctors down there. One of them's bound to have a car, and I'll ask him to come up to you. To-night . . . if he can make it. I'll give the anæsthetic . . . if they won't make any fuss about my practising without a Canadian licence. . . ."

The little man laughed and rubbed his stubbled jaw. Tony could see now that he was a Jew, with a strong New York accent. He said "hoit," not "hurt." It was an accent that sounded reassuring in this scene. "You see," smiled the little man—"I'm wanted. I did a little operation, you know . . . to accommodate a young lady. . . . And you know how those things will happen; she got puerperal fever . . . and was ungrateful enough to go and die on me. You know what women are! Friend slipped me some dope and I just dropped it into the beer of the cop that was taking me up to Sing-Sing, and, being hospitable for a moment, I took his key out of his pocket and unlocked myself from his handcuff in the taxi afterwards . . . and here I am."

"Short but sweet, your description," laughed Tony. "Why on earth did you chance giving yourself away by patching that high-rigger up? . . . I heard you hated him?"

The little time-keeper's amusing face suddenly creased with anger. "Hummm . . . didn't I! And didn't I answer it . . . do you know why I saved that big brute's life?— because he tortured me—he made my life hell for me. . . . The minute I saw him lying the way he was on the ground . . . that leg bent back . . . I knew that they'd probably have to take it off. And then the idea came to me—I wanted him to live. You see, that Finn, for all his great strength, will never climb a tree again as long as he lives. *Never!*"

Tony was awed by such intensity of hatred; he lay there, examining the wan little time-keeper's face silently. But Flick gave her low, rasping laugh. "My God! . . . That's *marvellous*!" she said, as if fascinated by such a clever revenge.

"You got it," said the little man, swelling before them with pride that his astuteness had been recognised: "Takes a woman to see a thing like that. If you can get that launch again, miss, we'll go down to the store now and telephone. I have to tell them what to bring up."

He nodded to Tony. "There's very likely some bone involved, so I don't think this is going to be very pleasant for you. Don't eat anything."

Tony had heard that so often that he went a step further in his imagination and already saw himself, with his nose under the mask, sucking in deep breathfuls of oblivion-giving chloroform . . . in a few hours more he would be on his way to peace and rest again. He took a new interest in his surroundings, asked Flick to get another pillow and shove it behind him, to give him the book he had been reading and leave the cigarettes by his side.

*   *   *

The surgeon was the same one who had amputated the Finn's leg, and came up immediately in his car from Quamicot. Flick and the little time-keeper waited down at the store for him and arranged to come up in Ken Cullen's boat. The surgeon had started at once, speeded, no doubt, by the curiosity of seeing who it was who had patched the high-rigger up, and whom he had hesitatingly agreed over the telephone to let give the anæsthetic. The time-keeper and Flick, who was questioned about Tony by a peculiar-looking man called Digger Bean at the store, accepted his invitation to come over to his place and have a drink of the real stuff while they waited. There, Tony learned afterwards, Felicity had gathered almost a complete story of his two years on the lake. Dove-tailed with what Aline and the Debenhams had told her, she had a refreshing picture. . . . The surgeon was a grey-haired, red-faced old-timer, who had also brought his trout rods with him. "I used them half as an excuse," he laughed, while he and the time-keeper professionally set about placing the lamps and getting Lynd ready for the operation. From the technical jargon that the surgeon spoke to the little time-keeper, Tony saw that they had lost every interest except in the mechanics of the case they were on. He shuddered a little as he watched them drop the knives and forceps into a bowl and wash their hands to put on the sinister red-rubber gloves. "Looks like I'm for it," he grinned to Felicity.

She was very pale, so white that the freckles looked like spots of mud on her face. . . . He closed his eyes as he saw the mask being held over his face and began to breathe . . . click, click, click, he was rising, swirling, drifting, floating, around and around and around. . . . He choked, and heard the surgeon saying something. . . .

* * *

* * *

He was lying by the lake on a bench made from some planks to which one of the Tread boys always helped him down every morning. It was out in the sun, where he could get the full strength of it, although Flick sat with a straw bathing hat to protect her eyes. Looking across the blue lake he could see the black char that had once been the old Count's place, the two sheds, still standing as a secret memorial of his efforts that night, the deep, embracing belt of fir forest that rose behind them, and then the tumbled grey of the rocks above the timber-line. For days there had not been a cloud in the sky.

"You have the patience of a Buddha," he said to Felicity—"the way you can keep silent. I do appreciate that."

Felicity gave her hoarse laugh. "Well, I've been good so far . . . very reasonable. But I'm not going to keep it up, you know. Not now that you're able to walk again. You know me."

"I do," he said, "I do . . . bless you."

"I don't believe in hitting cripples."

"Hunh, I like that. Even old Feather say he thinks I can throw away these home-made crutches soon. Nice the way he took all that, wasn't he?"

"Oh, everybody on this lake is simply *marvellous*! Your bashful Swedish boy friend is a *mar*vellous type of the world-roaming Scandinavian; and that stupid old goat Dr. Feather is a sterling character, and old Mrs. Tread has a heart of gold. . . . And it's just too damn' bad the way all these honest people would be upset if you and I went over and lived in your cabin together. . . . But you don't under*stand*!" she drawled vindictively, mocking him.

"Well, they wouldn't. In the first place the old Huns are still living in my cabin . . . there's no place for them to go, until someone is brutal enough to make it clear they've got to go back and live in his tool-sheds for a change. . . . And then . . . well, this lake is far worse than London in that respect . . . infinitely worse—in London, we could get away with that. Not here."

"So you've told me. Well, what are we going to do about it? I can't stay here for ever, you know."

"You'll be a great hit in Japan," replied Tony.

He knew that he had not wanted to say that—not that way. But Flick's independence always drove him to this. It was difficult to hurt Flick, or, at least, to make her show it. But he saw that this remark had got home. Suddenly he was terribly sorry for what he had said. "Forgive me, I didn't mean it," he asked. For answer she turned over on her face and began to read.

"Tell me," he asked, "why did you make that idiot Aline promise never to tell her mother that she knew you knew me . . . that she was to keep it a dark secret, the real reason why you came here? Didn't you know that would get her into no end of trouble? . . . All the money they had wasted sending her to England, and all that. . . ."

Flick had been swimming, and lay now in khaki shorts, bronzing her beautiful legs in the sun, "Because," she said, assuming a thoughtful position with her chin in her cupped hands, "she *is* such a bloody little fool. That was why. The night Patrick Byron brought her over to me . . . already stuffed with nonsense . . . I could see she was simply dying to rush off and write her darling mother she had met the *woman* who had wrecked Anthony Lynd's life! So I decided to stop that."

Tony chuckled. "You would, of course, with your scheming mind."

"Yes. . . . It was a little difficult; I was sitting with some people . . ." Felicity sucked in her breath and gave a few heaves of mirth. "So I said before everybody that she simply *must* see me before she wrote one word home. . . . I had something I wanted her to write to the lake about you. . . . You can imagine the effect?"

"On Pat Byron, too!"

"That little ——," growled Felicity . . . "and then, I cultivated her. I asked her to lunch in my place the next day, and I bared my secret heart to her."

Flick dabbed out her cigarette on an ant that was passing: "*That's* what I'd like to do to you, you little misery!"

"But why didn't you want me to know you intended to come out here?"

"Because I knew you—you'd run away. You wouldn't have the guts to stay and face me."

"Well, I'm facing you now."

"Yes, but you haven't got the guts to dare to talk about things. Have you?"

Tony was silent. "I have," he said finally. "I'll go with you. It would be the easiest thing in the world for me to pull up stakes here. In fact, as you're always so fond of saying, I could self-dramatise myself beautifully by making the two old Huns a present of my place. I could leave this lake in a blaze of glory; but——"

"Yes?" said Felicity.

She was strained now, every sense on the alert. And he had said too much now not to say all of it.

"I'd be no damned good to you," he said.

She opened her mouth, as if to speak, and then lay there with her lips open and her green eyes fixed intently on the grass before her. He knew well enough that this was her sign for him to say everything; she was waiting for it.

"You've a nice plausible way of putting things," said Flick suddenly, when he had been silent too long; "always thinking about *me*—what about your own bloody little self?"

"Well, it's my own bloody little self that I'm thinking about. I'm just tired. I'm fed up with using my emotions so much. When your letters came they simply burned the hide off me; they made me think that all the life I'd been living out here was simply so much sheer fantasy . . . an attempt to live a Thoreau in *Walden*. . . . And when I felt that the life I was living on this lake wasn't *real* . . . understand?—why, I simply didn't know what to do. Thank God I didn't know that you had set your mind on coming here. . . . I *would* have run away, just like you said I would. Then I'd never have known anything."

"And now what's the great truth?" asked Felicity.

"Just the fact that though I do love you, I don't want to be continually affected by you. And if I'm near you I know that's what would be happening to me for the rest of my life. I'd be continually played upon, just like some musical instrument. This, despite the fact that with you I've found some of the most amazing peace in my life. As far as man and woman go, you and I are ideal for each other."

"Well . . . I've heard a few contradictory arguments in my life!" began the appalled Felicity, "but——"

"I know it sounds like the most ungodly nonsense—but I want to live alone. *Alone.* Just that. Nothing more. Right here. And you, of course, simply can't conceive of such a thing. Why the hell do you think there are so many monks and . . . hermits?"

Flick rolled over on her back in the grass and simply yapped with laughter. "Tony, you—are—the—most—stupid . . . idiotic . . . incredible person! Never did anyone have a more troublesome monster. . . ." Then she changed, flung suddenly into a furious passion by the thought that this might be serious, instead of nonsense, and just sat there, staring at him menacingly.

It was an old trick that he knew, and feared. It was Flick's way of making him so uncomfortable that he would simply have to say something—usually, to make a retraction of some sort. He had often found it more intimidating than any other form of attack upon him. They were sitting there, locked like two wrestlers in the intenseness with which they were trying to read the thoughts behind each other's eyes, when Billy staggered past.

"Matt's shot," he cried.

"*Shot?*"

"Yes. Ken Cullen."

*   *   *

In a few minutes they saw the *War Eagle* coming up the lake, headed for the Tread landing. Smedley and two loggers came up carrying the body of Matt. They laid it on the veranda and stood there undecidedly. Then Smedley knocked gently on the Treads' door. Billy came out. And then Billy and his father carried Matt back into the house. Smedley shook his head as he and the loggers came past them. He came over.

"It was Virgie," he said in a hushed voice.

"Where?" Tony asked.

"Up in the woods, behind where the booms were. . . . Ken came right over to the store and gave himself up. Swinton's arrested him."

"Oh, ironies . . ." muttered Tony.

"I've got to go," said Smedley. "The police are coming up. Hard on the old Treads, isn't it?" Flick got up and walked down with Smedley to the boat. When she came back, she said: "Cullen apparently let everybody think he had gone down for the mail, and left his car on the road and came back. I wonder what we are going to do about you, with all this going on?"

Just when they were deliberating how to get Tony across to his cabin Shorty Murdoch came out of the woods from the trail that led to the Treads' logging camp. He came over and sat down beside them. "I knew this was going to happen," he said angrily. "She was always hanging around when we were down with a boom. And Aline Debenham's a lot to blame for it. I know . . . way she's treated Matt ever since she came back . . . as if she was too good for him. Well, she's found out now."

"What's happened to Virgie Cullen?" asked Tony.

"Her? . . ." Shorty stared insolently at Flick's shorts. "Oh, she's screaming the place down. Like any woman. . . ."

"If I were you, I wouldn't go into the house," he said to Felicity—"not in those."

Tony controlled himself and said evenly: "She's not. We were just wondering how I could get across to my place. I could row all right, if someone could put me in a boat."

"Nah . . . ye'll do none of that. I'll take you across, soon as I've seen if I can be of any use here. It's a peetiful way for a man like Matt to end . . . for a harlot like that." He stared again, angrily, at Felicity's legs.

"You needn't bother," said Tony. "I can get across without you."

"I doot it," said the Scot, getting up. "I'm thinking that the Treads will be wanting their boat."

Shortly after Murdoch had gone into the log house old Henry Tread came out. "You're staying here," he said to Tony. "Murdoch said you wanted to go. But that's all right. . . ." He stood there, dazed, staring off up the lake as if he were trying to make himself believe what had happened. Everything around him was growing as usual. He kept rubbing the stubble on his always unkempt jaw. "We'll bury him here," he said. Flick took his arm and walked back with him to the house. Tony saw that the old man was leaning against her.

When Flick came back she said nothing, but merely stared at Tony. She was weeping. He felt his throat clutching and gripped his crutches. "I think I'll go along to him," he said hoarsely. "Go over and tell the Debenhams and . . ." his throat was dry—"come back here later."

As he entered the room and saw old Henry Tread, lying with his arms outstretched across the table, he put his arm around the thin shoulders. He felt a fierce desire to help this stricken man.

*   *   *

With a bitter stubbornness, old Tread insisted that Matt should be buried the next night, and in the same way that all the old settlers had been buried. "It's no use," Tony heard him saying to Copey Debenham, "he's my son . . . and Billy and I can do all that is necessary for him. I know what's wanted."

The result was that Tony lay in his room and had to listen to the macabre sound of sawing and hammering the next morning. Old Mrs. Tread had kissed her son good-bye and had been taken over to the Debenham place. This also had been old Henry's adamant command. He had reverted, with Matt's death, to his very first days on the lake. He sent Shorty Murdoch away so that only he and Billy made the coffin. When the baffled police tried to tell him that he could not bury Matt until permission had been granted, he again said very simply: "He's my son. You go away from here and leave me alone with him."

They left, making, as an apology to Tony for their un-official soft-heartedness, the excuse that they had another job to do on the lake; they had orders to interview the time-keeper up at Jesse James' camp. Tony saw Digger Bean, who had brought them up in his launch, open his eyes wide at that. He felt the shock himself, but could not say anything.

That night Tony watched Billy and his father carry down the coffin to the grave they had dug that afternoon. He heard them working in the dark, and then, by the light of the two lanterns, saw them standing there looking down at the earth. Then he heard them come back and talking in the next room. In a little while Billy came in carrying a tray with some cups and the teapot on it. Tread came in and sat down by his bed. He drank his cup and sighed: "Ah, well . . ."

"Poor old Matt!" suddenly sobbed Billy.

The old man placed his hands on his knees and got up. He placed Tony's cup on the table beside him, took the teapot from the tray, and the sugar, and placed them beside that. Then he reached down and picked up Billy's cup from the floor. Billy suddenly rushed from the room, and his father followed him out.

He closed the door.

* * *

"I'm going," said Flick. "When I was down at the store yesterday I telephoned and bought a passage on the *Empress of Canada*. She sails Saturday. A car's coming up from Quamicot to take me down to-morrow morning. So this is our last day together."

He had known when she was so late in coming over, and when she appeared in a Tyrolean, grey-flannel suit, that she had made the decision. Her last gesture in self-defence had been to announce it to him after she had completed everything. "Everything's packed," she said.

They were sitting on the string-piece of the Tread landing, looking down into the boat in which he had watched her rowing towards him. He said: "Would you like to row across to my place—take a look? I could take you there."

"Why? What's the use? I'm not going to try and torture myself. I'm going to do what I always did, since I was a child—when I believed that I couldn't get a thing . . . that it was beyond me. . . . Then I made myself believe I didn't want it."

"And you'll do that to me?"

"Of *course*!" she said. And she gave her rasping laugh.

"Your quiet peaceful lake seems to be standing on its ear," she said. "The charming Mr. Swinton apparently blabbed to the police about Digger Bean's bootleg activities . . . so he's in trouble . . . and I can't use his boat. The heart-of-gold and sophisticated Mr. Axel Swanson has volunteered to come up to the Debenhams' and take me down to-morrow. He suggested that he could also take you along. He told me to tell you that the Germans have gone back to their place—he took up a collection of blankets and cooking things that had been donated by the Feathers and the people around the store. Your German, apparently, has not been very profuse in his thanks—has he?"

"I didn't expect it," said Tony. "He's a queer character."

"Like you . . ." mused Felicity. She said it sadly, staring away from him across the lake. "Like you, my little misery. . . .

"There is one thing," she said, turning, her lovely brow creased with a perplexed frown—"that poor little doctor who stepped in to save you. I almost wish we hadn't bothered him, and—and had let you take your chances. No, my sweet, I don't wish that—but I was struck by that man; there was no damn' nonsense about him. The police took him down with them that night they were up here. So, all in all, your little world seems rather upset, doesn't it? Even if, as you say, you are going to try and help the Treads a bit."

She lit a cigarette and then lighted one from that for him. From the selection of his own clothes that had been brought over to him by Swanson when it was known he could move, he was now wearing a pair of grey flannels and his old tweed coat. The only sign of his illness was the bulging woollen sock pulled over the bandages on his right foot, and the pallor around his sullen lips. He was unnaturally thin.

"It will pass," he said, meditating. "Another rainy season . . . and a winter. And it will rub all of this out. You have no idea," he said, slowly tapping his one good foot with his stick, "how it is when the lake opens . . . and you begin to live again . . . in the spring. . . ."

She looked at him queerly. "I'm going back," she said. "There's nothing to be gained by staying here and merely torturing each other. I won't come over to say good-bye to you to-morrow morning; we'll say it now, 'Good-bye.'" With an unexpected dexterity she dropped into the boat.

He watched her row off. Always, when he got out of her car to say "Good night" to her in London, he noticed that she drove away without looking back. Flick did so now. She rowed with her eyes fixed on something she seemed to see, over his left shoulder, in the blue sky. He sat there, slowly tapping his stick against his foot. Then he lifted his head and stared across the lake to where the forest stood still below the grey rocks all along the skyline.

It was hardly yet in the middle of the day, and he wondered what he would do.